Advance Praise for *Journey*

"This is that rare thing: a truly original novel. Imagine *Zen and the Art of Dentistry* co-written by Philip Roth and Larry David, and you *might* get an idea of how funny and unique *Journey of a JuBu* is. Reading stories of spiritual awakening can be like getting a root canal. Fortunately, Blaine Langberg knows how to apply laughing gas so that readers don't even realize they've been enlightened until they stop giggling."

— Chris Belden, author of *Shriver*

"Who can write with witty irreverence about deep spirituality, combining existential despair with laugh-out-loud humor? Blaine Langberg can! Sparked with charm and hilarious social satire, *Journey of a Jubu* is an earnest exploration of the meaning of life and the commitments of love by a suburban professional who attempts to navigate a world that has just about lost all sanity. A scintillating, fast-paced novel that lingers in the heart and mind."

—Valerie Ann Leff, author of *Better Homes and Husbands*

"*Journey of a Jubu* is part *Seinfeld*, part *Portnoy*, and a wholly new vision for understanding the mysteries of faith. It will keep you laughing throughout, but those beautiful, honest moments of introspection—they will keep you thinking long after you're done."

—Bill Wolff, author of *Bruce Springsteen and Popular Music*

"What happens when we put our dreams on hold for others? And how do we find them again? *Journey of a Jubu* cleverly serves up a book within a book, chronicling the parallel paths of author (Jacob) and subject (Adam) as each faces the greatest challenge of his life. At times poignant, at times hilarious, this book playfully inspires readers to seek a more enlightened and fulfilling life."

—Julia Bobkoff, award-winning poet and screenwriter

Dear Alison,

It's been great getting to know you and your family through the years. I've enjoyed creating and fine-tuning their great smiles! I hope you enjoy the book. May you be entertained and enlightened!

Blaine Langberg

JOURNEY OF A JUBU

How a neurotic Jew found his inner Bu

BY BLAINE LANGBERG

Critical Eye Publishing

Plymouth, Minnesota

Edited by D.J. Schuette
www.criticaleyeediting.com

ISBN: 978-0-9984293-4-2

Critical Eye Publishing
Plymouth, MN 55447

CRITICALEYE

Visit the author at www.blainelangberg.com.

For Rachel

Thanks for your love, support, and *infinite* patience.

CHAPTER ONE
October 26, 12:45 p.m.

"You want me to kill Adam Freeman?"

"Yes," Maggie says. "Adam Freeman must die."

I, Jacob Silverstein, Harvard-trained orthodontist, faithful husband of Leah, loving father to three girls, am being asked to commit murder. And not just anyone—Adam is my best friend. I want to lose my lunch, but I force myself to shovel more bacon, mushroom, and Swiss burger (I'm not a kosher Jew) into my mouth, buying time to think. I'm a tooth straightener, not a hit man. But Maggie's serious. Dead serious.

As I chew, she waits, Caesar salad untouched on her plate, sipping her iced tea. In her early forties, with brown, collarbone-length hair and a well-tended figure, Maggie resembles Season One Nina Myers in *24*—a beautiful woman in touch with her inner badass. I'm obsessed with pop culture, so you'll have to forgive me when I compare almost everyone I meet to TV and film characters.

"Well, Jake?" Maggie stares at her watch. "I haven't got all day."

I raise my finger to signal I'm still chewing. I've dealt with choices my whole life, some agonizingly painful, because I'm the guy who always does the right thing, even when it hurts. But lately, as I fasten braces to crooked teeth day after day, I've been wondering, is there more to life?

Maggie shifts in her chair.

"You know"—I swallow—"it's not as easy as you make it sound. Adam isn't some random schmuck. He's like a brother to me, and we've had great times together. If Adam dies, a huge part of me dies too."

She scoffs. "You know, Jake, sometimes you have to make a bold move to get what you want—"

"Dr. Silverstein?"

Our ponytailed waitress bounces over in her black "High-Priced Café" T-shirt to refill the water glasses. She smiles, flashing a row of bright whites. I can't recall her name, but I instantly recognize those teeth; I put braces on her a couple of years ago and straightened them to perfection. Now, her incisors are starting to crowd again—my beautiful work undone.

"Dr. Silverstein," she continues, "I'm glad I ran into you. I was on a roller coaster this summer and, like, my retainer fell out of my mouth when I was screaming. My teeth are, like, moving. I know I should make an appointment, but…could you, like, possibly take a look?" She bends over Maggie's salad and opens her mouth, pierced tongue just inches from the gluten-free croutons. Maggie shoots me a disbelieving stare.

Although I don't need a close-up to see that without the retainer her teeth have relapsed, I lean over to examine them. Fixing it means more money for me, but I'm so bored with braces, I could garrote myself with my wires. I grit my own teeth.

"Losing your retainer on a roller coaster ride, well, that's a first. Give the office a call, Abby," I reply, finally remembering her name, "and we'll get you in for an impression to make you a new one."

As Abby trots back to the kitchen, Maggie cannot conceal a smile. "Do you get that a lot, Jake? Patients coming up to you for free checkups and drooling over lunch?"

"All the time," I respond. "I've probably put braces on half the kids in Matingly."

"Well good for you," she continues. "How thrilling. Have you thought about my question? Or is your head still in that waitress's mouth?"

Something inside me snaps. Maggie has pushed mild-mannered Jacob Silverstein over the edge—or at least right up to it. I consider making a comment about where her head is in relation to another part of her anatomy, but a mushroom escapes from the bun I'm still holding and plops onto my tie.

"Dammit..." I wet my napkin and dab frantically at the widening stain. Hardly the composure of a cold-blooded killer.

Maggie eases her chair back and gets up. "I knew you didn't have it in you, Jake."

"Wait."

She pauses and sits down.

"You want a bold move?" I loosen my tie and unbutton the collar of my dress shirt, then carefully roll up each sleeve over my elbow.

"Yes, like the day we met. You were full of fire."

I think back to that day three weeks ago. Living my predictable, boring life as a successful orthodontist and writing at night. I had taken my girls to Kids' Fest in Matingly, Connecticut, and they tugged on my cargo shorts as they dragged me into Books on the Green. I almost dropped my cup of Dunkin' Donuts iced coffee when I saw mega-author Irving Sharf signing copies of his latest fantasy book, *The Swan*

Song of the Dragon Menace. Sharf, with his sweep of thick silver hair and horn-rimmed reading glasses perched on the tip of his nose, sat behind a stack of books, pen in hand, autographing copies of his enormous hardcover bestseller. The truth was, that should have been me up there.

Fifteen years ago, I struggled through dental school, inches away from a nervous breakdown. No one ever told me it would be that stressful. Working on live patients when you'd just learned how to do the procedure on a fake tooth the day before and knowing you could cause irreparable damage to a real human with one slip, was giving me migraines and nervous tics. One of my roommates offered me a Valium, but it only made me feel sick. Then I read an article that said dentists have the highest suicide rate of any profession. That fun fact hadn't been included in Harvard's glossy vocational brochure. When the same roommate who offered me the pills overdosed and nearly died before finals, I freaked. I told my advisor I wanted to quit. He referred me to a counselor at student health services, who urged me to do something creative—non-dental—as an outlet for my stress. During the summer between my third and fourth years of dental school, I took a creative writing class at Boston University. I wrote a novella and, on a lark, submitted it to the Academy of Writing Competition, a prestigious contest. Shockingly, I was chosen as a finalist from tens of thousands of entries.

The final step in the competition was to fly out to California to read an excerpt to a panel of judges who would determine the winner. The day of my flight, I received a frantic call from my mother: "Jacob! Meet me at the hospital! Your father had a stroke. He's conscious, but in intensive care." I agonized, but like I said, I'm the guy who always does the right thing, so I skipped the flight, withdrew from the competition, and joined my family at my dad's bedside. My dad recovered almost fully, and eventually I learned to manage my anxiety at dental school. I graduated, completed my orthodontic residency, and now own a thriving practice.

The creative writing class served me well. To this day I still write to reduce my stress. But who do you suppose won the competition that year, along with one hundred thousand dollars and a publishing contract? None other than Irving Sharf, the man right in front of me, signing autographs for the masses. And there next to him, I recognized local Matingly resident and literary agent extraordinaire, Maggie Christiansen—maker of bestsellers and master of the million-dollar advance—fresh from the pages of a recent profile in *Publishers Weekly*. Seeing Maggie rekindled something inside me.

As that bastard Sharf signed copy after copy, I waited in line for nearly an hour with my three girls bored out of their minds and spent thirty-two bucks on his 600-page monster—a book I'll never read and will probably use as a doorstop—to get a minute with Maggie. I was determined to pitch her the novel I'd been working on late at night. Maybe she could resuscitate my dream of becoming a writer.

Sharf beamed as he posed for selfies with his fans. Not a care in the world. Damn him. I wondered what it would be like to get out of the business of straightening teeth and into a life of true creativity, to realize the dream I'd dropped when my dad became sick. Just as I was about to walk up to the table, I heard my name.

"Dr. Silverstein!" I turned around and saw a woman with bleached-blonde hair smiling at me. "My daughter's bracket broke last night, and it's dangling in her mouth. She's in a lot of pain. Can we get in to see you…today?"

As I looked up, there was Sharf being hugged by an attractive female fan. I fake smiled to the blonde mother. "Come by at four o'clock," I said and turned around dejected, prisoner of my orthodontic practice.

Finally, I stepped forward and shook Sharf's hand. A hand that gets to spend all day writing. A hand that's never had to bend wires or bond braces.

"Who should I sign this to?" he asked.

"I'm Jacob Silverstein, one of the finalists with you in the Academy of—" But before I could finish, Sharf scribbled something inside my book and turned his attention to the next person in line. I opened the book and read: "To Jacob—Always Live Your Dreams!" over his enormous "Irving Sharf" signature. I looked around. Where was Maggie? As I backed up to let a Sharf groupie move ahead in line, I bumped right into her.

"Excuse me, I'm sorry."

Maggie lifted her eyes from her phone. At last, my *carpe diem* moment had arrived. But the only thing seizing was my throat.

I coughed and surprised myself by blurting, "I would love to pitch you my novel." Before she could say no, a surge of courage overcame me. "*The Adventures of Adam Freeman, DDS*"—I wiped sweat from my upper lip—"is the story, ahem, of Adam Freeman, ahem." I took a gulp of my cold coffee. "The story of a late 30s, Jewish, Yale-trained pediatric dentist, who—"

"A novel about a *dentist*?" She looked back down at her phone.

"A *pediatric* dentist," I clarified, "who goes on a quest for spirituality and enlightenment and finds it in unlikely places."

"Like between his patients' teeth?"

I was losing her. Suddenly I remembered reading in *Book Business* magazine that editors like to hear crosses and comparisons in pitches.

"It's *Seinfeld* meets *The Celestine Prophecy*," I managed. She looked up—a flash of curiosity in her eyes. I gasped, "I'm only an orthodontist, but I know this book can become a pop-culture classic."

"Slow down," she said.

I bit my lip to curb my enthusiasm as she finally stuffed her phone in her purse.

"You're interesting. Send it to me, and I'll give you feedback." She handed me a business card. I was all smiles, just like my patients when their braces come off. I walked through the rest of Kids' Fest in a daze, beaming at strangers, buying my daughters the cotton candy they'd been craving since ten in the morning. We went into the toy store and finally left for home after I ran out of cash.

"It was a great pitch, Jake."

"I know, and it's an even better novel." I take my napkin and wipe my damp forehead.

Maggie purses her lips. "Look, Jake, you're a fine writer for someone who spends all day wiring teeth. But I'll be blunt. *The Adventures of Adam Freeman, DDS* doesn't work as a novel, and Adam is a total douche. Using him as your alter ego drains the book of its authenticity. But…your book would work beautifully as a memoir." She pronounces it 'memwahh' with the accent on the second syllable. "Spirituality books are cash cows. People eat enlightenment for breakfast, lunch, and dinner. As a memoir, even by an unknown author, I could make *12 Steps to Spiritual Enlightenment* a breakout bestseller—the next *Eat, Pray, Love*. You have a fresh voice, Jake, and that could be *you* in Sharf's chair autographing copies. Adam Freeman is the only thing holding you back. If you don't kill him, I can't help you."

I sit up straight. "I can't kill Adam. And I won't. I spent six years creating him. And even though you don't like him…"

"I hate him."

"…I believe I can go deeper into my story, my journey to enlightenment, in *The Adventures of Adam Freeman, DDS* than in some twelve-step 'memwahh' published by Hazelden."

"Hazelden pays well, Jake. Are you done with your rant?"

"No. I'm not. I'm just getting started. I told you I lost my big break, my dream, of becoming a professional writer when my dad suddenly got sick. I told you how, after I established my practice, I came home after fourteen-hour days and exchanged my pliers for my pen. I told you how Adam sat down at my desk next to me, whispered in my ear, and begged me to tell his story. And you're playing on my fear of missing out again and trying to get me to write the book *you* want."

"The book *readers* want…"

"Look, Maggie, I know you're trying to clear a path to success for me. But the kind of suecess you're talking about is the bitch goddess who steals your soul. I need to take the road less traveled here."

"What, the yellow brick road, Jake?"

"Instead of following the money, I need to follow my heart. And if you can't help me with that…"

"Jake, this is a once-in-a-lifetime opportunity. Don't blow it."

"And my name is Jacob."

"Fine. *Jacob*, would you be kind enough to read me your opening page?"

I pick up the manuscript that's sitting on our table and begin to read.

The Adventures of Adam Freeman, DDS

by Dr. Jacob Silverstein

June 9, 2014—*Six Feet Under*

Am I dying? I think I'm dying. Can this really be it? My left arm feels numb, and pain is gripping my chest. I must be dying. I'm sweating, and I can't breathe. Shit. Is this the end? Is this how I go? At thirty-nine? A fucking heart attack? In bed? This must be how my own *Six Feet Under* episode starts. But what a boring death. Jim Fixx, the guy who wrote that running book, died while he was running. Steve Irwin, the crocodile hunter, got stabbed in the chest by a stingray. Adam Freeman, DDS? Ticker gives out watching late-night reruns of *Seinfeld*. Totally pathetic.

I should probably call 911, but I don't want to wake up my wife, Minnie. She just took her Ambien and fell asleep a few minutes ago, and when Minnie gets a good night's sleep, I've got a shot at morning nookie. But if I'm dead? I forget what they call that, necro-something or other. And if it's a panic attack, like the one I had before, how embarrassing to have the ambulance gurney me off for a false alarm—a mental problem—with all the neighbors watching. You can bet everyone on our street will be looking to see what the hell's happening at the Freemans' at 12:00 a.m., then checking online tomorrow for my death notice.

Arghhh, this pain, it's almost worse than death, and my left eye won't stop twitching. I'm ready to run my dental drill through it. I never thought it would end this way. Isn't my life supposed to flash before my eyes? Hello, God, turn on the projector! If I do croak, who'll write my obituary? Who'll come to the Shiva for miserable, old me? Who'll tell a bunch of funny, poignant anecdotes, sanitize the bad stuff, and make me out to be better than I was? Can I count on my buddy, Klein, or can I trust Errol to cover for me? Oh, God. Breathe, Adam. Breathe. Maybe it is just another panic attack. OK. The pain's a little less now. Try to go back to sleep...and hope you wake up in the morning.

* * *

Maggie looks up at me. "What is there to like about Adam? Why do we give a damn if he dies—or exists at all? He's a selfish, narcissistic, male chauvinist—a typical prick. 'Morning nookie?' Honestly, Jake."

I lower my head, trying to hide my dejection.

"And he's not your *friend*," she continues. "He's your fucking protagonist."

I look down at the remains of my burger and the mushroom stain on my tie. Maggie may as well have driven the table knife into my heart.

"But without Adam, I'm afraid there is no book," I whine.

"Without Adam, you have a future as a writer. I'll give you twenty-four hours. Meet me here at one o'clock tomorrow. I'll have a contract ready. If you want me to be your agent and sell your book, off Adam and move on."

She takes a platinum Amex from her wallet and signals for the check. Our waitress walks over with it. She must see the stricken look on my face.

"Dr. Silverstein, like, are you okay?"

"I'm fine, Abby." I force a smile. "And thank you for the lovely lunch, Ms. Christiansen."

"You know,"—Maggie snaps her wallet shut—"I'll pay tomorrow if we have a deal. This one's on you, Jake." And with that, she swooshes out of the High-Priced Café in her four-inch heels, leaving me with the high-priced tab. I look over at Abby the Waitress and shrug.

She smiles at me with one corner of her mouth and whispers, "What a bitch."

CHAPTER TWO
1:18 p.m.

I nearly run three stop signs driving back to my house, five minutes away, to grab a clean tie. I have a pit in my stomach the size of the Grand Canyon. Opening the glove compartment, I reach for my secret stash of Twizzlers Bites and shove a fistful into my mouth. It would have been much better if Maggie had said, "Love it! Let's get this book published." But instead she wants me to shelve Adam and begin a new book—a memwahh for Christ's sake—to expose my life experiences…Righhttt. She didn't even think that Adam was likeable. Sure, he's childish and inconsiderate at times, but he's a stream-of-consciousness kind of guy who's thoughtful, entertaining, and—at least to me—funny. And now it dawns on me: what does Maggie Christiansen, a Catholic woman who grew up in Connecticut, know about my protagonist—a neurotic, Jewish, Yale-trained pediatric dentist from New York? I'll be damned if she'll stop me from chasing my dream.

I enter the house and race past Leah sitting at her corner desk in our new designer kitchen. Leah, my Mary-Ann-from-*Gilligan's-Island* look-alike. She's petite with shoulder length, dark brown hair, and her gorgeous smile lights up the room. I enter the bedroom, pick a clean tie, and make my way back to the kitchen. While tying my Windsor knot in front of the dining room mirror, I tell Leah what happened with Maggie.

I'm out of breath when my monologue is complete, so I plunk down on the cushioned bar stool and pull myself up to our granite counter at the center island. Leah pours me a glass of lemonade. "I can't believe she wants me to kill off Adam!"

Leah smiles, looking around at our gleaming new kitchen. "I love your tenacity and determination, honey, but isn't creating beautiful smiles—and this beautiful life for your family—enough for you?"

"Well"—I take out the crystal bowl I bought Leah for her birthday last year and fill it with trail mix—"it's one thing to create a healthy, esthetic smile, but a whole other ball game to create a universe—a universe that readers enter and fall in love with. And learn from. And never want to leave. During their appointments, my patients sometimes experience pain and can't wait to get out of my office. But my novel? No one will want it to end. Today at lunch, I ran into this girl I treated who lost her retainer on a roller coaster. Now her teeth are crowding again, and we're back to square one. Every day in my office is like writing the same chapter over and over again. But with my novel, my very own book, I can work my way to the end of the story and create something everlasting!" I let out a breath, surprising myself with my own passion.

Leah sits down next to me and picks through the trail mix to get to the M&Ms. "I thought you were happy with your practice," she says, popping a handful of the green ones in her mouth. "Why do you need this?"

I look longingly at the candies in her mouth. It's as if she didn't hear anything I just said. I try a different tack. "You know I've been searching and looking for my truth. To be honest, I want this for my legacy. I want to be listed in the credits, like Larry David, not the invisible man behind the Invisalign."

Leah laughs, then turns serious. "That's sweet, Jacob, but this book's not going to pay the bills." She picks up my copy of *The Swan Song of the Dragon Menace* from the kitchen counter where it sits next to my manuscript. "I didn't know you liked this series. I've been looking forward to reading the new one." Leah makes her way to the living room, hugging Sharf's book.

With three quick steps I catch up to Leah and grab the book from her hand, startling her. "Six hundred pages of total crap. Instead of reading his book, you should be reading mine." Her mouth drops open. "Not once in the six years I've been writing did you ever ask to see my manuscript." She gives me a shocked look. My tone softens. "You know, I'd love your take on Adam. After you read it, tell me how delusional Maggie is for loathing my protagonist."

Leah shuffles back to the counter and sits. She sees the hurt in my eyes. "I'm sorry, Jacob. I didn't know you wanted me to look at your book. In my defense, you would hunker down in your office writing for hours on end. I assumed the book was personal. Do you have time to read me a chapter now? I don't want you to be late for work."

I check my watch. 1:39 p.m. "We start clinic at two. I have a few minutes, plus Dr. Smith can always cover for me." Picking up the manuscript, I turn to Adam's next entry and start reading.

The Adventures of Adam Freeman, DDS
June 9—*The Office*

"You look really tired today, Dr. Freeman. Are you okay? How was your weekend? Did you get my emails? Oh, and are you coming to the morning huddle? You haven't been in a while."

This is the barrage of questions that assault me from my office manager. Veronica is in her early sixties and has been with me the longest—over nine years. With her bright red hair and short, stout build, she looks like Mrs. Garrett from *The Facts of Life*. She has the gift of gab. Every topic of conversation eventually reverts to her grandchildren and her past job as an office manager at a podiatrist's office. Occasionally, I have to remind her that she now works at the *other end* of the body. Veronica is my most reliable employee—even coming to work once with a broken arm. I can't complain about her commitment, but I wish I could give her a plaque that reads "Silence is Golden."

I pick and choose which of Veronica's questions I answer. "I'm fine...tired. The little one was up all night again," I lie. I feel bad blaming my sleep-deprived night on my innocent toddler, but not *that* bad. It's like the time when I farted in public and blamed it on him. I had no choice. What was I going to say? That I was up all night because I had a panic attack? That my anxiety is becoming unbearable? I'd just as soon lie.

I tell Veronica to start the morning huddle without me. I used to attend them. The original goal was to make the workday run smoothly, but after a while they became bitching sessions: "How come extra work was performed on Suzie?; It looks like this appointment will cut into lunch; I have to leave at 2:30 today...." The whining was too much, so Veronica leads the meetings, and I pretend to be busy in my office as I secretly play Candy Crush.

Now is when I break the fourth wall—my Michael-Scott-from-*The-Office* moment when I speak to the reader. I knew that starting a practice would have its challenges, but I didn't think it would come with such intense headaches for eleven years straight. Managing eight women, ranging in ages from twenty-two to sixty-two is insane. These employees have given me a lot of premature gray.

I look at the schedule and see that I am beginning my day with Becky McDougall. I remember her as a cute little girl—one of my first patients. With her pigtails and bangs that hung down to her eyes, she could have been Punky Brewster's twin sister on the 1980s show of the same name.

My God, I think, as I enter the room, *Becky is not so little anymore*. She is twenty-one years old and back from college on her summer break—a very attractive young woman in a low-cut, V-neck T-shirt.

"How are you, Becky? Wow, you've grown up."

She laughs. "Hi, Dr. Freeman. I go by Becca now."

"Oh, sorry. I guess I've known you for too long then. You were one of my first, uh," I stutter, "patients."

My assistant, Sam, quickly covers up Becca's burgeoning cleavage. Mental note: make sure my daughters never wear a shirt like that until they are at least thirty. I don't want some perverted old man getting a free peep show. I know how guys think—and most of the time it isn't pretty.

I continue babbling, "Where are you at school again?"

"University of Florida."

"That's great, must be fun down there. Getting any studying in?"

She laughs nervously. "Yeah, I'm a pre-med major, so I take a lot of lab courses that keep me busy."

I pick up the needle to get her numb, and suddenly the room is spinning. I feel dizzy. To distract myself, I focus on the X-ray to visualize the cavity I'm about to fill. But the lightheadedness persists. "I'm sorry, Becky—I mean Becca, can you excuse me for a moment?"

I quickly remove my mask, take off my gloves, and walk out of the operatory into the hallway. It's not a great practice builder to faint on the patient with a needle in your hand.

"Are you okay Dr. Freeman? You're sweating. I'll get you some water." Sam rushes away.

Sam is a character. She started working for me at twenty-two years old, and four years later she's still with me. She resembles Lena Dunham, the comedian and writer of *Girls* on HBO, with her thick, wavy brown hair, high forehead, and round face. It would really make my life much easier if Sam came with an instruction manual. At first, she was very punctual, upbeat, and personable. She wants to please me, a great trait for an employee. But it's amazing how much drama some people create. Sam is the CEO of conflict. She smiles at you one moment, then goes behind your back and knifes you in her next breath. I don't completely trust her. So why do I keep her around? It's like the idiom, "better the devil you know than the devil you don't."

Sam hands me a glass of water and I take a sip. "I'm fine." I move my hand and wipe the sweat from my forehead. I hope it's not another panic attack—or worse, a stroke.

Buzz, buzz, buzz... Snapping out of my daze, I notice Sam's scrub pants lighting up. "Hey, is that your cell?"

"What? No! I just forgot to put it away this morning."

I snap at her. "You know my policy, Sam. No cell phones while we're with patients! How am I supposed to treat anyone when my assistants are off in the bathroom texting and checking their emails? Not acceptable."

Sam looks at me evasively. "It was a mistake, Dr. Freeman. I haven't been myself this week. I have my period."

Oh no, here come the full waterworks. For a moment, I look into her eyes and feel sympathy. I lean over to give her a hug but then I remember how many times I've warned her about this. "Sam, I'm sick and tired of the lies. I've given you a zillion warnings. Do I have to write you up?" Sam covers her eyes. "Look at me when I'm talking to you."

She lowers her hand. Eyes puffy and red, she stiffens her back. "After all I've done for you, this is how you speak to me? Forget about writing me up.

Save your paper. I can't take these conditions anymore. I quit." Sam walks out.

I stand there dumbfounded, then rush to Veronica's office. "Veronica! Sam just quit."

Veronica stands up from behind her desk. "What happened?"

"I told you. Sam left. I need your assistance."

"*Another* employee quit? What did you say to her? With all due respect, Dr. Freeman, how are we supposed to run an office with employees leaving all the time? You're gonna lose this practice if we can't keep a stable staff. What am I supposed to do?"

"I don't know. It's your fucking job to staff my office!" I storm out.

* * *

My cell phone rings, and I ignore it as I turn the page to start the next chapter.

"Aren't you going to get it?" asks Leah.

"Don't you want to hear more?" I ask excitedly.

"I want you to be on time seeing your patients." I see that Leah is right—it's the office calling. I pick up.

"Hey Janet. Sorry I lost track of time... Have Dr. Smith start the clinic... I know he's fresh out of school, but he can handle things until I get there... Okay, I'll see you soon."

Before Leah can object, I pick up the pages and keep reading.

The Adventures of Adam Freeman, DDS
June 9—All in the Family

My crappy day gets even worse when I arrive home. I breeze into the mudroom, talking on my Bluetooth, and my wife's voice echoes from the kitchen, "Adam, how many times have I asked you to get off the phone when you walk in the door?" My wife Minnie is no mouse. More like a shrew.

"I just got home. Hang on a sec." I put the call on mute. "Really, Minnie, give me a minute?"

"Your family appreciates your full attention."

"Gotta go, Klein. Talk to you later, buddy." Gone are the glory days of *All in the Family* when Archie collapses into his armchair and Edith mutely brings him a cold beer. I hang up and my words rush out unfiltered: "My God, can't a man get a freaking break? If you'd had my shitty day, you'd be yakking it up with your girlfriends. Get off my case. Go check your email, which you do half the time when I'm home anyway, and don't be so hypocritical." I stop to take a breath, a little surprised with my level of anger. I know I've hurt Minnie's feelings.

It's times like this when I wish life came with a DVR and a pause/rewind button. I regret my harsh words as soon as they come out of my mouth and wonder why I couldn't stop myself. I'm about to apologize before going upstairs to change into my post-work shorts, T-shirt, and hoodie when Minnie rebuts, "Adam Freeman, you're being an asshole. Don't you dare accuse me of not paying attention to our kids. I'm with them all the time, and if I have to answer an email, I don't need *you* making me feel guilty about it. Men..." She trails off, and I slink upstairs for the comfort of my sweats.

The kids are watching television and can sense the tension between their parents. I try to defuse things by throwing up the white flag. "Listen Minnie," I yell down the stairs, "we're on the same page here. I think *everyone* should put down the iPads and smartphones. We're enslaved to them. Remember last weekend in that restaurant? The couple next to us, each texting while their meals were getting cold? The conversation was nonexistent. For all we know, they were probably texting each other." I enter the kitchen waiting for Minnie to laugh, but her response is flat.

"Dinner is served. Let's eat."

All things considered, we have a nice family dinner. Minnie has always been good at hiding her issues with me in front of the kids, then handling things later in private. After dinner, I bathe our three-year-old son, Spencer, and Minnie reads to the two older girls. We meet up to do the dishes together, which we have agreed is the fair way to clean up. I may be a schmuck sometimes, but I'm not one of those guys who won't help his wife in the kitchen.

Minnie begins, "At the PTA meeting this morning..." My mind starts to drift back to my day at the office and Sam's departure after Cellgate. Did I react too harshly? Will Veronica be able to clean up my mess again? "I think Debbie will run the book swap."

I turn to face her. "What?"

Minnie turns off the water. I continue to dry. "Are you listening to me, Adam?" There's hurt in her eyes.

"Sorry, thinking about this cell phone incident at work today."

"I'm talking to you, Adam. We've been over this."

"What? I missed that last part."

"Oh my God, you're so ADD! I think you need Ritalin." She storms upstairs, leaving me to finish the encrusted lasagna dish.

I fill the dish with water to soak and turn on what's left of the Yankees game. I make the conscious choice not to go through the saved recordings on the DVR. I don't want to get sucked into one of my shows, even though we are 90 percent full, and I really should clear some space. I may have to spend this weekend catching up on my programs.

After the Yankees get down by four runs, I decide to go to bed. The iHome on my nightstand reads 10:38 p.m. I slide under the covers, prepared for a round of humbling pillow talk with Minnie, but she's fast asleep. What's that warning for couples about never going to bed angry? I don't enjoy apologizing to my wife for my behavior, but I do know it makes things better in the morning. Now I'm screwed—and also *not* screwed—and I can't even get Minnie's advice on losing Sam. I'm sure I have a patient or two who takes Ritalin. Maybe I can score a few pills. I'd rather take stimulants than go see a marriage counselor.

I put my head on my pillow, and my rapid heartbeat starts again. A wave of anxiety tenses my body, and my eye begins its twitching ritual. I'm already losing control of my body (God forbid I have Parkinson's or MS), and now I feel as though I'm about to lose my practice, my wife, and my mind.

* * *

I put down the manuscript and turn to my wife, anxiously awaiting her response. I prod her, "I'm dying to know what you think."

Leah cocks her head. "The writing's good. You've always had a way with words. And it's…entertaining."

I clench my fist and give a celebratory pump of my arm in the air. "Hah, you made my day!"

"But I can't disagree with Maggie. Adam is a jackass."

I look down at the counter. "But he's a man on the edge, beaten down and—"

She cuts me off. "He's mean to his staff and wife. If you were like that to me, I'd kick you out and probably divorce you. Don't get me wrong, I want to see where you're going with this, but why don't you think about writing a memoir like Maggie suggested? You're such a big fan of reality television, and we're both devoted followers of *Survivor* and *Naked and Afraid XL*. And it's impressive that she'd want to get your book published."

"But, Leah, I don't want to be that guy who exposes himself to the public both figuratively and literally. Those reality stars seem motivated by the fame, the money, the adventure. I want to create a work of art."

"With a total jerk as your main character?"

"Adam is a means to an end. I want my writing validated, and it almost was with my novella. But that came to a crashing halt when my dad was hospitalized. I thought that ship had sailed, but meeting Maggie was like a kick in the pants that brought back those desires. I need to share Adam's journey with the world."

"But why not write *your* story?"

"Because my life story isn't nearly as interesting as Adam Freeman's. Plus, I don't want to expose my crazy, neurotic thoughts to the world. You know my history with anxiety before I sought help."

Leah glances out the kitchen window and nods. She knows that when I was a kid, I assumed it was normal to go to the bathroom four to five times before leaving for school. Before big tests, I vomited uncontrollably for ten minutes straight. In social situations, I would hide in the corner while others talked and laughed. She lived through my anxiety and stress during dental school, and then in my practice before I studied Buddhism and became more enlightened. I didn't want to write my version of *Portnoy's Complaint*.

"If I tell the truth, Leah, people will laugh at me. And if I exaggerate, I could have a James Frey, *A Million Little Pieces* moment with Oprah chastising me in front of millions."

"Jacob, it would take tremendous courage for you to write about your anxiety and how you always wanted to be peaceful and to have a calm soul. Maybe you should think about that." I sigh. "And Oprah would eat it up," Leah adds.

"But there's no dramatic arc to that narrative. Seven years of schooling after college, starting my own orthodontic practice from scratch, being married to a loving and supportive wife"—I smile at Leah—"and having three amazing girls—all great accomplishments but hardly a page-turner."

"From what you told me, I think Maggie is interested in the anxiety you felt each day, your journey into spirituality from neurotic Jew to enlightened Buddhist, and how you conquered your inner demons. You could write about how you were obsessed with ridding yourself of your uncontrollable ear twitch."

I grimace. "I gave Adam an oscillating left eye twitch. And I had a wiggle, not a twitch."

"Honestly, I'm not sure of the difference, but fine, your wiggle. It was a cool party trick, anyway, before you lost control of it."

"I know, right? It had a mind of its own when I got stressed and went from an entertaining diversion to a disruptive part of my life."

"You hated it when people asked you if your ear was moving, and you told them it wasn't. You were in denial until you asked for help."

On this Leah and I agreed. I was so distraught with the wiggling and the fact that I was losing control of my body, that I went to a doctor to see if I had a brain tumor. The EEG showed my neurological system was functioning normally, ruling out any pathology. Although I ran three to four days a week and was over six feet tall and built like a beanpole, I went in for a stress test. The results were unremarkable. My heart was healthy. Still more visits to the doctor. Full blood work-ups and back to the hospital for a PET scan.

After the medical tests turned up inconclusive, I still had no idea what was causing the twitching. It became clear that something was wrong inside my head. Leah stepped in and took me to a psychiatrist, and when I didn't like him, she persisted in finding a mental health expert who could "treat me."

You might think that now is when I'm going to reveal deep dark secrets about my tortured life and the perils of growing up as a white, middle-class, Jewish kid in suburban utopian hell. I'm sorry to disappoint you, but even though I've always been melancholy, I have no bad memories of my upbringing. I was well loved by my supportive and caring parents. Shrink after shrink couldn't pinpoint what was wrong with me either, why I was anxious.

The key turning point came on my thirty-fifth birthday. I didn't want a baseline of sadness as I approached midlife. I had to get my act together and figure out how to settle my anxiety, ditch my ear wiggle, and soothe my restless soul. With traditional medicine giving me no answers, I decided to seek non-standard help. I found an amazing hypnotherapist. After a few sessions with her, during which, among other things, she encouraged me to write again, my ear wiggle miraculously vanished. When I put pen to paper, all I could think about was the universe I was creating—a universe over which I could exercise complete control. To get to the bottom of why I couldn't control my body, I invented a character with a similar problem and had him explore it and eventually solve it. With Adam, I could face my uncomfortable truths safely through fiction, then comfortably reveal my discoveries to myself. Adam's story resonated deep within me. Even though I was straightening teeth all day, each night I would make a beeline to my laptop and join Adam Freeman in his fictional world. With each stroke of the keypad, as I became more immersed in Adam's eclectic existence, I felt alive and free. Even though bags were developing under my eyes from lack of sleep, I felt euphoric. I was finally leaving my mark.

I turn to Leah. "Maggie thinks Adam is so snarky he needs to be given a fatal overdose of nitrous oxide so my real story can be told. I'd like to put that mask over Maggie's face instead."

Leah has a shocked look on her face, but it quickly morphs into a smile. "Listen, Jacob, if you feel that much passion for Adam's story then I support you. Whatever you decide. But remember, you have to decide soon. Maggie gave you twenty-four hours."

My cell phone vibrates again. I see the text, "Dr. Silverstein—clinic 1/2 hour behind. R u coming?"

"Leah, I've gotta run. Your support means the world to me. I love you." I grab the manuscript, give Leah a quick smooch, and dash to my car.

During my ten-minute drive back to the office, I ponder Maggie and Leah's feedback. They both have a point. Surprisingly, I didn't remember what a prick of a character I created. I must have writer's amnesia. I look down at the manuscript and address Adam as if he can hear me.

"What the hell are you thinking, man? Stop whining about your work problems and start treating your wife like someone you care about. If you keep treating Minnie this way, you might as well live in a monastery. She's working hard for you. You want her to manage your office, and she's already managing your life. This is exactly what Maggie didn't like in you. The stereotypical, misogynist, entitled, male attitude.

"Still, I can empathize with you, bro. I've lost count of the times I've said something stupid and hurtful to Leah—something I didn't mean and totally regretted. Getting into an argument with your spouse can make you regress and descend to a place where you're embarrassed about what comes out of your mouth. While I'm not proud of you, Adam, you've captured a pretty accurate portrayal of marital conflict. It rings true to the man you are at the start of the story and lays the groundwork for the man you need to become."

CHAPTER THREE
2:32 p.m.

Manuscript still in hand, I enter my office through the back entrance. I see Dr. Dennis Smith, my young new associate, remove his mask and gloves, and pat the patient on his right shoulder. "Great job with your elastics. See you in seven weeks."

The enthusiastic Dr. Smith walks into my office as I place the manuscript on my desk. "It's been real busy since lunch, Dr. Silverstein." He's in his late twenties, fresh out of his orthodontic residency at UCLA. This black surfer dude exchanged the fun and sun of Los Angeles to live near his wife's family in Connecticut. Smith resembles a young version of the actor Will Smith, no relation, and flashes a bright white smile that makes the moms swoon and the teenage girls giggle.

"I keep telling you, Dennis, please call me Jacob. You're making me feel old." He nods, but I know he won't stop addressing me as Doctor. "I apologize that I'm late, I had a meeting about my manuscript which took longer than I thought."

"Manuscript? You wrote a book?"

I sit down at my desk. "Oh. I thought I mentioned it."

"Nope, I would've remembered." He points to the pages sitting on my desk. "What's it about?"

It dawns on me that I have another chance to get a fresh perspective for my book. "Looks like you cleared out the clinic. Sit down and I'll read you a chapter."

The Adventures of Adam Freeman, DDS
June 13—*Mad About You*

Tonight's the Freemans' weekly date night, and it couldn't have come at a better time. I'm looking forward to recharging my batteries and reconnecting with Minnie. A weekly date night wasn't my idea (I'd be happy with once a month), but Minnie lobbied for it and I gave in. It's not that I don't like going out with her, but sometimes a guy just needs space. I mean, I love my wife and all, but I also love my time alone. Scratch that. I love my time alone more. But even I recognize I've got to compromise in this marriage to make it work.

When you think about it, marriage is a sacred bond between two people who decide to spend their lives together—and who can un-decide that too. But as kids we are thrust into this world with parents who have to accept us, flaws and all. And the truth is, our parents didn't really *choose* us. They ended up with us in the genetic lottery. In my case, my mother tolerated me while she adored my sister. Pretty much every family has a "golden child," and Hannah, my sister, was ours. When we were growing up, she was the one who was given an air conditioner in her room while I suffered and sweated, sleeping in my underwear because my bedroom was "between two rooms that already had AC." Then there were all the times my mom took my sister out for ice cream and shopping but, because I was lactose intolerant, I was left home with my quiet father whose idea of playing with me was reading *The New York Times* by himself. My dad did spend time with me, but only to watch sports. His other passion was playing one-on-

one basketball, but I grew frustrated losing to him. Once when I was fourteen and we were the same height, I took an 18-12 lead in a game, but he stormed back to win 20-18. Due to his ultra-competitive nature, he never played basketball with me again.

Minnie and I go out to dinner at a neighborhood bistro with white tablecloths where a piano/guitar duo is playing singer-songwriter tunes ranging from Simon and Garfunkel to Ed Sheeran by the fireplace in the back corner. I love listening to live music, and I'm in great spirits. After the wine comes and we order our food, Minnie gives me the recap of what's going on at home with the kids.

"I signed the older girls up for the early bird special at camp."

Gulping down a spoonful of French onion soup, I ask, "How much did that set us back?"

Minnie pierces a cherry tomato with her fork. "A little over six grand."

I drop my spoon. With a string of melted cheese dribbling from my lip, I blurt out, "I should have been a camp director! They must make some good coin!"

Minnie laughs. "Debbie spent eleven thousand dollars to send her boys to a two-week sleepaway camp, so this day camp's a bargain."

"A bargain?" I sputter. "How is six grand a bargain for four weeks in the woods behind the local YMCA? This day camp doesn't even provide lunch. Sounds more like extortion to me."

Minnie's face sours. "What's your problem, Adam?" she says between bites of her niçoise salad. "I saved you five percent by doing the early bird special. You're welcome."

I sigh. I guess these camps have to make enough money to take them through the winter, but it's still outrageous. People balk at how much I charge for a dental cleaning and X-rays, but I have a Doctor of Dental Surgery degree from UPenn and my specialty training from Yale, and I run an office of trained professionals, not a group of hormonal teenage counselors-in-training learning on the job. They say finances are one of the biggest problems a marriage faces. Minnie and I have a lot of hot-button issues, but fortunately money is not one of them. I may get cranky, but I make enough to give us and the kids a good life.

"Well, I'm sure the girls will enjoy it. I'll just have to take on a few more patients this year to cover it." Minnie nods and smiles her beautiful smile that can still make my heart skip a beat.

Now seems like a good time to update Minnie about my hellish work week. "Remember last month when I got upset with Michelle for not having the burs that I need when doing fillings?"

"Vaguely," she says. "I remember you were mad and almost fired her, but Veronica stopped her from leaving." She signals the waiter for another glass of Pinot Grigio.

"Yesterday she told me she doesn't want to do the ordering anymore."

"Where do these girls you hire get off telling the boss what they will and won't do?"

"I know, right? That's what I thought. But you'll be proud of me, honey. I told her I'd give her a fifty-cent raise for doing the ordering. She was psyched."

If looks could kill, I'd be dead and buried. Minnie lowers her eyes and bites her lip. "Why," she says, folding her arms and exhaling sharply, "would you give a raise to someone complaining and refusing to do her job? That's not a precedent you want to set."

"What do you mean?" I ask. "I thought you'd be glad I listened to her perspective and tried to do the right thing."

"Adam, I don't get you. You'll fire someone over their phone but give another person a raise when they refuse to do something. You've established a protocol for rewarding insubordination."

Talk about taking the wind out of my sails. "Damn it, Minnie, I hate it when you disagree with me. I was trying to help her out and solve the problem."

We sit without speaking for a few minutes, listening to the duo's acoustic rendition of "Satisfaction" and then the main course is served. Minnie's Chilean sea bass with whipped potatoes and asparagus looks much better than my seafood risotto. As usual, I reach across the table and take the first bite out of her dish. Minnie frowns. She grudgingly puts up with my neurotic belief that food always tastes better from her plate than mine. I brace myself for her reproach.

"Adam, it's over."

"What?" I stare at her. Does she mean our marriage?

"Stop pouting. The thing at your office. It's done. I would've handled it differently, but you made your decision, live with it."

"Minnie, I love working with teeth, but I hate being an HR manager. I'm not sure how much more of this I can take."

"It's part of the job, Adam. And you make a good living."

"But I'm sacrificing my mental health for that living. I'm not equipped for this. There was no course in dental school on how to deal with disobedient staff members. How tolerant do I have to be of them? First the cell phone thing and now letting myself get pinched for a raise. Last month it was the girls refusing to stay late with me to see an emergency patient. When does it end?"

Minnie eats her fish in silence. Finally she says, "You know the rules of date night. Are we done talking about your office?"

"Yes. I mean, no, not yet," I continue. "I need to solve this before I go back to work Monday, and date night or not, I need your help."

Minnie sighs. "My advice: take time to think about your decisions. But you're incapable of it. You certainly didn't think about how I'd react if you brought your work problems up on date night again. I thought we were working on this, but self-centered Adam is back."

"What are you talking about?" I say, grabbing her wine glass and taking a sip since mine is already empty. "Don't you realize I'm hurting here? I've had a horrible week. I'm exhausted. I'm twitching. I nearly passed out from stress today. Maybe you could be more sympathetic."

"Adam, these are problems of your own making. I'm not your office manager. And I can't be there for you any more than I already am. You need a good therapist. I think you're depressed."

"I am *not* depressed," I shout back, slamming my fist on the table and rattling the silverware. "I've never been depressed. Depression is for weak people who stay in bed, watch TV, and eat ice cream all day. I get up. I go to work. I face my problems even if I do a poor job of solving them. And I'm going to go in there Monday and show those girls who's boss."

Minnie pushes her chair away from the table. "Adam, anger isn't going to fix anything. You need help, and you probably need medication. Look what a little Lexapro and Atavan have done for me. The pills will get rid of your anxiety and negative feelings so you can calm down and think straight. Maybe they'll even help with E.T."

I scowl. "Minnie, I asked you not to call it that. It's not an alien. It's an eye twitch."

"Come on, honey, have a sense of humor." She smiles and reaches out to touch my hand, but I jerk my arm back. *E.T.* is Minnie's favorite movie of all time, and she likes to think of my eye twitch as an alien in my body with a mind of its own.

"For your information, it's been getting worse. The acupuncture you made me try didn't help to control it. But what would you know about stress, anyway?"

"I'm home with the kids all day. Try it if you don't think it's stressful."

"I mean real work. Calling a camp and spending my paycheck doesn't qualify."

Minnie gets up from her chair, and there is fire in her eyes. "What I do at home is not work? Taking care of the kids, schlepping them to their activities, running the house, paying the bills, making the dinner, doing your goddamn laundry?"

"Sure, you do a lot. But when I come home from a full day of work all tired and drained, I *still* have to help out with the kids and do the dishes and bring the laundry basket upstairs from the basement and take out the trash and change a goddamn light bulb or whatever it is you've put on the task list. I'm working two jobs here, and it's *really* tiring."

Minnie grabs her purse from under the table and turns to leave. "Sorry if asking you to help out with your kids is a problem. Screw you, Adam Freeman!"

By now, people in the restaurant are staring. The women are glowering at me, while the men have this look that says, "Bro, you're fucked tonight." I grab Minnie's arm to stop her from leaving.

"Let go of me."

"Listen, Minnie," I say, tightening my grip. "You signed up for this job. You wanted to stay at home with the kids, and I'm fine with that. And I know your life's not a cakewalk. But it would be nice if, once in a while, you acknowledged that when I come home and help out I'm doing part of your job too. My dad never did any of this stuff when I was growing up."

"That's rich, Adam. You want credit for doing part of my job, when you're practically asking me to manage your office—on the one night we're not supposed to talk about work or the kids. You think I sit on the couch all day and eat bonbons? You have some fucking nerve. I do everything for this family...and don't compare yourself to your dad. He was a man of his time, and he's also a gentleman who walks through walls for your mom. And what do I get from you?" She wiggles free of my grip and heads for the door of the restaurant. "I'm taking the car. You can call an Uber."

I sit down at the table and pick a shrimp from my risotto, but I'm not hungry. The other diners are no longer staring, but they're talking about us—about me. I signal the waiter for the check, then have the horrifying thought that a few of my patients could be here tonight. I blow out the candle on the table and duck out as quietly as possible after I've paid the bill.

I'm relieved; Minnie is waiting for me in the parking lot. I get in the passenger side, and we don't speak on the drive home. After a few minutes, I turn on my Back to the '80s Rockin' Mix to dispel the silence. After she pulls into the garage and we get out of the car, Minnie tells me to get back in to drive the babysitter home.

Our main sitter, Stephanie, is a tall, blonde high-school senior. On the drive home, she tells me all about how cheerleading competition is going. She is dating the high school quarterback, Jason, but has a few options as to who she'll take to prom. I want to put my arm around her in a fatherly way and tell her to enjoy being seventeen, beautiful, and free because being tied down in a relationship is the hardest thing in the world. Once you marry and have kids, the only way to get out is to hurt the people you love. But I refrain from sharing my pessimistic, neurotic thoughts and listen to Stephanie tell me all about how senior night went.

On the way home, I think about the mess—and the scene—I made at dinner. I know I hurt Minnie, but I'm hurting too, and she doesn't seem to understand. My twitch, which reared its ugly head toward the end of dinner, is now out of control, and I feel a dark cloud coming over me. I didn't want to say those mean things to Minnie. I felt so much rage and couldn't stop myself. Why do I feel this pain and suffering? Why can't I get a grip on my marriage—or my life? I think of the Buchmans in *Mad About You* and how there's always more under a marriage than meets the eye. We smile and laugh with our friends and put up a brave face around our kids, but it's all an act—a show we put on to avoid facing our real problems. I stare at my hands on the steering wheel, the wedding ring on my finger. I take it off at the office each day before I work on patients, but I always remember to put it on before I come home. Because marriage is home. And Minnie is home. And our kids...

I pull into our garage and swallow the lump in my throat, then wipe the tears from my eyes before walking back into the house. I know what I want to say to Minnie. I head to the kitchen, ready to pour us leftover wine, ready with my humble, heartfelt apology. But Minnie isn't in the kitchen or anywhere downstairs. She's up in our bed, sleeping. She looks peaceful, not angry, and I wonder if she had thoughts similar to mine while I was driving the sitter home. I put on my pajamas and slip into bed beside her. I look down at her angelic face, then turn my attention to my growing member. I think about caressing Minnie—we've had some amazing sleepy sex—but I know tonight is not the night for that. I apologize to my boy, Charlie, down there. "No post-date-night sex *again*, buddy." I can tell he's really pissed at me for sabotaging his plans. He can't even remember the last time we got laid. It's a vicious cycle—no sex leads to more stress which causes me to say stupid things to Minnie that make her not want to have sex with me which makes me more stressed which... I grab one of Minnie's Ambiens from the bottle on her nightstand and down it without water, then drift off into a dreamless sleep.

* * *

Janet, my office manager, who resembles Sally Field as Forrest Gump's mother with dark but graying wavy hair and soft features, peeks her head into the room. "Sorry to interrupt you, gentlemen, but the clinic is full of patients. We require your services."

"We'll be there in a minute." I turn towards Dr. Smith and eagerly ask, "What do you think, Dennis?"

"Dr. Silverstein!" Dennis slams his hand on the desk. "Did you record my last night out with my wife or something?"

"You found it relatable?"

"Most guys can relate to the stress at work, feeling overwhelmed, and then having to come home without any time to relax. It can make a man insane. You nailed it!"

I smile broadly. "I'm psyched you understand. And Adam, he isn't too much of an asshole, right?"

"Adam? He's a gigantic prick."

I jerk my head back in shock.

Dennis continues, "I admit, I've had those thoughts but would *never* say them out loud. Women will hate that guy."

"But he's real, right?"

"I know guys like that. But if he's your main man, he needs to be cooler. Or at least surround him with some good dudes. Like give him an entourage. Let's get to clinic, Dr. Silverstein." Dr. Smith claps his hands.

I look up at my dental and orthodontic degrees in their oversized mahogany frames and the Veritas symbols etched in gold across the custom-crimson matting. But the recessed LED lights from above my desk are shining brightly on the manuscript. I stare at the cover page, *The Adventures of Adam Freeman, DDS*. "You gave me a great idea. Can you cover clinic for me today?"

He shoots me a look. "Clinic's crazy busy; I'm not used to this patient volume."

I plead, "I need your help, Dennis. The literary agent I had lunch with today is leaving town in less than twenty-four hours, and she gave me a deadline, an ultimatum. I have to decide whether to rewrite my book as a memoir or stick with my vision. I want to pursue my dream just like when you joined the surfing tour for a year before your ortho residency."

"That year was lit."

Janet comes in again. "Doctors, we need you."

Dr. Smith pats me on the shoulder. "Janet, Dr. Silverstein is busy finishing an important project. I'll handle clinic this afternoon. You do this, Jacob. I got your back."

CHAPTER FOUR
3:04 p.m.

I take my laptop and jog to my car in the back of the parking lot. Dennis was right, Adam needs serious tweaking. I shut my eyes. Okay, I know I need to spice up Adam's life. His friends come into play later, but let's add a scene where we meet Adam's buddies in more depth and get to see what happens when guys hang out and keep it real. But none of this fake, *Entourage*, heightened-for-Hollywood crap. It has to be what happens when real dads in suburban America come together and hang out at the playground while their kids play. I climb into the passenger's seat, power up the laptop, wiggle my fingers to get the blood flowing, and start typing a new chapter.

The Adventures of Adam Freeman, DDS
June 14—*Entourage*

Finally, the weekend's here! After all the stress at the office and the tough date night with Minnie, I finally get two whole days away from work to relax and reload. I live for weekends. It's the only time I feel at ease and can be myself, and my eye twitch even goes into remission.

Sometimes I look at my kids—Paige, Rose, and Spencer—and wonder what I did to deserve these amazing children. When Paige was six, I put a baseball bat in her hands and tried to pitch to her. Instead of swinging, she used the bat as a microphone for singing. In that moment, I knew my girl wasn't going to be my athlete. Instead, now eleven, she's an artist, plays the piano like a prodigy—although I'm totally biased!—and loves to sing and dance. Rose, however, is a whole different ballgame, so to speak. She came out of the womb wanting a ball in her hands and ready to compete. At eight, she plays three sports really well: soccer, basketball, and softball. It fascinates me that two sisters with the same parents can be this different early in life. And what will the littlest one, Spencer, my three-year-old, end up liking? At this point he appears to have been put on earth for his older sisters to dress him up in their play clothes. He has become their living doll. One day last month, they made him a princess, painted his fingernails, and put makeup all over his face while Minnie was—you guessed it—checking her email. "For Christ's sake, he could end up wanting to be a woman or something," I snapped at Minnie when she demanded to know why I was yelling at the girls. She said I was being irrational, and who cares what his sexuality will be when he's older. On some level, I know she's right; we'll love him no matter what. But still, he's a boy—my only boy—and why encourage a gender switch? He loves playing catch with me, and he has a hell of a left-handed throw. I'm thinking he could be a hotshot flamethrower out of the bullpen for a long Major League Baseball career. I mean what the hell—a dad can dream, right?

I know exactly how to turn things down a notch after the date night debacle. I walk into our bathroom, which is dimly lit due to a burned-out bulb, and gaze longingly at Minnie through the clear shower door. In the semi-darkness, I can barely make out her lovely shape. I have to say, my wife still looks amazing after giving birth to three children and ten years of marriage. I'm a breast and legs man, and, well, Minnie still rocks it in both departments. After a minute or two of gawking, I realize I need to get out of there quickly because I feel Charlie starting to rise. Minnie would have no problem with it, but I don't feel like explaining to my kids when they burst into the bathroom why Daddy's pajama bottoms are bulging.

I speak loudly enough for Minnie to hear me over the running water. "I'll take the kids out to the playground today, Minnie. Then we'll all go to lunch so you can have a peaceful morning. I'll get the Four Horsemen together."

No, I'm not suggesting the apocalypse is coming—though it almost did last night at dinner. The Four Horsemen is what my three best friends and I call ourselves, and we often meet on Saturday mornings with our kids. I love these guys like brothers—after all, they are my very own version of Vinny Chase's *Entourage*.

I wait for her response. Minnie lets the water run over her wet, jet-black hair, a la Phoebe Cates in *Fast Times at Ridgemont High*. She finally replies, "That'd be helpful. I have to buy groceries and run errands today. Oh, and before you leave, Adam, make a list of what you and the kids want to eat, and change the light bulb in the bathroom. It's a little dark and creepy in here."

Dark and creepy? Change the light bulb? What a buzzkill on my fantasy.

"I was really enjoying the mood lighting," I say, imagining Phoebe Cates asking Judge Reinhold to change the filter before she comes out of the pool. Damn, my work is never done. All I want to do is take the kids out for some fun and hang with my buddies. "I'll change the light bulb later, Minnie, I promise."

I open the shower door to give her a kiss, but she frowns at me and sighs. "I was hoping you'd change the bulb now. I don't want to get ready in the dark."

I grumble and storm out of the bathroom with a full-blown hard-on, shift Charlie to get him comfortable down there, and make sure I untuck my shirt to cover up the evidence.

As I'm leaving the bathroom, I hear a scream. *"Shut the door. It's freezing!"* If there's one thing Minnie hates, it's being cold.

I yell back, "Sorry about that," and quickly close the door. The kids are downstairs watching the ever-present television and clinging to Minnie's phone and my iPad.

"Get off those electronics," I tell them. They ignore me.

After taking care of the great light bulb fiasco, I head back down and start to make my patented banana and chocolate chip Mickey Mouse pancakes for breakfast. While I'm waiting for them to turn a perfect golden brown, I pull out my phone to text the Four Horsemen to schedule our playdate.

My buddies and I came up with this name for ourselves one drunken night while playing poker. Ryan, the fanatical Christian of the group, decided to give Klein and me, the two Jews, a lecture on the Book of Revelation. Errol, the agnostic, listened intently as Ryan described the Four Horsemen of the Apocalypse—Death, Famine, War, and Conquest—and how they are harbingers of the Last Judgment. Klein, who has a wicked sense of humor, had the inspiration to name our group the Four Horsemen. Errol claimed Conquest, the White Horse, in deference to his exploits with women, and we all agreed. Ryan's choice was obvious: War, the Red Horse, which matched the Irish red hair of his children and the fact that he is a military buff with a large gun collection. Neither Klein nor I wanted Death, so we played one last round of Texas Hold'em to decide. When we revealed our cards, I was happy to beat Klein and become the Black Horse, Famine, leaving Klein as Death, the Pale Horse, by default.

Here's the back-of-the-baseball-card rundown on the Four Horsemen:

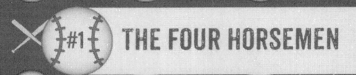

#1 THE FOUR HORSEMEN

JOSHUA KLEIN (aka: Death) ✕ **Entourage Persona: Johnny Drama**

Height: 5'8"   Weight: 178 lbs   Bats: Left   Throws: Left

Born: February 26, 1977   Home: Sunnyville, Connecticut

Wife: Joy(less)   Kids: Miriam (14), Tara (12), Nicole (8), Grace (4)

Look-alike: Josh Radnor as Ted Mosby on *How I Met Your Mother*

Stats: 1999 BA, University of Vermont; 2002 Masters in Education, UConn

Occupation: Teaches history at an all-girls school

Great guy who does anything for his friends. Examples include: helping with the backsplash in my kitchen, binge-watching *The Wire* with me, and installing a new generator to restore our electricity after a hurricane.

#2 THE FOUR HORSEMEN

ERROL NAISMITH (aka: Conquest) ✕ **Entourage Persona: Vinny Chase**

Height: 6'1"   Weight: 185 lbs   Bats: Right   Throws: Right

Born: April 5, 1977   Home: Scarsfield, New York

Wife: Kristy   Kids: Felicity (11), Tara (12), Joey (8), Courtney (4)

Look-alike: Combo of trainer Tony Horton and George Clooney in his *ER* days

Stats: 1999 BS, Tufts University; 2006 MD, St. Georges University; Residency in radiology from Weill Cornell Medical Center

Occupation: Radiologist at Swan Medical Center in New York City

Father was a physician who divorced three times. Due to Errol's poor college grades, he worked for a few years as a model then went to med school in Granada. He's always had a way with the ladies.

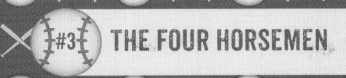

RYAN O'MALLEY (aka: War) ✕ **Entourage Persona: Turtle**

Height: 6'4"   Weight: 275 lbs   Bats: Left/Right   Throws: Right
Born: January 20, 1977   Home: Skandy, New York
Wife: Sally   Kids: Ryan Jr. (11), Sam (8), Ben (6)

Look-alike: Chris Sullivan as Toby Damon in *This is Us*
Stats: 1995 All-Section high school football player. Voted "Best Eyes" in our high school yearbook. One year at Skandy Community College
Occupation: Stay-at-home dad

The guy who always laughs the loudest in the room. He plays guitar and taught himself to play ukulele by watching YouTube videos. My first friend to embrace his baldness and shave his head. He now sports a cool goatee.

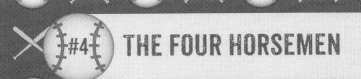

ADAM FREEMAN (aka: Famine) ✕ **Entourage Persona: Eric**

Height: 6'2"   Weight: 170 lbs   Bats: Right   Throws: Right
Born: October 26, 1977   Home: Davidson, Connecticut
Wife: Minnie   Kids: Page (11), Rose (8), Spencer (3)

Look-alike: Bradley Cooper (kidding), John Stewart from the *Daily Show*
Stats: 1999 BS (*magna cum laude*), Tufts University; 2003 DDS (*cum laude*) University of Pennsylvania; Pediatric Residency, Yale New Haven University
Occupation: Pediatric Dentist

Almost dropped by the doctor at birth. A neurotic, Jewish, Ivy-League-trained pediatric dentist who suffers from a nervous eye twitch. All this guy wants is to get rid of his anxiety and find peace and happiness in his life.

I get to the playground and see my good buddy, Klein. We joke that we Facebook—we stayed in touch by writing letters, talking on the phone, and taking the proverbial summer break road trips. Coincidentally, we ended up living one town away from each other as adults, and he has four girls similar in age to my kids. Klein and I hit the guy jackpot because our kids like playing together, so we can hang out while they keep themselves busy. Like Kramer in *Seinfeld*, he's the type of guy who always has something going on. In college, he traveled for two months straight to see his favorite band, Pearl Jam, perform. At one point he became obsessed with running marathons— and he still runs a few days a week—but now he's on a spiritual journey. Last summer, he took a trip to India where he studied Jainism and met a spiritual guru. Before that, he was learning about Buddhism and Hinduism, and now he wants me to attend his meditation class. Klein would make a great character in a book.

Klein's only albatross in life is his wife, Joy—nicknamed "Joyless" by the Horsemen. She's the quintessential tiger mom, and she doesn't like me or any of our gang. I forget if she's Chinese, Taiwanese, or Korean. I've never been good with all those Asian countries. I do give her credit for converting to Judaism, and Klein loves that she's embraced Jewish culture. But man, my friend married a real hard-ass. She gets off on control and runs that house like the CEO of a Fortune 500 company. She has their girls' schedules—for school and home—on a whiteboard in the kitchen, and each one knows exactly where they need to be and at what time. Klein receives event reminders from their family Google calendar on his phone telling him when it's time for dinner. Joyless has told Klein that the optimal time for him to come home is before 5:35 p.m., because if he misses his mark, he'll rile up the kids before bed. No matter how much advice and support the Horsemen give him, poor Klein seems unable to grow a pair to stand up for himself. Minnie and her honey-do list are nothing compared to Drill Sergeant Joyless.

If I were Klein, I'd throw bleach on the whiteboard, delete the Google calendar, and slip Valium into Joyless's morning cup of Jasmine tea. But, somehow, he keeps it together and perseveres.

Right after I see Klein, Errol Naismith, MD, struts into the park leading his kids. Dr. Errol has a cushy job as a radiologist where he can work from home or go into the office and congregate with his practice of twelve colleagues. At my encouragement, he now has a side business of reading dental cone beam CT scans to detect abnormal defects.

I call Errol "Doctor Suave" because even though I find his cockiness annoying, most people, and especially the ladies, find him charming. With his full head of hair, athletic and chiseled build, and prominent chin that can be seen before he enters a room, he could be straight out of casting for *Mad Men*. I am delighted to see he's graying at the temples, but even that look is handsome on him. Maybe one day his hair will fall out, but even then, he'd probably look like Derek Jeter. The guy lucked out in the gene department.

I don't mean to be jealous of my former college roommate; he's always been extremely nice to me and a class act, but it's amazing how some people seem to have it all at their fingertips. I worked my ass off taking dental prerequisite classes that did not allow me to have much of a social life. Errol, on the other hand, chose to go out three nights a week and come back to the room with "company" instead of hitting the books. I pretended to be asleep, but the moaning and groaning of his nightly girlfriends always kept me up.

Although Errol had a successful career as a model after college, he always wanted to follow in his father's footsteps and become a doctor. I didn't think he would do it because of all the hard work, but leave it to Errol to get educated in style. He studied in the Caribbean while I froze my balls off in the cold northeastern winters at dental school. Rumor had it that he slept with one of the Cornell admissions officers when he was interviewing for his residency, but that son of a bitch still won't confirm or deny, so the urban legend continues.

Errol walks up, holding a green smoothie and his usual egg white sandwich. "What's up, my friends?" I look at his breakfast and make a mental note to start eating healthier. "Hey, we missed you at poker last weekend, Adam. It was a blast. I got loaded and went out after and got a tattoo." Errol pulls up the sleeve on his bicep, exposing an enormous horse. "Come on guys, as members of the Four Horsemen, I expect you to do the same!"

I look at Klein. "Did you know about this?"

"No, I left on the early side."

"Holy shit. What the hell, Errol, how old are you? You're acting like a frat boy."

"Learn to live a little, Freeman."

"Come on, Errol. You're not twenty anymore. The concerts, the long weekend trips, and every time I see you, you've been out all night. Look at that six o'clock shadow. And now a tattoo?"

"Don't be so lame, dude. You should've joined us."

"Minnie had plans."

"Mah Jongg night again?" He smiles slyly.

"Yeah, I had to watch the kids."

"Your wife's such a party animal. I bet Charlie's getting a lot of action, you dirty dog you." Errol laughs from deep within his belly. I admire people who have the ability to share their love of life with everyone. This happens to be one of Errol's greatest attributes. He finds joy and happiness in everything, and I wish I could bottle up that aspect of his personality and drink it to help me get through my days at work. "Hey, don't forget to clear your wife's schedule. I hope you're still on for the trip to PR."

"Of course I'm going to Puerto Rico. I've been stressed at work lately, and I totally need a break."

Klein cuts me off. "You should come with me to this new meditation group I'm in. I am telling you, these relaxation techniques we're learning are the bomb. They've worked wonders for me."

Suddenly, Ryan O'Malley comes hobbling around the corner with a cane. His kids instantly run from him and onto the playground.

"What's going on with you? You look like an old man," Errol needles him.

"I threw out my back."

"How?"

"I'm embarrassed to say..."

"During sex no doubt."

"No, I wish," he says. "It happened when...I sneezed."

The three of us can't stop laughing. At least we're laughing with Ryan, not at him, because Ryan laughs louder than the rest of us. "I'm pissed because I was taking off the pounds recently, and now I can't exercise for a month."

Ryan is of Irish descent and as hearty as they come. He's also one of the happiest people I know. His wife is a big shot with IBM, and he gets to stay home and take care of the kids. Lucky bastard—I'd love to have his cushy job. One day he told me the secret that all mothers are afraid to admit—he loves it. He loves putting his headphones in, zoning out to his iTunes playlist, and folding mountains of laundry. "I love the smell of Downy in the morning," he said to me one time, doing his best Robert Duvall imitation from *Apocalpyse Now*.

I look Ryan over and notice that since my buddy dropped over thirty pounds, he's got more bounce in his step even though he's still fifty pounds heavier than in his glory days as a starting linebacker for our state championship high school football team. In his heyday, Ryan was a super-jock, and being his friend gave me high school street cred. We've been acquaintances since kindergarten, but we became buddies when I tutored him in tenth grade math. He helped me cross over the chasm between the studious nerd crowd to the popular jock clique. Life is strange. It seems like yesterday we were hanging out in high school, and now we're the next generation to contribute to the betterment of society.

Personally, I always thought that I could go through life and be content without having a family. It's nothing against my kids; I never wanted to subject children to the same painful childhood I had. The bullying I endured was unbearable. Kids teased me because I wore glasses earlier than most. At recess, I preferred to be left alone to play Dungeons and Dragons with friends instead of joining the kickball game. That made me an outsider and a target for insults like "dungeon boy" and "fantasy freak." I still remember Big Billy the Bully taunting me in front of his friends. "You're not from this planet...you must be an alien." That's another reason Minnie calling my twitch E.T. bugs the shit out of me.

Childhood is brutal and can scar you for life, and I didn't want to subject my children to the inevitability of human cruelty. But I knew if I wanted to marry Minnie—and I desperately wanted to marry her—I would have to have a family. In our late-night talks, Minnie said she wouldn't feel whole if she didn't become a mom.

I tried to protest. "You're already a whole person. You don't need kids to complete yourself. And besides, I want to focus my attention on you." Minnie told me that was sweet, but she didn't let up, and I realized this was a package deal. I decided to go with the flow and see what having kids would be like. As Klein likes to say, "Raising children is the biggest science experiment in the world, and it happens without a lab manual!" I'm overjoyed that I took the leap of faith with Minnie to have a family.

I focus on the group again. Klein says to Ryan, "Glad you could join us."

"I had to get out of the house. My wife's friend from college—that chick, Cierra—is over."

I try to remember Cierra. "The one with the bug eyes that looks like Crazy Eyes from *Orange is the New Black*? She lives with all those cats, right?"

"You watch *way* too much TV," Errol says to me, then looks at Ryan. "Is that the single one from your New Year's Eve party? Smoking body?"

Ryan continues, "Yeah. They sat in the kitchen for hours discussing whether they should change the light fixtures in Cierra's bathroom. How much time do you need to discuss that crap?"

Klein yells, "Girls, Mommy's going to kill me if we don't put on the sunblock!"

They shout back, "No! We're playing."

Ryan says, "I never talked to my parents like that. What's with the way kids act today?"

Klein laughs. "This is totally the Negotiation Generation. I see it in school and with my own kids too. They'll spend thirty minutes arguing with me about when they should go to bed. They have no respect for adults and no fear of the repercussions of their actions."

Ryan responds, "Mine know they need to be accountable for their words and deeds. Last week, Ryan, Jr. told me to 'suck it.' I almost smacked him, but I ended up taking away his Xbox for a week."

"Better be careful man," warns Klein. "You can get arrested for even threatening to touch your kid. At my school, I've heard about kids calling DCF on their parents. You can still have rules and discipline, but you can't lay a hand on them or you're seriously fucked."

Ryan replies, "I didn't hit him, but I did grab his arm and remind him who's in charge. He's lucky he was born in this generation. You know how many times I got the belt when I was his age?"

I'm about to say something when out of the corner of my eye I see Spencer is climbing up the slide from the bottom while another kid is racing down. I watch helplessly as the kid's feet swing up and smash into Spencer's face. My little one falls backwards off the slide right onto his head. He's crying hysterically.

I rush to Spencer and the guys follow. First thing I do is check that he didn't lose any teeth—my worst nightmare. Fortunately, he still has the full complement and no mouth injuries. There's a scrape on his elbow. Minnie is paranoid about concussions, but Spencer doesn't have any lumps or bumps, and that's a good sign. Trying to calm down a three-year-old is as hard as catching the wind. But some TLC and four dads to distract him seems to do the trick. Eventually, we all agree that Spencer is okay. Although my daughters didn't see the incident, the scrape may become evidence.

"I'll never hear the end of this," I tell them.

Errol agrees. "I still have equity because one time Courtney fell out of the high chair when Kristy forgot to buckle her in. I use that as my ammunition whenever she gets nervous leaving the kids with me."

"Good one. But I'd be nervous leaving my kids with you too," Ryan says, laughing at Errol. "It's hard dude. Last week I drove out of the garage and realized I left Sam behind in the house." They continue their banter as I hold Spencer tight in my arms. I feel guilty because he hurt himself on my watch and, despite the usual weekend respite, my eye starts twitching again.

"I've got to get out of here." I can feel my eye going crazy and my anxiety rising.

"Dude, you're sweating," Errol tells me. "You okay?"

Ryan is concerned. "You're not going to drop dead of a heart attack here, are you?"

Great, I wish Ryan had never said that, because that's another one of my paranoid fears. I'm playing with my kids and I croak in front of them. Despite the happy childhood I've tried to provide, that would totally ruin their lives. I didn't bring my children into this crazy world to desert them with an untimely death.

* * *

Beep. I look down at my cell phone. It's a text from Janet, "Don't forget Yale Grand Rounds Lecture tonight."

The timing couldn't be worse, but I know I'll lose my privileges if I don't make an appearance. I text Leah, "Won't b home 4 dinner. Yale Grand Rds 2nite."

CHAPTER FIVE
4:44 p.m.

I speed through the backroads of Matingly only to reach a dead stop on I-95 North. This is the one time in my life I'm thankful that Connecticut's roads resemble a parking lot. Might as well make good use of my time, so I decide to read more of Adam while I'm stuck in this mess.

The Adventures of Adam Freeman, DDS
June 16—Arrested Development

I pull into the parking lot and try to psych myself up. I'd really like to have a good day at work. I've just listened to a self-help podcast called *The Power of Positivity*, and I'm determined to implement what I learned. I open the car door, see an empty bubble gum wrapper, pick it up, and put it in my car garbage bag. I'm OCD when it comes to litter. Candy wrappers, soda cans—you name it, I'll trash it. But I do have limits. I draw the line at used condoms and rotten food. These cleanup efforts are my little contribution to help improve the environment. Minnie often asks me why I don't have this same obsession with picking up my laundry or clearing my dishes at home. I can't explain it. It's the way I am.

I'm in a surprisingly good mood, feeling wonderfully self-righteous after throwing out the street trash, when I notice that my large sign on the building has been vandalized. Instead of seeing:

DR. ADAM FREEMAN
PEDIATRIC DENTIST

I now see:

DR. DAM PEEMAN
FREDIATRIC DENTIST

Goddamn it! It's the second time this year someone's messed with my signage. They didn't address how to react to vandalism in the positivity podcast, so I have no strategy to stop me from fuming. I walk into the office, and Veronica is at the front desk smiling, almost as if she thinks the joke is funny. "Can you believe it, Dr. Freeman? They got to our sign again."

I don't say good morning with a big bright smile, the way I practiced in my rearview mirror. Instead I blurt out, "Call the landlord and have them take it down, now. Look into signs that can't be defaced this way. I don't want to be dealing with this crap. All I want to do is fix kids' teeth."

"I'll take care of it," she responds. "Oh, and Tiffany's out sick today."

"Again? That's the third time this month. When it rains for me it doesn't pour, it typhoons!" I look down at my phone, and there's a Facebook instant message from Klein.

"Hey there, Dr. Peeman. How are you? I saw what those damn pee vandals did to your sign. You must be pretty pissed." I put my phone away with a scowl. The day is flushed, and it's not even 9:00 a.m.

As I walk towards my personal office, I notice a few assistants and hygienists acting strangely, so I decide to attend the morning huddle. Are they laughing at me because of the sign? Did I say something wrong already today? Is there cream cheese from this morning's bagel stuck to my chin? After the huddle, I'm still stumped. I ask Veronica if she knows what's going on. She hesitates then calls in Jackie, one of my hygienists.

Jackie comes in and stares at the floor. She starts speaking without lifting her head. "I'm not proud of what I did this weekend, Dr. Freeman."

There is a deadly silence. Could she be the one who vandalized my sign? Did she steal something from the office? Or maybe she got drunk at a party and threw up—but why would that be any of my business? Instead she tells me, "I'm sorry. I took off Tiffany's braces."

I pause to put this news in context...and now I remember that Tiffany, my newest assistant, hired three months ago, has—oops, *had*—braces from her old orthodontist in Ohio. She told me she was going to transfer her care to a friend of mine, Dr. Richard Clarity, an orthodontist in Davidson, but she hadn't gotten around to making the appointment.

Veronica interjects because she can see I'm still not getting it. "Dr. Freeman, they came into the office over the weekend and removed the braces here."

"Here? How? What?"

Jackie explains, "I used to work for Dr. Clarity, where I learned to remove braces. We came in on Saturday morning, and I took her braces off. You don't have to pay me, though."

"What? *Pay* you?"

"Oh, well, we clocked in."

"Clocked in?"

I feel like I'm in the middle of an *Arrested Development* episode. My dysfunctional staff is like Michael Bluth's spoiled and eccentric family.

I move closer to the two of them and stand to my full height. "Let me get this straight. You came into my office over the weekend, removed an employee's braces without my permission, thought there'd be no consequences, *and* you'd get paid for your time? Are you insane?"

Veronica whispers to me, "Dr. Freeman, with all due respect, you're being snippy."

"Snippy? I'm being snippy? I'm not the one who came in and snipped the wires now, am I? What were you two thinking?"

Jackie starts to tear up. "Tiffany called me over the weekend. She had a big date with her boyfriend," she says, breaking into hysterics. "She really...wanted the braces off...and said they were going to...come off anyway. She begged me...and I felt bad saying no. I realize now it was a lapse of judgment."

Veronica stares at me, waiting for my reaction, ready to place her body between Jackie and me if I lunge at her. I look over at this sobbing woman in front of me and my heart softens. It's hard for me to be angry with Jackie because she has her own *Arrested Development* issues. At twenty-eight, she still lives with her mom and her two older brothers while saving up for her own apartment. Her dad is in prison—for drug abuse. She's a reliable and hardworking employee, trying to create a life unlike the one she grew up knowing.

"Okay. It was a *huge* lapse of judgment. If something had gone wrong, I would have been liable. And my insurance premiums are already sky-high. Fortunately for you, nothing did. Don't let it happen again."

Jackie leaves the room with her head down, and I'm left with Veronica. "Can you believe this shit? How am I supposed to run a practice when my entire staff lacks impulse control and adult judgment? I should fire the whole lot of them. But then I'd have to go through the hiring process again. I'm basically fucked."

My eye is going crazy, and Veronica can't help but notice.

"Are you okay, Dr. Freeman? Your eye is twitching a lot."

I'm sure my staff has seen me twitch before, but this is the first time someone's addressed it. I think about Minnie's suggestion that I take medication, but that only makes me angrier. I take a deep breath and exhale, but it comes out like a growl.

"I'm fine," I respond crisply. "Is my first patient ready?"

I sit down at my desk and pull out a hand mirror from the top drawer. As I stare at myself, I think of Selina Meyer in the HBO show *Veep*, who develops a nervous eye twitch before a debate, and her whole staff focuses on it. I worry I have now become Vice President Selina—the caricature of a neurotic, self-absorbed person everyone mocks behind their back. I'm supposed to be my own boss, but I'm losing control of my body every time I come to my office.

Suddenly, I let loose a primal scream and slam my head down on the desk. I want to numb the pain. The pain of having no control over anything in my life. The pain of not being respected by anyone, including myself. I keep slamming until I hear a crack. I don't know if it's the desk or my skull. And I don't care. After that, everything goes black. When I come to, I'm looking up at a fluorescent light with my staff hovering over me. Everything is hazy. My head is throbbing. I close my eyes. I am jostled awake again by

Veronica. "Dr. Freeman," she whispers, "you passed out. The EMTs are taking you to the hospital."

* * *

Part of me wants to shake Adam and ask him what the hell is going on, but another part wants to comfort him in the ambulance as he's being rushed to the ER. Although I'm an orthodontist, I know from others in the field that being a pediatric dentist can be stressful, and everyone has a breaking point. On a good day, a pediatric dentist clears a few thousand dollars without breaking a sweat. On a bad day, the screaming patients who want to bite you and your dysfunctional staff are enough to make you want to hit your head on the table—but most people don't knock themselves unconscious. I think my main character suffered a nervous breakdown.

HOOOONK. I lift my head up from the manuscript and put the pedal to the metal. Swallowing hard, I bring my heart back from my throat to its normal anatomic position and speed towards the hospital to be on time for Grand Rounds.

My thoughts are racing as fast as the car, so I try to quiet my mind by switching the radio to NPR. I'm startled when I hear "All Things Considered," with Robert Siegel. "Tonight I'm speaking with critically acclaimed author Irving Sharf who is on a national book tour promoting his new bestseller, *Swan Song of the Dragon Menace.* This is the latest book in your epic Dragon Menace saga, Mr. Sharf?"

Sharf again? Maggie's golden boy with the silver hair is everywhere. "Great to join you, Robert."

"Thanks for taking time from your busy schedule. Let's start by asking you what many of our listeners want to know. Tell us about your journey to becoming a bestselling author."

"Well, I was in my early forties and managing a Blockbuster. I wanted more out of life. One night, I was online and came across a six-month writing course. I had dabbled in writing short stories but soon lost my way after high school. I had always intended to go to college to study literature but, before I knew it, I was a middle-aged man with a family and needed a job to pay the bills. As I tell the attendants at my seminars, always live your dreams and take risks, because you never know what lays behind the next door you open. On a whim, I submitted my work from the course to a prestigious competition. Lo and behold, I won the Academy of Writing Competition that year. It allowed me to use my novella as an outline for my books."

"Mr. Sharf," Robert continues, "Showtime bought your book rights to make it into an epic drama. Critics are calling it the next *Game of Thrones*."

"As you can imagine, I'm tremendously excited to bring my book to a new medium. There are many talented people at Showtime, and I can't wait to work with them."

"Tell me about your characters. They're quite interesting. I remember loving Queen Catherine from the moment I started reading. And the Knights of Ricochet Canyon are memorable."

Click. I turn off the radio. I can't take it anymore. Sharf is everywhere. Some guys get all the breaks. But he puts in the time, which I don't have as an orthodontist and dad. I should forget the whole thing—novel and memoir. I don't have Sharf's talent, drive, and certainly not his charm. What was I thinking? I'll stick to straightening teeth.

I pull into the parking lot, turn off the ignition, and look at the time—6:07 p.m. I'm late. I race towards the lecture hall and arrive outside right before it's about to start, print my name on the sign-up sheet to get credit for my attendance, and fill an empty paper plate with my dinner of complimentary hors d'oeuvres. I almost drop my free crackers and cheese when I sit down and look up at the first slide. It says, "Adam Freeman, DDS: Forensic Dentistry."

The doppelganger of my alter ego! What are the chances of that?

CHAPTER SIX
7:17 p.m.

After the lecture, it takes me a few minutes to recap what's transpired in the past seven hours. First, I have to get the images of the slides I saw out of my mind. That Forensic Dentistry lecture by Adam Freeman—a real-life Adam Freeman, DDS—was not for the faint of heart. Simply put, it was gruesome. This Adam showed numerous pictures of people with bite marks on all different areas of their body, including the genitals—areas never meant to be bitten. It made me wonder whether he was Adam Freeman, DDS, or Adam Freeman, BDSM.

During my drive home, I finally let go of how deranged people in this world can be and turn my attention to today's synchronicity. First, I get the news that this hugely successful agent can't stand the main character of my book and wants me to write a memoir. I hate her for saying this, but I have to admit—at least in what I've read—Adam isn't as likable as I thought he was when I first wrote the opening chapters. Part of me wants to thank Maggie, while another part wants to garrote her with some orthodontic wire. Then, there's the lecture with a real, live, flesh-and-blood Adam Freeman. You can't ignore a sign like that when the universe sends it. To attend a lecture by a dentist with the same name as my very own fictitious character is like something I'd see on an HBO series. I keep fingering this figurative Mobius strip, trying to figure out how to untwist it. As hard as I try, I can't disentangle my relationship with Adam, can't unlink myself and break my bond with him. It doesn't feel right, the way your bite feels off if your orthodontist hasn't done his job. Well, I have to fix it. As I drive home from New Haven, I know what I need to do. But first I need fuel—not for the car, but for my body.

I pull off the highway and immediately see a Walgreens. Confession: I have a major sweet tooth and, don't worry, the irony is not lost on me that as an orthodontist I love candy. Somehow, I'm still skinny despite all the junk food I eat. I guess there's something to be said for having a fast metabolism. I buy myself a six-pack of Red Bull, a party-size bag of Cool Ranch Doritos and another of Tostitos, shredded nacho cheese, and a box of microwavable popcorn. Then, with laser focus, I rush to my favorite aisle where I stock up on Twizzlers, Junior Mints, and several rainbows worth of Skittles. And, of course, I can't leave without putting a giant-sized bulky bag of peach rings in my overflowing basket. I put my Lexus through its paces on the winding suburban roads on the way home, with the bag of candy and junk food buckled safely into the passenger seat, right on top of my manuscript. It's going to be a long night.

When I arrive home, the house is quiet. Leah must be upstairs, putting the kids to bed. Ordinarily, I'd run up and kiss them good night—which makes Leah mad when they're almost asleep—but tonight I pad silently up the back stairway with my stash of candy and the pages of my book to avoid disturbing them. I need every extra minute I can get. I change quickly out of my work clothes and slink into the bathroom to start reading. I'm about to send Leah a text letting her know I'm home and taking a few minutes to chill when my phone pings: "Please come down and empty the dishwasher." I swear she has the tracking skills of a bloodhound. While I'm putting away the dishes, she comes tiptoeing down and wipes off the kitchen table as we talk about her day and the kids. I tell her about the lecture at Yale. "…I can't believe there's an actual Adam Freeman out there."

"That's a really strange coincidence," she says.

"It's more than a coincidence! It's a sign!"

"What Jacob? From God? I think you're taking this a little too far."

"Too far? No. I'm not taking it far enough. Adam's name was plastered across a massive screen tonight in front of a large crowd of people. I can't let him die."

Leah shrugs. She knows from previous experience not to stand in my way when I get an idea in my head. "Okay, do what you need to do. But don't stay up too late tonight—you have to work tomorrow."

I hold up my bag of junk food and the manuscript. "I'm diving back into the book, even if it takes me until morning. I have to decide if I should kill Adam or let him live before Maggie leaves town."

"Come on, Jacob, you're going to pull an all-nighter? You're not a college student anymore, and you can't afford to be exhausted at work. What if, God forbid, you make a mistake with someone's teeth?"

"Leah," I say, swaggering up with my best John Wayne imitation, "a man's gotta do what a man's gotta do." I take the manuscript and my diabetes-inducing treats into my office and shut the door to begin reading the next chapter. Will Adam survive his nervous breakdown?

The Adventures of Adam Freeman, DDS
June 17—Touched by an Angel

I had only been in the hospital overnight once before to get my tonsils out in the first grade, so I had little experience being "the patient." All I want to do is sleep, but that isn't possible. Countless doctors and nurses come in at all hours to check on me. I have a nasal tube down my throat and a catheter up my schlong. How prophetic that altered sign in front of my office had been. Although admittedly ironic, it wasn't funny then, and I'm not finding it funny now.

I have a bandage over my head and must be on serious narcotics, because I'm feeling only a dull twinge of pain. After I woke from unconsciousness, I was a poor historian of events. I didn't reveal that I purposefully smashed my head on my desk; everyone assumed I passed out before impact. I've had an MRI, blood work, PET scans—you name the test, I had it done. I'm shocked when a pack of doctors report they've found nothing physically wrong with me. That means I have to deal with the pain in my psyche. The silver lining? I'm relaxing and recharging. My eye twitch even feels better.

It's a relief to find out that I'm physically healthy. Being a typical guy, the last time I had a physical was when I needed more life insurance and the company sent over a visiting nurse. If that exam was good enough for the insurance company to dole out three million bucks in term life insurance, it was good enough for me to avoid a physical with a real doctor. I never told this to my life insurance agent—my premium would have skyrocketed—but I have always felt like I was living on borrowed time. When I first woke up in the hospital, I was amazed I'd made it back alive. I never really imagined myself living past my teenage years or going to college after high school. Then after college, I never thought I'd be a dentist, but suddenly I was studying pediatric dentistry at Yale. Over time, the life I had never envisioned for myself unfolded and grew more complex. I married Minnie and kids started to appear. One day I realized that—*holy shit*—I was responsible for running a dental practice, raising three kids, and supporting a family.

Speaking of my children, they approach the foot of my bed and my body floods with joy. I don't need painkillers when my children are around. Tears form in my eyes when I see Paige holding out a picture she drew. That gap-toothed grin that Rose always sports makes me smile, and Minnie is holding our son Spencer tightly, making sure he doesn't knock over any medical equipment.

"Daddy, here's a picture I drew for you." Paige hands me her rendering of a dolphin swimming in the ocean with the sun shining above. It makes my heart melt.

"I love you guys. I'm coming home soon, and we'll play and have the best time in the world! Give me a Freeman Family Hug," I say, fighting the frog in my throat. After the group hug and outpouring of emotion, I'm suddenly extremely hungry. I've had nothing but fluids for twenty-four hours. I sit up in bed and reach towards my lunch tray, but the pain in my head stops me. I motion for Minnie to slide it over and, as she does, I notice my chocolate chip cookie is missing. Somehow, it has found its way into Rose's sweet little mouth. I lunge for the cookie and manage to grab the edge, leaving half of it in Rose's mouth, dropping the other half on the floor as pain shoots through my neck.

"Now look what you've done!" I shriek. "I wanted that cookie!"

Rose looks at me wide-eyed with tears forming. Then she spits the half-eaten cookie from her mouth and offers it to me.

Minnie stares at me in disbelief. "Really, Adam?" She grabs a napkin and scoops the mix of saliva and cookie from Rose's hand then tosses it in the trash.

"Goddammit, Minnie! I was looking forward to that cookie. It's one of those soft and chewy ones."

Moments ago, my family was hugging me. Now the kids all look sullen and afraid. Minnie shakes her head at me and tries to calm Spencer, who has started to cry. Despite her efforts, he keeps thrashing, and as she shifts him to her other shoulder, his foot knocks over a vase of flowers on the bedside table. Cold water splashes all over me. With nothing on but my thin hospital gown, I start shivering, and Minnie can't help cracking a small, satisfied smile before she contains it and turns to the kids.

"Daddy's still not quite himself yet. I think we should go and let him get some rest." She turns to me. "I'll ask the nurse to come in and change your sheets," then leans down and whispers, "but you better change your attitude, buster. I got the kids dressed and we schlepped over to see you, and..."

"I'm sorry, Minnie. Something's still not right with my head."

"I'd like to believe that, Adam, but this little accident didn't suddenly make you selfish. It's a preexisting condition."

"Please, Minnie. I want to get warm and dry now. Can't you stay and take care of me? I'm in agony."

"I have to take the kids home now. With the pain meds they're giving you, you'll feel better in the morning."

After Minnie and the kids leave and my sheets are changed, I feel better. I think about texting Minnie to apologize, but I'm determined to write. I've started scribbling on a napkin, like the legend about Lincoln and the Gettysburg Address. And besides, Minnie's going to stay mad at me for at least one score and four hours. When I've covered both sides of my makeshift parchment with ink, I buzz the nurse to ask for paper. When she brings it, the attending physician, Dr. Rosen, is with her. I can't help but notice how good-looking he is. With his wavy black hair and radiant smile, he could be a stand-in for McDreamy on *Grey's Anatomy*.

"We'll release you tomorrow, Adam," he says, "but you should give yourself a week of rest before going back to the office."

"A week? A whole week? I can't afford to miss that much time. Can we maybe do two days?"

"You took a pretty hard hit to the head, and our staff has observed erratic behavior." I stare icily at the nurse. "I'm willing to chalk it up to stress, which is what I believe caused you to pass out. I need you to take downtime before returning to work. Doctor's orders." Rosen turns on his heels and leaves the room, white coat flapping, as Klein walks in. He pulls a chair over and gives me a warm smile.

"You look good, my friend. For someone suffering from extreme stress, I don't think I've ever seen you more relaxed."

"It's easy to be relaxed when you're helpless."

"Not exactly helpless. I hear you managed to steal a cookie from a little girl."

"Half a cookie. You must've talked to Minnie on the way in."

"Yeah. She had some choice words for you, but I think I managed to calm her down a little. You can thank me later. Here, I brought this for you to read while you're home on bedrest," he says, handing me a copy of *The Celestine Prophecy.*

"What's this?"

"A great book. It really helped open my eyes."

"Another one of your spirituality books, Klein? You know I'm not into that bullshit."

"Calm down, Freeman. Maybe we should up your meds. Nurse!" He moves his hand to the call button, then stops and leans in close. "I've been dying to ask... Did you experience any visions or maybe words from God while you were passed out?"

I knew it. Klein has been reading a lot about near-death experiences, and he's like a kid in a candy store waiting to hear about my unconscious experience. I flutter my eyelids and pretend to fall asleep for dramatic effect. Then I grab his arm. "Like that old CBS show, buddy, I was *Touched by an Angel!*"

"Oh my Lord, really? Where did the angel touch you?"

I haven't seen Klein this excited since we discovered his father's porn collection—a huge stash of *Playboys*, *Penthouses*, and *Hustlers* under boxes in the corner of his garage. I continue, "When I was unconscious, I met a talking red-eyed eagle that flew up to me. It was right in my face. So vivid. The eagle told me to listen to "Heaven is a Place on Earth" by Belinda Carlisle. I felt like he was about to reveal the secrets of the universe when he suddenly burst into bright blue flames."

"That's amazing! Did you hear any other voices?"

"I sure did. A bright white orb appeared in front of me, and it hummed the chorus of the song.

Klein has a tear in his eye. "Oh my God, that's beautiful. I knew it—*love comes first*. Do you think God was speaking to you through the orb? Was God the orb? You need to write this down, Freeman. Did you have a life review?"

"Yes! My whole life flashed before my eyes, and the eagle came swooping down again." Gradually my lips begin to curl up.

Klein sees my smirk. "You fucking prick. You didn't see shit, did you? Minnie's right. You're an asshole."

I burst out laughing. Klein punches me in the arm, sending spasms of pain up to my neck. "That's not very spiritual of you, man," I tell him as I rub my bicep. "Sorry to disappoint you, but I got nothing—only Belinda Carlisle's song. I wasn't *Touched by an Angel*. I didn't meet God, Jesus, or Belinda."

Klein finally smiles. "You know Belinda's still alive."

"Not dead yet," I say, shaking my head. "I mean, it's not like Jesus would come to me, anyway. I don't think he answers to Jews."

"What are you talking about? Jesus *was* Jewish, for Christ's sake. I'm sure if you asked him he'd answer."

I hadn't thought of this option, and I give it serious consideration. "If I met Jesus, I'd ask him how I can find peace in this fucked up world." A wave of melancholy washes over me. "Can I be honest with you, Klein?"

"Sure."

"This morning when I woke up after the accident and saw these tubes in me, I freaked. I don't want to die. I don't want to leave my family. I'm not ready. And I'm scared." I shut my eyes and breathe deeply.

"Freeman, are you crying?"

"No," I tell him quickly.

Klein reaches over and hands me a box of Kleenex from the table by the bed. After I'm done dabbing my eyes, he says, "Listen, there's nothing to be afraid of. I can give you some great books to read about life after death. The last one I read was by this Yale-trained physician who studied children in India who were in a coma and wrote a book about what he saw. It was fascinating that each of them reported the same thing. They saw a bright white light and then they heard the voice of God."

I pay no attention to Klein, since there's no scientific evidence in the books he reads. "You seem to be getting more and more out there. When did you become a religious freak?"

"I'm no zealot. Religion's caused a lot of harm in this world. I'm more spiritual."

"Meaning?"

"My Indian guru defined spirituality as the belief in a higher being— that the universe has a divine plan for us. We have to have faith in this being."

My first instinct is to slap him and call him a crackpot, but I decide to keep my mouth shut.

"In the Ashram we learned we're part of God's creation. Since everything good comes from this source—call it God, the Divine, the Creator, Mother Nature, or whatever—we're all perfect. However, people believe we're separate from God now and, because of this illusion of separation, *we* create the bad things that happen to us. I am convinced that if we give ourselves up to the universe, we'll all be in a better place."

Klein used to complain to me for hours about how life was kicking his ass. He was one miserable son of a bitch, but he's totally changed his tune since coming back from India. Maybe I need that kind of journey.

Klein continues, "My family frustrated the hell out of me. I would get pissed at them, but then I started to read this stuff, and it really opened my eyes. Now I always strive to show them love. When I meditate, I ask God to watch over my children and help them in their quest for a happy and peaceful life."

"Are you sure I'm not hallucinating this conversation? I know they gave me powerful pain meds."

"Adam, I'm serious. These discoveries, this new way of being, it's changed me."

"All this Almighty God stuff makes me nervous. People expect religion to cure everything. I want to know how I can deal better with all this pressure I feel in life. I've worked hard to get into a good profession. I make good money and have an amazing family. These are supposed to be the good years, the salad days, but I'm not feeling it. I'm not fulfilled. I want a 'Peaceful Easy Feeling,' like the Eagles song."

As Klein is trying to find the song on his iPhone, Dr. Rosen walks in with a determined look on his face. "Dr. Freeman, I've been thinking about our conversation earlier. I cannot emphasize enough the need for you to take time off after we discharge you. Quite simply, stress kills. Here's a list of psychiatrists you can call to schedule an appointment. I like you, but I'd rather not see you back here again under these circumstances."

Klein is smiling. "I like that guy," he said as Dr. Rosen walked out. "He reminds me of one of those TV doctors."

"I don't know. Do you think I really need time off?"

"Seriously Adam? Look at you. Think of it this way. You can take off, and no one can say a damn thing about it. Plus, you'll have time to read the book I gave you."

"Well, if you look at it that way…" I grab my phone from the bedside table and text Veronica to reschedule my patients so I can take the rest of the week off.

"How does that feel?" Klein asks.

"Not bad. Better than I thought."

"Well, now that you've invested a little in self-care, I think you should come with me to one of my meditation sessions."

I let out another breath and sink back into the bed. My life is taking an unexpected but not entirely unwanted turn, and I feel I have no choice but to go with it.

Klein continues, "The teacher is amazing. She has this gift of reading people and telling you what your spirit guides are advising."

"Spirit guides? Really, Klein? And I thought *I* was losing it. Here, you need this more than I do," I say, handing him the list of shrinks that Rosen gave me.

"Seriously, Adam. You should try it."

Maybe Klein is right, but something—call it my bullshit detector—holds me back. I'm all for meditation, but spirit guides are a little much for me. I remind myself I'm a scientifically trained medical professional and say, "I don't think that'll work for me, Klein. I'll have to decline your invitation."

* * *

I reach into the Doritos bag, but my sticky orange fingers come up empty. I lick off the powdered cheese, and since there is no napkin in sight, I use the next best thing—my pants leg. I feel sick to my stomach after consuming a whole bag of Doritos, and I'm equally nauseated by Adam's obnoxious behavior towards his family. I couldn't imagine acting that way towards Leah and the kids.

Frustrated with Adam again, I decide to take a break and treat myself to the Skittles. My mouth is bursting with artificial flavor, and my heart is bursting with love for Leah, tinged with the worry and fear of a guy who knows he got lucky when he thinks about his amazing wife. Before I dive back into the manuscript, I lean back in my desk chair and reassure myself that Leah and I have been in a good place lately—actually for a while. I like to say that marriage is like a baseball season, filled with streaks of happiness and joy, like going four-for-four in the birthday, anniversary, Valentine's Day, Mother's Day lineup, getting on base on fifteen straight date nights, or knocking one out of the park with "just because" flowers. Then, sometimes without explanation, you go into a slump, like striking out four times in the same conversation—a version of the Golden Sombrero—making a string of unforced errors or going a dozen date nights without scoring.

Since I became an evolved man with a different perspective on life, I appreciate all that Leah has sacrificed for us. Working full-time while being CEO of our family is exhausting for her, and some days she doesn't even have time to take a shower. (Note: delete this before Leah reads this draft.) I realize now how selfless one must be to put the kids above everything else, which Leah does daily. I can honestly say that my wife is the most caring, loving, and compassionate person I know. And I'm not saying that because, unlike poor Adam, I got laid last night! Okay, maybe that has a little to do with my euphoria, but trust me, I am speaking from the heart.

Adam needs to wake up and realize that Minnie is the glue holding his family together. I'll keep reading and see if I need to write in a chapter of Adam groveling back to Minnie.

The Adventures of Adam Freeman, DDS
June 18—*Homeland*

I'm home resting, with clearance from Rosen to return to work this coming Monday. I can't abandon my job, but the thought of going back to the same anxiety-provoking atmosphere that put me in the hospital makes me feel sick. For me, there's no better way to deal with problems than escaping them, so I decide to hunker down and hide myself in the man cave. I fill my NY Giants mug with an icy cold root beer and make myself comfortable in the leather sofa that faces my seventy-inch Samsung Ultra HD flat screen. I rest my head on top of the Yankee head pillow and bring my Nana's crocheted blanket up to my neck. It's going to be a heavenly day of television!

After researching shows worthy of my vacation time, I decide to alternate between *Homeland*, Season Three and an old classic, *The Sopranos*, which, unbelievably, I never saw. I start with *Homeland* since I want to see how Carrie and Brody resolve things. I should be able to knock off both shows by Monday.

I make it through the first four episodes of *Homeland* with a little bit of fast forwarding. Season Three isn't as engaging as the first two. But I relate to Carrie not wanting to take her Lithium meds because they dull her ability. Both Minnie and Dr. Rosen are trying to medicate my mental anguish. I look down at the list of psychiatrists from Rosen and feel disturbed at how mentally ill people like Carrie Mathison are often stigmatized. I toss the list in the trash can. I'm going to kick this thing on my own.

I'm bored with *Homeland*, so I switch to *The Sopranos*. Right away, I become addicted. As a neurotic, Jewish dentist who runs his own practice, I connect with Tony Soprano—a neurotic, Italian mob boss who suffers from panic attacks. Like me with my eye twitch, he has a hard time controlling his body. Of course, I'm not a sociopath or a murderer, but other than that, I relate to Tony Soprano wholeheartedly. If macho Tony Soprano can see a shrink and take pills to get better, maybe it wouldn't kill me to get real help. It would certainly get Minnie off my case. I pause the show, pick up my phone, and text the one person who understands my situation. "Count me in."

CHAPTER SEVEN
8:45 p.m.

I look up from the manuscript to see Leah walking in. She looks down at my pants dotted with orange powder. "Jacob, you're filthy. How about using a napkin next time instead of your pants?" She reaches into my candy bag, takes the whole box of Junior Mints, and pops a single chocolate-coated mint into her mouth, sucking on it until it melts away.

I point to the Junior Mints box longingly. "Those are my favorite, but you enjoy!"

She frowns at my Skittles. "You'll thank me later, junk food fiend! Oh, and Jacob, please change the light bulb above the table in the living room. The Mah Jongg girls are coming over tomorrow." She walks out of the office.

This is why it took me six years to write *The Adventures of Adam Freeman, DDS*. I'm always being interrupted; there's never a peaceful moment. I'm about to say, "I'll do it in the morning" with a tinge of resentment, but I catch the negativity and realize that's what Adam would say. Instead I answer, "Sure. Give me a minute."

On my way to get a bulb, I walk past a stretched-out Leah on the sofa watching *The Bachelorette*. She seems to be enjoying the Junior Mints as much as she liked the sex last night. Note to self: buy Leah

Junior Mints more often. While changing the bulb, I think back to my courtship of this woman who matches me in the sweet tooth department.

Although I dated a few girls in college, it wasn't until I met Leah that I understood what love was. We met when we were both nineteen in sociology class. She was the classic girl next door—cute, sweet, and Jewish. Although I didn't care much about religion, it meant a lot to my parents, and it also meant we had a lot in common from our upbringings. I found her personality hypnotic, and we spent countless hours on the phone philosophizing about life. Our relationship grew closer when we became pen pals senior year during my term abroad in Scotland. Upon my return, I made my move one evening. Leah came over for dinner, and later that night we decided to watch a movie. I suggested she'd be more comfortable if we pulled out the sofa and made it into a bed, thinking to myself, *Smooth move Silverstein.* Needless to say, I don't remember much of the movie.

Here we are, over twenty years later, in our early forties with three kids. We have our issues, like any married couple, but as the Ketubah, our Jewish marriage contract, symbolizes—we're in it for the long haul. It's invigorating knowing that she is a part of my life, and I am committed to being a better person, husband, and father. As I turn to the next chapter, I remember that Adam, for all his flaws, wants to become a better human being too.

The Adventures of Adam Freeman, DDS
June 19—*Long Island Medium*

The kids are in school and Minnie is running errands. I'm in the man cave continuing my *Homeland* and *Sopranos* marathon. I've reached the end of

Season Five of *The Sopranos* when I get a text: "Let me in." My body is practically glued to the sofa after five hours of binge watching. I peel myself off, stretch my atrophied muscles, and ascend the stairs to open the door for Errol. He's dressed in a tank top and spandex shorts. We head back down to the cave.

He sees the television paused on a close-up of Tony. "*The Sopranos*. Classic. Adam, I've been thinking, dude—you need to be more active. You should join us at boot camp. It kicks your ass, but it's rewarding."

"What are you talking about?"

"Remember, I was telling you about my boot camp? The group meets every day at 5:30 a.m. We bring in personal trainers. It's intense. Feel the burn."

"I'm not sure that's my thing, Errol," I say, sinking back onto the sofa. He puts his arm around me for a moment in kind of a mini bro hug. I know he means well, but I know my body is not up for this boot camp thing.

"It'll pump you up. Look at me." He flexes his massive biceps and his new Horseman tattoo gallops up and down. "*Mens sana in corpore sano.* A sound mind in a sound body. When I don't take time out of the day for me, I'm off and no good to anyone. You need something like this. It's no secret you've been stressed out."

"Since when did you learn Latin?" I ask.

"That's the sound mind part. I can concentrate way better after I work out."

"You're telling me your brain is as ripped as your abs," I say, looking at the solid wall of muscle under his tank top, then instinctively squeezing the spare tire around my midsection. Errol notices my pile of junk food on the table near the sofa, and I look down, ashamed.

"I don't need your judgment," I say. "I feel shitty enough already, and I don't need to hear how glorious your life has become because of your fitness regimen."

"Give it a try when you're feeling a little better." With that, Errol's phone pings, and he rushes out to do the grocery shopping. After he leaves, Klein walks in.

"I was psyched to get your text last night." He beams at me. "You ready to go, Freeman?"

Minnie knows not to expect me for dinner tonight. She has been giving me space since I've been home. On our drive to the session, Klein is like a kid in a candy store. "I know I've been hounding you, but I promise, this'll totally be worth it. What made you change your mind?"

"Tony Soprano."

"Ah, the fat man in the bathrobe who wants to do his hot Italian shrink. Don't expect Jennifer Melfi here. This is purely professional."

"And yet you talk about it so orgasmically."

"These sessions are amazing, Adam. And I'm excited because I want to share them with you. God knows Joy doesn't get it. The time I spend meeting Hope inconveniences Joy's schedule. But it's rocking my world. It's like Hope has special powers. I swear she reads my mind."

"Klein, you're a well-educated man. You teach the country's next generation of thinkers. I hope you realize this woman's no mind reader. She's probably a mentalist, using little things you've told her, stuff she observes, and probabilities to make you think she's a psychic. She's scamming you."

"No. She has a true gift."

"You've heard the story that Houdini challenged any psychic to give him a reading, right? If the psychic guessed the word his mother told him on her deathbed, he would give them a hundred thousand bucks."

"When I've had readings from Hope, it's like being on a live episode of *Long Island Medium*," Klein says. "I'm putting it in TV talk so you can understand."

"I don't watch that crap."

"With all the shows you're addicted to, *that's* the one you don't watch? Theresa Caputo rocks," he said before getting back on topic. "Tonight we're meditating. The key to meditation is 'Quiet the mind.'"

I sigh. "Might as well give it a try since nothing I've done up to this point is working. My mind is like a heavy metal concert with the amps all turned up to eleven. By the way, Houdini never had to pay up."

Klein and I walk into a room packed with people, all waiting expectantly for Hope. Never in a million years did I think I'd be going to a meditative workshop. I was schooled in the science of the body—physiology and pathophysiology. It strikes me as odd that people put their faith in this woman with such passion and certainty. In their minds, this "medium and healer" has abilities that can't be explained scientifically. I promise Klein that I'll keep an open mind, but my gates of skepticism are already closing as I start to survey the crowd.

I'm expecting to see circa 1970 hippies: women in flowery dresses, men in tie-dyed shirts, Yoko Ono hair, and John Lennon glasses, the stink of body odor in the air. But this group looks like the crowd in my local Starbucks—well-dressed, well-groomed, well-deodorized professionals ranging in age from late twenties to early sixties. I'm surprised by how many people are here. There must be over twenty-five, mostly women and a handful of men. They're getting comfortable, sitting on throw pillows scattered across the floor. Klein and I grab a space in the corner, and he nudges me to take off my shoes. I lean back against the soothing yellow walls and dig my feet into the plush white carpeting. From the conversations I overhear, I glean that a lot of the people know Hope from when she worked on Wall Street. Klein has told me that the group consists of local business owners, nurses, a psychiatrist, a bunch of housewives, and a few retired men, as well as several executives at Fortune 500 companies. I guess Hope takes corporate Amex.

Suddenly the lights flicker, then dim, and Hope, medium and healer, strides into the room. She is not what I expected. Mid-forties, dressed professionally, she must be close to six feet tall. I strain my neck to give her a once-over. She's knockout gorgeous; think Rebecca Romijn's long legs, bleached-blonde hair, and radiant smile. Klein told me that after she made a pile of money at Morgan Stanley, she ended up having a nervous breakdown. While recovering in the hospital, Hope began to receive messages from spirits. After studying with mystics all over the world, she wrote a book and launched her own spiritual practice. I figure being a spiritual healer is not much different from being an investment banker— either way, you're taking money from suckers.

The class starts off with Hope talking about Sufism as the mystical part of Islam, which I have never heard of.

"Those who practice Sufism, practice love," she proclaims as we sit together in a wide circle. "When we embrace our relationship with the Beloved, we become mystics in our own right. Mysticism is one way to describe your relationship with God."

I whisper to Klein, "Will a relationship with her bring me closer to a relationship with Him?"

"For Christ's sake, Freeman," he whispers, elbowing me. "Grow up."

Hope continues the lesson, and we learn about a man called Rumi, a famous Sufi poet in the 1300s. Rumi was a lawyer by training, well-respected with a wife and children. Then a mystic named Shams (no symbolism there) entered his life and taught Rumi how to express himself through poetry. Rumi left his family to study with Shams and devoted his life to God, becoming a world-famous poet. He wrote about pure love through his relationship with the Beloved.

"Rumi's main teaching was that it is not what God gives us but what we give God. We have been separated from God," Hope concludes, "and we need to bridge the gap and get back to our Creator."

I take a deep breath. This is a long way from my scientific research lab at Yale. The whole thing is pretty hokey, but I keep thinking back to Tony Soprano and how Dr. Melfi helped him figure out the causes of his stress. He didn't stop being a sociopath, but he did stop having panic attacks, so I'm willing to give whatever Hope's selling a try.

Hope reads a portion of Rumi's poetry while playing Enya and asks the group to close our eyes.

"Concentrate on your breathing," she intones, "and relax your bodies and minds." *Mens sana in corpore sano*, I think to myself.

At first, I try to keep my eyes shut, but I can't help peeking at the people meditating around me. I'm surprised no one else is peeking too. The scene is fascinating; the lady across from me has a large grin on her face, the older man next to me is swaying back and forth, like a Jew davening during prayer, and I almost burst out laughing when I see that Klein appears to be sleeping. I listen to Hope's words and try to match the rhythm of my breathing to hers. I close my eyes and try to let go, but my eye starts twitching uncontrollably. I find no solace in the music and the Rumi poetry I've just listened to. My mind is in chaos, and my eye's blinking like a strobe light. This goes on for over ten songs.

"For those of you having trouble relaxing," Hope says gently, as if speaking to only me, "envision the words coming out of my mouth. Imagine," she continues, "you are a bird gliding through the clear blue sky into an enchanted garden of roses."

Hope's imagery takes me to a place both foreign and familiar and, despite my efforts, I can no longer control my feelings. Gradually, my eye movements calm down, and the tension and tightness begin to drift away. I am a bird soaring through the heavens. I spread my wings and descend over fields of weeds to land in a magical garden. The sweet smell of roses is overwhelming. I breathe it in, and I can see every petal on every flower as the blooms unfold to greet the rising sun. I feel the heat pleasantly pulsating through me.

"Let go of your body. Free yourself of your chains."

I lose myself. I'm flying like a bird, floating and doing aerial somersaults across the heavenly sky. Words pop up in my bird brain. I don't necessarily hear them, but I feel them. The phrase 'have faith' fills my soul.

Suddenly, my vision shifts. I'm in a smoky, foggy swamp, but I can see a bright star shining. I want to get to this star more than anything. I'm looking for a way to get there, following the light. I can no longer control my feelings. My eyes are watering, and I realize I'm crying, releasing my pain.

Then it dawns on me that over twenty-five people are gathered in this room, but I don't care—this weeping is long overdue. Hope interrupts my heartfelt release of emotions, "Everyone, take one more deep breath and open your eyes."

I'm not ready to come back to reality, but I can feel the group staring at me. When I finally open my eyes, I feel a strange sensation—peace. I haven't felt this way in months. We go around the circle to talk about our experience during the meditative session, and I skip my turn. I can barely speak, much less articulate what transpired.

At the end of the session, Klein grabs my arm and drags me over to meet Hope. I come clean to her. "This is the first time I've ever meditated and," I hesitate, "something shifted. You've made me feel better."

She stares at me. I start to feel fear. Can she read my thoughts? Does she know I think she's hot? But she puts me at ease.

"Joshua told me you're a dentist. That's lovely." She blinks her eyes and smiles. "Well, I have a question for you. A dental question. I am petrified of needles and want to know if you use laughing gas. I have a cavity and don't want to use Novocaine."

I'm used to people peppering me with dental questions, but this one catches me by surprise. I can't believe Hope is afraid of anything. I fantasize for a moment about her beautiful body lying supine in my dentist's chair, her arms limp and her eyes closed as the nitrous takes her into la-la land. But half an hour of heaven with Hope isn't worth half a year of purgatory with Minnie if she found out about my new "adult patient," or worse, half a life with my kids if she divorced me over an affair.

"I use nitrous," I tell her, "but I'm a pediatric dentist. I only work on kids. That's what I trained at Yale to do."

She continues to stare through me. "You seem very troubled. Your spirit guides tell me you recently had trauma to your head. I will pray for you." I mumble a thank you as she turns and speaks to another attendee.

Klein has a smile as large as Jack Nicholson's Joker. "I never told her of your injury. See, she's good."

I point to the Band-Aid on my forehead. "Give me a break, Klein. My ten-year-old could have come up with that."

On the ride home Klein lowers the Rockin' Mix I have blaring and wants to know what I thought of the session. I'm honest. "I'm not sure how she did it, or if she's for real, but I do feel better."

Klein cannot contain his enthusiasm. "I *knew* she'd help you. You already seem more relaxed and comfortable in your own skin."

"Yeah. I'm pretty happy I went."

"Dude, I know you felt something—I heard you whimpering."

I describe my vision of the rose garden while Klein listens, giving me his full attention. This is one of the things that I love about him; he has this special ability to make you feel like you're the only person in the room, though in this case I am the only one in the car with him.

"Still," I say to Klein, "there's one thing bothering me. What's the deal with this spiritual woman being deathly afraid of needles? Isn't that ironic?"

"How do you figure?"

"Well, couldn't she meditate before going into the dental chair and get over her fears like she teaches her students?"

Klein responds, "Listen, Adam, although Hope has a talent, she's human. We all have our fears and insecurities, and that one happens to be hers. Incidentally, you were rude and condescending to her."

"What are you talking about?"

"You tend to throw that Yale thing around to people. To be honest, it makes you seem pretentious."

"Dude, that's bullshit."

"You don't realize how it comes across. Remember you thought dropping the 'Yale-bomb' on girls would get you laid? It was funny then, but it isn't now. Try to be humble and let go of your ego. I know the real Adam Freeman, and he doesn't need to sound snooty and condescending about his education."

"Thanks for the unsolicited advice and the giant buzz kill." I hurry out of Klein's car and slam the door behind me. Let go of my ego. Klein's such an asshole.

* * *

All of a sudden, I smell something delicious. I turn around, and Leah is in my office holding a plate of nachos. My absolute favorite! Tostitos topped with chunky salsa, spicy pepper rings, and black olives, all draped with perfectly melted shredded cheddar. The nachos call out to me: "Dr. Jacob Silverstein, we are here for your eating pleasure."

Even though I'm stuffed with junk food, there is always room for nachos. And with all due respect to Forrest Gump, he got it wrong. Life is *not* like a box of chocolates—it's way more like a plate of nachos. I share my thoughts with Leah. "Thanks honey, this looks amazing. Did I ever tell you how a plate of nachos is like a metaphor for life?"

Leah nods. "There you go again with your Forrest Gump analogy. While eating, you could dig into a delicious bite of chips, salsa, and melted cheese, yet in the very next serving you could get a hot pepper mixed in, which changes your perspective on the meal completely."

"Exactly! What's the occasion for serving up my favorite dish?"

"You've been cooped up in here for a bit, and I thought you'd like another snack. How's it coming? Are you almost done?"

"No, it's getting juicy. Adam started learning about meditation."

"OMG, Jacob, is this your autobiography? You told me it was fiction."

"OMG? Leah, our girls are rubbing off on you. No. Adam and I are completely different."

"What about his wife? You're not writing stuff about me in there, are you?"

"Absolutely not. You and Minnie have nothing, I mean, almost nothing in common."

"Almost nothing?"

"Well, there is one thing. You and Minnie are very attractive." At this, Leah blushes, then reaches over and delicately extracts a nacho.

I can't match Leah's skillful nacho maneuver. Instead, I scoop up a huge handful of chips, cheese, and salsa, and throw a hot pepper on from the other side of the pile. As I lift my hand to my mouth, a glop of salsa splashes onto the leg of my sweatpants.

"Ever heard of napkins, Jacob? You're the messiest eater I know."

Leah heads to the kitchen to get me a washcloth. We've acted out this scene before.

While she's gone, I down a few more handfuls of nachos, then spread salsa on the crotch of my sweatpants.

When Leah returns, she looks down and laughs.

"Jacob, that is not where you spilled the salsa." I gently guide her hand towards the stain.

"Men." Leah shrugs. "It's all food and sex." I make my best hurt-puppy-dog look. "Oh, Jacob, I'm kidding. You're not like that. You grew up—although it took you nearly forty years."

"Better late than never."

She begins wiping gently with the washcloth. "I can get your pants clean, but your mind will always be dirty." The scrubbing feels good, and I sense movement down there.

"Take off your pants," she orders. "I'll put stain stick on them. And I *am* in the mood…" As much as I'd like to get naked with Leah, I can't leave Adam alone after his meditation session. He may be starting to evolve.

"I'm at a crucial scene here, and I need to read the next chapter before I can be of service." As she turns to leave the room, I can see her pouting.

"I'll be upstairs, waiting for you."

I'm into Adam's story and need to see what comes next. However, if I don't head upstairs soon, I'll miss the moment with Leah, and then it'll be a while before the next invitation is offered. "Forty minutes and I'll be up."

"You have a half hour while I do a load of laundry and take a shower. Don't be late. I'm losing steam." I take out my phone, click on the clock icon, and set the timer for thirty minutes. Like my boys Daft Punk, I'm about to "Get Lucky."

The Adventures of Adam Freeman, DDS
June 20—*Crossing Over*

When I get home from the meditation workshop, Minnie is already snoring lightly with a half-smile on her gorgeous lips. I climb into bed and curl up next to her, inhaling her scent. My eye has stopped twitching, my whole body is relaxed, and I fall into a deep sleep straight through until morning.

I wake and want to let Minnie know how good I feel. She's still sleeping, so I go downstairs, make her a cup of Earl Grey tea, and bring it up for her. This is one of my favorite times—when we can relax in bed together for a few minutes before the kids get up. Minnie squints at me through sleepy eyes and lets out a contented sigh when she sees the teacup on her nightstand.

"Thank you for the tea, Adam," she says, the thickness of sleep still in her voice. "How was your meditation session?"

My scientific mind wants to attribute my anxiety reduction to the placebo effect, but I can't deny the correlation between seeing Hope and feeling more relaxed. I recap the night for Minnie as she sips her tea, summarizing Sufism and quoting some choice lines from Rumi.

"Isn't it amazing that Rumi could break free of the chains in life and feel bliss and happiness?" I ask.

Minnie wrinkles her adorable nose. "At the sacrifice of his family."

"I wish you heard his poems. The lines I remember don't do them justice."

"I've seen his poems all over Facebook. A lot of people share them when they're trying to sound deep."

"Well, his words sure had a deep impact on me. I'm definitely feeling more relaxed. Life finally seemed simple last night in a room full of people who all want love and harmony. It felt like we were moving together with God's purpose, like ripples in water on a windy day. If only everyone could feel that spiritual connection."

Minnie frowns. "Who are you? Anyway, I don't see how a just God can create this much sadness in the world. My mom died an awful death from breast cancer. My sister's fighting leukemia. People suffer, get shot, and blown up all over the world. How can any of that be a good thing?"

I think about Minnie's personal pain and the degree to which tragic world events affect her. I'm immensely grateful for her compassion towards me, and I begin to see how her sensitivity makes it hard for her to see suffering in the world. I feel powerless to change it.

"Well, last night Hope said that everything happens for a reason. We don't know the reason—only God knows it. Everyone must die; it's the cycle of life."

"That's callous of you, Adam. Where's your empathy? I understand everyone dies, but people die in pain, and we're unable to help them."

I thought telling Minnie about the peace that last night brought me would help her feel better. But it only makes her more upset.

"You're confusing spiritual enlightenment with fatalism," she continues. "Why take my Mom right after she retired? She'll never see her beloved grandchildren grow up. And now my sister?" She thumps her pillow with her fists, then starts thumping on my chest as tears fill her eyes. "Goddammit, Adam. Why can't you agree with me that this all sucks—big time."

I channel my empathic side. "Minnie, your mom is looking over us now—watching out for you and the kids. And Klein tells me that Hope can see spirits and speak to them. Maybe we should go there and try to contact your mother."

Thump—her fist lands hard on my solar plexus. "Adam, I love you, but you say stupid stuff sometimes. We die and get buried. No one's communicating with the dead. One meditation session with some crackpot—the money manager turned medium—and suddenly you're *Crossing Over* with John Edwards? It's typical for you to fall head over heels without stopping to think; can't you do *anything* in moderation?"

So much for empathetic Adam and my last shred of self-control. My fight or flight response kicks in, and I go on the attack. "You're wrong, Minnie! The grand totality of life isn't chaos and coincidence. You can't deny the presence of a higher power." I stare deeply into her eyes. "Last night I was part of something bigger. I came to know that we're all loved by God, and everything we experience has a higher, unknown meaning. You need to look beyond the obvious in your life and search for the deeper truth behind why things are happening to you."

"Are you listening to yourself? I am a trained nurse. There's no 'why' for these things, no deeper truth. People get sick and they die. And it hurts when they leave us. Look at your job. Is there a deeper truth to why kids get cavities? No. Brush better. You're a Yale-trained dentist who now suddenly believes in ghosts and spirits? Sure, let's break out the Ouija board and talk to my mom. Maybe she'll tell us what an asshole you're being." Minnie throws herself into her pillow and starts sobbing. I stand there, staring at my heartbroken wife. All my good vibes from last night are gone. My eye twitches uncontrollably. I reach over to comfort Minnie, but she balls up like a baby inside its mother.

"Minnie, you're right. It's all a pile of crap. I don't know what came over me."

She turns toward me and swallows, then wipes her nose with the back of her hand. "You have no right to talk to me about God. We joined the temple, but you never go with me. You probably know more about Sufism now than you do about Judaism, your actual faith."

I want to say, "Look who's talking; you don't even believe in God. You're not even remotely religious or spiritual, yet you dress up and go to the Shabbat show at temple with the girls every Friday." But I bite my tongue and tone it down. "Just because you go to Shabbat..."

"I go because I loved our family Shabbat dinners growing up. Maybe you could at least go with us one time. You are still Jewish, aren't you? Or did last night's meditation include a conversion ceremony?"

"You know a relationship with God has nothing to do with going to temple every single Friday and Saturday or even at all. I don't need to be seen inside a synagogue to make a show of my faith. I communicate with God privately."

"I'd love to hear that conversation. Look, Adam. We're not getting anywhere with this. I'm asking you to go to temple with us tomorrow—as a family. Paige is going to become a bat mitzvah in a couple of years."

"Minnie, I was born Jewish, had a bar mitzvah, and suffered through religious school, but I feel no connection to Judaism," I pause, "other than my neurotic personality." I smile, hoping my joke will make Minnie laugh. But she's having none of it. I wish with all my heart I could make her feel better and share the joy and peace that I felt last night while meditating. All she wants right now is for me to go to temple with her. I lean over and wrap her in my arms. "Honey, I can't stand the rabbi's zeal for Judaism, and his proselytizing makes me feel uneasy. I love you dearly, but you're not getting me to go to temple.

* * *

Adam's story has me hooked. And while he can be so annoying you want to shake him, I don't hate him. And I'm confident readers won't hate him either, because they'll see a part of themselves and their struggles to be better than they are, in him.

It's like rubbernecking on the highway—I can't look away. Even after his panic attack and the help the universe is giving Adam, he's *still* stuck in the same prison of his petty, selfish, and egotistical thoughts. He has his first chance at enlightenment with Klein, but he blows it by refusing to go to temple with Minnie. I want to kick him, then tell him to get his act together. I got mine together a bit more easily, but it still took some doing.

CHAPTER EIGHT
9:41 p.m.

My first foray into the strange, new, non-scientific world of spirituality and enlightenment started about seven years ago when I was in my mid-thirties. One Sunday afternoon, I followed my wife into Restoration Hardware. She'd bestowed upon me the job of occupying the kids as she browsed. While sitting with my girls on the plush, white couches and trying to keep them away from the overpriced dinnerware, I spied an impressive coffee table book. I became engrossed in the pages, and I barely noticed my three-year-old daughter prancing towards a bar cart covered with decanters and cocktail glasses. "Eva, get away from there!" I yelled. "You'll break something!" Then I turned to see her older sister rinsing her hands in a zen fountain. "Autumn," I shouted. "You can't do that. And there are germs in there! Rina, take Autumn to mom and get hand sanitizer."

The two older girls went off to find Leah, and Eva snuggled next to me on the couch, playing with a pair of folding binoculars, leaving me free to return to my reading. The book I had found was an introduction to Buddhism. I felt like I was in the world's fanciest petting zoo as I sat between the overstuffed pillows and faux fur blankets. I ignored the frowning customer on my right who kept shaking her head as a saleswoman sifted through a catalogue the size of a Charles Dickens novel, and I tuned out the shouting match between a clerk and his customer returning a chair that was delivered with a scratch. Soon enough, *All About Buddhism* absorbed me. There were beautiful images of Tibetan, Indian, Japanese, and Chinese Buddhist temples, and statues of the Buddha from all different cultures interspersed among pages of short paragraphs in large type. Here's a passage I remember:

> Prince Siddhartha Gautama had the world at his feet. His father was the king of a region in India. Although born to tremendous wealth, Siddhartha felt unhappy. His father heard a prophecy that Siddhartha was destined for greatness and would one day leave the kingdom. The king did not want to lose his son, so he lavished him with an abundance of riches. When Siddhartha was still not satisfied, the king provided the most beautiful women in the kingdom for his heir to do with as he pleased. Siddhartha remained sad. Even after Siddhartha finally chose his bride and had a boy of his own, the prince continued life unsatisfied and unfulfilled.

The feeling Siddhartha was experiencing felt familiar to me. If a rich prince with all the wealth in the world, all the women he could want, even a kingdom at his feet, still couldn't feel peace—then *damn*, what were the chances the rest of us mortal men could feel harmony and peace in our lives? No wonder that even in my blessed life as an orthodontist, I still felt anxious and unsettled. I didn't stand a chance of having inner peace if Siddhartha, the prince and future king, couldn't be happy.

"Are you watching them?" Leah chimed from across the store.

"Of course," I responded without looking up and continued to read about how Siddhartha became a Buddha, which literally means the 'awakened or enlightened one.'

> Siddhartha could not be placated by the lavish lifestyle, so he decided to shed his earthly possessions and leave the comfort of his kingdom to find his utopia or, as he put it, his *nirvana* (heaven on earth). He studied with scholars and mystics from all over the land and trained in meditation for six years, but peace and inner harmony continued to evade him. Then, realizing he was close to attaining full enlightenment, Siddhartha perched himself under a Bodhi tree, assumed meditation posture, and vowed not to rise until he had obtained eternal happiness. He had visions of infinite past lives. He uncovered different worlds and planes of existence. Finally, he broke through his barriers and attained enlightenment, achieving his inner peace. Siddhartha had a palpable clarity about life that everyone around him could detect. The way to eternal nirvana was unlocked.

I decided to start reading everything I could about Buddhism and to commit to meditating. Short of joining a monastery, it was the best way I knew to put myself on the path to enlightenment.

Then I heard a crash followed by a scream. I turned to see Autumn standing frozen in place over the scattered shards of a glass light fixture.

"Oh my God, Autumn, what happened? I thought you were with Mommy." She looked up at me with fear in her eyes. A store clerk came over and found the price tag amidst the broken glass. Autumn had toppled the "Restoration Globe Room Surround Light," which went for $398.00.

"Autumn Silverstein!" I screamed.

"Daddy, it wasn't my fault."

"Oh really?" I snarled. "Did it fall over and break by itself?"

Autumn unfroze and started shuddering, her big brown eyes filling with water.

"Jacob," Leah gasped, having arrived at the scene. "How could you let this happen on your watch?"

"Now it's my fault?" I retorted. "Autumn's the one who knocked it over."

"She's a child, and you're the responsible adult. *You* were supposed to be watching the kids." Leah bent down to get on Autumn's level.

"It's okay, honey, accidents happen. We'll take care of it." A manager came running over, and I felt my ear start to wiggle uncontrollably. I remained silent as I pulled out my wallet and extracted my credit card to pay for the broken globe and my new coffee table book. While signing the receipt, I looked forward to going home and reading more about how Siddhartha finally attained peace and enlightenment—both of which I badly needed after we left the store. Maybe this highly anxious, neurotic, Jewish dude I had become could learn something from the Buddha.

Over the next several months, I read everything I could find on Buddhism, and I turned my spiritual education into a research project. Do you have any idea how many different ways there are to meditate? They all boil down to the same idea of clearing your head, freeing your mind of thoughts and distractions. The great thing is you don't need any fancy equipment or expensive workout clothes. All you have to do is get comfortable and express your wish for self-transformation and a desire for others' well-being and the alleviation of their suffering.

Meditation is a way to cultivate the basic human qualities that can reduce suffering in life. Your mind becomes more stable and clearer, you achieve emotional balance, and you begin to develop more love and compassion. We all have the potential to grow this way, but these qualities can remain latent if you don't make an effort to develop them through a practice like meditation. And, it is just that—a practice rather than an activity, a way of being rather than a daily ritual. Poor Adam was in tremendous pain and so ripe for transformation that he achieved an instant benefit from meditation, while my growth and the gifts I've received from it have come more gradually.

When I first started meditating, my mind would not stop thinking about other things, so I had to learn calming techniques. The first one was called focused attention—taming and centering the mind in the present moment while developing the capacity not to get distracted. Even after several months my mind was still not focusing on the present. I tried mindfulness—cultivating a detached reactive awareness to emotions to prevent thoughts and feelings from spiraling out of control and creating mental distress. That lasted a couple of months, too, and then I fell right back into the dismal abyss of my melancholy state. Finally, I learned to meditate with compassion and loving kindness, which helps foster an altruistic perspective towards other people.

Eventually, I learned to combine all three techniques. Given Adam's impulsive nature—I mean, the guy ripped a cookie right out of his kid's mouth—his journey to enlightenment is more like a sprint from start to finish compared to my steady jog along the path. I admire his ability to dive into things—and feel bad for him when he belly flops or hits his head on the bottom of the pool.

* * *

BEEP, BEEP, BEEP—my timer goes off, reminding me that the nirvana of the bedroom awaits. Leah can hang tight for one more minute. After all, life is suffering, according to the Buddha. Each one of our hellish moments has meaning. There is a master plan. Mindfulness is the first step on the pathway to peace.

I'm in a dilemma. Adam has experienced his first step towards enlightenment, but my wife is waiting upstairs for her own lightbulb moment. Well, if this is the worst situation I find myself in this month, life's pretty good. I decide to go on a reconnaissance mission and sneak upstairs to see what Leah's up to. If she's doing her usual pre-sex rituals, I might be able to read a few more pages. And, in fact, she's still in the shower. My wife likes to get clean before doing the dirty. I open the door a crack to gather more information. "Are you ready yet, hun?"

"Shaving my legs so they're nice and smooth for you. Oh, I almost forgot, I need you home early this Friday. We're doing the refreshments for Oneg Shabbat. Twenty more minutes and I'll be ready." Unlike when I say twenty minutes, Leah really means twenty minutes. I have until 10:10 on the dot.

"All right, Schmoopy. I'm running downstairs for a moment; give me a shout when you're ready."

"Okay. But shut the door," she yells. "It's freezing." I close the door behind me as I rush downstairs.

Leah's reminder that we're going to temple this Friday stirs up deep feelings. My wife knows I'm more spiritual than religious, but I'll go to temple because it makes her happy. Religion—in my humble opinion—is man-made. And the idea that only one religion is right, at the exclusion of others, strikes me as absurd. If God is omnipotent and omnipresent, can't we all share Him or Her? There must be a common "religious denominator," a Venn diagram that shows the intersection of all religions in a common core—one that will deliver truth to humans. During my journey into enlightenment, I made it my unofficial mission to find the overlap, the shared center of all religions, the set of beliefs and principles that makes them one. Searching for that overlap helped me get closer to my inner peace. I want Adam to get there too.

Moment of epiphany here! What if, instead of rejecting Minnie's request to go to temple, Adam acquiesces and joins the family at temple for the Sabbath?

I run down the stairs two steps at a time, throw myself in front of the laptop, highlight "but you're not getting me to go to temple" and change Adam's response. This is going to be a classic scene!

The Adventures of Adam Freeman, DDS
June 21—*The Bible* miniseries

"Minnie, I was born Jewish, had a bar mitzvah, and suffered through religious school, but I feel no connection to Judaism." I pause before adding, "Other than my neurotic personality." I smile, hoping my joke will make Minnie laugh. But she's having none of it. I wish with all my heart I could make her feel better and share the joy and peace that I felt last night while meditating. But all she wants right now is for me to go to temple with her. I lean over and wrap her in my arms. "Okay, honey, I'll go to temple tomorrow morning with you and the girls."

"Thank you. I'll text your mom to sit for Spencer."

Minnie goes into the bathroom and shuts the door. I lie in bed and feel a stirring in my lower parts. I lift up the covers and whisper to Charlie, "Finally buddy, maybe we'll get laid tomorrow and end the dry spell. I think it's a mitzvah to have sex on Shabbat!"

The kids are still asleep and Minnie's in the shower, which gives me time to check my phone. I see that Klein emailed me links for meditation sites. I grab my laptop and rush down to the man cave to read them. There are hundreds of scientific articles from peer-reviewed journals, and I'm not sure where to begin. I notice that meditation has been studied in fields ranging from clinical psychology, preventive medicine, and even education. I never received the memo that meditation was becoming mainstream.

With little time to spare, I focus on an article in the November 2014 *Scientific American* that addresses various benefits derived from meditation. Depression, chronic pain, and stress all seem to respond positively to meditative practices. Universities have reported that meditation may be clinically effective in helping the body fight off inflammatory diseases. It catches my attention that a study using magnetic resonance imaging discovered that experienced practitioners of Buddhist meditation have shown decreased volume of the amygdala—the fear processing center in their brain.

I know I'm in a time crunch, so I bookmark the pages. Now I have scientific ammo to use the next time I talk to Minnie. I shut the lights off, get comfortable in my leather chair under my Yankee Stadium poster, and close my tired eyes to meditate.

My second deep breath is interrupted by Minnie yelling, "Adam, are you ready? I don't want to be late." I open my eyes, and it hits me why Siddhartha and Rumi left their families—it's impossible to get a moment of peace when you're surrounded by your loved ones. Today's meditation session will have to wait.

I rush up to our bedroom and see Minnie's scowl as she looks at my sweats. I ask her what to wear. It's been a long time since I've gone to temple, and I wonder if people still wear suits. She removes my dress pants, a button-down shirt, and a lightweight blazer out of my closet and hands them to me.

"Can I wear a hoodie over this?" I ask her.

"It's temple, Adam, not a sports bar. Now please get the kids ready."

It's easier corralling animals than getting all three of my kids in the car. After a missing hairdryer, arguing over matching clothes, and jostling over which one will take the middle seat, we manage to get out of the house as a family in a reasonable amount of time. We drop Spencer off at my parents' house and arrive on time for the start of Saturday morning services. To my delight, Minnie picks a row in the back, and the Freeman family files in. Sitting down on the cushioned chairs, I pick up a prayer book, and Minnie rolls her eyes at me as I open it the wrong way. She grabs it, pulls it open from the right, and hands it back to me.

I didn't think there'd even be a minyan—more than ten people—but much to my surprise there are over fifty worshippers. The group is split evenly between elderly Jews, who have no better place to go on Saturday morning, and the families with upcoming bar and bat mitzvahs.

I want to please Minnie, so I immerse myself in the service. Benjamin Edelman—Rabbi Ben—is not your typical old-school rabbi. Mid-thirties and handsome, he acts like the hip, progressive Ben Stiller character Rabbi Jake Schram in *Keeping the Faith*. Minnie told me he was first in his class at Duke Law School and on his way to a big law firm in New York City when he felt the "calling." Rabbi Ben is still single, and the older Jewish mothers are all over him like cream cheese and jelly on matzah trying to fix him up with their daughters. Good thing he's a rabbi, not a priest, or he'd miss all that action.

Half an hour into the service, despite my best effort to pay attention and learn something, I am bored. The temple's bigshots, or as Minnie calls them "the machers," open the door of the ark and bring out the Torah. We stand as they walk the Torah through the aisles. I'm about to reach out and touch the Torah, but I miss my chance when I feel my pants pocket vibrate and sneak a peek at the text: "Meet me in the bathroom, NOW -K."

What? Klein's here? No way. Then it dawns on me that his daughter Tara's bat mitzvah is coming up. He needs to be here every Saturday. "I'll be right back," I say to Minnie, "I've got to pee." I get up and stride quickly to the restroom. When I rush in, Klein is waiting for me.

"You're a sight for sore eyes, Freeman. What the hell are you doing here?"

"Long story, but it's your fault. Last night Minnie told me I knew more about Sufism than Judaism. She coerced me..."

"You mean convicted."

"Right. Convicted me into going. What about you? I thought you're anti-religion."

Klein laughs. "If I want to stay married, I've got to put in my time. Joy knows more than a lot of the people here. Plus, she has a crush on the rabbi."

"She could do worse," I say.

"Yeah. I like the guy, even if he is better looking than I am. I went to his viewing of *The Bible* miniseries last month and, afterwards, he led a great group discussion."

"That's cool. I didn't know they did things like that here."

"It's why they raised all that money for the multimedia room."

"You mean I can come watch TV in temple?"

"You bet. I guess you never read the newsletter. Ben's a cool dude. Salt of the earth."

"Kosher salt of the earth."

Klein chuckles. "Funny you should say that."

"Why? I've never eaten kosher in my life. And I couldn't give up kung pao shrimp if my life depended on it."

"Sounds pretty shellfish of you. Seriously though, I've been doing a lot of reading about why Jews keep kosher."

"And what'd you learn?" I ask.

"Keeping kosher comes from the body of Jewish law that deals with what foods we can and cannot eat, called Kashrut."

"So I can eat Baby Kash Ruth bars?"

"Touché on the puns, okay? The word kosher describes the dietary laws of the Torah. God told Moses that Jews cannot eat certain foods, and what they do eat has to be prepared a certain way. For example, you can't eat meat and cheese together. Nothing from a pig and no shellfish because they dwell at the bottom of the ocean."

"I thought they dwelled in the kitchen at Little Hunan."

Klein lets out a deep sigh. "Can't you take anything seriously?"

"Okay, I have a serious question for you. Will God judge me because I eat lobster and love a mushroom bacon Swiss burger?"

"I don't know the answer to that. I once read online that you are what you eat, and kosher is God's diet for spirituality. Jewish mysticism teaches that non-kosher food blocks the spiritual potential of the soul."

"The scholars think I'm going to hell after my bacon Swiss burger-induced heart attack."

Klein laughs. "Jews don't believe in hell. Remember the eleventh commandment. 'Thou shalt watch thy cholesterol.'" Klein looks at his watch.

"Shit, Joy will kill me if I don't get back in there. I'll see you after the service at the Kiddush." He runs out.

I wait a few minutes before heading back into the service so it won't look like we had a meeting. When I sit down, Minnie glares at me. "How was your men's room rendezvous with Klein?"

"What are you talking about?"

"Don't play dumb, Adam. I saw him walk back in."

"Look, Minnie. I came here for you—and the kids. My best friend happened to be here, and I was excited to see him. A friendly face in a foreign land." Minnie's stops scowling at me when the rabbi leads the congregation in a silent prayer. I close my eyes, and it starts to feel like a form of meditation. I begin to wonder what the difference is between meditation and prayer. Note to self: ask Klein.

After services, everyone heads to the reception room for lunch. *Now* the Freemans and the Kleins can congregate freely. The surprise gift of hanging out with Klein overshadows the intimidation I feel when I'm around his wife, Joy. At least she and Minnie get along, and they chat as the kids run off towards the sweets table. Mine will come back dipped in chocolate and dusted with powdered sugar, while Tiger Mom's troupe will return showing no traces of the single rugelach they're each allowed to eat. Klein and I join the conversation our wives are having about the party preparations for Tara's upcoming bat mitzvah.

Klein interjects, "For what we pay for our temple membership, they should give us the party for free."

"I know, right? Why pay five grand per year to belong to a temple, anyway?" I add.

"Of course, they've got maintenance and upkeep, but still, it's absurd. There are less expensive ways to show devotion to my creator." Klein looks at Joy. "We should have joined Chabad—they don't charge these outrageous dues."

"Chabad?" I ask. Minnie rolls her eyes at me. I scowl at her to indicate that I hate when she does that.

Klein answers, "Chabad is one of the orthodox sects of Judaism. You remember seeing the Mitzvah-Mobile in college and those guys in dark coats who would walk up and ask us if we were Jewish?"

Joy jumps in, "It may be more economical to join Chabad, but they're way too zealous for me. I love being Jewish, but I'm not going to shave my head or wear those hideous clothes."

Now Minnie piles on. "I don't get it. Why shouldn't the men shave their heads too? Most barely have hair anyway! And boys only become a bar mitzvah, not girls. They don't consider us worthy. Spare me the sexism, please."

"Did you know," interjects Klein, "that when a woman menstruates she has to sleep in another bed, because the orthodox men believe she's dirty?"

Minnie shakes her head. "Unbelievable. Why doesn't a man leave the house when he has an erection? He should sleep in the car. These rules are ridiculous. Who makes them up, anyway?"

"If I had to sleep in the car every time I had an erection at home," I comment, "I'd be living in a mobile home." Everyone laughs. The conversation ends when Rabbi Ben arrives at our table. He puts his hand on my shoulder and leans in.

"It's nice to finally meet you, Adam. Minnie's told me a lot about you. I heard about your hospital stay and have been praying for you. How's it going?"

I pause, wondering who else Minnie has told about my incident. "I'm good, thanks for asking, Rabbi. I've been under a lot of stress at work lately."

I feel my twitch starting and rub my eye to hide it. "I feel fine," I continue, "but I have to admit I've been doing some soul searching."

The rabbi puts his arm around my shoulder. I'm not one of those guys who's into bro hugs, unless it's with the Four Horsemen, so I shrink back a bit, then try to relax, not wanting to offend him. "That's wonderful, Adam. I'm delighted to hear you're looking inward. In tough times, people can lose their faith in God. It is completely normal to have doubts and to be angry at what life throws at you." He turns to Klein. "Speaking of which, how're you doing on your spiritual quest? Did you enjoy *The Bible* miniseries?"

"I did, Rabbi. I recruited Adam here to join me on my last meditation retreat. Speaking of which"—he smiles at the rabbi—"I've got a question for you."

"Oh God," Joy says and grabs Minnie's hand. "Let's go. I don't even want to know what *fakakta* questions my husband has for the rabbi now." I smile at Asian Joy speaking Yiddish. She's the most Jewish person at the table besides Rabbi Ben.

Klein continues. "Last week I went to my reiki expert, and I had an out-of-body experience during our session. What do you make of that? Is it possible for our souls to escape our bodies? While I was out, I visualized a past life. I know Jews aren't big on reincarnation, but this felt entirely real. Is this a sign I'm going crazy?"

"Yes," I answer, "and it isn't the first sign." I glance at the rabbi—maybe I shouldn't joke in the presence of this holy man.

Rabbi Ben grins. "Contrary to what your friend believes about you, Joshua, you're not going crazy. Did you know that, traditionally, Jews believe our souls come back to earth again and again to get things right? In that sense, reincarnation is part of our belief system. You'll find it in the Zohar."

"*What*? Jews believe in past lives?" I blurt out.

Klein has a huge smirk on his face. "I knew it! What's the Zohar? A mystical text?"

"The Zohar, gentlemen, is the written book of Kabbalah." I give the rabbi a blank stare, and he goes on. "Simply put, the Torah, or Word of God, consists of the five books of Moses that were written down for the Jewish people to have as a guide. You may be familiar with the Talmud, which provides scholarly commentary on the Torah. The Kabbalah explores the deeper meaning behind the literal translation of the Torah's words. The Zohar is the primary text of the Kabbalah, presumably written by Rabbi Shimon Bar Yochai, known as Rashbi, who lived in the second and third centuries. It was meant for Jews who had already achieved a higher level of spiritual awakening, and it describes all the stages of the evolution of the soul—125 to be exact. It reads like a set of stories to the spiritually unaware, but if you're a Kabbalist who's already achieved spiritual growth, it's a practical guide for even deeper learning. When the high Jewish priests studied the Zohar, they deemed it intellectually inaccessible to the public. About 250 years ago, another rabbi interpreted the Zohar and wrote the Tanya, a layman's guide to the Kabbalah, which became a self-help book for the Jews of the time. It offered guidance for people dealing with life's struggles, emotions, and the various stages of their lives."

"I had no idea about this," Klein says.

"If you're both interested, I'm teaching an intensive, week-long class on Kabbalah next month."

Klein responds, "Count me in!"

I hesitate. "Honestly, too much religion for me," I tell the rabbi.

"Well, when you're ready, Adam, we'd love to have you join us. I hope to see you more, and I'll see you soon, Joshua."

Klein looks disappointed. "Look," I say, "maybe later. But after today, I've maxed out my religious quota for the month."

When Joy and Minnie return, Klein informs, "Hey Joy, I'm going to take a Kabbalah class with the rabbi next month. Is that cool with you?"

Joy sighs. "Another class? All right, text me the link, and I'll add it to the Google calendar."

Minnie looks quizzically at me to see if I have signed up. When I shake my head, she smiles and adds, "Adam, why don't you take that class, too?"

"Because meditation is all I can handle right now."

Klein starts in with me on spirituality and science when Minnie's phone pings, and a worried look crosses her face. She turns to Klein and Joy. "We have to go. I got a text from my brother-in-law. My sister is back in the hospital. Adam, round up the kids—now."

On the ride home, Minnie decides to visit her sister in Maryland. It's not the best time for me to take on the added stress of solo parenting, but it's the right thing to do. I consider trying to soothe Minnie with Rabbi Ben's explanation of reincarnation, but then I think better of it.

* * *

All this writing about religion and God is making me hungry. I reach for my very own Holy Grail—the jumbo bag of peach rings. I was hoping to hold out until at least 2:00 a.m., but I can't stave off my craving any longer. Peach rings are my weakness, my sin of gluttony. Like Eve tempting Adam, they are calling my name. I open the bag and pop four succulent, chewy rings into my mouth. There must be a God, because peach rings are like heaven on earth. My phone vibrates.

The text from Leah reads: "JACOB...I'M READY! ♡" Oh Lord, there's the call.

"I'M COMING... 😳" I text back. I grab one more handful of candy, stand, and head for the stairs.

CHAPTER NINE
10:10 p.m.

I'm sitting on the edge of our bed, enjoying an especially chewy peach ring. I can hear Leah blow-drying her hair in the bathroom. Giving Adam a brief synopsis of Kabbalah was a blast from the past for me. Minnie's crack about Adam knowing more about Sufism than his own religion could just as easily have been leveled at me a few years ago. I had boned up on Buddhism after my trip to Restoration Hardware, but I knew shockingly little about Judaism. I decided that, before I disavowed the religion I was born into, I would take classes in the Kabbalah.

My first foray was a ten-week online course with the Harvard Divinity School. Although pricey at $1,895.00—it was Harvard after all—it didn't seem smart to skimp on enlightenment. Besides the ten, hour-long webinars, the course involved a ton of reading and writing.

"We're not taking Madonna's Kabbalah class here," was the bespectacled Professor Bernard Gilbert's opening comment, followed by, "Kabbalah is based on the Alter Rebbe's writings called the Tanya, which is a self-help book based on the Zohar. The book took him twenty-two years to write, and it addresses who we are as spiritual beings. It also gives us tools and teaches us lessons to live by, to help bring light back into our lives."

The only way to interact with Professor Gilbert was by email—I had decided not to spring for the half hour of video chat with the professor for an extra $195—but I needed a live person to talk to about my discoveries. Leah suggested I meet with our temple's rabbi, Emmet Shekl.

Rabbi Shekl, a dead ringer for comedian and actor Billy Crystal, was eager to meet and discuss what I'd learned each week from Professor Gilbert's lectures. Thursday nights after work I drove to the temple and shared my thoughts with the rabbi over a glass of wine. According to Kabbalah, humans have two souls—the animal soul that encompasses our wants and needs, and our Godly soul that is an embodiment of the Transcendent. The animal half is about survival; it can be selfish and passionate and can cause you to do what you need to do to feel better. Our Godly part is altruistic and seeks Godliness above all.

Rabbi Shekl explained, "God told Isiah, 'I have made two souls.' It is written concerning Adam," (Bible Adam, not Freeman Adam) "God breathed into his nostrils a 'soul of life,' which can be interpreted that we all have a part of God within ourselves. In fact, we're all an embodiment of our Creator."

Gilbert's lectures introduced the *Sefirot*, the ten building blocks that form the anatomy of the soul. Three of these building blocks—understanding, knowledge, and wisdom—make up the intellect, or the cognitive aspect of the soul. The other seven—severity, kindness, compassion, humility, endurance, bonding, and sovereign—make up the emotive aspect.

Rabbi Shekl was happy to expand on this. "The attributes, or the *Sefirot*, are expressed through the three garments: thoughts, speech, and action. In essence, our two souls, each having ten faculties, fight over those three garments."

When I told him that he'd lost me, he patiently continued, "Bottom line, there's a battle going on inside us where the animal soul tries to control our thoughts, speech, and actions with selfish deeds. But we must think, speak, and act in a Godly way, and not egotistically. We must bring love into everything we do, which makes our deeds and thoughts limitless and infinite on a Godly level. Even though we'll experience animalistic urges and desires, we need to control them and have mindful, pure, and holy thoughts. Don't entertain these evil thoughts when they approach our mind."

I'm absorbed in the memory of the pleasant nights the rabbi and I spent together when suddenly my Godly soul is distracted, and my animal urges take over as Leah emerges from the bathroom wrapped in the sheer white robe I gave her on our last anniversary. Suddenly, the robe slides to the floor, and she's standing there naked. Everything is pert, but her face falls when she sees the faraway look in my eyes.

"What's wrong?" She leans closer, her breasts inches from my face. "You don't want this?"

"God no…I mean yes…I mean…you're as beautiful as you were on our wedding night."

She smiles. "Thank you, Jacob."

"And seeing you all in white makes me think of—"

She interrupts, "*The Dress?*" I look down at her feet sheepishly.

"Yes. *The Dress*. You know what it does to me." Leah lets out a long breath as she pulls the robe back on.

"Listen, Jacob, I know my wedding dress turns you on, but it's not exactly the most comfortable thing I have. I'm happy to indulge your romantic memory, but tonight I was hoping we could—"

110 JOURNEY OF A JUBU

"You don't want to relive the best night of our lives?"

"It was a great night. But I like to believe the best is yet to come." I snicker, and she smiles, realizing her unintended joke. "And tonight I'd like to be in the here and now."

"But…"

"Come on, Jacob. What happened to the Buddhist who lives in the moment?"

"He's here. Now. But how about Jewish…tradition." I sing it *Fiddler on the Roof* style. "That dress…does something to me. I guess I'm equal parts nostalgic Jew and well-balanced Bu."

Leah blushes. "It's tight and uncomfortable. And it's down in the basement. But I'll do it because it turns you on."

"And I love you for that." Leah pulls her robe on, cinches the belt, and brushes past me to head downstairs.

I call down to her. "At least my fetish is recreating an actual moment you and I had—not some nurse or schoolgirl fantasy thing." I smile—she's going to be a while. I grab the manuscript I'd brought up—just in case—and keep reading.

The Adventures of Adam Freeman, DDS
June 22—*Family Feud*

I'm sitting here all alone on this rainy Sunday evening. I wish Minnie had left for Maryland in a better mood, but we had an argument and she's pissed. It started innocently this morning when I was lying in bed as she was getting ready to leave. She was packing clothes neatly in her hot pink suitcase—easy to spot at baggage claim—and she asked, "Ready to go back to work tomorrow?"

A wave of melancholy came over me. I could have said, "As ready as I'll ever be," but I decided to speak from the heart. "I don't know, Minnie. I mean, I make a good living, but I don't have a passion for my work anymore. My body is ready to go back to the office, but my mind is screaming, 'No, no, *no!*'"

She turned from her packing and stared at me. "Now is not the time for you to have your midlife crisis—not while my forty-seven-year-old sister is dying. I know your office is stressful, and I get that kids' teeth may not be your passion. But I need you to be rational. And I need you to be here for me. I can't handle losing my sister and you leaving your job."

"My job, Minnie, is killing me. It provides us a nice living, but I'm sacrificing my health and happiness to pay the bills. Sure, I'm my own boss, and I work in a nice, clean office. But managing my staff is driving me insane." Minnie continued packing.

"Adam, leaving your job would be insane. You have a successful practice, and your staff works hard for you. The problem is managing yourself. Grow up and get a grip."

"I tell you, I don't get no respect," I said, doing my Rodney Dangerfield imitation. "Maybe I should retire and start enjoying life."

Minnie slammed her underwear drawer shut and turned to face me. "My God, Adam, you're not even forty years old—you can't retire. You've got a family to support."

"I'm living vacation to vacation. I read a fortune cookie once that said you should build a life that you don't need to escape from. Besides, look how much fun your dad is having in retirement. He is my idol."

"My dad is seventy and worked really hard to retire."

"When you're retired, every day's like Sunday! He told me that."

"Stop channeling my dad," Minnie admonished, shoving a handful of bras into her suitcase. She was biting her lip hard. "You've got a whole bunch of Mondays left before you throw in the towel—or in your case, give up the drill."

"The first thing I'd do is write a book about my office. A self-help book for other dentists trying to run their own practices. Or a novel about hygienists' fantasies when the patients are sedated. I'll call it *The Dirty Hygienist*. Get it? The hygienist cleans teeth, but she's dirty..."

Minnie threw her shoes into another travel bag. "A book? Be serious, you can barely write a prescription for painkillers. Your grammar sucks, and you write way too many run-on sentences." This is the side of Minnie I both love and hate. The side that is unafraid to tell me the truth, even when that truth hurts. I consider something horrible to say back to her, but I'm not the kind of guy who attacks his wife when her sister is on her deathbed. The truth is, I could use her help editing my diary. But now is not the time to ask.

"Hey, maybe we should all go on *Family Feud*. I've always been good at that show! And, I bet I could win a pile of prize money!"

"You're a family dentist, not a *Family Feud* contestant. And I don't need this shit before I leave!" Minnie struggled to close her overstuffed suitcase. "You're irrational and depressed. You need a therapist, not a career change."

"I am not depressed!"

"Let your therapist be the judge of that. They'll probably put you on medication. You know it's helped me a lot with anxiety and negative feelings."

"Stop pushing drugs. I know it works for some people, but it's not for me. They never taught us how to deal with this stuff at Yale. It would be nice if you showed empathy for my pain."

"Empathy? My sister is dying. *Dying*! And all I've done is support and coddle you. Maybe I need to go the other way and give you tough love. So here it is: Stop acting like a baby and grow up. Everyone has problems. It's how you handle them that separates the men from the boys."

Minnie slammed her suitcase closed and yanked it from the bed. The weight nearly pulled her to the floor, and the case toppled onto its side. I went over to help her, but she rebuffed me. Then she delivered the coup de grace.

"By the way, your eye is twitching. *Again*. Kids, Mommy's leaving!"

That was my morning. Fun, right? And now I'm sitting here all alone with plenty of time to relive our fight and reflect on my role in it. Minnie makes good points, but I don't want to go on medication. I don't want to numb my pain. As a dentist, I'm trained to look for the root of the problem, to drill out the cavity and restore the tooth to health. A filling is useless if you don't eliminate the rot that's destroying the tooth. I know antidepressants help, but a pill will only mask my symptoms, which are signs of a deeper malaise. How do I deal with what's really bothering me? Who will listen, and where do I start? The meditation I did with Klein is the first thing that's made me feel even remotely good in a long, long time. I decide to call Hope in the morning to see if she can fit me in for a session.

* * *

Jesus, Adam. Don't make me kill you. Just when you show your redeeming qualities—your love for your children and the fun you have with your friends, you regress to idiotic, child-like behavior with your wife. Why are you antagonistic with Minnie? Can't you see she is being a supportive and caring wife? I know you don't realize you're being misogynistic, but man, you are walking on thin ice. I can see why my potential literary agent extraordinaire, Maggie, wants more of me and less—or none—of you, but I'm rooting for you, and I want to see you evolve. So evolve, dammit, so I can spare you from extinction!

I stuff three juicy peach rings into my mouth. I'll need the sugar rush for my rendezvous with Leah.

My thoughts are interrupted as my beautiful wife enters our bedroom—a vision of loveliness wrapped in a white brocade bodice with swirls of tulle beneath. Some guys get turned on by women wearing Frederick's of Hollywood lingerie or clad in leather, but not me. There's nothing like Leah's wedding dress to get me all worked up. The way *The Dress* hugs her curves makes her body look heavenly.

My heart stops, and I drop the manuscript onto my nightstand. Leah takes a step closer. "Oh God," I exclaim, "You still look incredible after thirteen years of marriage."

"So it took me wearing *The Dress* to finally get you to put down your book."

"You're not threatened by Adam, are you?"

She laughs. "I don't think Adam would look very good in this dress. And I doubt you'd want to see him naked."

I grin and whisper, "Leah, come over here. I have a surprise for you."

I open the drawer of my nightstand and take out the instant heating massage oil I bought when I'm startled by Leah's scream: "Goddammit!" I see a Barbie doll go flying across the room. "How many times do I have to tell those kids to clean up after themselves?"

Leah is sprawled out on the wood floor. I jump off the bed to make sure she's okay. "Maybe Barbie's jealous of your dress?"

"Where's Ken when you need him?"

"Here, let me help you over the threshold." I bend down to pick her up after she tripped over Barbie.

"Jacob, watch your back. You're not twenty-five anymore, and I don't need you in bed on painkillers missing work for a week." Leah laughs as I sweep her off her feet and inch towards the bed. I make it three steps and can feel my back tightening. I gingerly put her down.

"It's the thought that counts, honey." As she goes over to lock our bedroom door, I close my eyes and inhale. I still remember the smell of *The Dress* on our wedding night, the dress Leah wore not only at our wedding ceremony and the reception that followed but also later that night, in the honeymoon suite when we made love. Why did she keep her dress on? It all goes back to when my old Harvard roommate, Larry DeFazio, had popped the question, and his brother Joe and I took Larry out to celebrate. I'll never forget the scene in Daisy Buchanan's—a Boston landmark bar at the time—when Joe leaned into Larry with his elbow on the bar and said he wanted to pass down one of the best kept secrets a guy should know on his wedding night. I moved closer to hear the sage advice, but I couldn't make out what Joe was saying as Neil Diamond's "Sweet Caroline" blasted through the bar. When I pressed Larry later that night, he wouldn't tell.

Two weeks later, Larry and I celebrated the end of our root canal practical by getting drunk. That night, Larry was plastered enough to share the words of wisdom his brother had imparted. "According to my Casanova brother," Larry slurred, "every guy has to make love to his wife while she wears the wedding dress."

"Really?"

"Yeah. Joe said, 'Trust me—this is the best piece of advice I've given you since I told you where to buy your fake ID in high school.'"

Larry not only tried out Joe's suggestion but urged me to carry on the tradition. It took me a while to broach the subject with Leah, but I finally asked her about a week before our wedding, not wanting to surprise her on the night of with that request. "This may be crazy," I stammered, "but Larry D and his brother vouched that making love to your new bride in her wedding dress is a once-in-a-lifetime experience."

"I should certainly hope so," she answered. Much to my surprise, she continued, "I'm willing to try it."

That night, in the Presidential Suite of the Four Seasons, as I lay Leah back against the crimson headboard, roses lined the bed and a light summer breeze floated in through the open window. Leah looked ravishing—both innocent and sexy—in her dress. As I thought about the logistics of making love while she was still wrapped in all those folds of gossamer white, I wondered whether Larry and his brother were messing with me and playing a big joke. I mean, the first thing you want to do when you get your bride alone in your hotel room is rip off her clothes, right? But as my hands slowly caressed her elegant neckline and made their way gently down to her breasts, my mind cleared. And then Leah made it easy. She simply lifted the sheath skirt of her wedding gown and invited me in. As she put her hands on my waist and pulled down my tux pants, she whispered, "You were right. This makes tonight sexy." And it only became better after that. I couldn't believe that this geeky guy had gotten so lucky in love, and that I would get to spend the rest of my life with this beautiful, intelligent, exciting woman. Like all great secrets, the rest of the night is best left unspoken. I'm not about to write my version of *Fifty Shades of Grey*. Suffice it to say, Joe and Larry's piece of advice is one I'll never regret taking.

And while Leah is not as into reliving history as I am, she has indulged me on many occasions by putting on *The Dress* to recreate the romance and feelings of bliss we experienced on our wedding night. And we've still got it after all these years! After we finish, Leah whispers as we're cuddling, "Jacob, that was like an out-of-body experience. While you were inside my body, I was leaving it." She sighs. "It was intense. I don't know about you, but I'm exhausted, and

I'd love a glass of water." I hop out of bed buck naked, head to the bathroom, and return with a glass of cool water from the tap, but Leah is already asleep when I get there.

Perfect.

CHAPTER TEN
11:23 p.m.

I pull the comforter over Leah, put on my shorts and a T-shirt, and slip out of the room with my manuscript and head downstairs to keep reading.

The Adventures of Adam Freeman, DDS
June 23—Who's the Boss?

As if getting the kids ready for their respective playdates isn't hard enough, I've had to pee five times already this morning. Maybe I *am* the damn pee dentist. I'm nervous about going back to work. Everyone is conspiring to help me get there. Klein's wife, Joy, picks up Rose and Spencer to watch them for the day, and Minnie has arranged for me to drop Paige off at her BFF's house. I commute to my office in solitude and ponder how my first day post-nervous breakdown will go. I decide to break my day up into thirds to avoid getting overwhelmed. The first third will be before lunch, and I look forward to calling Hope the Healer after the morning huddle with my staff.

The first thing I see when I pull into the parking lot is a new inlaid sign above my office door. That's a good start to the day!

I join my team at the morning huddle, and Veronica runs it smoothly. I didn't think my staff cared much about me—other than as the one who pays their salaries—but they seem genuinely glad I'm okay. I make a two-sentence speech about how I'm happy to be back and put the incident behind us. No one makes eye contact with me, but that's fine. I am not in the mood for small talk.

My morning clinic session with patients is uneventful until I begin doing sealants on my last patient before lunch—eight-year-old Karly, who, with her wavy blonde hair pulled back in a ponytail, resembles one of the Olsen twins in their *Full House* days. We're still short an assistant, so Veronica sets up my chair while I glove up. Karly's mom asks, "How are you feeling, Doctor Freeman?" I panic for a moment, not wanting to recap what happened last week.

"I'm good, thanks." I put my mask on and begin working. "Open, Karly." I continue talking to Karly's mom through my mask, eager to change the subject from myself. I know she's involved with our local art museum, so I ask, "How's it going at the museum?"

"We're excited to be showcasing Steve DiBenedetto this month. It took me a while to get him to display all his works in one showing. He has a paranoid fear they'll be consumed in a fire." I'm about to say he should try meditation to calm his nerves, but I quickly realize this will start a line of conversation I'm not prepared to finish. She continues, "His paintings have a prophetic, philosophical, and mystical undercurrent to them."

I remember reading those exact words in the museum's newsletter last month. Rinsing the etchant from Karly's teeth, I indulge her mother. "It's amazing that our little town has such a prestigious museum."

She nods. "Yes, we're very lucky."

The insides of my cheeks feel dry, and I have that malodorous bad-breath taste in my mouth. I need a pick-me-up, so I remove my gloves and mask and quickly pop a Pep O Mint into my mouth. I put my new gloves back on and lean over Karly to place the sealant. "Does he live local—"

As I reach for my mask, I lose control of the Pep O Mint, and like something out of *Curb Your Enthusiasm*, it falls out of my mouth and into Karly's. I nearly pee in my pants. Sign or no sign, damn pee dentist strikes again.

"Veronica, suction, quick!" I shout. She hands me the suction, but I can't grab the mint. "Get me a cotton plier, now!" I quickly pull the Pep O Mint out of Karly's mouth.

I press a button on the side of the dental chair and Karly slowly ascends. I sit there frozen. Veronica finally breaks the ice. "Well, that was a first. Karly, why don't you rinse with this?" She hands Karly a plastic cup partially filled with Listerine. How embarrassing. And now my eye is twitching with a vengeance.

I stand there ready for an outburst from Karly's mom, slumping my head to cover up my twitch. She smiles. "Not a big deal, Dr. Freeman. Shit happens. It's kind of funny, like a Seinfeld episode." I'm not a big fan of cursing in front of kids, but like a Life Saver, it's *refreshing* that she finds humor in this awkward situation.

With the Pep O Mint debacle behind me, I have a free moment in the schedule to call Hope the Healer. I need guidance concerning why my wife doesn't appreciate my new journey. I want Minnie to understand the amazing contentment I felt while I was meditating. Who knows—maybe it will help her deal with how sad she is over her sister's illness.

Klein told me she's hard to get in touch with but, surprisingly, Hope answers. I skip the small talk and go right to what's on my mind. "Why can't I connect with my wife the way I did with the people in your group?" I ask.

Her answer is simple and makes perfect sense. "You can't force your beliefs on people. Everyone has their own journey."

"But my wife and I are on a journey together, and I want to be able to share this special experience with her."

"I understand, Adam, but you'll have to wait until she's ready, if she ever is. You know the saying about how you can lead a horse to water..."

"Well, dammit, I want to make the horse drink. I want Minnie to find the inner peace I'm starting to experience. God knows she could use it."

"I have another call coming in, but I have a suggestion. Why don't you bring your wife to one of my sessions and see how it goes?"

"All right. She'll pooh pooh it, but I'll try." She hangs up abruptly.

Even though I forgot to make an appointment with her, I still feel deliriously happy. Not because I'm overexcited about something, but because Hope has helped to channel my longing into the desire for peace. Somehow, the more peaceful I feel about my situation, the more I'm able to feel happiness and true joy. Giddy, I call Veronica into my office and tell her to order lunch for the staff. "It's on me!" She gives me a quizzical look. "For the great job everyone did running the office while I was out."

"That's very kind of you, Dr. Freeman. We're all really glad to have you back."

The rest of the afternoon clinic runs perfectly. My staff is attentive and cheerful with me. My work goes smoothly, and it's pleasurable. On top of that, all my patients and their parents seem genuinely glad I'm back at work.

For the first time in a long time, positive thoughts flow through my head as I pack up. I feel like a new man. I didn't know meditation could have such a powerful effect. In one day, I'm evolving from the uptight and controlling Angela Bower in *Who's the Boss?* to the laid-back, live-in housekeeper, Tony Micelli.

I'm rolling my work suitcase out the door when Veronica stops me. "Dr. Freeman, Mr. and Mrs. Cain are here to see you."

"Cain? Do they have an appointment?"

"No, but they insisted that you meet with them about Reggie."

"Okay," I sigh. "Give me a moment." I return to my desk and pull up their child's chart. Reginald "Reggie" Cain. Who names their kid Reginald these days anyway? I skim his chart and see I haven't seen Reggie in over two years. I remember the dad likes to hear himself talk. He's older, with grey hair parted to the side and resembles Mr. Drummond on *Diff'rent Strokes*. His short, stout wife with short curly brown hair sits hunched over. The Cains are obsessed over their only child Reggie. Despite their concern for his welfare—which surely included enforcing twice-daily brushing—he suffered from serious tooth decay. They questioned why there wasn't more I could do to prevent the problem. The truth is, while proper oral hygiene helps, some people are genetically predisposed to cavities. During one appointment I had to extract three baby teeth, and Reggie was supposed to have come back for placement of a space maintainer while we waited for his adult teeth to erupt. Curiously, the Cains never returned to purchase the appliance, despite diligent follow-up on the part of my staff.

Mr. and Mrs. Cain enter, and we exchange a handshake. "Good to see you both. It's been a while. What grade is Reggie in now?"

Mr. Cain answers, "Starting seventh this year. Let's skip the pleasantries, Dr. Freeman. We're here about a serious problem." He pulls out a pocket-sized, wire-bound, spiral notebook and continues. "You took out Reggie's baby teeth a while back."

"It was traumatic for him," Mrs. Cain chimes in. "He could only eat Jello and smoothies for a whole month."

"He should have been able to eat solid foods after forty-eight hours."

"That's not the point," Mr. Cain interjects. "We took him to an orthodontist who said Reggie needs braces and additional teeth taken out. Apparently, if a space retainer had been used, we could have avoided all this."

Mr. Cain removes his reading glasses, crosses his arms, and glares at me. My eye crinkles a bit, which I recognize as pre-twitch mode. I stare into his beady black eyes, and his head jerks back. We didn't learn about delusional parents in dental school, but I can draw a few lessons from my own childhood. I pause to gather my thoughts. I glance over at his wife, whose pungent, strawberry-scented perfume has turned my office into a Yankee Candle store and is giving me a headache.

"If you'll recall," I say, mimicking the tone Reggie's father used with me, "Reggie had severely infected baby teeth that required extraction. As is standard with such procedures, I informed you that Reggie would need a space maintainer, and my staff scheduled a follow up appointment. Unfortunately, you never returned. Nor did you respond to repeated attempts to reschedule."

"Well," Mr. Cain harrumphs, "you may have told us about the space invader..."

"Space maintainer..." his wife corrects.

"...Space retainer," he continues, "which I recall as being quite expensive. But we were never told that Reggie would need orthodontics because of crowding." He waves his memo pad at me as if it's the smoking gun. "The orthodontist said that if a space"—he looks at his wife—"maintainer had been placed, we wouldn't need braces. It's your fault!"

I lean forward. "Incidentally, who's the orthodontist? I'd like to confer with them."

"None of your business," Cain bellows. "If we knew that Reggie would need over six thousand dollars in orthodontic treatment, we'd have gotten him the six-hundred-dollar space maintainer."

I resist the temptation to say, "Penny wise, pound foolish," knowing that if the Cains didn't listen to me when I was treating Reggie, they won't listen to me now. The Cains are examples of annoying future thinkers; they ask a ton of questions but never listen for the answer because they're thinking of what to say next. I take a deep breath.

Mr. Cain doesn't wait for my response. "In light of your egregiously unprofessional and harmful treatment of my son, we'd like our money back for the fillings we paid for as well as cash compensation for the orthodontic treatment Reggie will need." He slams his memo pad down on my desk and rests his case.

I smile and let out a long breath of air. I should have known the whole thing was about money. Cain is probably out of work or strapped for cash and thinks I'm an easy target. I look over at Mrs. Cain and give a patient, measured response. "I'm not responsible for the fact that you didn't bring him in for his follow-up appointment to get the space maintainer."

Mr. Cain glares at me. "I want twenty-five hundred dollars for the work you did and sixty-five hundred dollars for the orthodontics. If you don't pay," he hesitates, "I'll report you to your board and pursue legal counsel."

Any sense of serenity I had from my meditation is shredded. Even though my case against the Cains is solid, I'm in my own personal hell, struggling between the relief of giving these robbers a refund and the satisfaction of slapping them both across the face. I can't see into the middle distance or find a way to stand up for myself that doesn't involve provoking the Cains's ire.

My alter ego bursts out screaming in my mind. *"You are both nuts! I treated Reggie over two years ago and did a damn good job.* You *missed his appointments and now you're asking* me *to pay for your carelessness. That's bullshit."*

Then my softer side, the Adam who wants to make the problem and the stress go away, says, *"This family is crazy with a capital C. They are going to raise your blood pressure and make your life miserable one way or the other, so give them the nine thousand dollars."*

From its perch on my other shoulder, my alter-ego responds, *"Don't give in to this lame-ass couple that's clearly playing you. They're totally bullying you. You did nothing wrong, and you're a fool if you pay them."*

After a few moments of staring at the Cains's smug faces, my chosen words come out carefully. "Mr. and Mrs. Cain, I've built a successful pediatric dental practice with thousands of happy patients. You never brought your son back to me after you were explicitly told he needed a space maintainer. I resent your accusations concerning my abilities and my professionalism, and I'm not going to give in to your extortion. Good day to you both."

As I leave my office, I look up at my new sign. Note to self: change sign to "Jean-Claude van Damme P. Freeman, Dentist."

* * *

Whoa, Adam. That's badass! Where did those balls come from? I admire how you didn't back down and stuck up for yourself against that couple. Maybe you could give me a backbone transplant. I had a similar situation with bullies once in my practice—a lying, manipulative couple that took me for a ride. I failed to check the facts before I wrote them a thirty-five-hundred-dollar refund check, and I kicked myself when I found out later that they had lied about their story. I even heard from a colleague that they had scammed him too. I could learn a thing or two from Adam Freeman, DDS.

Down to my last handful of peach rings, I savor the flavor, placing them gently in my mouth one by one. Then I wash them down with my second can of Red Bull. Pulling this all-nighter brings me back to my days at college, which is also the time when my run-ins with bullies hit their zenith. Freshman year, my roommate was brutal. He would have sex in the room while I was trying to sleep. *What a dick*, I would think to myself as I covered my head under the blanket. One time he stumbled in drunk and trashed my stereo, spilling a cup of beer all over it. He'd refused to pay for a new one, telling me my stereo had been in the way of his beer. But, living with him was a walk in the park compared to the guys I lived with during my junior year. I was assigned to their suite after my term abroad in Scotland, and these dudes were brutal.

The group consisted of their ring leader—a privileged, spoiled nineteen-year-old Sri Lankan kid, a short guy from Russia with a Napoleon complex, and a waspy, all-American cowboy from Texas. They would steal my toothbrush, take all the toilet paper out of the bathroom, and put big orange construction cones in my bed. They stepped up their game when I refused to be riled. They put ketchup in my shampoo bottle and mustard in my conditioner, and I had to parade through the house in my towel to find replacements. The last straw for me occurred when they baked brownies laced with LSD and offered them as a late-night snack. I came super close to eating one before one of their girlfriends stopped me.

Eventually, I went to the Dean of Students and asked for a transfer. Before he agreed, he insisted that I visit a counselor. Mental health had a three-week waiting list. Thankfully, the very next day, I found a listening ear and a quantum of solace in my English Professor, Daniel Jorkins, who looked and acted like Steven Keaton from *Family Ties*. While visiting his office for help with my *Paradise Lost* essay, I felt a bond form between us. Most of the students mocked this esoteric hippie still stuck in the '60s, but I saw past the tie-dyed shirts and flip flops. That day, my roommates had stolen my alarm clock, causing me to be late to an exam. As the rain drummed against his office window, my pent-up sorrow—laced with a heavy dose of rage—exploded. I screamed, "Why are people so cruel?"

"Listen, Jacob. People can be evil-spirited and hurtful, but these are life lessons. You have every right to be angry and feel hurt. Don't hold in these emotions; let them loose."

My sobs came uncontrollably, matching the torrential downpour outside. After I stopped shuddering, Dan—his preferred salutation—handed me a tissue, patted me on the shoulder, and said, "I'm getting you new roommates tomorrow. But listen carefully, Jacob. I know these guys are assholes, but you can still show love and compassion in the face of adversity. You need to forgive them, or you'll hold on to this anger forever. Can you do that for me?"

I slowly nodded.

"Nevertheless, do me a favor tonight. When they're all sleeping, take each one of their toothbrushes and piss on them! I know that won't be very compassionate of you, but it'll feel good and start your healing process."

I smiled. "With pleasure."

Maybe Maggie was right; I guess I have a little more Adam Freeman in me than I thought! And speaking of Adam, I better keep moving along.

The Adventures of Adam Freeman, DDS
June 24—The Odd Couple

The kids are in bed, and I'm waiting for Errol and Klein to come over to watch the Yankees. My patented nachos are bubbling in the microwave when my phone dings with a text from Hope. I'm expecting a meditation tip or an invitation to another session, but instead it's a bill for my phone call with her. Is this woman for real?

"Phone consultation 6/23. $75.00. PayPal, AMEX, MC, VISA Accepted."

I shove my cell phone at Klein as he walks into the man cave. "Can you believe this?"

Klein sits down in my leather recliner and reads the bill. The Yankee pregame show is on the seventy-inch screen. "She usually doesn't even take phone calls; she's by appointment only. You're lucky you reached her. Her time costs money and, besides, it looks like she gave you a 10 percent discount."

"I spoke with her for fifteen minutes. These are like lawyer fees. She's more concerned with her wallet than the welfare of her clients."

Klein gets up from the chair and stands to his full height. "Freeman— stop being such a cheap bastard! That's chump change for you."

"It's the concept. And to think I was going to take Minnie to her. I thought someone like that could help us. She's a fraud. By the way, I'm not cheap. I'm frugal."

I reach over and click the baby monitors on. Minnie would be proud of me. I always forget. I see Spencer sleeping soundly and the girls reading in their beds.

"You know, Adam, you have to admit, you felt better after seeing her. You were starting to make progress, but now your eye twitch is back."

"Shut up," I say, rubbing my eye furiously. "I'll pay her, but I'm done! Anyway, I've been meditating by myself the past few days."

Klein nods. "I'm proud of you, man. Keep it up and see where it takes you. Me? I couldn't go on this journey alone. I need a guru."

Errol walks in, and Klein continues, "This journey through life is treacherous. Someone to help guide you onto your spiritual path can be useful. Right now, I'm starting to renounce my material possessions."

Errol, catching the tail end of the conversation, chimes in. He and Klein are like the *Odd Couple* when it comes to spirituality. Errol thinks Klein is being brainwashed, and Klein thinks Errol is an ignorant heathen. "Material possessions? Really Klein? What are you giving away—your dad's old VHS porn collection? You know you can get that all on the iPad?"

"Glad I don't have boys, I'd be worried that they'd overdose on cell phone porn," Klein says, then turns to me. "Remember when your cousin showed us his porn stash, and we looked at those magazines and videos for hours?"

Errol shakes his head. "Those days are gone, my fellow Horsemen. Our kids will never know the thrill of being introduced to the secret stash. It's all here now." Errol taps his phone as he grabs a plateful of nachos and a beer from the stocked fridge. "God, I love this invention. Do you think Steve Jobs had any idea of the boon this device would be for the pornography industry?"

Klein says, "You know, I've heard it's pretty scary what's out there."

"Man, have you seen some of those chat rooms?" Errol asks. "People are into strange and kinky shit."

Klein's eyes are the size of saucers. "Like what?"

I chime in, "Errol, let's be real. I've seen my share of porn sites, that's a fact. But going into live chat rooms, you're setting yourself up for trouble."

Errol shrugs. "It's no big deal. Seeing how the other half lives."

"Minnie would have my balls in a vice if I went into a chat room. That's cheating."

"Fuck you, Adam. What makes you holier-than-thou?" Errol stands up. I cower back but am relieved to see that he's getting more nachos and a second beer.

Klein sees it's getting heated and heads for the fridge. He comes back with a Mike's Hard Lemonade and changes the subject. "I told you before, I'm in the middle of purging my possessions. I started with the easy stuff, like old clothes and mix tapes, but it's tough getting rid of sentimental stuff like cards from my kids."

"I'd have a hard time getting rid of my collections," I tell Klein.

"Collections?" Errol asks.

"Yeah, baseball cards and comic books."

He laughs. "I had baseball cards when I was nine."

Klein jumps up and flails his arms at me in dramatic fashion. "Dude, you should use this as an opportunity to cleanse your soul. You need to ditch the baseball cards and comic books. That would be symbolic. Shed your past and rid yourself of material possessions. Connect to the universe without constraints."

Before I can respond, Errol laughs. "Honestly, Klein, you sound crazier than ever. It was fun in the beginning seeing you transform into this religious person, but now—"

Klein interrupts him. "Spiritual person."

"Whatever... Same thing." Errol stands and fills his plate with more nachos. I take the opportunity to refill my plate too. I'm suddenly famished. Errol continues, "You know, Klein, if I wanted to hear someone preaching about God, I'd go to church."

"Well, you'd feel more peaceful if you realized that spirituality plays a major part in your growth as a person and in your journey here on earth. When I was in India—"

"Oh God," Errol says. "Not India again. Why don't you take your vow of silence now, and shut the fuck up?"

Klein doesn't miss a beat. "—and took my vow of silence, I swear I could communicate with my spiritual guru Ris Ris by looking at him."

"Klein, I'm looking at you." Errol moves his face a few inches from Klein's. "Can you read my mind?"

"Errol," I say, "you're going to wake the kids." I continue looking at my own version of Felix Unger and Oscar Madison.

Felix to Oscar: "You seem troubled, Errol. Clearly something's bothering you. Maybe you should try meditation like Adam. You might be able to find peace and happiness."

Oscar to Felix: "The only peace I want is you not telling me how unhappy I am and that the answer to my problems is your religious bullshit. I have a great life. I don't need you preaching to me," he says, then turns towards me. "Or you."

Klein takes a slow sip of his Mike's. "Listen, Errol. No judgment here. I don't live your life. I only know what you tell me and what I observe when I'm with you. I get that people don't like to be told what to do. If you're satisfied with your life, fine. But if you feel like maybe there's more, something that you're missing..."

"I don't think you're preaching, Klein," I say, looking at Errol. "You're trying to share what you've learned to help out a friend."

Errol hangs his head for a moment. His shoulders slump, and I wonder if Klein's message has gotten through to him. Then he stands up abruptly. "I'm done." He throws a nacho at me, splattering salsa on my Pearl Jam concert T-shirt, then grabs another beer and storms out.

Klein and I sit there dumbfounded. Derek Jeter steps to the plate. "I can't believe he got so pissed," I say. "That's a record. We didn't even make it past the first inning."

"Give him time," Klein says, sipping his drink. "He'll come around."

* * *

That exchange with Errol reminds me of when I tried to share my newfound belief system with Leah. She didn't throw a nacho at me, but I learned quickly that a spiritual view of the world cannot be force-fed. People have to find spirituality for themselves.

Leah always encouraged me to be open to new ideas, so I thought she would be interested in Buddhism, the Kabbalah, and my newfound spiritualism but...

"Jacob, can we talk about something else?" she asked, as I was delving into my latest Kabbalah discoveries.

"Aren't you fascinated by this? I mean, this ancient wisdom is applicable—"

Leah cut me off. "It's not that I don't find it interesting. I do. But every time you bring it up, there's a part of you that wants to convert me. If you want to go down this path, I support you, but please stop trying to drag me with you."

I thought about Abraham, Moses, Buddha, Mohammed, Jesus, and Mary and how they found clarity in the Universal Source and connected with the masses. How their teachings to people became both a blessing and a curse. Some followers turned their teachings into strict religion which, in my opinion, tainted the message. There is not one cookie-cutter recipe for how to achieve inner peace. Manmade religion imposes a rigid belief system, which can disconnect us from our inner God. Each person has his own journey to go through to find his or her inner truth and achieve eternal happiness. My spiritual education helped me find my connection to God, and I wanted to share the intense joy of that with Leah. As hard as it is, though, you can't force the journey on anyone. You have to let them find the path themselves.

CHAPTER ELEVEN
11:39 p.m.

I rub my blurry eyes and stand up for a stretch. It's been a long time since I've read the whole manuscript, so I'm just as surprised as a new reader when I reencounter Adam's details. The crisis he's about to experience, though, is one that's burned into my memory. Some people, like Maggie, might be critical of Adam for his faults here, but I'll withhold my judgment until I revisit how he holds up under pressure. I see him as an ordinary human, like all of us, wonderfully imperfect. I'm still rooting for him to do the right thing and prove Maggie wrong.

The Adventures of Adam Freeman, DDS
June 27—*Sons of Anarchy* meets *Game of Thrones*

It's amazing what a difference twelve hours can make in your life. Just when I thought I was getting my groove back, everything went to shit, and my life exploded into a million pieces. The whole thing was a preventable accident. But I choked. We like to think we are masters of our own fate and that our nobler instincts will carry us to glory. When we confront a situation that tests us, we don't always choose the righteous path. Sometimes, we don't even choose at all. We stand there, frozen, watching with horror as a huge boulder comes rolling towards us, threatening to destroy all we have built. We realize in that moment that our final destiny is not under our control as the boulder flattens us and everything in its path.

Twelve hours ago:

I'm finishing my morning coffee and reading over resumes that Veronica assembled to replace Sam. Veronica bursts through my office door with a panicked look on her face. "Dr. Freeman, we need you over here stat," she implores. Like most men, I have trouble redirecting myself when I'm deeply involved in a task.

"What is it?" I ask, not looking up from my stack of papers.

"Dr. Freeman, this is serious."

"What, Veronica? What's going on?"

"I don't know how to tell you this."

I feel myself losing my patience, but I maintain my composure, trying to keep new version Adam 2.0 from regressing after only one week back at work. "Yes, I'm listening."

"Uh, Danielle is doing a cleaning in Room Three with Timothy Hedon, and there's a situation."

"A situation?"

"Well...he took a selfie with his phone, and Danielle thinks that her butt was in it. And you know what teenage boys do with pictures like that."

All I want is one peaceful week—one simple, boring week. Is that really too much to ask the universe? I'm not being unreasonable, am I? I push these negative thoughts out. "What do you think he did with the picture?" I ask Veronica.

"Who knows? Instachat? Snapgram?" Veronica is pushing sixty, and technology isn't one of her strong suits. She continues, "Danielle's really upset."

I stand up. "I'll bet." I shake my head. Can't I just do dentistry?

"It would be nice to only focus on dentistry, wouldn't it?" remarks Veronica, as if reading my mind.

I take a deep breath and gather my thoughts. I've always found Tim's sarcastic wit and quirkiness amusing. He's always appeared harmless enough. But making my staff uncomfortable is taking things too far.

We approach Danielle's treatment room, and Danielle runs up to us hysterical. I'm thinking to myself, *Come on, this isn't that big a deal,* when Danielle blurts, "Doc, I went out of the room to take bitewings on Tim, and now he's fondling himself."

Jesus Christ! "You're absolutely sure of this?"

Danielle nods.

I want to give Tim the benefit of the doubt. Maybe they caught him doing "the shift." I was a teenager once—my wife still thinks I am—and sometimes you need to move it around a bit to get comfortable. I know firsthand it can be a battlefield in your pants with a soldier who doesn't listen to your commands. Maybe his trooper decided to "salute" Danielle—a good-looking, twenty-five-year-old woman who could easily inspire movement down there. I admit I occasionally feel a twinge when I'm talking with her. I may be married, but I'm not dead. I try to get clarification. "Are you sure that he wasn't excited and trying to make it inconspicuous?"

"Look for yourself," says Danielle. I lean my head into the room and, sure enough, his right hand is in his pocket fiddling with something. I don't think he's rubbing a rabbit's foot for good luck. I give myself five seconds and ask Danielle what procedures she has left.

"I need to floss and prophy."

"Okay," I tell Danielle and Veronica, "you two stay here. I'll finish."

I walk into the room, and Tim jumps when he sees me. "Tim, put your hands by your side. I'm going to finish your cleaning, and then we'll talk about your amateur photography." His eyes widen like saucers, and he quickly moves his hands to make them visible, dangling from either side of the chair.

"I'm sorry," he mumbles, as I put the contra-angle, slow-speed handpiece into his mouth.

As I polish Tim's teeth, I notice he has nail polish on and bangs covering his eyes like Justin Bieber circa 2009. It's always interesting to see how much these teens change in six-month intervals.

I complete the cleaning and fluoride treatment and dismiss Tim, then realize I still have to confront him over taking pictures of Danielle. My adrenaline is pumping when Danielle runs up to me. "Did you talk to him?"

"I'm going to right now."

"Well, you may want to speak with his mother, too, because he's hysterical in the waiting room, cursing at her right now."

"This has gone too far. Bring them both back to my office." I make a good living as a dentist, but this stuff is above my pay grade and definitely not my forte. There's a reason that I didn't become a trial lawyer or a fighter pilot—I don't think fast on my feet, and I make mistakes when I'm stressed or pressured. Dentistry was the perfect choice for me. Everything happens in a controlled environment, and the surprises are mostly predictable. With excellent training, the proper tools, and a steady hand, you can overcome any challenge. But a masturbating teenager taking pictures of a staff member and having it out with his mom in my waiting room—that's way more than I'd ever bargained for.

Tim and his mother shuffle in and sit across the desk from me in my guest chairs. Mrs. Hedon has shoulder-length, disheveled black hair and is as plain Jane as they come. She looks like the mom on *Malcolm in the Middle*, and I'm about to ruin her already bad day. I begin, "There could be a misunderstanding but, um, Tim may have taken an inappropriate picture of my hygienist when she was working on him." They both stare at me like zombies in *The Walking Dead*. I continue, "Then we noticed that his hands were in his pocket, um...rubbing his..." I don't want to have to finish the sentence, but the mother gives me a blank look. "...groin area." She purses her lips tightly. Tim is looking down, as if surveying the part of his body he was fiddling with earlier. "I run a professional office, and I'm responsible for what happens to my staff. Patients are not allowed to use their phones or take photographs while we're working on them, and"—I look directly at Tim—"it's inappropriate to touch your private area when you're around women in the workplace. It's called sexual harassment."

Mrs. Hedon's mouth is agape. I move on to explain, "This is an important lesson to learn, Tim—you don't want to make anyone uncomfortable. Taking a sexually suggestive picture of someone without their permission and sharing it with your friends is a problem. My staff members were engorged—I mean *enraged* by your behavior."

Tim's mother looks at him with disgust. Tim flicks his head to the side to push his bangs back and speaks for the first time. "Mom, I swear I didn't do anything! I was playing with something in my pocket. And I took the picture accidentally when I was checking my texts. I joked with Danielle that I was going to share it. I wouldn't do that stuff."

Of course, denial, what else could I expect? I answer, "Tim, I don't know what you were doing with your hands, and I'm willing to give you the benefit of the doubt. But my employees saw *something*. I want to make sure we don't have any problems here in the future."

Mrs. Hedon gets up and pulls Tim out of the room by his Bieber bangs. "Thank you, Dr. Freeman. We'll deal with this at home." I take a deep breath and realize my eye is surprisingly not twitching. Standing up for myself and sticking up for my staff felt good. I might finally be finding the balance between angry Adam and passive-aggressive Adam.

I'm on my way to the front desk to boast to Veronica about how I handled this delicate situation when out of the corner of my eye, I see Jason the Jock—a high school kid who looks like he could be in college—harassing Tim as his mom pays the bill. Jason is an all-American football player who plays quarterback on Davidson's high school team. He dates my babysitter Stephanie and could be straight out of a casting call for *Friday Night Lights*. It's obvious these guys don't run in the same social circles, but as I listen to their argument, it sounds like Tim also has affection for Stephanie.

I pretend I need printer paper and linger behind the front desk. I open the cabinet, grab a ream, and continue listening. Tim is already having a horrible day. I hope it doesn't get worse.

"How was the prom, Tim?" Jason the Jock asks.

Tim flips his bangs over his eyes. "You know I didn't go."

"Oh. Couldn't find a date since Stephanie decided to go with me?"

"Fuck off, asshole. I don't need your bullshit."

I don't need any F-bombs exploding in the middle of my family practice, especially during the "rush hour" 3:00–5:00 p.m. time slot when my reception room is filled with kids and their parents. I'm about to say, "Language, gentlemen," when Jason takes out his cell phone and snaps a picture of Tim. "I'll meme this one 'Prom Reject.' Maybe it'll go viral."

Tim has a crazed look in his eyes, like Jax Teller before a blowout in *Sons of Anarchy*. Suddenly, he flips a switchblade from his pants pocket, springs it open, and rushes at Jason. Before I can blink, Jason crouches, then lunges at Tim's legs like a linebacker sacking a quarterback.

"*Stop it, boys!*" screams Veronica.

"Holy *fuck*," I yell, and Veronica stares at me along with the dozen parents in the reception area."

"Dr. Freeman! *Do something!*"

I feel like I'm watching an episode of *Game of Thrones* as I hide behind the desk. Tim and Jason the Jock are locked in a death battle in the middle of my reception room. Tim's mom screams hysterically. Jason grabs the knife from Tim, then Tim grabs it back. They wrestle each other, the blade flashing between them. Then—*CRASH!*—they fall together onto the long glass table, sending shattered glass everywhere. Still frozen, I watch in horror as the knife, now in Tim's hand, pierces Jason's stomach in slow-motion, then the film suddenly speeds up as blood gushes from Jason's midsection onto my expensive, new Persian rug. Mothers are backed up against the walls shielding their small children, and one family is making a run for the exit. The thought that someone should call 911 slowly enters my brain, but I remain motionless, watching this unfathomable scene unfold.

Jason pulls the red-stained knife from his stomach and tries to hold off Tim with the other arm. Blood is splattered all across the front desk, and my office now looks like a crime scene. I hear a dad yell, "Call the police!" Jason's fist connects with Tim's face, and his head whips back from the blow. Another father seizes the chance to break up the brawl. He's built like a tank, with a square jaw and a military buzz cut. Hero Dad lifts Tim up and throws him across the room, then wrestles the bloody knife out of Jason's hand. With the fight broken up, he deftly tucks the knife in his pocket and shouts, "Call 911."

"Already done," Veronica replies,

Hero Dad now shows off his medic ability. "Doc, where's your first aid kit? This kid's bleeding out of his stomach, and I think the other one has a broken nose." He strips off his Notre Dame Football jersey and hands it to me after I venture out from behind the front desk. "Apply pressure to the wound."

I look around at the mess, and my body slowly regains motion. But I don't run to the injured boys or step boldly into the middle of the room to take charge and calm everyone down. Instead, I gingerly edge into the waiting area and suddenly my legs slip out from under me, and I fall backward onto broken glass. I roll over and crawl towards Jason to press the shirt against the open wound. Out of the corner of my eye, I see Tim across the room lying in his mother's lap as she holds her balled-up scarf against his bloody nose.

Danielle arrives with the first aid kit, and she removes the bloodstained Notre Dame jersey. She crouches down next to Jason and places a large gauze pad over his wound. "Hold this here," she says to me as she reaches for the tape and scissors. Jason lays motionless now. I replace the sodden shirt with the fresh gauze, mumbling to myself, "God, please don't let this kid die! Please, don't let this kid die."

The sound of sirens pierces the uncomfortable silence, and they're like music to my ears—help is finally here! Hero Dad briefs the EMTs who rush in. I give way weakly to the paramedics who swarm around Jason, tending his wound and taking his vitals. I hear one of them shout, "Hospital stat," as they load him into the ambulance which screeches away.

A female paramedic comes over, examines me and notices a piece of glass from the table lodged in my neck. She informs me that the shard narrowly missed my carotid artery, and I'm lucky to be alive. I don't feel lucky. I feel sick to my stomach as I try to answer questions from the police and pray they don't ask me why I didn't intervene. The paramedic tells me I should go to the ER to get stitches to be sure the bleeding stops. Forget that. I want to go home. I want to disappear and pretend that none of this ever happened. Why couldn't I have been like Captain Dick Winters in *Band of Brothers* and pulled the boys off each other before Tim stabbed Jason? Instead, I acted like Lieutenant Norman Dike. I sit dumbfounded amidst the rubble of my reception area—upended chairs scattered across the floor, glass everywhere, and a large splotch of dark red where Jason bled onto my rug.

With a pit in my stomach the size of the Grand Canyon, I realize I can't go on working here, that I can barely go on living. The inhumanity of it all makes absolutely no sense to me. And my reaction—my *non-reaction*—baffles me and leaves me cold. What kind of a God allows this violence to occur? And why wasn't I able to stop it? Why did I freeze and become useless?

As I sit on the floor, shuddering and weeping, Veronica tries to comfort me, but I push her away and tell her to go home.

"I'll cancel all your appointments for tomorrow, and I'll get a crew in to clean up this mess," she offers.

"Thank you," I mumble, "but it's hopeless."

"What did you say, Dr. Freeman?" she asks.

"I said go home." I didn't want her to know the extent of my despair. "You've been a great help, and there's nothing more you can do now."

* * *

Poor Adam, flat on the floor at his failure to act and inability to make sense of it all. Poor Jason, who got knifed in the gut. And poor Tim, who got a nose job he didn't ask for. What on earth was I thinking while writing that scene? I must have been high as a kite on junk food. Or maybe I'd finished binge-watching Season One of *Game of Thrones* or had just seen the brutal Opie jail scene in *Sons of Anarchy*. It's one thing watching fights on television, but real-life violence makes me sick and numb. I was so devastated to hear about the school shootings in nearby Newtown, Connecticut, that I could barely get up and go to work that week. I nearly lost it a few times while I straightened teeth for innocent, angelic elementary school kids. At home, every time I tucked my own children in at night, I held onto them a little longer than usual. Perhaps the violent scene in Adam's office was my way of dealing with the emotional devastation from the tragedy that I'd never fully processed and addressing the unresolved and unresolvable questions that still haunted my mind. The wrestling match was a kind of cosmic mix of real-life events, my favorite TV shows, and my vivid imagination. What surprised me was how Adam responded to the crisis. I remember beginning the scene with the intention of having him be the hero, but just as he couldn't move during the fight, I couldn't alter the words that were flowing through me onto the page. In fact, I barely remember writing the scene at all. I wonder if other writers experience this amnesia.

As I read it over now, I'm pretty pissed at Adam. I want to say to him, "One minute you're acting all holier-than-thou and the next you— my protagonist and would-be hero—huddle behind a desk while a real hero saves the day by breaking up the brawl. Then you have the audacity to act like a victim of circumstance rather than reflecting on the trauma all the kids and parents suffered from Jason the Jock's bullying and Tim's violent reaction. I wonder if you were more upset about the blood on your new carpet than you were about one of your patients being stabbed.

"You know, Adam, the heartbreaking thing about this scene is that, in the beginning, you were doing well. You handled yourself admirably when dealing with the alleged self-pleasuring of Tim, the angry, young lost soul. You were endearing and in complete control when employing the right amount of delicacy and authority with Tim and his mom. But when push came to shove—or taunt came to stab—in the ensuing stressful and intense moments when the fight erupted, you regressed. Ducking for cover instead of getting out there to break up the fight and protect the other patients was a poor choice—assuming it was a choice at all and not a freeze response. You did your best George Costanza, shouting, 'Screw women and children first, how about me? White, middle-aged man coming through!' I have lost my love and respect for you, Adam Freeman. Forget about me killing you. You're killing *me!*"

I close the laptop as my hand instinctively jumps to my abdomen. I'm feeling quite nauseated as a tidal wave rises in my stomach. I rush to the bathroom and kneel over the toilet. Out comes a bright stream of all the diabetes-inducing junk food I ingested. Every color is there in the amalgamation of the Doritos, Skittles, Sour Patch Kids, yellow and orange peach rings mixed among the nachos. I look down and see a rainbow of colors swirling in the white, porcelain bowl. I feel like shit. Still on my knees, I wipe away the sweat misting on my forehead. I flush the toilet, washing away all the sweetness of the night.

It's after midnight, and I've invested all this time in my hero's story. But now, Adam seems more like an anti-hero. Maggie was right—Adam is self-obsessed with few redeeming qualities. This guy needs to grow up and start acting like an adult—or maybe I'll take her advice and rewrite the scene again, letting Adam bleed out through his carotid artery. Minnie, I'm glad you have a good life insurance policy on Adam.

Head down, shoulders slumped, I walk to the fridge and pour myself a ginger ale to soothe my flaming digestive tract. I walk back to my office and shake my head at the manuscript. A flood of negative thoughts comes crashing into my mind: first doubt, then recrimination, and worst of all, self-hate. Maybe Adam Freeman should never have been born. Does anyone really care about him besides me? And, if Adam is an extension of me, am I a coward too? Would I react the same way if violence erupted in my office? The competition in dental school was intense, but I've never been in a knife fight in my life. Irving Sharf's characters are strong and tough— heroes with heart who don't take crap from anyone. And here's Adam, weak, flawed, tragic, and, dare I say, pathetic. Adam, you've hit bottom, man. You need help.

And me? Maybe I *should* write *12 Steps to Spiritual Enlightenment* instead of *The Adventures of Adam Freeman, DDS*. Remember, memoir is hot and Maggie can sell memoir.

Maybe I should stick to straightening teeth and take up other hobbies that dentists do, like golf, tennis, perhaps sailing. I used to dream of opening up a bagel shop in England or applying for a job on the Good News Network—journalism always interested me. I have a million ideas in my head that I can pursue rather than wasting time writing a novel.

"Waaaahhhh…" I hear my youngest daughter crying. Usually this sends pain through me in the middle of the night. Leah and I play rock, paper, scissors to see who gets out of bed to take care of her. Tonight, I find myself welcoming the distraction. I rush upstairs to Eva's bedroom and bring her to the bathroom. After she goes, I put her back into bed, and she asks me to snuggle with her. I take off my slippers, lay my head down, and make the mistake of closing my eyes for a second.

CHAPTER TWELVE
October 27, 1:15 a.m.

When I open my eyes, I'm shocked by the time. I look at Eva lying there like an angel, and suddenly I have a moment of clarity. Who am I to judge Adam Freeman? Not everyone in life can be a real-life hero in a real-life emergency. We're human. We panic. Even though I'd like to think I have a more enlightened way of looking at things since delving into meditation, I have no idea how I would react in Adam's situation. I might have found myself cowering behind the desk too. The fact that Adam didn't rise to this particular occasion doesn't make him worthless or his story not worth telling. And it's not fair of me to act like I'm holier-than-he. I have to accept him for the tragic hero that he is and bear with him as he—hopefully—grows on his journey. After all, he has more than half a book left to get his shit together, and I have half the night left to finish reading and revising *The Adventures of Adam Freeman, DDS*.

Re-energized, I jump out of Eva's bed and run downstairs. I'm suddenly famished. I rush to the kitchen and grab my secret stash of Pringles Sour Cream and Onion chips from the back of the cabinet above the oven, score a Red Bull from the fridge, and scamper to the office. I have no time to waste.

The Adventures of Adam Freeman, DDS
June 28—*Lost*

After leaving my office, the scene of the crime—the crime of my cowardice and inaction—I sat in my car for what seemed like hours. But when I looked at the dashboard clock, twenty minutes had passed. I texted Klein to let him know what happened, and Joyless showed that she was not compassionless by offering to keep my kids at their house for another day. I picked up my phone again to text Minnie, then realized her being away was a blessing. I didn't have to talk to her about this yet and deal with her judgments. I could sort it out, try to pull myself together, and give her the rundown from a place of strength. Besides, given all she's been struggling with, I didn't need to burden her with this now. I drove home, holed myself up in the man cave, and fell asleep eating stale Pringles and binge-watching *Lost*.

I wake up in my recliner, barely able to move my body. I check my cell and see there's a text from Veronica. "Jason still in surgery. Not out of the woods yet." I feel like a lead weight has settled on my chest. My legs feel paralyzed, like John Locke's pre-airplane crash in *Lost*. If only I could have been as courageous as he was during Season One. Instead, I'm praying that Jason will survive.

The sour taste of Pringles lingers in my mouth and I have to pee, but I don't have the strength to get up and walk to the bathroom. I can barely reach the empty can of Red Bull that fell to the floor when I dozed off last night. I fill it with my stream, then curl back up in the fetal position under my blanket and sleep for another hour.

The beep of the garbage truck backing up into my driveway wakes me from my slumber. I panic, thinking it's a news truck coming to interview me for their lead story:

"Cowardly Dentist Watches as Knife Fight Erupts in Office, Victim Dies on Operating Table."

Except I would title the story:

"Davidson Dentist Seeking Peace Through Meditation Gets Confusing Message from Universe."

It hits me that I need to take control of my story, and to do that, I need to write in my journal. I start writing the reporter's intro—background about me, my dental practice, the troubled adolescence of Timothy Hedon, and the interrupted life of Jason the Jock—but all I can do is relive the horror and release my self-destructive thoughts. Like the island in *Lost*, yesterday's mayhem has become today's living hell for me. I got a close-up glimpse into the devilish eyes of a disturbed teenager. And it sunk my whole office, my whole life, into his abyss of terror.

In between flagellating myself with words, I check my phone every few minutes for any news on Jason the Jock, and finally, around noon, Veronica texts me to say, "Jason out of surgery. Prognosis good." Jason won't be playing football this year, but the doctors are optimistic that he'll make a full recovery like Kima Greggs did in *The Wire*. My Irish yenta always gets the town gossip, but this time it's news I want to hear. The knot in my stomach dissolves—I am not an accessory to murder and won't have to close my practice and move to another state—and my appetite, along with my ability to move my legs, returns. I immediately go for the cold leftover General Tso's chicken from last weekend. I down it in three mouthfuls and go to wash it down with my Red Bull, but as soon as the liquid touches my lips, I remember what I used the can for this morning. I run to the bathroom and puke.

I doze off again and am awakened by the door opening and Minnie's voice, saying, "Adam, I'm home," followed by, "Why on earth are you sleeping on the couch?"

I sit up, and right away, she notices the bandage on my neck. "What happened?"

"Well," I begin, "I'm alive."

"Was that ever in question?" she asks.

"Yesterday, in my office, a patient stabbed another patient with a switchblade."

"Oh my God. Was anyone seriously hurt?"

"The kid who got stabbed lost a lot of blood and ruined the new carpet. He nearly died. But he'll be fine. The other kid has a broken nose. And I almost killed myself when I tripped and a shard of glass pierced me"—I finger my neck—"and just missed my carotid."

"The new glass table I picked out?" Minnie stops herself. "I mean, who cares about that. Thank God the kids are okay. And you, only a flesh wound. I thought you got stabbed too."

"I almost died, Minnie. One centimeter and…"

"Well, I'm glad you're okay. My sister is dying, I can't take another tragedy." Minnie looks around. "Where are the kids?"

"They're over with Joyless Klein, who really came through for us. Sit down, and I'll tell you the whole story." Minnie sits at the end of the sofa and rubs my feet as I start from the beginning, telling her about Tim playing pocket ping pong and snapping a picture of Danielle's derriere, then Jason taunting him about the prom. She can read the shame of my inaction, and I expect Minnie to lay into me for doing nothing, but she responds with understanding and grace.

"You can always look back and think about what you would have done differently. But it's really hard to be perfect or even functional sometimes in the moment. I mean, I spent part of this weekend fighting with my sister. Fighting! About something completely stupid. And she's dying. Things ended up okay, but we wasted two precious hours of however many she has left."

We sit in silence for a few minutes. Minnie has been brave and vulnerable with me, and I want her to hold me as I tell her I feel like my whole world is coming apart, but instead I act like a turtle in my shell. I poke my head out briefly to say, "That was kind of dumb, fighting with your sister."

Minnie gives me an icy stare. "I know you have a cut on your neck, Adam, but words can hurt more than shards of glass. I'm trying to be sensitive to your pain while I'm in horrible pain myself. And the last thing I need right now is your judgment."

I remain mute. Minnie stands and lets my feet fall from her lap. "Adam, you have some serious work to do." She grabs an apple from the bowl on the coffee table and takes a bite. "And your socks stink. Go take a shower. And brush your teeth. Your breath smells like piss."

Minnie deserves a medal of honor for being with a schmuck like me, and I didn't mean to hurt her. I was mad—and jealous—because she was able to open up the way I want to but can't.

Suddenly, I'm filled with rage, and I throw my Red Bull across the room, knocking over Minnie's favorite lamp.

She screams, "You psycho freak! Why are you throwing things?" She starts crying. "What's wrong with you? You know I have a big issue with acts of aggression."

"Stop telling me I have to 'work' on myself. I almost got killed in a knife fight!"

Between her sobs she replies, "Adam, I get that yesterday was traumatic for you...but no permanent harm was done to anyone, including you. And you couldn't even bother to ask me about my sister. I'm being as supportive as I can for you with your incident, and you can't offer me a shred of compassion during a tragic life crisis? I lost my mom already, and now I'm losing my sister to cancer. The least I could have is a supportive husband..."

At this, I shrink further into my carapace, then poke my head out one more time to say, "You'll never understand."

"I understand that I already gave you three kids...I don't need to raise another one."

The angry part of me wants to start throwing everything in the room, but the sad part collapses on the couch and starts crying. I bury my runny nose in the sofa and wipe it on the pillow—the one Minnie's mom embroidered with the names of our three children on it. There is a soft hand on my head, and I look up through teary eyes to see my wife.

"Adam, you *have* to do something. Please, for me...for the family."

Deep inside my shell, I know that Minnie is right. Today I will rest. And tomorrow, I will get some help. This cleaner of teeth will try to clean up his own life.

June 30—*M*A*S*H*

I slept the whole day yesterday, only getting up to pee. Waking up today, I feel like Gregor Samsa in Kafka's *Metamorphosis*, only worse. My sadness is crippling.

Minnie—my wonderful, forgiving Minnie—tries to cheer me up before lunch by bringing in my DVD collection of *M*A*S*H*, one of my favorite comedies from childhood. But not even Hawkeye and Trapper John can cut through my despair. All I focus on is the theme song: "Suicide is Painless."

Though I promised myself, I still haven't done anything about getting help, and Minnie ever so gently prompts me. "Adam, I got some names for you to call for help." I stare blankly at the yellow Post-It note she hands me with names and numbers penned in her elegant handwriting. "Maybe I'll call for you."

I've been nibbling the marshmallows from some Lucky Charms while lying in bed, and I stick Minnie's note to the box. "No, I'll do it myself," I say.

When I refuse to get up for lunch, Minnie goes into crisis mode and stages her version of an intervention. I'm finishing writing down the words to the *M*A*S*H* theme song when Errol and Klein walk into the bedroom.

"Oh, I loved *M*A*S*H*," says Errol. They sit on the love seat across from the bed. I put my journal down. Errol continues, "Listen, dude, you've been through some rough shit, but keep this in perspective. It could have been a lot worse. You've got to pull yourself together—if not for you then for your family."

I look at Klein for sympathy. If anyone can understand me it's him. But Klein's not having any. "Adam, he's right. No one was murdered, and your family needs you. Think about what Minnie is going through with her sister. You have to be strong for her."

Errol takes over. "We're not trivializing what you experienced but be realistic. You need to move on. You need to—"

I interrupt him and, as if on cue, my eye twitching starts again. "Guys, you're not helping me here. It was like a war zone in there. And I was like a commanding officer who ran from the battle instead of leading his troops."

Klein turns off the television. "Cut the shit, Adam. No one expected you to break up the fight. What's really eating you?"

I close my eyes and lean my head back against the headboard. I hear Errol saying, "I think we should leave him in peace. He needs time to sort stuff out."

"You can go, Errol," Klein tells him. "I've got this. I'm going to charge the paddles again and see if I can resuscitate the patient. Clear!"

Before Errol leaves, he adds, "One last thing, Adam. I've arranged coverage for your office while you recover."

"You did?" I ask. "How'd you manage that?"

"You know how I do 3D radiology readings for dentists? Well, I asked around and got Paul Nelson in Greensand to see your patients in his office for a couple of weeks. That way you can rest and get your office cleaned up."

Finally, some of my load has been lifted. For the first time since the incident I feel a little bit better. My patients are not being abandoned. "Thanks, Errol."

"The Four Horsemen have to look out for each other, and I know you'd do the same for me." Errol flexes his tattooed-horse bicep and gets up to leave. "Plus, Adam, you have to find a way to get out of this funk. We need you ready for our trip to Puerto Rico!"

After Errol leaves, Klein speaks to me softly. "Look Adam, I know you feel like a huge failure, but you did all you could. You have to let go. Remember what Lao Tzu said: 'If you are depressed, you are living in the past. If you are anxious, you are living in the future. If you are at peace you are living in the present.'"

"I don't know who Lo Tzo is and—"

"It's Lao Tzu. He was a great Chinese philosopher who founded Taoism."

"All I know is that this was my one moment to stand out and be the hero, to step up for someone besides myself, be great, and I froze. I did nothing while violence erupted."

"Dude. You're already great. You're a great—well, a good husband—and a great dad. And a great friend. You don't need some heroic shit to go down in your office to prove that you're a mensch."

"That kid could've died while I literally fell over myself. It makes me question what kind of stuff I'm made of, what kind of man I am, or if I'm even a man at all. I hid behind the desk until a real man took action."

Klein brings his face up close and stares at me, dead serious. "And what if that real man had gotten a knife to the heart? What if that real man was a dead man, and he was you?" He crosses his arms. "The *Three* Horsemen would be going to your funeral."

I look down.

"We don't know how God works, but your inaction may have saved you—and your family—from something much worse. And everything still turned out okay. So stop beating yourself up and get some perspective. Try saying affirmations about what a valuable person you are and how much you mean to the people around you."

"I'm past the point of affirmations. And last I checked, you were a middle school teacher, not my psychotherapist."

"That's true; you need more help than I or even Minnie can provide. And I know you can't kick this thing by yourself. You, Adam Freeman, need the help of a professional."

I know deep down he's right. I turn over in bed and lay facedown on my pillow. The turtle withdraws into his shell again. My emotions flood through me, but all I can manage to say to Klein as I sob is, "I give up. I can't go on."

"We're all worried about you. Do you want me to commit you? Should I call 911?"

"Fuck no!" I answer, my turtle head poking out to snap at Klein. "I may be de...*down*...but I can go on my own power."

"Say it. There's no shame in being depressed, Adam. Your first act of courage is admitting you need help."

"Mmm hmm," I mumble.

"You know," he says, "I take Prozac."

I sit straight up and feel a crack in my turtle shell. "You never told me that. You meditate, have gurus, see healers and—"

"Yeah, take meds. I have a chemical imbalance. There's no shame in helping my neurotransmitters function properly so I can explore what is transpiring in my mind and body without going off the deep end."

"I've always worried that chemicals would treat the symptoms and mask what is really behind my anxiety. But you—why didn't you tell me?"

Klein sits down next to me. "Honestly, Adam? You can be so judgmental and condescending. I didn't want to deal with your snark."

"I always considered you the beacon of light—a shining example of how we can resolve our personal suffering without resorting to drugs."

"That's exactly what I meant. Now shut up. We are going to a mental health facility to get you help. It's all been arranged."

I give up. There's no point in arguing anymore. I slowly dress as Klein grabs the suitcase Minnie has already packed for me. I inch down the stairs to the family room where Paige and Rose are playing Candy Land. Minnie is sitting in the corner of the couch, knitting yarmulkes for Paige's bat mitzvah, and Spencer is curled up in her lap. "*Daddy!*" the kids yell when they see me.

"I'll load your stuff in the car and meet you outside," says Klein. Minnie follows him out, where he's obviously briefing her on the breakthrough he made with me.

"Daddy, play with us," implores my game-loving Rose.

"Daddy has to go, my sweetheart," I tell her, choking back tears.

"Please," Rose and Paige beg in unison.

"Do your Scavenger Hunt for us today, Daddy," requests Paige.

"Yeah, those are fun," shouts Rose. Minnie reenters the house and stands behind Rose.

My heart is bursting open with sadness, but I know what I have to do. "You know I love you all very much, but Daddy has to go away for a little while with Uncle Klein."

"Where are you going, Daddy?" asks Rose.

"Daddy is going away to get better." I kneel down. "Now give me a Freeman Family Hug." I can barely see anything through the tears in my eyes as my kids engulf me. Minnie gives me a huge hug and whispers, "I hate that you're leaving, but I know this is what you need. And when you come home, I'll have my husband back."

I stare out the window as we drive down the scenic, narrow, and windy roads of Davidson on our way to the highway. We take the on-ramp, and after a few miles we pass the "Welcome to New York, the Empire State" sign in silence on our way to get me psychiatric help.

CHAPTER THIRTEEN
1:35 a.m.

Although under different circumstances, like Adam, I suffered from severe anxiety and stress as a middle-aged man. I felt pulled in too many directions as a father, husband, orthodontist, and boss. The responsibility and the trappings of working to support the family, the mounting expenses, the need to work harder for more "things," and then needing even more money—the whole vicious cycle—was spiraling out of control. There was no way that I could get off the carousel of life without making a radical change.

Just when my monkey mind was about to drive me insane, I shared with my hypnotherapist how writing was cathartic for me back in dental school. Getting out my emotions on paper lessened life's burdens. One day while traveling into New York City for an orthodontic conference, I remembered my hypnotherapist's advice.

I took out my journal and noticed my fellow travelers on Metro North keenly. Two rows ahead of me sat this three-hundred-and-fifty-pound man stuffing his face with a Big Mac. A punk rocker on my left had multiple ear and nose piercings and leaned against her heavily tattooed boyfriend, who was incessantly clearing his throat. And the man next to me was drowning his sorrows with a flask. That moment I realized *everyone* has issues, and my experiences and thoughts could inspire people to find the courage to face their own problems.

Like God creating the universe, I wielded my Pilot V-ball very-fine-tipped pen with black ink and gave birth to my characters in the spiral-bound journal that lay in my lap. I carved the outline of Adam Freeman's journey on that train ride, from the Harlem 125th Street stop to Grand Central Terminal. Out came this story that seemed to write itself. To this day, it wasn't me writing Adam; it was more like Adam needing to share his story with the world. Writing became my ticket out of the daily drudgery of straightening teeth, managing a staff, and dealing with parent complaints.

"Daddy?"

Startled, I turn around. "Oh my God. You scared me. Are you okay, sweetie?" It's my middle daughter, Autumn. She has a habit of sleepwalking. I stand up from my chair and grab the small, soft palm of her hand and we climb the stairs. Autumn crawls into bed, and I pull the covers gently over her body. I lean over, kiss her on the forehead, and whisper, "Don't worry love. Daddy's not going anywhere. Please get some sleep. God bless you." This is my nightly ritual that reminds me to be there for my kids, while making it clear I'm not the one ultimately in control of my girls' lives.

I peek in to see that my oldest daughter, Rina, is sleeping peacefully. When I enter Eva's room, she is upside down in her big-girl bed. I take out my phone and snap a picture. So cute; how can I resist? As I rush downstairs to continue reading, I look at the photo and am grateful for all the precious family moments.

I think back to the time in my life when I needed help. I never needed to check myself into a mental health facility. Mine was more the impulse to run away from my family and go to a Tibetan Buddhist monastery and have tea with the Dalai Lama. Much like the Buddha who left his wife and son to pursue enlightenment, I thought that was my destiny too. I almost clicked "Book Your Tickets" on Expedia. But after tremendous soul searching—and remember, *I'm the guy who always does the right thing*—the answer was no. Unlike Siddhartha, I could not bear to desert my family to achieve peace and happiness. Although it's a lot of pressure, and sometimes more than I can handle, I'm the one who they rely on for support. I'm the one who they need, and I made peace with staying home and honoring my commitment to my family. For me, it was the only choice.

But Adam, that lucky bastard, he's not stuck making my choices. He's a free man after all. He can take the road less traveled and realize the unfulfilled parts of my life that will only happen in my dreams. I know I made the right choice for myself, but Adam should go for it and take some big risks. I'm in front of my computer ready to change the direction of Adam's life again.

The Adventures of Adam Freeman, DDS
June 30—*One Day at a Time*

I stare out the window as we drive down the scenic narrow and windy roads of Davidson on our way to the highway. We take the on-ramp, and after a few miles we pass the "Welcome to New York, the Empire State" sign. Twenty minutes later, Klein exits onto a scenic road, and he continues to drive in silence.

Suddenly I yell, "*Stop*! Turn the car around!"

"What? I'm not taking you back home. We're all *really* worried about your mental state."

"I said, *stop*!"

Klein pulls over onto the shoulder.

"No...not home...there." I point to a sign about a hundred yards behind us.

Klein looks at me quizzically. For the first time in a week I give a genuine smile. "No mental health center for me, my friend. Yes, this feels right."

"What'd the damn sign say?" Klein asks.

"The Ganden Monastery," I tell him. "I'm going to become a monk."

Klein hasn't said a word in the last fifteen minutes. As we turn onto a long, tree-lined driveway that leads to the monastery, I break the silence. "This is no coincidence, Klein. I'm meant to be here. I need to do this."

He doesn't answer. For a moment I think he is furious with me, but he replies, "You have to go with your gut." I relax. He continues, "By the way, I've been here before. This place is tremendous; it will transform you. I went to a workshop, and it really helped center me. You're taking a chance, Adam, but this could be good for you."

"I knew you, of all people, would understand. I can't deal with another bunch of doctors who've read all the medical studies but never opened a spiritual book. I don't want to go where they'll do Rorschach tests and pump me with drugs, or worse, put me in one of those padded cells. I'm not crazy. I just need to learn how to control my emotions and deal with this deep sadness I can't shake. This feels right."

"I hear you, brother. But before I drop you off, I need to know why you're completely ruling out meds."

"I don't know, Klein. It's a visceral feeling. I don't want to put up any more masks. I don't want to pollute my body with drugs that will relieve my symptoms but hinder my growth. I need to find out who I truly am. I don't want to achieve better living through chemistry. I want to achieve inner peace—in my own way, on my own power."

"You know, I'm a big believer in the Eastern Medicine mind-body philosophy, but it's not like you've failed if you have to go on meds. There's nothing wrong with Western medicine. Ask Steve Jobs; he tried to treat his pancreatic cancer with Eastern medicine and regretted not going the Western medicine route sooner."

"I can't ask him because he's dead."

"Exactly."

"Well, my condition isn't life threatening. I mean, I may be depressed, but I'm not about to off myself. If I'd wanted to do that, I would have blissed out on nitrous in my office. If this doesn't work, I can always take meds, but I'm not ready for that yet. I want to conquer this thing myself."

Klein nods. "I get it. And I support it. But you know when Minnie finds out she's going to go apeshit."

"*If* she finds out."

"What do you mean, if? You know I can't hide this from her. What the hell should I say?"

"You'll figure it out. Be in the moment. And remember the bro code."

"You're impossible, Freeman."

"And you're amazing. You'll know what to say."

Klein stops the car. We have arrived at the gate to the monastery, and the sign reads "No Vehicles Beyond This Point." He helps get my suitcase out of the car and gives me a crushing man hug.

"Jesus, the things we do for friends," he says.

"Thanks, man. I can take it from here."

Checking myself in to a Buddhist monastery is the last thing I ever thought I'd be doing. But walking down the path, I feel a pull in my heart. As I round a bend, the building comes into view. I was expecting a renovated Victorian house—a sort of "This Old Monastery" with a porch where the monks sit and quietly meditate. I mean, this is New York, not Nepal. It's not like I'm going to the Maya Devi Temple, which enshrines the Buddha's birthplace at Lumbini.

I couldn't have been more wrong! I'm looking at an eight-sided tower stretching seven stories up towards the sky. I feel like someone cut out a section of the Orient and dropped it into the woods in this unassuming, blue-collar town. The pathway leading to the temple is lined on both sides with stone pedestals that support miniature three-foot statues of the Buddha. As I approach the entrance to the temple, I suddenly get cold feet. This place looks hard core. Maybe I should have let Klein drive me to the mental health facility. There are monks walking around in robes with shaved heads. I reach up and run my hand through my hair, wondering if I'll have to part with it. I'm suddenly afraid I don't belong here—a non-religious Jew trying to find spirituality to avoid a total nervous breakdown.

I'm reaching for my phone to call Klein to come back and get me, when I notice a monk who appears to be in his mid-sixties. He is about as tall as my eldest, Paige, who measures 5'4". He is trimming the bonsai trees that surround the outside of the temple. His bearing is self-assured, and he seems completely at peace with the world and his role in it, like a man who doesn't care how long it will take to arrive at his destination. I catch myself staring at this old-school Buddhist monk with his shaved head, wearing a traditional pale-yellow robe with a red sash that loops around his right shoulder. I've always been curious about what those sashes symbolize. I stand there, entranced, watching him wield his shears, and when he turns to look at me, his eyes emanate a pureness and kindness unlike anything I have experienced before. I feel a palpable positive energy and stream of compassion flowing towards me as I stand in his presence.

"I'm sorry," I say. "Am I in your way?" The monk gives me a smile so bright for a man of his age that I wonder if he bleaches his teeth. I try to put all thoughts of dentistry out of my head as I stare into his brilliant blue eyes. I am mesmerized. I want to feel the calm, inner peace and happiness that this man exudes.

"What is your secret?" I ask him.

He looks up at me and squints. For a moment, I worry I have offended him. But he looks more amused than angry. He breaks into a half smile but doesn't speak. *Oh no*, it dawns on me. Maybe this man has taken a vow of silence like the monk in *The Hangover Part II*. And maybe I've broken a rule by speaking to him. I'm relieved when he begins to speak.

"Buddha encourages us to rise above the muddy roots like a lotus flower whose roots are embedded in the sludge, under the water, but whose petals are above water and remain untouched by any such dirt that is below."

I nod, although I have no idea what he means. I'm still pondering the metaphor as he continues. "Even though you are living in this world, your actions and thoughts should never be at a lower level. All of our sights should be set skyward, and we must remain cognizant of those below us. With purity in our hearts, control in our speech, and compassion and endearing behavior, that is how we should lead the days of our lives."

"That sounds great," I say. "But easier said than done. I experienced a horrible tragedy. How do I begin?"

"You begin at the beginning."

"Well, even before the incident, I didn't feel happy or content with all I've accomplished. I make good money, I help people in my job, but still I'm searching for that missing something."

"Success is fleeting. Nothing is permanent. We must accept impermanence and the idea that life is ultimate suffering. We must remain humble and compassionate. With this attitude, it is not possible for your state of mind to enter into depression or unhappiness."

"So how...how can I be that way, live the way you're suggesting?"

"To embrace this way of being and become an individual who practices the traits of humility, compassion, generosity, patience, forbearance, diligence, truthfulness, forgiveness, and tranquility is tremendously difficult."

I nod enthusiastically. "You got that right!" I say loudly before I can control myself. I raise my hand to give the monk a high five, but he leaves me hanging. I drop my hand sheepishly.

"There is a simple reason the practice is quite difficult. There are many distractions and evil forces that steer us away from this path. It takes a great deal of fortitude to overcome these temptations, to ignore the lures of evil passions and unhealthy desires to enter the realm of total goodness."

"And I thought it was hard to go on a diet," I mumble to myself. The monk places his shears down on the ground and opens his arms widely. "Do come in, my friend. I invite you to walk around the grounds and spend some time here."

I'm ecstatic. This monk has found the inner peace I'm seeking. I want to learn everything from him, to pump him for all his secrets. His views seem logical and clear to me. I need to know how to implement them, how to make inner peace happen on a daily basis when I have to work a job and deal with my family. I imagine myself driving calmly through Davidson's stop-and-go traffic at the end of the day, listening to sacred music, with a bumper sticker on my car that reads, "Buddhism is AWEsome!"

I turn to address the monk. "You mean I can stay here? My friend has told me a few things about Buddhism, and I would love to learn from you, and from your community here, how to practice it. But I'm Jewish by birth. Can I still become a Buddhist?"

The monk smiles broadly. "Buddha inspires everyone to achieve inner peace and then share with others. It does not matter what the past is, only what is happening in the here and now."

"Yes." I meet his eyes with mine. "I have no...I need to find my source of inner peace. I'm tormented. I'm...desperate."

The monk seems to contemplate this, staring at me as if he is looking deep within my soul. I wait patiently, expecting him to say something profound. Finally, he breaks the silence. "We only allow monks to stay here."

I'm crushed. My shoulders slump, and I turn around and take out my cell phone to call Klein, but his voicemail answers. I hang up and kick the shears the monk has left on the ground, and they land about an inch from his feet. He turns.

"You suffer deeply. You are angry with the world and the way you think it is treating you. But it is *you* and not the world who needs to change." He picks up the shears and resumes clipping. I'm about to walk away, when he says, "We offer retreats here for those interested in the Buddhist philosophy. We have one beginning at 7:00 p.m. tonight."

"For how long?" I ask him.

"Ten days."

"How much does it cost?" I ask, reaching for my wallet.

"There's no set price, but we encourage donations from our participants. However, I would like you to be our guest here. My hope is that you will be able to free yourself of your sadness, your anger, and your pain. You can decide afterwards how much that is worth."

I'm speechless, blown away by the synchronicity of events. I saw the sign, made a split-second decision to come here, and now I'm being offered a free ten-day retreat to learn all about Buddhism and find the peace I have been seeking.

"I'm extremely grateful," I say. "By the way, my name is Adam. Adam Freeman. I've come here from Connecticut. And you are? I mean, how should I address you?"

"Please follow me. I am Venerable Pannagavesi—the residential monk, and a Priory here at the monastery. I'm also the leader of the retreat. Residents call me Venerable Panna for short."

I follow the monk through the entrance to the Buddhist temple. We walk down a hallway with tiny offices on both sides of the corridor, and I try to make small talk as we enter one of them.

"Where are you from?"

"Sri Lanka."

"What brought you to America? And, by the way, your English is excellent."

He does not answer. Instead he hands me a piece of paper from a pile on the desk and whispers, "Please read this sheet carefully and commit it to memory. It explains the rules of the retreat. You may walk around the grounds, but please return to the Great Hall no later than 7:00 p.m. At that time, we will have an introduction and then begin the retreat. Please excuse me. I must finish my task." And with that, he smiles, escorts me out of the office, and bows.

I return the smile and say, "Thank you," but he remains standing there, motionless, facing me. I realize I'm supposed to bow back. As I raise my head, he turns and walks away.

I walk out of the temple into the hot summer evening and sit down on a newly-painted green bench. Feeling inspired, I take out my phone, pop in my earbuds, and open the Spotify app to listen to some tunes. Music always cheers me up, and I'm starting to feel more hopeful, so I click on my Rockin' Meditation Mix and play the theme song from the classic show, *One Day at a Time*.

As I'm humming along with the music, I take the time to diligently read through the document that Venerable Panna gave me:

Protocol of the Retreat:

The Eight Precepts:

(All meditators are expected to mindfully observe the eight precepts during their stay.)

1. Harmlessness: not intentionally taking the life of any living creature
2. Trustworthiness: not taking anything that is not given
3. Chastity: refraining from any sexual activity
4. Right Speech: avoiding false, abusive, or malicious speech
5. Sobriety: not taking any intoxicating drinks or drugs
6. Renunciation: not eating after midday
7. Restraint: not wearing make-up, jewelry, or immodest clothing; not playing music or musical instruments; refraining from dancing and singing; refraining from the use of adornments and ornaments
8. Alertness: refraining from the use of high and luxurious seats and beds

Meditators are required to strictly adhere to the rules of the retreat and to practice diligently according to the instructions given by their teacher.

Noble Silence:

Meditators are asked to maintain strict "noble silence." That is, not engaging in any talk with each other or anyone else, unless it is necessary during the retreat.

All guests must turn in their cell phones and other means of communication.

As I finish reading, I think to myself, *Jesus...I mean, Buddha, it's going to be tough as per #6 not to eat after lunch. Shit, that really sucks*. As Minnie can tell you, I get extremely cranky if I miss a meal. *To do this for ten days is going to be brutal! Uh oh, did I violate rule #4? That was bad to write "shit and suck." Wait, what's this about #7? No music? You've got to be kidding. Damn it, there I go again, not following #4.*

I take out my earbuds, exit the music app, and put my phone away. Like the Venerable Panna said, "It takes a great deal of fortitude to overcome these temptations..." Fuck. This is going to be harder than I thought.

CHAPTER FOURTEEN
2:05 a.m.

I look at the picture of my girls staring at me in the wooden frame on my desk. I know for a fact that the females in my family cannot go for five minutes without speaking, which is evident in one car ride or even at a single meal with my wife and three girls. There is a constant barrage of chitchat and details of events beyond anything that my minuscule male brain can sometimes take. I love my family dearly, and could never desert them, but now I'm wondering if they have any extra spaces on Adam's ten-day retreat? If all goes well, maybe I'll join him, depending on what I can come up with this early morning during my rewrite.

The Adventures of Adam Freeman, DDS
June 30, evening—*Curb Your Enthusiasm*

I take a self-guided tour of the monastery's gorgeous grounds to get myself in the right mindset. I'm in awe of the magnificent statues of a thousand "little Buddhas" (individuals who have achieved enlightenment) that grace the entrance of the complex. The babbling brook running through the path of enlightenment looks so tranquil.

I can't believe this peaceful oasis exists right here in Lemrac, New York. And I can't believe that I, a Jew, am beginning a Buddhist journey, combining my Judaism with Buddhism. I am now officially a JuBu for short.

At 6:45, as daylight is starting to falter, I walk up to the Great Hall. I take a deep breath and approach the twenty-foot door. My heart is pounding. And the room? The room is gloriously plain. There are no gilded ceilings or stained-glass windows like you'd see in an ornate Italian church. No bimah at the front of the room with a decorative ark for the Torah like in temple. No rows of benches like at a Southern Baptist Church. Only a gigantic statue of a Buddha, which they claim is the largest in the Western Hemisphere. The rules of the monastery are written on the walls. The floor is carpeted, and I follow the directions to remove my shoes.

Venerable Panna and four other people are sitting in a circle under the enormous Buddha. I sit down on an empty cushion. Venerable Panna addresses the group. "Before we embark on our retreat, I'd like each of you to tell us, in two minutes, the reason you are here. Keep in mind, these will be the last words, written or spoken, that you will use with each other for the next ten days. You may, of course, address the monks as necessary in our breakout sessions."

The first person to speak up is a fifty-year-old former priest from Ecuador. With his gray pompadour full of hairspray, he looks like a Latino version of Richard Gere. He has studied all different religions and is still not sure what he believes in. This retreat is his first foray into Buddhism. Next is a knockout beautiful, thirty-year-old psychiatrist who has been advising her patients to meditate and decided she should try a dose of her own medicine. The other two students are a couple; the woman is in her late forties—a recent divorcée—who is attending the retreat with her yoga instructor. He got her interested in Eastern medicine, which she claims helped cure her arthritis. I miss the rest of what they are saying because I'm wondering if they're an item and if their relationship caused the divorce.

My turn comes, and my heart feels like it's beating a hundred times a minute. I can't decide if I want to play the class clown or spill my guts out. Then I remember we only have two minutes, so I start speaking and let the words flow. As I begin, a benevolent force seems to help me along. "My road here feels like it started a long time ago, and I know that this is my destiny." The others look at me with surprise, but they're not as shocked as I am to have uttered these words. I continue, "I'm here to seek guidance on how to feel peaceful in my life, how to accept the constant stresses I face, and handle them with equanimity." I pause. Did I really use that word? "I've recently been through a traumatic experience, and I want to free my mind from the chains that bind it." I have everyone's attention, and I sense I'm on a roll now. "I feel paralyzed in my life, and I need help getting unstuck."

I am about to say more when Venerable Panna interrupts me. "Thank you. From this moment on, there will be silence. Before you leave the Great Hall, please get your robes from Venerable Kshantii."

Doing my best Larry David impersonation, I reply to Panna, "You know, I had like thirty seconds left."

Venerable Panna smiles at me. "We are strict about our protocols here. Your time is up. But your journey is just beginning."

He turns to face the group. "The focus of your time in meditation is to increase awareness of your bodily sensations and to practice objective observance of what you feel rather than to crave those feelings. Your goal for the next ten days is to sit with your sensations, both physical and emotional, in silence, and not try to change them or hold onto them but simply to experience their impermanence."

I look down at the floor and see a giant spider crawling towards me. I am about to squash it with my foot, but I decide to experience my fear instead of changing it. The spider crawls closer, and I freeze, trying to stay serene.

Venerable Panna continues, "By letting go of your thoughts, you will strengthen your capacity to tolerate and practice non-reactivity. And remember, the principle of Buddhism teaches: "Do no evil. Cultivate good. Purify one's mind.""

Now the spider is crawling up my right leg. It's taking all my restraint not to swat it off and kill it. I am sweating, and a small, frightened gasp escapes my lips.

Venerable Panna stops speaking. All eyes are on me. The monk walks over and gently brushes the spider from my leg. "A harmless creature," he says. "No need to fear it. Still, you wanted desperately to take its life."

My face is bright red, and my eye is twitching like crazy. "I—"

"Silence, Adam Freeman," booms Venerable Panna.

I am breathing heavily, and my inner peace is in the toilet, which I would like to find right about now. This is going to be a tough ten days.

* * *

Just as I'm hitting the all-nighter wall—the time between 2:00 and 3:00 a.m. where your body has to decide if you're going to crash with your clothes on or stay awake until dawn—things are getting really interesting. The time in the monastery will be pivotal for Adam's personal growth. Will he smash a bug or strike up a conversation with a pretty participant and get himself kicked out, or will he make it through and finally find the inner peace he seeks? And while he meditates and learns about Buddhism in silence, how can he document his journey if he's not allowed to write? When Adam Freeman wants something, he's a pretty resourceful, even devious guy. That's why I'm betting that he'll find a way to keep up his journal entries without being discovered. Only one way to find out. I better keep revising.

The Adventures of Adam Freeman, DDS
July 1—*The Wonder Years*

I lie in this uncomfortable little bed, my long legs hanging over the edge, in this ten by ten foot room, and I can't sleep. My mind races a hundred miles a minute. I turn on the light and pull out the Protocol of the Retreat sheet that I keep in my robe pocket. Although I'm a strict rule follower, I break Protocol #8: "Alertness: to refrain from using high and luxurious seats and beds." The pathetic pillow they have on this bed is the size of Rose's Unicorn Pillow Pet, and it's beyond uncomfortable. I take my robe off and place it under my head to make sleeping bearable. Following Rule #7 is going to be a challenge, since I play music to relax. I look at the clock. It's 3:49 a.m. Despite the adjustments I've made to my bedding, I still can't go back to sleep. I decide to go for a walk through the grounds.

As I stroll through the dense fog rising from the ground, I feel like I'm in a dream. The predawn dew on the grass is soaking my feet, so I take a detour along a dirt trail that travels into the woods. The trail meanders for a bit, and then a large oak tree appears in the middle of a clearing. I sit down at the tree's wet base and do a double take. Is that what I think it is next to my foot? I bend over and grasp the end of it... Yes! It's a black, ballpoint pen. I pull it from the dirt and stare at it like some foreign object.

I think briefly about Rule #2. "Trustworthiness: not taking anything that is not given to you." I look up to my Jewish God and ask, "Should I pick up the pen? Is it considered contraband, or is it a sign from you?"

A voice inside my head that I know is not mine says, "*There will be valuable learning here.*"

Usually, I keep Post-It notes in my pockets at all times to write down thoughts that come to me. Minnie will often find them when she's doing laundry and set them aside, but she's given up on trying to decipher my illegible scrawl. I surrendered all writing implements and materials at the start of the retreat. I really shouldn't pick up this pen, but it was obviously placed in my path by a divine power.

As I hold the pen, it seems to radiate energy in my hand. It makes me feel whole. I'm itching to document everything I learn in this majestic place. My Buddhist monastery visit needs a narrative voice, like Ted's voice-over in *How I Met Your Mother*. Imagine *The Wonder Years*, one of my favorite sitcoms from the late 1980s, without those excellent nostalgic ruminations of the adult Kevin Arnold as we watch his adolescent self struggling through his teens. The voice-overs put things in perspective and provide life lessons with which we all can identify.

I put the pen down for a moment and feel instantly deflated. I know I can't leave here without a record of my experience. So, I place what I have deemed the *pen of enlightenment* in the pocket of my robe and head back to my room, where I lay in bed writing microscopically on the back of the protocol sheet until the 4:30 a.m. meditation.

With no sleep but more energy than I've had in months, I jump out of bed and race over to the Great Hall. I'm excited to learn how to meditate Buddhist-style! I anticipate receiving detailed instructions from Venerable Panna on exactly what to do. Maybe a tutorial, YouTube video, or manual of some kind, but we receive only limited advice.

Panna keeps his remarks brief. He tells us we can sit in the Great Hall under the watch of the Giant Buddha, do moving meditation, which involves hand movements to keep us in the present—all I can think is that the monk looks like he's doing the Macarena as he demonstrates—or we can do walking meditation in the Hall or outside on the grounds. I'm eager to walk, but everyone else has already formed a circle, eyes closed, palms up on their legs, sitting Indian style, sorry—the kids now call it crisscross apple sauce. I don't want to exclude myself from the group, so I join the circle.

I know I'm supposed to clear my mind, but I keep thinking back to last night. Why did the monk interrupt me? That was rude. Shouldn't he have been more "monkly?" My mind's playing tricks on me. I realize I'm creating drama that isn't there, I try to ignore my negative thoughts, but I'm incapable of acting on this knowledge. If awareness is the first step, I'm badly in need of the second. I feel guilty that I am violating many of the rules of Buddhism—but not guilty enough to stop. Clearly, at this point, I'm more Jew than Bu.

After morning meditation, we are encouraged to walk the grounds and find private places for quiet reflection. I return to the clearing where I found the pen, thinking I will try to scribble my observations on the morning ritual, but as soon as I sit and lean back against the tree's enormous trunk, I fall sound asleep until I'm awakened by the bell signaling lunch. I stretch and make my way groggily to the Great Hall.

I was expecting Asian cuisine—authentic Chinese or Thai food. But the Chinese food truck outside Yale-New Haven Hospital is far better than what they serve here. Since I can't talk, I'm not able to ask what we're eating, but I suspect it's some kind of vegetables over rice. The others in the group seem to enjoy the food, but it's much too bland for me. I didn't come here for the culinary experience, but I find myself craving Chinese takeout.

* * *

The *pen of enlightenment*? Not sure how I came up with that one, but good for you Adam! You're really going with the flow. Now I have you exactly where I want you, experiencing—and writing, albeit secretly—about Buddhism! Even though the food stinks, I would gladly trade places with you. I had to learn about Buddhism from books, but you, lucky dog, get to take instruction directly from the monks. I know—it wouldn't work for you any other way. Some of us can absorb knowledge by hearing or reading it, but you're a visceral person who needs to ingest information by taking action. Learning can't be passive for you. So, there you are, in the monastery, with your contraband pen trying to write down everything that's happening, beginning your metamorphosis. I'm thrilled for you, but also the slightest bit jealous.

The Adventures of Adam Freeman, DDS
July 1—*Weeds*

After lunch, we're each given jobs for the afternoon. I pray to my Jewish God that I will get a fun, not-too-taxing chore to do. God answers my prayers. They assign me to weed the lush gardens. I know I'm not going to make millions of dollars working with these weeds like Nancy Botwin did in Showtime's famous series, but I feel like I have won the Buddhist Lottery! (Note to self: Find out if Buddhists gamble.) I love being outside, and I get to avoid the monotony of scrubbing floors like Elizabeth Gilbert did in *Eat, Pray, Love.* Indoor cleaning isn't my thing.

I'm escorted out of the Great Hall with the Richard Gere-look-alike Ecuadorian ex-priest, and we exchange smiles. He looks as excited as I am to be working out in nature. I glance back and withhold a snicker when I see the spiritual psychologist being led into the kitchen and the NYC debutante and her yogi boyfriend being handed gloves and a bucket filled with soapy water while they kneel at the base of the Buddhist statue. I wink at the giant Buddha looking over me as I go through the door and out into the hot sun.

I'm led by another monk into the colorful gardens filled with roses, lilies, irises, and Gerbera daisies, and those are only the flowers I recognize. A stretch of sunflower stalks promises a swath of fiery blossoms later in the season. I sit down and pull out the weeds one by one, as the sun beats down on me. I look around and wish I could ask someone for sunblock. My pale, white Jewish skin is reddening, and I'm looking more lobster-like every minute. I did come here to exercise my spiritual muscles, but this isn't how I wanted to feel the burn. Maybe scrubbing floors wasn't such a bad task to get after all.

I'm focusing intensely on pulling each weed out of the ground, like the monks instructed, but my mind starts wandering after the first hour. I stare at the ex-priest and am desperately jealous of his sun hat with a neck flap. Smart man—I wish I had thought of that. Then again, I didn't exactly prepare for this adventure. I wonder if the ex-priest's Christian God told him he would need a hat for the burning sun, the way ours told Noah he would need an ark for the flood. I wonder what his Christian God looks like. I was born Jewish, so I'm not supposed to believe in Jesus as God's son. But while Judaism is my birthright, I have free will and am entitled to my own beliefs. There's nothing stopping me from becoming Catholic, Muslim, Hindu, or even Buddhist. In fact, I wish I had been exposed to different religions earlier because I could have made more informed choices about spirituality as an adult. I blink hard to focus my thoughts again on the weeds in front of me, when suddenly...*bzzzzzzzzzz*!

I wave my hand to shoo away the yellowjacket flying by my ear. I pull another weed. *Bzzzzzzz*! This time I swat at the wasp, which flies off, then zooms back, circling my head twice before dive-bombing its stinger straight into my leg.

"*Jeeesus!*" I scream out loud. The four monks, along with the Ecuadorian ex-priest working alongside me, look up. According to the rules, I should stay silent, but I'm in serious pain, and now that I've screamed, I might as well explain why. "Grrrr." I grimace. "I was stung." My words fall on deaf ears as the monks and ex-priest go back to weeding.

I look down at my leg; it's throbbing and starting to swell. I should add that I have a very low pain tolerance. I feel like Tim plunged his switchblade into my calf instead of Jason the Jock's stomach. The pain is white hot. I try to focus on picking more weeds and tell myself the sting is a sign reminding me that I need to control my mind and focus on the moment. But the moment hurts like hell. What do I do with this pain? It could be worse, I remind myself. At least I'm not allergic to wasp stings the way I am to poison ivy. I doubt any of the monks are carrying an EpiPen.

After we have finished weeding, I limp back to my room and examine the damage. My leg has a welt the size of a half dollar, and I'm convinced the stinger is still inside me, releasing its venom. I consider going to the office and asking if they have a first aid kit, but I convince myself that acceptance is part of the transformation I need to undergo to achieve true peace. I'm dying for dinner, but we're not allowed to eat after midday. (How, I wonder, did the Buddha get fat?) I nap until the evening *dharma*—the teachings of the Buddha.

During the dharma talk we learn that the monks, *bhikkhus*, live according to the Vinaya, the code of monastic discipline established by the Buddha. The Venerable Panna tells us that "in accordance with this discipline, the monastics are alms-mendicants, living lives of celibacy and frugality. Their training is a means of living reflectively and is a guide to keeping one's needs to a minimum." The frugality part I could handle, as I've never been an extravagant spender, except when it comes to bootleg concert tickets or buying rounds of drinks with the Four Horsemen. But celibacy...? I think of my longest dry spell with Minnie—about seven weeks—after I messed up and forgot our seventh anniversary. "A week for each year," she had told me. "This way, next year, you'll remember." By the end of week five I was begging her for even a hand job, a quick jerk, but she held firm to her resolve. As soon as my punishment was over, she couldn't wait to jump my bones, and I could tell it had been a challenge for her as well. After that, the forgotten anniversary and the seven weeks of famine were never mentioned again. That's one of the amazing things about Minnie. She never holds a grudge. Once she's said her piece and we've made peace, the subject is over, and unlike some guys I know, I don't have to hear repeatedly about stuff that happened years ago. I find myself missing Minnie's companionship and her care—she would have found something soothing for my wasp sting—but I know I have to endure my time here and try to learn how to be a better partner and a more emotionally healthy adult. I shake my head to bring myself out of my reverie, drawing a few sidelong glances.

As the monk continues, I find a host of unorthodox questions forming in my mind. I doubt that my retreat colleagues possess the intellectual rigor that was drilled into me at Yale, where I was trained not only to question but also to challenge assumptions, told to take no idea's truth or integrity for granted, and encouraged to raise my hand early and often. But here, I find myself simply absorbing an abundant flow of unfamiliar concepts and premises, doubting my own doubt, questioning my right to question. Maybe it's the robes the monks are wearing, which convey both trust and a sense of spiritual seriousness, the way a simple white lab coat imbues a doctor with the air of infallibility and an unchallengeable authority. As I sit and squirm, adjusting my leg, which is swollen like a drumstick, thoughts too bizarre to voice pop into my mind. For example, if these monks are leading a life of celibacy, are they masturbating to relieve their sexual tension? If not, do they have wet dreams every few weeks, like sex-starved teenagers? I know these questions are entirely inappropriate, but they're also very real to me, and enquiring minds want to know. I shake my head again and try to keep my mind focused on more wholesome thoughts.

I enjoy the teacher's dharma, even though it is hard to hear him over the rumbling of my starving stomach. My meager breakfast of tea and buttered bread, my pathetic lunch, and my afternoon of hard outdoor labor, have rendered me hungry and tired and extremely cranky. They don't even serve any cookies with evening tea. No wonder bedtime is 9:00—everyone is exhausted from food deprivation. Incidentally, I now know what it feels like to be a contestant on *The Biggest Loser*. Hey, I have the newest Mark Burnett reality show—*Birth of a JuBu*. All we need is a boatload of cameras following me around and a place to do the confessionals—except that I can't talk!

CHAPTER FIFTEEN
3:10 a.m.

Adam, my brother, it's like you're breaking free from my body and creating your own universe with its own set of laws—or lack thereof. It's embarrassing to have my alter ego wondering if monks masturbate and acting like an adolescent in the serene setting of a Buddhist monastery. Like all guys, I have my share of sex on the brain, but even Jacob unchained is nothing compared to the side of Adam we're seeing here. It's Adam's mind that needs to be rid of the weeds overtaking it, not the monastery's garden. Although these pages are coming from my fingertips, I'm beginning to wonder if I have a twisted writing muse who pumps Adam full of adolescent thoughts.

I've been with you so far Adam. I've tolerated your shenanigans (there must be a better Yiddish word for that) but now is your time to show us what you're made of. Grow up, man. Get your act together. I've given you the tools to make a change in your life, to bust out of your neurotic thoughts. This is not the time to be reflecting on a monk's sex life or a new reality show. Sure, you've got me chuckling, but we need to supply Maggie with ample evidence to overturn your trial, conviction, and execution. One stroke of the keyboard and you're history. And a part of me will die with you. So don't make me do it. Instead, make me proud.

I stand up to stretch and walk to the pantry to get myself another 5-Hour Energy Drink. But when I open the cupboard, I realize I need to finish this manuscript without any more stimulants. I put down the can and walk back into my office with a glass of ice-cold water and a large, overripe banana. I know what Adam would say about the banana, and I banish those thoughts from my head.

Before returning to the manuscript, I stand in front of my spiritual books that neatly line the shelves above my built-in desk. Damn, I did a lot of research when I was writing this book after my serendipitous enlightenment moment at Restoration Hardware. On my shelf, I see *Many Lives, Many Masters* by Yale-trained psychiatrist Brian Weiss, along with *You're Not Going Crazy, You're Just Waking Up* by Michael Mirdad; *Anatomy of the Spirit* by Caroline Myss; *Way of the Peaceful Warrior* by Dan Millman; *The Power of Now* by Eckhart Tolle; and *The Celestine Prophecy* by James Redfield.

I take a swig of the ice water and feel the cold liquid give me the jolt I need to stay awake.

The Adventures of Adam Freeman, DDS
July 2—*Survivor*

Oh no.

I wake up and my arms are on fire!

I can't open my left eye; it's swollen shut and itches like crazy. I must have touched poison ivy while I was weeding yesterday. This is *not* good news—I'm highly allergic—and I feel like scratching all my skin off down to the bone. Now I really wish I had been assigned to clean the Buddhist statue.

Fuck this. Why did I come here? Why did Klein let me come here? Fuck him. It's all his fault. What kind of a friend agrees to drop you off at a

Buddhist monastery when you clearly need to go to a psych clinic? I'd be much happier bound in a straitjacket, shuffling around in my nice, clean padded room, pleasantly sedated, but instead I want to scratch myself like a cat clawing new furniture. I came here to find the new me, but that wasn't supposed to involve shedding my skin—literally.

At first, the feeling of my nails digging into my flesh soothes the itching sensation that pulsates through my body, but the relief is fleeting. The itch comes back—with a vengeance. Like a drug addict needing his next fix, I furiously rub the bumps on my arm, promise myself I'll stop, then start again a minute later. I want to drench myself in a bathtub full of calamine lotion. Like my unfiltered thoughts, the poison ivy is merciless.

I lie in bed, stuck in the hell of the present moment, wondering how I'm going to get out of this. There really is no choice. If I don't get help, it won't stop spreading, and I'll need to be hospitalized, wrapped from head to toe in gauze. So instead of making my way to morning meditation, I head to the office and approach a monk filing papers inside. Without thinking, I break my vow of silence. "Excuse me, Venerable One. I need to see a doctor." I show him my swollen eye and bumpy arms, which are now oozing.

The monk escorts me to Venerable Panna's office without saying a word. When I enter, the elder monk is hunched over a book, whispering to himself. The office is bare except for a light to the left of him and a hard, wooden chair across from his desk where he motions me to sit. Venerable Panna looks up. "Yes, Adam Freeman, how may I help you?"

I reply hysterically, "I got poison ivy yesterday while weeding. I'm extremely allergic and need to see a dermatologist. Last time it got so bad the doctor had to inject steroids in my ass. Oh sorry, butt."

Panna laughs. "We are a Buddhist monastery not a hospital. There are other ways that you can address this poison ivy."

I look at him incredulously. "I doubt it. Last time, the poison ivy even spread to my scrotum. Look, it's in my eye."

"You're funny, Adam. The body can be healed without traditional medicines."

The disbelieving Jew in me shakes my head. "No. Not with this. I'm telling you, I get it bad."

Panna brings his hands together and rests his chin on them. "Adam, you must trust me. The mind can control how the body responds. I'll teach you." He moves his chair out from behind his desk and sits face-to-face with me. I continue to scratch. "Put your hands at your sides," he says. I obey his command, though it takes every ounce of my willpower. "This is but one way that life has chosen to impart suffering upon you. Remember what you've learned so far, that the mind is very powerful when controlled by meditation. Meditation will cultivate the basic human qualities that will reduce your suffering."

I am not convinced. "How can meditation get rid of my poison ivy?"

"By meditating, you can enrich the mind to be more stable and clear, develop love and compassion, and achieve emotional balance. Once the mind is healthy, it will facilitate the body healing itself. In most people, this power remains latent, but you can make an effort to develop it through meditation, and it will serve you well."

I give this some thought. "Maybe. But I'll be honest. I don't feel we've gotten good guidance on exactly how to meditate."

"And that's the problem right there," Panna says, smiling. "You use the word exactly. But meditation is very personal, and you can go crazy reading up on all the various ways to meditate. The truth is, they all achieve the same result. You choose the one that works best for you. They all involve getting in a comfortable physical posture and wishing for self-transformation and a desire for others' well-being and for the alleviation of their suffering. The focus is on others, not the self. As you progress, you stabilize your mind, which is all too often disorderly, as it is occupied by a stream of what we call monkey chatter. To master the mind, you must free it from the automatic conditioning you've received your whole life and your resulting inner confusion. Only then will you achieve clarity."

"You're saying there's no right or wrong way to meditate?"

"Not exactly. There are many wrong ways but also many right ways. It's just that there's no *one* right way. For example, some people have success with *focused-attention meditation,* in which we tame and center the mind in the present moment while developing the capacity to not get distracted. Others engage in *mindfulness meditation,* which involves cultivating a less emotionally reactive awareness to emotions, so that thoughts and emotions in the moment don't spiral out of control and create mental distress. There is also *compassion and loving kindness meditation*, which fosters an altruistic perspective towards others."

The short-in-stature-but-huge-in-knowledge monk rises, and I open my mouth to speak. He cuts me off. "Please, I would like you to now maintain your vow of silence again and practice what I taught you. It is time for my dharma talk. You will find this one especially enlightening. Follow me."

As I follow Venerable Panna into the Great Hall, I am feeling trapped and miserable inside this monastery. I'm like a contestant from *Survivor* who has been voted onto Exile Island. I now must deal with this dreadful poison ivy and try to meditate it away before it consumes me. Is this guy for real?

During the dharma talk, I try to concentrate while my itching arms beckon my fingernails. Panna speaks about the three essential characteristics of the Buddha's teachings: *anicca* (impermanence): everything we have can be taken away and nothing ever lasts forever; *dukkha* (suffering): life is suffering, and it is our job to eliminate the cycle of life and get to paradise—

or nirvana—through enlightenment; and *anatta* (egolessness): letting go of the ego and freeing the craving that the ego wants us to pursue.

As I rub my itchy eye, he continues. "Only when you experience impermanence as suffering can you come to the realization of the truth of suffering, which is the first of the four noble truths basic to the doctrine of the Buddha. When you realize the subtle nature of suffering, from which you cannot escape for a moment, you become truly disgusted with your very existence. Only then can you look for ways to escape beyond suffering and get to eternal peace and happiness—nirvana.

As my arms start to bleed, I am truly disgusted with my very existence. I want to scream, "That's it! I've been searching for nirvana, but how can I escape suffering when I can't even stop scratching?" Only my vow of silence holds me back.

As if reading my mind, Panna continues. "You have to get rid of your *karma*—only then will you come to the end of suffering as you know it. *Karma* or *sankhara*, gives energy to sustain your life. When there is no sankhara, then there remains no necessary energy to sustain the person in any form of life. To reach anicca—this is the state of inner and outer calmness and balance that leads to nirvana—one must meditate."

All I know is if I don't *medicate* to make the itching stop, I'm going to have to get rid of my arms to come to the end of suffering as I know it. I want to raise my hand (before it gets severed) and suggest there's another kind of meditation—amputation meditation—in which the loss of one or more limbs causes one to realize the truth of suffering. Somehow, I force myself to focus, because Venerable Panna is talking about karma and, apparently, it's not at all what I thought it was—i.e., getting poison ivy on your scrotum for speculating on how monks handle their sexual desire. I understand karma to be "doing a good deed which benefits the do-gooder in the future," or the opposite, doing something bad and having it come back to bite you. But these monks are talking about an entirely different concept. They are saying one needs to free oneself of karma, or energy, to get off the cycle of leading a suffering-filled life. To buy into this, you must believe in the reincarnation doctrine. At this point, I'm having a hard time believing I was another person in another life, although I would love to be someone else in a different place with a different set of non-itching arms right now. And I would like to see the scientific evidence behind the theory of reincarnation.

Then Panna concludes, "By learning to breathe and connecting with the universe, you will see right mind and body."

If I have it right, the key in Buddhism is that the mind controls the body, and we have to get complete control of our mind in order to banish negative, impure, and evil thoughts from our thinking. When the mind is properly developed and you reach the state of annica, this will strike at the root of your physical and mental illnesses and will gradually eliminate what is bad in mankind. I close my eyes and ponder this for a while, as I try to visualize the poison ivy disappearing from my body.

* * *

"Oh God, you startled me!" I say to Leah as she walks into my office. I stop typing. "What are you doing up?"

"I could ask you the same question. Have you been down here all night?"

"Yes, you fell right asleep after we made love—that's usually my job."

Leah laughs. "Yeah, I know. Usually I get all worked up and can't sleep and *you're* lights out. What's gotten into you?"

"I've been editing my book. It's my mission to finish it this morning."

"I thought it was done."

"I thought so too. But while re-reading the book, I've gotten some ideas that enhance Adam's character and give the story more legs."

Leah sees *All About Buddhism*, the book I bought at Restoration Hardware, open next to me. I've been using it as a guide to help me with the last chapter. "You know, I remember when you bought that thing. You were on such a kick to learn everything about Buddhism. Remember when you made us go to the Buddhist temple for brunch?"

I smile and think of Adam stuck in the monastery for almost two weeks, hoping to get the CliffsNotes version of enlightenment. "That was a fun family adventure we had." I hear a whistle and she stands up from the recliner. "Would you like some tea?"

"No, I'm good."

"I'm making myself green tea. I'll be back."

"Okay, I'll be here," I respond, burying my head in my laptop again.

The Adventures of Adam Freeman, DDS
July 3—from *Oz* to *Fantasy Island*

By now, the poison ivy has spread. My left eye is swollen shut. I feel like I'm at the Oswald State Correctional Facility (*Oz*), instead of a Buddhist monastery in suburban New York. This stay is supposed to help foster my spiritual growth, not make me a prisoner in my own body.

It takes every ounce of energy to get out of bed and try one last time to see if meditation can help heal me before I forsake the monks in favor of steroids in my ass.

I'm the last to arrive in the Great Hall, and everyone else's eyes are closed, so no one can see my left eye, which is the size of a golf ball, or my arms that look like red jelly beans. I sit down on a cushion and first try focused meditation. My mind visualizes a waterfall, I'm feeling heavenly. But without warning, my right hand instinctively begins scratching at the bumps. With every step forward, I'm being pulled backwards with a strong desire to relieve the itching in my arms. I'm too distracted by the fire engulfing my body for my mind to let go.

I try being mindful, less emotionally reactive to my situation. I try being apathetic towards the itching, but I can't stop myself from being angry because of my carelessness during weeding. I should have known better than to be so nonchalant about it. There's a point where I'm almost winning the battle, but suddenly a monk taps me on my shoulder, bringing me out of my groggy state. When I open my one good eye and look up, he is shaking his head. It appears that almost falling asleep is seriously frowned on here.

Now that the first two methods have failed, I might as well try compassion and loving kindness. I begin to picture each of my children the very last time I saw them. I'm hovering in our family room, looking down at myself hugging Paige, Rose, and Spencer. I feel the joy in their hearts when I'm around them and giving them the love and attention that children need. I think of how amazing my family is and how I'm blessed with such an understanding wife, two incredible girls, and a young son who is the apple of my eye. Precisely how long I meditate I don't know. The other members of the retreat have long since left, but I sit there, cross-legged, in a trance, directing all my energy into blessing each of my family members. I miss lunch and the evening dharma talk. By the time I finish the meditation, my bumps have miraculously disappeared. I can open my left eye, and oddly, I feel no desire to scratch. It is 5:04 p.m.—time to get ready for bed.

Somehow, during the time I was sending love and compassion to my wife and three children, I didn't have a care in the world. I've always known deep in my heart that love is the only thing that matters in the universe, but now I feel it wholeheartedly. Suddenly, the depression that has been crushing me these past few weeks lifts, along with my lifelong anxiety, like the morning fog when the sun rises up. I've moved from *Oz* to my very own *Fantasy Island*.

I experience my own miracle this day, because never in a million years would I have thought that the pulsating itching sensation in my arms and the swollen eye would be cured through meditation alone, but I could be a case study. My friends in the Yale lab would never believe me. But as I lie in bed recapping my day, I can say with all my heart that what usually takes me weeks to recover from has been cured within one compassion and loving-kindness meditation session. I am amazed, confused, but most of all happy. So happy I want to jump for joy, but I'm afraid if I do I will jinx the feeling. I do it anyway, dropping the last vestige of neurotic fear. I jump. I land. The feeling holds. This must be a glimpse of nirvana!

July 4—*Growing Pains*

It's the fourth of July, Independence Day, and instead of going with my family to see the colorful fireworks display (of which, incidentally, I'm a proud sponsor) in our hometown of Davidson, Connecticut, I am sitting on a threadbare cushion in the afternoon dharma talk in the Great Hall under the large statue of the Buddha. I should be unhappy about this, but I'm ecstatic. I know I'm missing a special tradition with my family, but I focus on the fact that this Independence Day is about achieving my freedom from the chains of my mind—a revolutionary change that will bring about the birth of the new Adam Freeman Nation when I return.

Venerable Panna begins by addressing the Buddhist's belief in God. "Everyone thinks that Buddhists don't believe in God. The truth is that the Buddha never explicitly said whether he believed that there was a God or not. He did not say for sure that there is a Creator, because he wanted each of us to discover for ourselves the universal truths. We know he preached that there is no one who can lead another to nirvana. One must get there alone. You cannot rely on praying to get you to peace. The universe has given us a map that leads to enlightenment."

I resist the urge to lift up my healed arms and say, "If there's no God, then who did this?" If I'm called on, I'll tell the cross-legged occupants in the room—who are all nodding like marionettes in unison—that "I'm having a hard time with the concept that the Buddha did not specifically expound on a belief in God because I think there's a Source of the universe. And if the Buddha achieved enlightenment, don't you think that he could have given a little credit to a higher power. I mean, Abraham, Mohammed, Jesus—why couldn't Buddha acknowledge the big guy?" But I can't argue with the other concept that Venerable Panna introduces, the idea that we all have God within us. Once, when we were driving back from Yom Kippur services, I asked my Paige, when she was eight, if she believed in God and she said, "We all have God in us, Daddy." I have never forgotten her answer.

Thinking of Paige on this holiday that our family always spends together, makes me suddenly homesick. The joy that flooded through me only a short while ago evaporates, and the positive energy I worked so hard to cultivate the previous day dissipates in a flash. The Jewish father in me feels guilty that, before I departed, I was unable to think of my children with love in my heart. I miss their angelic faces, their smiles, even their tantrums and fights. I imagine them missing my neurotic preparations—long-sleeve shirts, ponchos (in case it rains), bug spray, glow sticks, flashlights, bottled water, and making sure everyone uses the bathroom before we leave the house—for our short drive to the town green and for the half-hour fireworks display. A wave of sadness engulfs me; I'm not being a good father while in this monastery. Ignoring my children—and abandoning my wife—in a selfish quest for spiritual fulfillment. My arms begin to itch again, though I don't notice any marks on them, so I know I am experiencing a psychosomatic reaction.

After the dharma talk, I can't take it anymore. I march into Venerable Panna's office and begin to sob uncontrollably. In a low whisper I say, "I've learned a lot here, but I need to go home and be with my family."

"We would never force you to do anything you find uncomfortable," he says, "but before you make any drastic decisions, I suggest you see the abbot."

I understand this is not a suggestion but a subtle command, so I soon find myself standing outside of the door of Venerable Rinsho's office. I am surprised to learn that he is Canadian, in his mid-fifties, and with his deep seated radiant brown eyes and wide smile, he's a ringer for Dr. Jason Seaver in *Growing Pains*—except for the shaved head. I feel an instant connection with him. If he has good advice like Dr. Seaver gave to his kids, Mike, Ben, Carol, and Chrissy, then I'll be in good shape. He is carefully trimming a bonsai tree—*is that what everyone does here?*—on a small table, and he stops as soon as I enter.

"Please, let's sit," he says, gesturing towards the larger of two pillows on the floor. "Tell me what is on your mind so we can get to the bottom of your perceived troubles."

I want to say, "I see what you're doing there, with 'perceived' troubles," but I decide to trust him. And in any case, I can always decide to leave. He pulls up the pillows, and we sit down opposite each other. My voice is raspy. "I was beginning to feel peaceful here, but I miss my family. I'm anxious, unhappy now."

"You must let go of attachments," says the monk. I look at him intently, and the serenity he exudes tells me he speaks the truth. "That is the reason you will always have anxiety and feelings of unrest."

"Let go of *things*? We're talking about people. The people I love and care about most. Are you saying I should leave my family behind?"

"Of course not. I would never suggest that. You have built a life for yourself back at your home. But now you are here, with us, trying to heal yourself so you can return to that life and live it as a better person, with a greater sense of purpose. I encourage you"—another subtle order from the boss—"to let go of your past, focus on the present moment, and use your precious time here to heal yourself. Search for your nirvana, then you can go home and be the best father and husband that you can be."

"I strive for that feeling of bliss and happiness. It would be ecstasy for me."

"Ah, there you go again, striving. You're falling into that trap. Stop striving and desiring things. Even craving peace or happiness, as lovely as they are, is dangerous. Your work here is all about letting go of everything that you want and living in the moment. No striving. Living the Noble Truths, eh?"

I repeat the Noble Truths we were introduced to in the first dharma talk. "One, the truth of suffering. Two, the truth of the cause of suffering. Three, the truth of the end of suffering. Four, the truth of the path that frees us from suffering."

"Very good. I see that you have been busy learning. Anyone can memorize words, but what do they mean to you, eh?"

I elaborate, "The first Noble Truth, dukkha, is translated as life is suffering."

Venerable Rinsho continues, "Everything in life is dukkha, even something precious and enjoyable because it will end. We can extend this to the nature of the self. We *all* are temporary. Finally, before we can understand life and death, we must understand the nature of self."

I tell him, "The second Noble Truth teaches us that suffering is caused by craving or thirst."

He adds, "We continually search for things outside ourselves to make us happy. But no matter how successful we are, how many material things we accumulate, we never remain fully satisfied. The Buddha teaches us that this thirst for more grows from ignorance of the self. We go through our life grabbing onto one thing after another to get a sense of security about ourselves. People attach to physical things and ideas and opinions about themselves and the world around them. Then they grow frustrated when the world does not behave as they think it should, eh?"

"The third Noble Truth tells us that through diligent practice, we can put an end to the craving." I give a smile, self-satisfied with my memory.

"Ending the infinite quest for satisfaction is called enlightenment, or *bodhi*. The enlightened being exists in a state called nirvana. And what is the fourth Noble Truth, Adam?"

"It is to follow the Eightfold Path to enlightenment."

He stands up. "Excellent. These are rules that one must live and indoctrinate into one's life, not just believe in. You are very smart, but we must see if you are wise. Come, let's go for a walk."

CHAPTER SIXTEEN
4:20 a.m.

Leah walks in with her tea, and I lift my head up from the computer screen. "Do you mind having company while you're writing? I'm having trouble sleeping." She reaches down and takes the last bite of my banana, then lifts up *All About Buddhism*. "This really helped you, didn't it?"

"Yes. You know I've never felt completely comfortable in my own skin. I always had this emptiness inside, like there was a piece of me missing, and then there was my ear wiggle. Before my spiritual journey, I felt like I was not in the right time and place. I wasn't living in the moment. I needed to let go of my past and live in the present. It's helped tremendously, in every area of my life."

She smiles. "My Jewish-born husband has embraced the concepts of Buddhism. What did you call yourself that day? A JuBu?"

"That was my aha moment, my epiphany. I am a JuBu! I now incorporate the Buddhist doctrine into my Jewish faith and heritage."

"And what's that Bu part all about again?"

"Buddhism is about living in the present moment by putting the past behind you and the future out of your mind."

"I could have told you that much. I'm not sure why you needed a gigantic book to learn that being in the here and now, instead of somewhere else all the time, is what life's about."

I'm a little miffed, but I know Leah is not making light of my spiritual awakening. "I know it comes innately to you. But I tend to overthink things, to agonize over decisions, in case you hadn't noticed."

"I noticed." At that, we both laugh.

We hear a cry from upstairs that ends our philosophizing. "Oh dear, I think that's Eva. Let me check on her. Jacob, are you going to get some sleep?"

"No, I need to finish writing this. Thanks for taking care of our baby."

The Adventures of Adam Freeman, DDS
July 4—*Sex and the City*

Venerable Rinsho and I pass a line of yellow and orange wild lilies in bloom. The Buddhist version of the late Alan Thicke seems proud of me after my description of the Four Noble Truths. He elaborates: "The Buddha's teachings on the Four Noble Truths are sometimes compared to a physician diagnosing an illness and prescribing a treatment. The first truth tells us what the illness is; the second truth reveals what causes the illness. The third holds out hope for a cure. Finally, the fourth truth is the prescription that the Buddha has written as a cure to our illness." I nod, and he continues. "I thought that you would like that analogy—with you being a healthcare professional. Now, I would like you to start following the Eightfold Path: Right View, Right Intention, Right Speech, Right Action, Right Livelihood, Right Effort, Right Mindfulness, Right Concentration."

We walk by a large fountain with a Buddha sitting in the middle of a lotus flower. I stop to watch the water pouring out of the flower. I'm beginning to relax when, out of the corner of my eye, I spot the gorgeous thirty-year-old psychiatrist, the NYC debutante divorcée, and her yogi boyfriend doing yoga poses in an open field with a younger monk in his twenties. I stop dead in my tracks. I feel like I'm watching an episode of *Sex and the City*. The divorcée and her boyfriend start to kiss. The monk, standing behind the psychiatrist, begins fondling her breasts while the male yogi reaches around under the divorcée's robe and mirrors the monk's ministrations. Both women moan loudly. The monk slowly lowers his hand to touch his partner's midsection, then continues south. The monk and the shrink lie down. Her long legs stick out from under the shorter monk's robe, and they start to gyrate on the grass. The divorcée kneels in front of the yoga instructor, wraps his robe around her head, and begins bobbing up and down. By now Charlie is throbbing, and I feel like I might explode. Fortunately, I'm wearing a loose-fitting robe. I turn to Venerable Rinsho, eyes wide, mouth open in shock, but he simply motions for me to continue our walk. As I adjust the folds of my expanding robe, it dawns on me that he is looking where I'm looking but not seeing what I'm seeing. I blink and rub my eyes, then look again at the open field. The couples I saw going at it moments ago are meditating serenely around a statue of Buddha.

It takes me a moment to let go of my late-night-Cinemax hallucination and refocus on the monk. Slowly, Charlie returns to his normal, unaroused position. Venerable Rinsho continues. "The Path is divided into three main sections: wisdom, ethical conduct, and mental discipline. Developing wisdom involves following Right View and Right Intention. Right View is not about believing in doctrine, but in perceiving our true nature and the world around us. Right Intention refers to the energy and commitment one needs to be fully engaged in Buddhist practice. Emphasizing Right Speech, Right

Action, and Right Livelihood are the components of the Ethical Conduct Path. This calls us to take care in our speech, our actions, and our daily lives to do no harm to others and to cultivate wholesomeness in ourselves. Finally, through Right Effort, Right Mindfulness, and Right Concentration we develop the strict mental discipline to cut through delusion. We meditate to achieve clarity and focus of mind, eh?"

He senses me deep in thought—though I'm certain he has no idea what I've been thinking about—and smiles. I break the silence. "The anger that swells up inside of me when I don't get what I want is so hard to control. I'm not sure that I am programmed to be able to follow the Four Noble Truths and the Eightfold Path."

"You need to keep at this," the abbot responds. "To persevere. Don't let your mind influence your thoughts."

I try to wrap my mind around that one.

"Do you believe that I can do this?"

"You should not care what I believe or what my opinion is of you or your devotion to Buddhism. The belief and Buddhist teachings have been around for centuries, and they will continue to survive with or without you. I know you have come here to achieve enlightenment. Can you reach nirvana? I don't know, but I'm proud and pleased that you are trying. I can only pass our teachings along to you. It's up to you to make your own conclusions and decisions. It is your call whether you quit or persevere."

We reach the end of the path, and Venerable Rinsho escorts me back to the Great Hall. All my thoughts of leaving the monastery are gone. I miss my family, but I will be with them soon enough, and I will bring back a better version of myself. This man has given me a challenge—expressed gently, but a challenge nonetheless—and if there's one thing about me, it's that I've never been a quitter. The monk concludes, "You will continue your vow of silence upon entering the Great Hall. And you will follow all the rules of the retreat from now on."

I open my mouth, the word "But..." forming on my lips, and he brings a finger to his own lips to shush me. "Without exception," he adds, then walks slowly away.

* * *

OMG! What the hell did I write? Adam hallucinating that soft-core porn scene in the monastery garden seems pretty gratuitous. Sure, it entertains the reader. But does it move the plot along? Does it help Adam grow? Or did I have sex still on the brain? Maybe I should cut it from the final draft? But it says something about where Adam's mind was in that moment and how he's still clearly susceptible to distraction.

I get up to stretch, and my eyes fall on a book about Judaism on the shelf. This starts me thinking about the two isms in my life—Judaism and Buddhism. The founders of these religions were about as different as two people could be: Abraham for the Jewish people and Siddhartha for the Buddhists. And there are enormous differences between the religions, like the fact that Buddhists don't believe in a personal God. They teach that we are continually reborn from past lives until we reach our nirvana. Jews, on the other hand, believe that we are made in God's image and come into the world with the capacity to do good or evil.

As I witness Adam's evolution, it occurs to me that the isms are not too far apart. The Buddhist teachings of the Four Noble Truths and the Eightfold Path parallel the story of my long-lost relative Moses and his Ten Commandments. It's so obvious I don't know why I didn't think of it sooner. Both religions have a holy book. For the Jews it's the Tanakh, for the Buddhists the Tripitaka. While Buddhists believe that the gateway to enlightenment is through the Four Noble Truths and the Eightfold Path, for Judaism, it is through studying the Hebrew Scriptures, observing the six hundred and thirteen mitzvoth—good deeds—and living by the Ten Commandments.

The nerd in me wants to lay it all out in a Venn Diagram to show the areas where Ju and Bu overlap. But if I don't get back to finishing Adam's journey, I'm going to miss work tomorrow, and then my wife will be far from Right Mind and Right Conduct.

The Adventures of Adam Freeman, DDS
July 5—No cable service. Check your internet connection.

Although I missed Independence Day with my family—along with the sparklers that I do with my kids every year—I found solace last night in the solitude of peaceful meditation. I was beginning to sense not only calm but also euphoria coming over me—an unusual combination of emotions. It was amazing. My mind was finally beginning to let go of everything, and I understood my role in the world. It was up to me to maintain as clear a mind as I could, uninhibited and undistracted by life. No kids screaming, no cell phones, no radio, no dental drills, and, most importantly, *no cable.*

All the background noise of life is just that—distractions that keep me away from the real truths and meaning of life. I cannot put this blissfully serene feeling into words. Being human with a limited capacity for language, I can only say it is beautiful and incredible times infinity.

I can't pinpoint the source of my happiness, but I know it's something universal that I have tapped into. Bottom line: if I can do this, anyone can; you need to let go and view yourself from afar. By stepping outside of myself, I was able to let go of my fears and anxieties. I had faith and trust in this process, beyond my understanding, which enabled and empowered me to become a vehicle for something greater. Last night, I had one of the best nights of sleep ever. This morning's light breakfast was amazingly filling. I feel full of boundless energy and fresh new purpose. I'm enjoying life—*my life*—which is saying a lot considering where I was only a few days ago. I feel transformed into the person I am meant to be.

During my afternoon chores, I am instructed to clean the white pebbles that surround the garden's glistening roses. I'm hard pressed to find even a speck of dirt on these rocks, suggesting they are cleaned frequently, perhaps even daily. I get down on my knees and, with the small brush and bucket of soapy water I've been given, apply the same skills that I use for cleaning teeth to the pebbles' round edges. Unlike the stresses I feel at my office, which cause my eye to twitch uncontrollably, the tension of this work feels healthy, and though I am laboring in the garden, I feel light and free. My mind doesn't dwell on the heat or the drudgery, it's simply blank. This allows me to enjoy the moment, and the usual set of worries that plagues me has been left behind.

July 6—*Breaking Bad*

I wake up this morning feeling lighthearted and refreshed. I decide to go for a walk before breakfast. As I stroll through the grounds in my Buddhist robe and bare feet, I suddenly realize that this is the closest I've ever felt to peacefulness. Have I reached nirvana?

I come across the same oak tree where I discovered the *pen of enlightenment*. This beautiful tree seems to be inviting me to nestle into its base like a comfortable chair. I sit down and lean back against the trunk. I feel one with the kaleidoscope of nature. The soles of my feet are invigorated by the touch of wet morning dew from the grass. The crisp air sharpens my sense of smell, and the vivid green and brown of the forest are accentuated by the clear, blue sky. Joy is flowing through my body, but instead of shouting it out to the world, which would violate my vow of silence, I take out my pen and paper to capture my feelings on the remaining space on the Protocol of the Retreat Sheet. I am writing as fast as I can, and I can't wait to share this—the intensity, the revelations, this miracle—with Minnie, with Klein, with the rest of the Four Horsemen. I want them to know what I'm feeling so they can feel it too.

Peace and tranquility flood through me as I continue to write. Suddenly a shadow falls over me. I tilt my head up and there, looming over me, is Venerable Panna.

He says nothing. He stares at my hand, which has stopped writing.

My heart sinks. Hank has caught Walt in *Breaking Bad*. I've been busted. I never thought it would come to this.

Finally, Panna speaks. "Pen and paper please." I feel like a little kid getting caught shoplifting. I sheepishly look at him and hesitantly hand them over. "Adam, on your first day here you took a vow of complete silence, which means verbally and with the written hand. You break this vow with every pen stroke."

I speak in a faltering whisper, "I had no bad intentions. I felt such happiness that I needed to document what I was experiencing so I wouldn't forget it. Please, don't be angry with me."

Panna sits down next to me and puts his hand on my back. "I'm not angry. I understand your motivation, and I don't judge it. But you did not abide by the rules and policies of the retreat, and your violation of those rules has consequences. I will speak with Venerable Rinsho. Please meet us in his office after breakfast."

"But—"

He lifts up his hand and places a finger to his lips. "Remember, you are still on this retreat and subject to its rules until dismissed. That means maintaining your vow of silence."

Until dismissed. Those words echo through my mind, bouncing wildly around now that it is clear of all the crap I'd been keeping in there.

Even though I'm starving, I barely touch my breakfast. I sit in the dining hall and stare at my food, feeling the joy ebb from my body. Moments ago, under the tree, I felt content, and now I'm a nervous, anxious mess—a middle school boy sent to the principal's office waiting for my detention. To settle my mind down, I try to convince myself this is no big deal. I mean, how serious can it be. I'm not a drug kingpin like Gus Fring on *Breaking Bad.* Maybe they'll give me a slap on the wrist. If this were a Christian church, I could probably say a few Hail Marys and be back in action. In my Jewish temple, I would atone while I fast on Yom Kippur, to cleanse myself. What do they do in Buddhism? Maybe they'll put me in solitary meditation for a day? Anyway, they like to live in the moment and forget the past, so I'll probably get off easy.

I finish my breakfast and walk up to the opened office door. Venerable Rinsho greets me. Venerable Panna is seated in one of the guest chairs, and he offers me the other. Venerable Rinsho begins, "Adam, we are all impressed by how much you have grown during your stay here. You're clearly more at peace with yourself, and I can see in your eyes how much you have connected with the teachings of the Buddha."

I smile. This is going even better than I thought. "Yes, I have. It hasn't been easy, but I can honestly say it's been an enlightening journey. I'm looking forward to continuing and completing my education."

He continues. "Venerable Panna filled me in on what transpired this morning. We made a contract with you that you'd maintain your silence. By taking notes, using this pen and paper, you violated that contract. Here at the monastery we take such obligations and commitments very seriously. Our work depends on them. Disobeying the rules is a serious and punishable infraction, so unfortunately we must ask you to leave."

All I can say as the air leaves my chest is, "Are you serious?"

"Yes, Adam. You have made great strides, but your lapse of judgment cannot be ignored. It is, for this retreat, the final lesson you will learn."

"But all I did was record my experiences here. I wasn't communicating with anyone. I've been, as you said, an excellent student, and I've done nothing else wrong. Can't you find it in your hearts to forgive me?"

Venerable Rinsho replies, "Our decision is not about compassion, which we both do feel for you. One of the most important truths that we are teaching you here is to let go of the past and live only in the moment. You understand, eh? By documenting your time here, you became a prisoner to your mind. You were experiencing the pleasure of sharing your notes with family and friends after your departure instead of experiencing your moments of joy fully in the present."

Venerable Panna offers me a flat smile and a barely perceptible wink. Both men stand. Venerable Rinsho folds his arms, and Venerable Panna ushers me out the door while handing me my cell phone. "Thank you, Adam Freeman, for entrusting us with your healing. We're sorry to see you leave, and we give you many blessings."

Not so sorry that you'll let me stay, I think to myself as I head back to my room. I quietly pack my belongings, turn on my phone, and ignore the twenty-three text messages and seven voicemails. I immediately text Klein, Errol, and Ryan to see who can come to pick me up. Errol responds first.

As I wait for my ride, the rest of the members of the retreat walk by me. I want to run up and tell them the truth about what happened, to dispel any rumors that may have been circulating. But then I remember they can't speak, so there shouldn't be any rumors. I guess that's one advantage of the vow of silence. Who cares anyway if they think I'm not there because I quit or that I got kicked out for some egregious action. I'll most likely never see any of them again.

I sit at the entrance to the monastery with my knees folded towards my chin waiting for my lift, and I see Venerable Rinsho ambling towards me. For a moment, I allow myself to hope he's changed his mind. As Errol's car pulls up, Venerable Rinsho sidles up next to me and places a folded piece of paper in my hand. I take it, and he bows to me. Out of respect for him, I bow back. As I put my bag into the car trunk he smiles and whispers in my ear, "Share this with the world, my JuBu friend." I unfold the piece of paper and see that it is all the notes I wrote during my visit. I smile. That sneaky Canadian monk read my diary, and I think he liked it!

CHAPTER SEVENTEEN
5:38 a.m.

Adam didn't finish the retreat—I kicked him out of the monastery halfway through. He appears to have grown tremendously in the five days he was there. But he didn't get the full ten-day experience—like stopping an antibiotic before you take the full course—and I'm hoping that the lessons of Buddhism stick with him. I don't want him obsessing on the past. I don't want him to be that judgmental, controlling, selfish, pre-monastery person. Most importantly, I want him to grow up. I know that the Buddhist teachings have made a big impact in my life, and I'm optimistic they can also help Adam, whom I've decided to keep alive... Unless he makes me look like a fool again.

The Adventures of Adam Freeman, DDS
July 6—House of Cards

Errol gets out, we embrace like long-lost brothers, and I suddenly start sobbing in his arms like a newborn baby. Reading the situation perfectly, he lets me cry it out. I don't know how long we man hug—it could have lasted thirty minutes if it lasted five. To break the awkward silence after we release, I say, "Nice beard."

"Yeah, I've been growing it out. So a Buddhist monastery, huh? What's the deal with that?" We get in the car and drive off.

"Long story," I respond. While driving through the winding roads of Connecticut I review the retreat with Errol.

"That sounds intense. I can't believe those fuckers kicked you out. I mean, aren't monks supposed to be about preaching tolerance and forgiveness? To nail you for writing down some thoughts, that's crazy."

"It's okay Errol. I broke the rules. I need to live with the consequences."

"That's such bullshit. Rules are meant to be challenged. I can't believe you're not pissed about this."

I look at Errol and see the anger in his eyes. His ears are burning red. "These are the same people who taught me to treat people with love and kindness. And kicking me out was their final lesson. I would have learned nothing in the retreat if I had reacted with anger and hostility. Instead, I can get in touch with my sadness and disappointment, feel it, and let it all go. This is a great way for me to incorporate the Eightfold Path in my thinking. Lead my life according to the Four Noble truths. You should try it."

"You're not going to convert me. And what the hell's the Eightfold Path?" asks Errol.

"It's like the Ten Commandments in the Bible or Jesus's Covenants in Christianity," I respond.

"Whatever. Same stuff. Different names."

"Errol—I connected with their teachings. I'm taking away what I found valuable to my soul. I'd like for you to respect that."

"Yeah, sure." Errol pats me on the shoulder. "It's great to have you back, buddy. Are you officially done with your nervous breakdown?"

I burst into laughter and tear up again, but this time from humor—a feeling I haven't enjoyed in a long, long time. Errol smiles and turns on his left blinker. "Mind if I stop at home for a minute?" he asks me.

"No problem, but I'd like to see Minnie and the kids soon."

Errol seems deep in thought. "This won't take long."

We pull up to his gated house adjacent to the beach. He loops around the circular driveway and parks in front of the guesthouse, which sits in front of the monstrosity of his McMansion. Errol calls this place his West Wing. The Four Horsemen have had some good times here, from poker nights to Super Bowl parties.

I follow him into the house-sized cottage. *That's strange*, I think to myself. The West Wing is usually empty, but there are dishes in the sink and a laptop on the kitchen counter. There's also a fresh coat of white paint on the walls (I can smell it) and some new IKEA furniture half-assembled in the corner. "Is someone staying here?"

Errol looks at me sheepishly. "I won't bullshit you. Kristy and I have been having some trouble lately, so I'm sleeping here while we sort things out."

"Are you serious? We had dinner with you guys a month ago, and everything seemed great."

"Yeah, we put up a good front."

"I can't believe it."

"You're not the only one. But we've been having issues for a while."

"What's going on?"

Errol leaves the main room and comes back with his briefcase. "I can't believe I forgot this. My mind's been scattered lately. They teach you to focus at that monastery of yours?"

"They sure did, and your fly's unzipped."

Errol zips up, and I follow him out to the car. I sit shotgun, fidgeting in silence, waiting for Errol to reveal how his marriage went off course. After he pulls out into the street, he finally addresses me. "I think I told you, we've been hanging out a lot with another couple lately."

"Doug and Sue, right?"

Errol nods. "We'd go out to dinner and alternate going back to each other's houses for a nightcap. It was a lot of fun—"

I interrupt him. "What—did you guys become swingers or something?"

"It wasn't like that. Kristy and I were having a good time with them. We'd chill out in our Jacuzzi, play board games, go dancing—it was harmless."

"What went wrong?"

"You know how you have those breakaway conversations with the other husband or wife on a couple date? Well, Sue and I were having more and more breakaway conversations. We had a...connection."

"A connection?"

"Yeah, and each time we met, it got more intense between us. One night after drinking too much...one thing led to another..."

As Minnie often tells me, I have no shame, so I ask, "What exactly did one thing lead to?"

Errol stops at a light. "Let me put it in a way you can understand. I finished the first season of *House of Cards* last night while crashing in the West Wing. I was Frank Underwood and she was my Zoe Barnes."

"Good one. So you slept with her."

Errol doesn't like to kiss and tell, but his smile gives it away. Then he confirms. "Kristy has a zero-tolerance policy for banging other chicks."

"Yeah, most women aren't as liberal as Claire Underwood and wouldn't tolerate your cheating. She kicked you out?"

"Yeah. I've been impeached." Errol leans in towards me. "The crazy thing is, man, it was a fucking rush when I was with Sue. To have someone love you for who you are, no strings attached?" He continues, shaking his head. "Being with her was so raw, so animalistic. Our attraction was like two planet-sized magnets. I felt like I was on ecstasy when I was with her."

"But what about your kids? For Christ's sake, you have a baby at home."

"I know," he says, hanging his head. He looks up in time to see a red light and slams on the breaks. He takes a gulp from his coffee mug. When the light turns green, he remains in the intersection.

"Errol," I say, "green light." He looks up and hits the gas.

"We lost our passion, man. We were going through the motions. What was I supposed to do? Turn down an amazing experience with this incredibly hot chick?"

"Yes," I say, "you were supposed to turn it down."

"Trust me, turning Sue down was not an option. I could either stay trapped in a life less lived or embrace a different, uh, more fulfilling path."

"I think what you mean is embrace a different body. Errol, are you really going to throw your family away for tits and ass."

"*Perfect* tits and ass."

"I assume you're still seeing Sue, then?"

"No. Once Kristy saw how close we were getting, she and Doug started getting closer, and that was getting super weird. Anyway, I cut off couples' night. We stopped seeing them."

Trying to practice my new Buddhist philosophy with my old friend is proving to be quite challenging. "Wait a minute, you're telling me that it was fine for you to get intimate with another woman, but when you saw Kristy getting close to a guy, you freaked? That's pretty hypocritical of you, Errol." He shrugs, so I ask him, "Where does that leave you and Kristy now?"

"I don't know. She and I were doing well after we stopped hanging with Doug and Sue and after a *lot* of therapy. But now Kristy's feeling insecure again because Sue started calling me. I mean, we only spoke a few harmless times, but Kristy saw Sue's number on my phone, and she went apeshit. That's when she kicked me out."

I try not to judge him. It takes every ounce of my energy to erase these thoughts. I remember early last month when Minnie and I were lying in bed with the kids. We were under the covers and reading them a book. Rose was snuggling with me and put her freezing feet on my warm ones, then started laughing. Paige put her cold hand on Minnie's face. Without warning, Spencer jumped into bed, and we all began cracking up. For me, it doesn't get any more perfect than that.

I try with all my mental might to ignore the thoughts of how stupid Errol was to risk those precious, intimate moments with his wife and children for sex with another woman for an adrenaline rush. I know I couldn't do that to my family—or myself. I channel my inner JuBu and say, "Errol, whatever you need. I'm here for you."

He pulls up in front of my house and says, "It's great to have you back, buddy! Now get back to your family—and don't fuck it up!"

* * *

Adam, I'm proud of you! Your sojourn in the Buddhist monastery is making a difference in your thinking. You started to judge Errol, you caught yourself, and you were there for him without reservation. I have to say, I felt the same way you did when Errol confessed his infidelity, but I loved how you caught yourself with your hand raised and decided not to throw the stone.

Now that you are bursting out of your turtle shell, I'm really hoping you can sustain the change when you get home to Minnie. You've got a tough road ahead of you.

The Adventures of Adam Freeman, DDS
July 6—*The Facts of Life*

I've come through my red front door thousands of times, but I'm desperately nervous as I approach my house because none of those entrances came with the backstory I have now. As I enter, the kids come running over and jump on top of me. I wrap Paige in a hug and start tickling Rose and Spencer. They knock me over, and I lie on the floor with them, oblivious to the uncomfortable hard wood on my back. I don't want this moment to stop. I swallow a few times to shove down the frog in my throat, and after a minute the girls and Spencer get up and disperse. Minnie approaches. There are tears in her eyes. I pull her close, and we rock slowly and softly, side to side, like slow-dancing teens at a middle school mixer. We finally break and move over to the kitchen, and I sit down at the island as Minnie pours me her world-famous lemonade. I'm dying to know what Klein told her about where I went and to tell her about my transformation.

"I missed you, Adam. We all missed you. How are you feeling?"

I can't stand the suspense, and I don't want to deceive my wife, so I blurt out, "Minnie, I want to come clean, I wasn't—"

"I know where you were."

"You do?" I let out a long breath. How the hell did Klein tell her without making her mad?

"Of course. Klein told Joy where he dropped you off, and even though he swore her to secrecy, she gave me the goods on you."

"That jerk! He broke the bro code." I shake my head, then stop myself. "Wait, that was the old Adam Freeman talking. You know I would have told you."

"I know. Did it help you?"

"Minnie, it was surreal. It helped me put everything I've been going through in perspective. I learned the facts of life from a Buddhist point of view." I look around at my familiar surroundings: the plates and glasses we picked out together stacked neatly in their glass-doored cabinets, the tiles Minnie made me splurge on for the backsplash, our kids' artwork on the fridge. "God, it's good to be home."

"It's good to have you home, Adam. Being without you has been hard on the kids. And me. I don't want you to have to leave again. Do you think this change will really take—without therapy and meds?"

I'm furious, no—*disappointed*—that she doubts me, but I also can't blame her. I wish, like Dumbledore in the Harry Potter books, which I am reading now with Rose, that I could take a magic wand and say "Obliviate" to erase her memory of the things I'm ashamed of. Then I'd cast a new spell, "Intimate" to recreate the passion and intense connection we once felt towards each other. I want to rekindle those flames and, in my heart, I know it is possible because when we both look into each other's eyes there is fire. I love this woman, and I'm lucky that she loves me. The fear of losing her is real, though, so I'll have to work my ass off. Suddenly, relief sweeps over me. I know I'm healthy because I feel that fear, because I'm living with it in the moment, because I'm finally not numb anymore.

"Yes, Minnie. Yes, I can do this. I will do this. For you. For us. For our family."

"From your mouth to God's ears. Or Buddha's, if that's who you're praying to now."

"You don't exactly pray to Buddha." She gives me a look that says don't push it. I backpedal. "But that's beside the point. Hey are you hungry? I'm starving." I get myself a V8 from the fridge, grab the cutting board, and start slicing apples and bananas to make us a fruit salad, something I often do on weekends. "Would you like pineapple in the salad too?"

Minnie nods but doesn't make eye contact. She picks at her cuticles and bites her lip. I grab the pineapple and start chopping. I look at her to gauge where she is, to see whether she feels the change the way I do or is worried I'll blow it again. I need her full confidence and support. I need my wife to believe in me. But her head is down, and I can't see her eyes.

"Honey?" I ask, tilting my head to get a glimpse of her expression. Suddenly the knife slashes my index finger. The yellow pineapple slices are dripping with red. I instinctively stick my finger into my mouth and suck the blood. "Damn!"

"Adam, are you okay?" Minnie looks up and sees me sucking. "Run it under water. I'll get the first aid kit. Let's hope you don't need stitches."

Minnie moves swiftly to a cabinet and grabs Bacitracin and Band-Aids. She washes her hands, rubs in the ointment, and bandages my finger. She gets BooBoo Bunny—the ice pack for kids' injuries—and applies it to my bandaged cut. We smile, knowing our inside joke that I am a baby when it comes to getting hurt. Minnie diagnoses the cut as a flesh wound, so no hospital visit.

Minnie walks me into the living room, and we sit down next to each other on the couch. "Adam, we both made a commitment to each other when we got married. In sickness and in health. I'm still getting over the things that have happened, and I'm...skeptical of your spiritual transformation, but we're in this together. I believe you can do this. And I'll give it—give us—a chance."

I am overcome with joy. I think of Errol, sleeping in the West Wing, and I am grateful that I'll be getting a good night's sleep in our marital bed. Through my tears of happiness, I reply, "I know I can give more of myself to this family. I can, and I will. I promise."

"Adam, if you put half the time and energy into our marriage that you put into your 'spiritual journey'"—she uses air quotes—"we would be okay. We'd be more than okay. If we're the most important people in your life, you need to make us feel that way. You need to make it real."

"I'm committed to making you and the kids my first priority and to changing my mindset so that I consistently express the love and joy I feel in my heart for this family."

"That's all I ask," she says. "That you make those words more than words." She leans into me and, much to my surprise, plants a passionate kiss on my lips as we fall back on the couch together. I think I have found my heaven on earth.

She gets up, goes into the kitchen, and comes back with a piece of notepaper. "Are you up for a few household chores?"

I force a smile. "You bet," I say. "Bring it on."

CHAPTER EIGHTEEN
6:01 a.m.

I want Adam to make it. And I think he can. Adam, my man, you are finally seeing the light. It's like watching your child take his first steps. I mean, it's kind of pathetic that you're still taking baby steps after more than half a book, but that's kind of what makes you lovable. At least, I hope so. You're on the brink—almost there. I'm hoping Maggie won't be able to delete you after this rewrite.

The Adventures of Adam Freeman, DDS
July 7—*The Brady Bunch*

For my welcome-home dinner, we order in from my favorite Chinese restaurant. I have no signs of anxiety sitting with the kids and Minnie playing our family games, like Number Buzz and Guess What I'm Thinking. Even though it's fattening as hell, I treat myself to General Tso's chicken as well as shrimp with lobster sauce, egg rolls, and steamed pork dumplings. Minnie comments that my order is very un-Buddhist, but after the dreadful food in the monastery, I can't help myself. The Chinese-food-loving Jew in my JuBu is in charge tonight.

"I never asked you how the food was," Minnie says.

"Two meals a day, breakfast and lunch. By evening, I was starving, and we couldn't eat after midday. I could've eaten cardboard, and it would have tasted like lobster." The kids laugh at my lame joke. I've missed the silly sense of humor we share.

"Speaking of lobster, tomorrow I am going to make that seafood gumbo you love from my *Cookin' Caribbean* cookbook," Minnie announces.

"Oh, that sounds scrumptious," I say, my mouth full of General Tso's chicken. I put down my chopsticks and sink deeply into my kitchen chair. I am such an asshole. I don't deserve my amazing wife. After a slow sip of my water, I clear my throat and deliver the news, "Um, speaking of the Caribbean, the trip to Puerto Rico with the Four Horsemen is this weekend, but I'm not going, Minnie. There's no way after all that time away I can justify leaving the family again."

* * *

I get up again to stretch. The morning sun is filtering through the window. I decide to go outside for a break, and I see that weeds have begun to grow in our front garden. I go back inside, get my iTouch and headphones, and put on my Rockin' Weedin' Mix. I don my gardening gloves—don't want to get poison ivy; like Adam, I'm highly allergic—and start picking the weeds out from among the blooming lilies, purple coneflowers, and blue hydrangea that line the beds.

Weeding a garden is like taking care of your mind. You have to remove the negative and poisonous thoughts that can creep in while you're not looking. I know it sounds new agey, but being mindful about the thoughts I allow to take up space in my head has been vital to my newfound peacefulness.

As I make a conscious effort to pull the weeds up by their roots, I ponder Adam's journey. If I can get Maggie to read my rewrite, I think she might come to appreciate this Jewish dentist's journey into an enlightened, Buddhist mensch. Well, he's not quite a mensch yet, but he has some chapters left.

I yank up a particularly nasty weed and ponder a question that Maggie's concern raises. If Adam isn't likable, and he's my alter ego, maybe a part of *me* isn't likable. Like Adam, I wanted to change the melancholy feeling that burdened my psyche. And like Adam, I didn't want to be sad and anxious. I wanted to feel love, hope, and forgiveness. I craved peace. I wanted what Adam was searching for, and I thought those desires made me selfish. But seeking happiness isn't selfish, as long as it's not at the expense of others. In fact, if you have a family, wanting to be happy and at peace means you want to be a better person around and *for* them—and that's not selfish at all.

I sit down in our garden and look around at the beauty Leah and I created together. Moments like these are priceless, and I enjoy immersing myself in the splendor of the flowers, plants, and trees. Sunbeams fall on the green grass, and it reminds me how the fresh outdoors rejuvenates me. I wish that Adam hadn't rejected going on the trip to Puerto Rico so quickly. Maybe he'd benefit from some fun in the sun. It's an opportunity for Adam to employ the mindfulness that he learned in the monastery to everyday life with his buddies.

I'm back in my office, fingers ready. I know Adam is on his way to the same blissful place I inhabit, but first, he's got a flight to catch.

The Adventures of Adam Freeman, DDS
July 7—*Freaks and Geeks*

"Oh, that sounds scrumptious," I say, my mouth full of General Tso's chicken. I put down my chopsticks and sink deeply in my kitchen chair. I am such an asshole. I don't deserve my amazing wife. After a slow sip of my water, I clear my throat and deliver the news, "Um, speaking of the Caribbean, the trip to Puerto Rico with the Horsemen is..." I wince, bracing myself for Minnie's reaction.

"This weekend." She finishes my sentence. "Adam, I've had your trip on the calendar for months. I was wondering if you'd cancel it, but..."—she holds back a swell of emotion—"...it's okay. I understand if you need to go. It's something you look forward to all year, and I wouldn't ask you to sacrifice your time with your friends. I know how important they are to you."

I am flabbergasted. I thought she would rip me a new one. I'm so moved by her tolerance that I suggest staying home. I know the guys would understand. "No, Minnie, I can't go after leaving you and the kids for so long. That's not fair. I'll go with those freaks and geeks another time."

"It's not about fairness, Adam. And I would rather have you here. But you should go. The monastery was hardly a vacation, and you need a little time off before you go back to work. You'll regret it if you don't go and resent me if I make you stay."

"Are you sure, Minnie?"

"Yes. You're going. The Four Horsemen need one last hurrah, and we start the clock on the new Adam the day you get back."

"Oh my God," I exclaim, "you're totally the best wife in the world!"

"I should hope so," she says, feathering her long, dark hair and giving me a sexy smile. "And besides, Errol needs your support now with all that he's going through."

"You know about that, too?"

"Of course, Adam. The great and powerful Minnie is omniscient!"

"How in the world—"

Before Minnie can answer, Rose interjects, "Let's play another game, Daddy. I am thinking of something."

"Is it a person?" asks Paige.

"Yes," answers Rose.

"Is it Daddy?" asks Paige.

"Yes," Rose smiles gleefully.

"You two must be sisters, you totally think alike," says Minnie, and we all break into peals of laughter.

It's good to be home.

July 8—*24*

Ryan and Klein ring the doorbell, and I ask them to hang on. This time, I only need a few minutes with my family. My bon voyage isn't the tear jerker it was last time, and I know I'll be back soon—rejuvenated after a week in the sun with my boys.

It's great to see my smiling friends again. Every summer after college, the four of us embarked on our "brodeo." (I can't take credit for that moniker; we stole it from *How I Met Your Mother*.) We've had some memorable brodeos in the past. Like a season of *24*, you never know where a brodeo can take you. There was the "Flipping Over the Speed Boat," incident of '92, the "Naked Half-Mile Crawl" of '97, and the "Mile High Club" of '99. Thank God these guys have mellowed over the years.

You never know what adventures are in store... Puerto Rico brodeo, here we come!

With busy schedules and our kids in the mix, the brodeo has become like the summer Olympics: our committee of wives sets a different venue every four years. Honestly, the quadrennial meeting is fine with me because every time I come back from a brodeo, I need a real vacation. But at Minnie's urging, here I am, embarking on another adventure.

We're piling into Errol's Porsche 911, and Klein calls shotgun. "Really," I say, "how the hell am I going to sit in that back seat?" Klein crams himself into the back with Ryan. Ryan's knees are up to his chin. I laugh. "You guys look like you're in a clown car."

"Jealous of my ride?"

"No, Errol. I'm not a sports-car kind of guy. I can barely fit in these things. And it's a good thing I travel light," I say, stuffing my small travel bag into the already full trunk, which is where the car's hood should be.

Ryan interrupts, "Hey, dude, I'm glad that you're doing better. I hear you're a Buddhist now."

I laugh. "Sort of, I'm calling myself a Jewish Buddhist."

"A JuBu!" Klein exclaims.

"Is that a thing?" asks Errol.

"Yeah it's a thing," says Klein. "Haven't you read *The Jew in the Lotus*?

"No, but I heard a joke about a Jew and Lexus," laughs Errol.

"Not funny," Klein and I say simultaneously.

Ryan continues, "I've always wondered. What the hell do they wear under those robes? Boxers or tighty-whities?"

"We free ball it, man!" The guys all laugh again. Ryan turns serious, leaning forward and putting his hand on my shoulder, he says, "Man, you look good. I admire how you handled your crisis."

Errol interrupts him, "Hey, you two. Cut out the sentimental bullshit, this is Brodeo Twelve not *Brokeback Mountain*. If you want to make out, go get a room!"

Klein interjects, "Errol, don't be such a meathead. It's good to have Adam back."

Errol snickers. "I'm dying to know how much Jew and how much Bu there is in the new and improved Adam Freeman."

After we arrive at LaGuardia and snake through the maze of security, Klein and I sit next to each other while waiting to board. He leans over. "Hey man, how did Minnie handle the whole monastery thing? Did my leaking it to Joy so she would leak it to Minnie have the desired effect?"

"It was brilliant. You're a master manipulator."

"I figured if I told Minnie, she'd give me the third degree, but if she got the secret from Joy, it would feel like a win for her and, uh, temper her..."

"She wasn't upset. More pleased to be a step ahead of me. Didn't dump on me—or you—at all. Speaking of dumps, I have to take one."

"Go for it. Using the bathrooms on the plane sucks."

"I'll be back." I get up and walk towards the bathroom.

I sit down on the toilet and text Minnie that we've arrived at the airport safely. Suddenly, I notice some graffiti scrawled on the partition: "4 Best Hummer Ever call (555) 229-5014." I wonder what the story was behind this vandalism. I reach for my pocket journal to copy the message, but I've left it and my pen back at my seat. So I take a picture on my phone. No, it isn't for a future BJ. One of these years, I'm going to write a book documenting graffiti throughout the U.S. I've always wondered, does NYC graffiti differ from Midwestern graffiti in Iowa? Minnesota? It will by my contribution to social science.

July 8—*Shameless*

Errol, being Errol, has booked us in first class. He insists on traveling in style, and he's used a bunch of credit card points to reduce the cost of the tickets. Even though it ended up only a couple hundred more than coach, I was against the idea because it felt like wasting money. When I complained to Errol, he accused me of being "a cheap bastard" and wrote me a check to cover the difference. "I'm a frugal bastard, not a cheap bastard," I told him, and I ripped up his check.

As I sink down into the comfort of the jumbo-sized seats, I smile at Errol and give him a thumbs-up. I hate to admit it, but he was right: traveling in first class is a whole new world. The Buddhist in me is pushed aside by the Jew enjoying the discount deal on the extra leg room, free liquor, and instant service from the flight attendants—not to mention the great selection of reading material. I push my seat back and dive into my *New York Post* Sports section to get my fix of Yankees, Giants, Knicks, and Islanders.

Errol is finding life in first class even more enjoyable. He comes to the rescue of a busty blonde having trouble putting her carry-on in the overhead compartment. She sits in front of us, and Errol instantly starts flirting. She's part of a rambunctious group of women on a bachelorette party. Dr. Suave is on his game. The attractive blonde's laughing at his lame jokes. A few minutes later, Errol excuses himself to go to the bathroom.

The drinks are flowing fast enough to make Frank Gallagher from *Shameless* proud, and the airline is definitely losing money on the unlimited booze. We're all feeling loose and carefree. After my third gin and tonic, I need to take a piss, and I stumble down the aisle. When I return, Errol is seated next to the blonde. They have a blanket over them, and the woman's hands are nowhere to be seen. Errol has a look of ecstasy on his face.

I sway back to my seat, and a few minutes later when Errol plops down across the aisle, grinning widely, I shake my head at him, trying to pop his bubble. "You're still married, Errol."

"Barely," he says, his words starting to slur. "Don' judge me, Adam. You don' know the whole story. Kristy and I are working things out, an' we *both* agreed that this week we're allowed to be completely, uh, free. We are coming back nex' week with a fresh star'."

"Man, you're shitfaced. You got a free pass? I thought that only happened on TV and in the movies. People really do that?"

Errol smiles. "Iss called an open marriage. And dude, truth is stranger than fiction. If anyone should know that, it's you."

The inside of the plane is spinning. I close my eyes and prepare to pass out, deciding to forget what I saw. It won't do anyone any good for me to reveal it.

CHAPTER NINETEEN
6:52 a.m.

As moralistic as I can get, I have to give Adam credit for distancing himself from Errol's foibles and not taking on the burden of guilt by association, a stance he wouldn't have adopted in June. Adam's growing—kudos to my aspiring JuBu!

And now I get to travel back to beautiful San Juan. What a great city. I have an affinity for its old-school charm—the cobblestone streets mixed with the historical forts built by the Spaniards in the late 1700s. I love the combination of the island's natural beauty—from the rainforests to the gorgeous beaches—with the adventure you can find kayaking, snorkeling, and swimming.

Leah and I went for her fortieth birthday with the kids last year. It was peaceful and calm—and it helped rejuvenate our marriage. I hope it puts Adam in a better place too!

The Adventures of Adam Freeman, DDS
July 9—I Love Lucy

Last night, we checked in and slept off our first-class hangover. Now, we're ready to begin the day. The property at the Wyndham Grand Rio Mar Beach Resort is immense. Seeing all the cool activities for kids, the water slides and pools, makes me yearn for my family. I reach deep inside for my inner Bu and make a vow to live in the moment and enjoy this trip for what it is—reconnecting with my good friends and reinvigorating myself.

Klein and I are roomies, and after we unpack, Errol and Ryan come in from their adjoining room. "I'm going for a massage," Errol says. "Who's in?"

"I'll go! I'll go!" squeals Klein.

Ryan takes out his bathing suit. "I'm going to sit poolside and enjoy the view."

I'm not much of a massage kind of guy. I don't like any woman touching me other than my wife. "I'll join you, Ryan, but I'm bringing some reading." I grab my towel and *The Celestine Prophecy.*"

Ryan and I plop down in the cushioned blue lounge chairs adjacent to the long pool. He's brandishing a copy of *Guns and Ammo* magazine, and I've got my book. He hands me his sunscreen.

"Thanks. I always forget when I'm not with Minnie how easily I turn red." I begin to lotion up.

"Don't talk to me about sunburn. My Irish skin burns like kindling."

I laugh and then there is silence.

I can talk spirituality with Klein all day long, and although Errol will argue with us, he keeps things lighthearted as he shares his agnostic views. But Ryan is a born-again Christian. Our conversations get twisted, or don't happen at all, because I become nervous talking about religion and spirituality with him. It's like maneuvering through a minefield, he's so dogmatic. One of the many pamphlets I saw in his church when I attended his wedding read: "Those who do not bear witness to the words of God and accept Jesus into their lives will not be saved by God when Armageddon comes to Earth." When I asked him what it meant, he said, "If one doesn't believe in the Lord Savior Jesus Christ, then they're surely going to Hell."

"You do know I'm Jewish, right?" I asked him.

"Yeah, I know," he replied. I looked amused, thinking he was joking, but he didn't smile back. That was my rude awakening to his rigid religious beliefs.

Underneath the clear blue sky and tropical palm trees of Puerto Rico, I'm feeling peaceful. I finish rubbing the last of Ryan's oily white sunscreen into my face, hand it back to him, and decide to risk it. I say, "Ry, after my Buddhist visit, I feel more tranquil and at peace. I'm such a big fan of meditation now. Have you ever tried it?"

He turns from his *Guns and Ammo*. "No. Look at this," and like a kid looking at a Playboy centerfold he thrusts a photograph in front of me. But instead of a beautiful naked woman, I'm staring at a picture of a gun. "This Glock is badass."

I continue, "You should take a class with Klein and me. Being at the monastery really taught me how much the body can be healed by the mind. I believe we all have a connection to—"

He interrupts me, "Your face is all white, Adam. Rub that shit in more."

I take out my phone and reverse the camera to see that I look like a mime. I snap a selfie to send to Minnie, then begin rubbing my face again. Ryan waves a server over and orders two Bud Lights.

I know it will start a fight, but I ask him anyway. "Do you really still believe that anyone who doesn't believe in Jesus Christ as their Lord and Savior is headed for hell?"

Ryan is quiet. We turn our heads simultaneously to stare at two tanned, twenty-something girls with hard bodies in string bikinis. We shake our heads as if to say, *those were the days*, and give each other shit-eating grins. Then Ryan's face darkens. "Of course, I still believe in the doctrines of my church."

There goes my peaceful feeling, and since I'm past the point of no return, I question him further. "God only saves those who believe in Jesus?"

"Like it reads in the Bible."

"It also says God created Eve from Adam's rib."

"Well, some of it you take literally, and some of it you look for deeper meaning."

"The deeper meaning of God only saving Jesus lovers is that Jews like me are going to hell."

"You can always choose to accept Jesus. He died for all of us."

The woman lying on the chair next to us turns her head to look at Ryan. She's mid-to-late thirties with short blonde hair, like the rocker Pink and is wearing a black and white polka dot bikini over a long, well-toned body. She's holding a large book in her hands, but I can see she's eavesdropping on us instead of reading. Ryan doesn't notice her.

"I can't accept someone I don't believe in," I say. The server brings over our Bud Lights and, as is our tradition, we cheer to the Four Horsemen. I make eye contact with the blonde woman, but she quickly covers her face with her book. I notice that it is *The Tibetan Book of Culture*.

Ryan looks at me in horror. "You don't believe in God?"

"Of course I do, Ry, but I believe in a loving and peaceful God. Not one that chooses certain people to go to heaven and rejects others. And I don't believe that Jesus was both God and his son. How could that be possible?"

"You think the Bible's made up, then?"

"I don't believe in a book that is exclusionary and condemns people to eternal damnation."

"This book you are talking about is the Word of God—the bestselling book in the world. How can you reject that? What the hell beef do you have with religion anyway?"

"I don't have any beef with any religion, as long as it comes from a place of love and joy. Isn't Christianity about spreading God's message of love, forgiveness, and oneness?"

Ryan interjects, "Our God is merciful. 'For I know the plans I have for you,' declares the *Lord*, 'plans to prosper you and not to harm you, plans to give you hope and a future.' Jeremiah 29:11."

I protest, "But your church talks about an exclusionary God that doesn't tolerate nonbelievers. Would our Creator really exclude one group over another?"

"It's not complicated," Ryan tells me. "Everything you need to do for salvation is laid out in the Good Book."

The blonde in the bikini puts down her book and turns sideways to address Ryan. "Your friend's right. When religion starts using God's name for the sake of causing harm to those who don't share the same belief systems, it's not religion anymore. It's a way to hold power. That's when humanity gets into major trouble."

Ryan turns his head towards her. "I'm sorry—I don't remember asking you your opinion."

"Ryan," I admonish him, "I'm sure you can respect other people's views."

The woman takes a drink of her giant strawberry daiquiri. "I apologize. I don't mean to butt in. My name's Lucy."

"I give her my best smile. "I'm Adam. This is Ryan." She leans over and shakes our hands, and I'm surprised by her firm grip. "I couldn't help but overhear your conversation. Religion is a touchy subject with people, but I had to speak up. I have such a hard time reconciling in my mind how religions can cause so much death and destruction in the name of God."

"I completely agree with you, Lucy." I say. "It sickens me that because people are born, say Jewish, they can be subjected to such violence against their religion by those who believe their faith is superior. Think about all the persecution and slaughter that the Bible has been used to justify. It may be called the Good Book, but it's not all good."

Lucy nods. "I don't believe in a God that is vindictive and punishes people by sending them to this so-called hell."

Ryan is deathly silent. He downs the rest of his beer and stands up. "I'm going to go get another. Either of you want anything?"

"I'm good," I tell Ryan. Lucy shakes her head, flashing her pearly whites. I can't help noticing her beautiful teeth. Then she picks up her book and says to me with Ryan out of earshot. "Your friend is quite, um…rigid."

I smile at her. "Yeah, he's got a stick up his ass. I've been on a spiritual journey lately, a Buddhist journey, and I was curious how Ryan would react to my new philosophies. Big mistake. I should have kept quiet."

Lucy lifts up her book. "Funny you should mention spirituality. I've been reading *The Tibetan Book of Culture,* and it's talking all about how there are whole cultures, communities, religions that have based their existence on reincarnation, meditation, becoming one with the universe, with our Creator. How can anyone say we die and go to heaven or hell when there's such great evidence out there about reincarnation and past lives?"

I start to process what she's saying. "I recently spent some time at a Buddhist monastery where we started to delve into the concept of past lives. It goes against my scientific training, but I—"

Lucy's phone rings. "Sorry, I have to take this call. Hello… Hi sweetheart… Okay— You're here? Great, Mommy will be there in a moment… Tell Louis to… Hold on one second, Siena." Lucy stands up and starts packing her yellow beach bag. "I've got to take off, but it was nice meeting you, Adam. See you in another life." She picks up her phone, and my eyes land on her heavenly ass as she exits the pool.

Ryan comes over, beer in hand, as if our earlier conversation never happened. "Dude, let's go explore this place."

"I need a minute."

"Why?"

He looks confused. I point to my expanded crotch and whisper, "Charlie." Ryan nods. I continue, "That woman got me all riled up. And this place is full of hot bodies covered in nothing but thin strips of waterproof spandex."

Ryan looks down at my bulge. "What, are you like fifteen again?"

I laugh. "Honestly, yeah—I have the erection frequency of a teenager."

"That's impressive. I wish I could say that for myself. Sometimes I need a little, you know, *help*."

"Really?"

"Yeah. I gotta tell you, those pills are magical; they really help get the engine running!"

I shake my head. The one thing I know is I won't need a prescription for Viagra anytime soon. My boy Charlie gets out of control very quickly. He can give a standing ovation to a hot chick without warning. Usually, I can untuck and mask him. Thank God I'm not European, because those tight-fitting, tiny Euro-bathing suits would be no fun at all.

"Come on, dude. Let's get going," Ryan says.

I use an old trick—thinking about washing dirty dishes—and Charlie starts to deflate like a Tom Brady football. "Okay, I'm good now, let's get some healthy snacks."

Ryan smiles. "You're such a big fucking kid."

* * *

Uh oh. Adam was doing so well, but I can see he's starting to regress. I feel like he's either on the brink of implementing the lessons that he learned at the Buddhist Monastery or he could fall back down the mountain that he's climbing. He's teetering. Having him travel to a tropical paradise exploding with attractive women is a good test of how serious he is about his spiritual journey. And Ryan is another roadblock, maintaining the superiority of his strict born-again religious views over the Buddhist doctrine.

I don't want Adam to relapse and end up like my patients who forget to wear their retainers. The other Horsemen are his friends, but maybe they aren't the best influence on him right now.

The Adventures of Adam Freeman, DDS
July 10—*The Flintstones*

The thing about golf is you need a lot of time and discretionary income. With three young children, student loans, and a supersized mortgage, I have neither. Although I have fun playing golf, I honestly suck at it. Some people say that and then proceed to drive the ball 250 yards. Me, I'll hook that sucker into the rough. Thank God my buddies are patient with me.

We take the hotel shuttle bus to the course, rent our clubs, and approach the first hole. "Why so nervous, Freeman?" Klein pats me on the back.

"I haven't played in a while. You leisure-class types get more practice than I do."

"It'll take a few holes," Klein says, "but you'll get your groove."

In a blink, Errol grabs his Big Bertha driver and wallops the ball straight down the fairway, over 250 yards. Ryan, ever the competitive athlete, even if he has put on a few pounds, outdoes Dr. Naismith as his ball bounces another ten yards past Errol's. Shit, these guys are better than I remembered. Klein's average drive is my only saving grace. The old Adam wants him to hook his first shot into the woods, so that he'll have to take a penalty stroke, but I'm happy when Klein launches his bright green golf ball about 150 yards, after which it rolls downhill another few feet. The guys are all high-fiving him. Then they turn their attention to me.

I place my orange ball carefully on top of the tee, and my heart rate speeds up. The butterflies awaken. I'm nervous that I'll not only muff the shot, but I'll also miss the ball completely. Like a self-fulfilling prophecy, I swing really hard and hear the whoosh of hitting nothing but air. I try to pretend it's a practice swing, but everyone sees through it.

I hear Ryan say to Klein, "Ouch! That's embarrassing."

Errol claps and shouts, "Do over. You got this, Freeman." I clench my teeth and begin my swing for the second time. I feel like it's the bottom of the ninth, two outs, bases loaded, and down by a run and...strike out...I whiff again.

There is muffled laughter from the two foursomes behind us. Although they are only eight people, I feel like a stadium crowd of fifty thousand is jeering. For the first time in over a week, my nervous eye twitch reappears, and I start to feel sick. I thought that I had cured myself of the twitching thing, but under the clear skies of a Caribbean paradise, my arch nemesis—E.T.—has resurfaced. I'm covered in sweat.

I take a step away from the ball and remember my training at the monastery. Take deep breaths, let go of negative thoughts, and focus attention on the present moment. I collect myself as the crowd grows silent. After a minute, I get back in front of the ball and channel my inner Venerable Panna. I picture him swinging a club with effortless ease. Finally feeling relaxed, I swing my club back and thrust it forward.

Crack! I make contact with the ball and it soars past Klein's and bounces up a foot behind Errol's. I am ecstatic. This Buddhist, live-in-the-moment stuff, really works!

I try to maintain my discipline, but my performance is erratic. It takes me two strokes for every one of Errol's, and I shoot a one hundred on the front nine. But I don't care. I'm having fun, and the Four Horsemen are back in action. We finish three six-packs and recount brodeo stories as we meander through the course.

Things get interesting when we tee up for the back nine. A foursome approaches that looks like they could be in a Sam Adams beer commercial. One is broad-shouldered with a bulging beer belly, dressed in khakis and a kelly-green golf shirt and sporting a "Boston Strong" hat over a sheaf of black hair. Another is clad in crisp, white shorts and a canary-yellow polo, sporting blonde hair under his Red Sox cap. The pair looks like they could be partners in the Wicked & Cool Law Firm. These two are accompanied by a hulking, tanned gym rat wearing visor shades and a Patriots hat who could trounce Rob Gronkowski in an arm-wrestling match. And of course, the fourth is the short and stout sidekick, the Barney Rubble of the group. They approach us while Errol places his tee on the tenth hole marker.

We hear the tail end of the conversation between the Gronk and Barney: "...you know what they say, Italians are like Jews but with better food!"

The alpha of the group, Boston Strong Hat, approaches Errol. "Hey, you dudes mind if we play through? We've been behind you all day and we're playin' fast and furious."

"Yeah, I noticed a couple of your balls came pretty close to us," interjects a drunken Ryan. "Not cool."

Errol whispers to Ryan, "Don't start." He addresses Boston Strong, "That's fine. You guys go ahead." Errol picks up his tee and steps back towards the rest of our group.

Ryan says loudly to Errol, "Why're you letting the Flintstones go first?"

Klein quickly approaches Ryan. "We're not twenty-five anymore, Ry. Let them go. We don't want another Conquering Whitney."

Errol approaches Boston Strong. "Don't mind my friend. He gets feisty when he's been drinking. We got him under control."

Gronk is about to tee off when he looks back at Ryan and scowls at us. "Tell your friend to calm down. I got no patience for a hothead that doesn't show respect."

I lean against a wooden pole that displays a map of the tenth hole. I notice it's a challenging par 5. There's a dogleg that runs along a public road for at least a hundred yards before it abruptly turns. I'm glad they're going first, because the sand trap next to the road looks tricky.

Gronk tees off. He slams his driver into the golf ball with a crack, and it skyrockets over the well-manicured grass. "Nice stroke," says Errol, who is next to me. I'm bad at following balls in flight, so I lose it in the sky. Suddenly, a *thud!* reverberates through the air. Gronk's face looks confused, then displays a smirk. A split second later, *Crash. Honk, Honk, Honk.*

Klein exclaims, "I think your ball hit a car."

Errol jumps into the golf cart, and the rest of the Horsemen join him as he slams his foot on the gas. Moments later, we pull up to the scene, which is worse than we expected. The stricken car has driven off the road, onto the fairway, and into a palm tree near a large sand trap. The front bumper looks like it's been in a demolition derby. The big white balloons of the front and passenger airbags, splattered with blood, bulge beneath the shattered windshield, enveloping a man and woman about our age. The man is groaning in the driver's seat and appears to be in shock. The woman, her face bloodied, is trying to comfort a girl around my daughter Rose's age who is crying in the back seat. The car's horn is still blaring.

Errol parks and jumps out of the golf cart first and runs to the car. "I'm a doctor. Are you guys hurt?"

The mom and dad answer affirmative. Errol says, "Don't anyone move. I'm calling 911." He dials. "Grand Rio Mar golf course. Tenth fairway. Car accident. Multiple injuries." He turns back to the car. "It's going to be okay. I want you all to sit still. Take deep breaths. Let's wait for the paramedics... Any teeth injured? We have a dentist here too."

I shoot a glance at Errol. Is he messing with me? He knows that I'm not good in emergency situations. Errol shouts, "Adam, no mouth injuries!"

Although this could have been my chance to step in and redeem myself after freezing during my office stabbing incident, I'm relieved that no one needs my services. My hands are shaking, and my eye is twitching like crazy. The sound of the horn is earsplitting, and I want to go back to the hotel.

Gronk arrives, panting heavily as he takes in the dented car. "Shit."

Boston Strong drives up behind him with the rest of the group and yells, "Come on you idiot, get in!"

"What happened?" asks Barney Rubble from the back.

"Looks like Smitty's ball hit a car that then crashed into a tree," yells Boston Strong. "Let's get the hell out of here."

Red Sox Hat, riding shotgun, nods. "Yeah—you don't know what kind of crazy these people are. We gotta split before they see us."

Without thinking, I turn around and plant my feet in front of their cart.

"Get the fuck out of the way you prick!" Boston Strong screams.

I take a deep breath, center myself, and stay perfectly still, as they inch closer. It's a Mexican—or should I say Puerto Rican—standoff. I give my best Dirty Harry imitation. "You're not going anywhere."

Gronk leaps from the cart and glowers at me. "You heard the man— *move.*"

I stand my ground as I hear the sound of sirens approaching. The sound of the eight-year-old girl echoes in my mind. This is my turn to be the hero. "You're not leaving the scene of this accident."

"Fuck it, let's back up and go around him," shouts Boston Strong as he flips the cart into reverse.

I continue to hold firm as Gronk looms over me. "I said you're not going anywhere. There are injured people in that car."

I hear Klein's voice in the background. "Freeman, the cops will be here soon. Let them handle it."

"I got this, fellas," I say.

Gronk shoves me hard. I go down and tumble over the edge of the sand trap and hit my head on something sharp. I lay there for a minute and feel a stabbing pain on my forehead. I bring my hand to my head and see blood on my fingertips. I slowly get up and climb out of the trap to see Ryan standing over Gronk, who is laid out on the grass. Boston Strong is swinging at Errol. Klein and Barney Rubble are watching from the periphery. The ambulance arrives, followed by golf course security, who take control of the situation and detain the Flintstones while they wait for the police. Play time is done. We spend the rest of the day giving statements at the local police station. The couple and their daughter are going to be okay. We get vouchers to play the course for free the next time we're in Puerto Rico.

It turns out that my cut is a surface wound, and I don't need any stitches. To be honest, I kind of wanted sutures; they'd make me look tough. But I am satisfied with a gash across my forehead to prove that I stood up to a Rob Gronkowski body double. The Horsemen all agree I am one tough motherfucker.

* * *

Bravo, Adam; you did the right thing! You showed courage and strength in a tough situation. I couldn't be prouder. All the hard work you've put in and the time you spent reflecting in the monastery seem to be paying off. Enjoy the rest of your vacation!

Making the right choices—especially ones with personal consequences—can be challenging, but those Boston shnooks should be ashamed of themselves. I vividly remember one Kabbalah class with Rabbi Shekl, when he discussed that a person can either be a *tsaddik*— a righteous and perfect person, or a *rasha*—an evil person with impure thoughts. Most of us are in between a tsaddik and a rasha, in that gray area, trying to become *benoni*—a good human being who has the ability to master his thoughts and enlighten himself to do Godly things—like being able to live life by the Eightfold Path. Adam's no tsaddik, but he's not a rasha either. He's in solid benoni territory now.

The Adventures of Adam Freeman, DDS
July 11—*Flight of the Conchords*

Errol and Ryan opt for snorkeling this morning. Klein doesn't want to go because he's out of contacts and hates wearing glasses underneath his snorkeling mask and can't see anything without them.

I decide to stay back with Klein, and we take a walk around Old San Juan. We stroll along the cobblestone streets of the quaint city center and admire the passion of its inhabitants having animated conversations along the storefronts. I stop in front of a bearded vagabond sleeping on a bench. I take out my wallet and slip a $20.00 bill under his soiled blanket. We continue walking.

"What was that about?" asks Klein.

"I'm feeling—"

Klein cuts me off. "Hey look at that." He points up at an LED billboard overhead flashing a picture of the rock group REO Speedwagon just as the digital display transitions to Air Supply.

I shake my head. "You want to see REO Speedwagon and Air Supply in concert? Come on Klein, I thought you had better musical taste than that."

"Come on Freeman, those bands rock! But no, look at the next ad, there it is."

I read the flashing billboard quickly. "Come See the World-Famous Hypnotist...The Sensational Vegas."

He continues, "Dude, have you ever seen one of these shows?"

"Can't say I have."

"I saw a hypnotist show in college once and it was extraordinary." We stop to cross the street. "I went to it with this girl I had the hots for. She got hypnotized and was up on stage with five other people in front of the crowd. I swear, if I didn't know her, I would have thought she was a plant. It was hilarious. She danced around like Madonna. Waddled like a penguin. But, the craziest part was when the hypnotist told everyone on stage they'd be really horny that night. I couldn't believe my luck. I had such a crush on this girl, and she was being served to me on a silver platter. When she came back into consciousness, she was all over me the rest of the night. We *have* to go." Klein points to a sign that reads, "Flight of the Concords Café" and says, "Hey, let's get some lunch."

"Yeah, that sounds good." The light turns and we cross the street. "So? What'd you do at the end of the night?"

"I really wanted her—God was she hot. But," he sighs, "I couldn't bring myself to do it. It was like I had slipped her a hypnotic roofie. It wouldn't have been of her own accord. But to this day I still think 'what if.'"

We walk into the restaurant, and a shaggy-haired guy with horn-rimmed glasses and a toothy smile wearing a blue T-shirt and jean shorts seats us. He hands us menus, and in a New Zealand accent says, "Take your time, mates. I'll be back to take your order."

"Is it my imagination or did he look like Jemaine from... Oh, forget it." I read the overpriced tourist menu. Eighteen dollars for a grilled cheese sandwich? I look up at Klein and continue our conversation, "Not very spiritual of you, Klein. I think you have to work on letting that fantasy go."

"I know, but I'm still a guy. If you saw her body, you'd be dwelling on her too!" We give our orders. Klein takes out his cell phone and reserves tickets for the Four Horsemen to see The Sensational Vegas, then sends a group text to the other guys about our new plans for the night.

July 11—*Fame*

Fast forward to this evening's performance. First off, I am surprised to see that the Teatro Tapia is sold out. There must be over seven hundred people here to see this woman. I begin to think we are in for a memorable night.

When The Sensational Vegas walks out on stage, I feel like I am on fire. Her sizzling red hair is the color of Deborah Ann Woll's from *True Blood*, and she has the mad curves of Christina Hendricks from *Mad Men*. I imagine her backstory: a child from a dirt-poor town in southern Mississippi with a preacher father and stay-at-home mom. At the age of eleven, she runs away to join the circus. On her travels, she meets a magician, falls in love, and works as his assistant. His career as an illusionist takes off, but their love flames out and Vegas becomes tired of being in his shadow. Her passion for entertainment and desire for fame consume her. She quits and takes intensive training with a master of hypnosis in San Francisco, who teaches her the trade. And here she is, rocking the stage as The Sensational Vegas.

My imaginary history for Vegas is clearly off base because she addresses the audience in a British accent. "This is a safe environment," she says, then continues, "I won't do anything you don't want to do. And I pledge to give you a fun and entertaining evening with the help of hypnosis."

Since I hate losing control, I worry about being called up. I sit down, confident that I will soon be laughing my ass off at other people's uninhibited actions. Vegas starts to relax everyone in the audience by having us close our eyes, clear our minds, and visualize a peaceful place. I look at Klein next to me. He is already asleep. I nudge Errol, who has a big smile on his face.

Maybe it's due to our late-night drinking, but my eyes become heavy as bricks. Yet my mind is clear, like when I'm meditating. The lights go out in the theatre and in my rational brain. Then the voluptuous, red-headed Vegas, firmly takes my hand, and reaches out to grab Klein's arm. She leads us both onstage. The rest of the night is a blur, and Errol and Ryan fill us in on the details. All I know is that the show must have been memorable and entertaining because later that night someone recognizes me on the street and tells me how great I was on stage. My five seconds of fame.

The guys inform me that I ate a whole onion that Vegas told me tasted like an apple. That explained the horrible taste in my mouth. She also made me gallop across the stage like a horse. Even though I was funny, I was the opening act to Klein—the main attraction. Vegas had him put on a wig and wear a dress as he performed the Macarena. For an encore, he led the crowd in "YMCA." Errol and Ryan said they laughed their balls off. Vegas told us at the end of the show that we'd not be embarrassed or ashamed of what we did on stage but that we'd feel peaceful. I have to admit, I'm feeling pretty amazing—relaxed and less burdened than normal. And my eye hasn't twitched all day.

July 12—*Twin Peaks*

Today is our beach trip. Klein falls asleep and, being mature friends, we bury him in the sand. Klein transforms into a mermaid with huge breasts. He has seaweed on his head stretching down onto his shoulders to represent his long hair, and we give him a long tail like Ariel's from *The Little Mermaid*.

When Klein wakes up, he has a good sense of humor about it, although he gets pissed when Ryan puts the picture on Instagram: #themerman.

While lying on the beach, I realize I am feeling lighter and more energetic ever since the hypnosis show. Although Klein is still trapped as a mermaid, he catches my attention and tells me he's also feeling less inhibited since last night—like there has been a weight lifted off him.

I say, "That's funny, I literally was just thinking about last night. Can I tell you something? I'm still mesmerized by Vegas and her bright red hair. I know this'll sound strange, but I feel like I've seen her before. It was like déjà vu. Ever get that feeling?"

"Of course I have. Go on."

"A memory resurfaced last night while I was in bed. I hadn't thought about it in years. When I was a teenager, I used to have this vivid dream." I chuckle at the image of Klein's head sticking out of the female mermaid body. "I dreamed of a woman with bright red hair. She was magnificent, by far the most beautiful woman in the world. She reminded me of your cousin."

"Who...Sara?" asks Klein. "Her hair is more strawberry blonde."

"No, you idiot. Ariel, the little mermaid."

"Nice reference to my sand body. Get me out of here anyway, will you?"

"No," I laugh. "I want to admire your gigantic tits one last time. Those *Twin Peaks* are amazing!" I start stroking Klein's sand breasts.

"Hey! Hands off my boobs!" he orders.

"Sorry," I say. "They're irresistible. So pert and shapely."

"This is sexual harassment. I'll get you for this, Freeman."

I return to my childhood dream/vision. "She radiated a bright light from her body, and when she touched me, I felt at peace—in complete harmony with the world at that moment. It wasn't even sexual. You'd think that I would have woken up with the bed all sticky, but—"

Klein interrupts me, "Which I bet happened often when you were a teenager!"

I smile. "No doubt. Anyway, when I woke up, I had this air of calmness about me. No small feat since, you'll remember, I was an extremely anxious adolescent. I still remember the dream to this day. I didn't know who that woman was...my future wife? An angel? A figment of my imagination? I never told anyone about this dream."

"Wow, I got chills. Maybe she was your guardian angel. Hope says that we all have spirits who help guide us."

I frown. "That sounds far-fetched, and besides, you know how I feel about Hope. The fact is that I was always searching for my dream girl. Even after my marriage to Minnie, I eventually forgot about her until last night. I swear, when I saw Vegas at the show something deep down was stirred. You believe me, right? I'm not crazy."

"Well you are crazy, but aren't we all? Yes, Freeman, I believe you."

"Klein," I pause, not really comprehending what I am about to say. "I want to find her. I have to meet Vegas."

In unison I hear, "We're in, let's do it!" I turn around and see Errol and Ryan standing over me.

"Excuse me?" I ask them.

"We heard everything you said. It'd be cool to meet that chick; she was hot. Let's find her!" Errol gleefully exclaims.

The Four Horsemen Detective Agency is formed. Of course, it's Errol who works his magic. Talk about six degrees of separation. His cousin is good friends with a high-powered agent in Las Vegas who is well-connected with some important players. After an hour of Errol working his peeps under the Puerto Rican sun, he is able to track down Vegas's manager. Incredibly, her manager says we can meet her backstage after the evening show ends at 10:00 p.m. It's that easy. It must be meant to be.

CHAPTER TWENTY
7:32 a.m.

Come on, Adam! Two steps forward and three steps back. The rogue streak I gave you is really showing now. Remember that you have a family at home, and don't do anything that you'll regret later.

The Adventures of Adam Freeman, DDS
July 12—*Married with Children*

The rest of the day flies by, and we finally get back to the Teatro Tapia at the appointed time. The guys leave me alone backstage as I wait for Vegas. I still can't get my dream girl's bright red hair out of my mind and how, thirty years ago, she made me feel peaceful.

Vegas finally emerges at 10:37 p.m. And boy is she worth the wait. She looks even more beautiful in person. As she speaks, her white teeth glimmer behind bright red lips.

"My manager, Louis, tells me you're a super-fan. Nice to see you again, Adam. I smile, speechless. She continues, "By the way, you gave me a memorable performance last night."

"You remember?"

"Of course I do. You and your buddy were absolutely hilarious. It was one of my best shows this year."

I wipe my damp forehead. "I'm not sure what you did to me, but I've been feeling great since the show. Would you have a free moment to join me for a drink to help me understand why I feel so good now? I want to know how I can keep this going."

There's an awkward silence. I look down, then back up at her. Finally, in her infectious English accent she says, "It's my policy to not go out with people from my shows."

My face flushes and my eye starts twitching again. "I get it. You don't mix pleasure with business, but that's not what I was after."

She eyes me. "Policy or no policy, I have to admit, you radiate energy I find very attractive, and your performance made an impression on me. You were one of the most interesting subjects I've hypnotized in a long time."

Hot damn, I was *interesting*! I reach into my pocket and pop a breath mint into my mouth. I stick my hand out. "I'm Adam."

"Yes, I know that. You can call me Lucy. How'd you get that scratch on your forehead?"

"Oh, it's a long story." I pause. "Lucy? That's funny, you're the second Lucy I've met this trip."

"Vegas is my stage name." She has a big smile on her face. Without warning, she takes off her hair. I'm now looking at a woman with short, blonde hair, like the rocker Pink. Holding her wig, she speaks again, but now with an American accent. "Now do you recognize me?"

"Lucy...from the pool? *No way*!"

"Yes way."

"But your red hair. Your British accent."

"Everyone loves a redhead, right? And Brits sound sophisticated. Did you know that studies show Americans will believe what a British person says about 62 percent more than someone with an American accent? Every night,

I transform myself into a British goddess with big boobs. Thank the good Lord for the push-up bra."

"Talk about a small world."

"It's no coincidence I picked you for my show. I remembered you from the pool. I wanted to get your *Guns and Ammo* friend, but he didn't close his eyes. When I saw you went under, I couldn't resist. And as I thought, you didn't disappoint." She gives me a big smile. "There's a cool little bar across the street. Give me one moment to say goodbye to my crew." She walks away, and I quickly text the guys letting them know where I am going and that I'll meet up with them back at the hotel.

She's back in five minutes, grabbing my hand and escorting me across the street. We walk quickly through the humid night and up to the entrance. Lucy flashes the bouncer her bright white smile. "Thanks, Leo," she says to the hulking Puerto Rican bouncer with two earrings.

"No problem, Luce. How'd the show go?"

"Marvelous. When are you going to come see me, sweetie?"

"Oh, I'm not letting you mess with my mind and make me look like a jackass in front of thousands of people."

"Ha, it's not that bad, is it, Adam?"

"Nah, I'm used to looking like a fool in front of a crowd." They laugh, and we walk into the dimly lit bar. It is decorated in eye-popping fluorescent colors.

We get a table away from the loud steel-drum music. I ask Lucy how she became interested in hypnosis. "It's a long story. I was a dental hygienist in New York—"

I interrupt her, "No way. I'm a pediatric dentist."

"Yes way. That's too funny. I liked being a hygienist and I was good at it, but acting was always my passion. I performed in local plays during the weekend. One time a patient, who was an agent, got me an audition for a commercial. But it was in L.A., and I've always been afraid to fly. I needed to conquer my fear, so with the encouragement of a coworker, I went to a local hypnotherapist and it worked!"

"No kidding?"

"Yeah. It helped me gain a sense of self and an understanding of why I was afraid to fly. I went on the audition and got the part. After minor roles in *Law and Order* and *CSI*, an agent approached me. We started talking about an innovative way for me to carve out a niche for myself in the industry. I told him about my experience with hypnotherapy. Coincidently, his wife had used hypnosis to stop smoking, and he'd used it to lose weight. He convinced me to enroll in an intense course to become certified in hypnotherapy. We decided to combine my new skills as a hypnotist with my passion for entertainment to embark on this new career. Why are you smiling?"

"When I was in the audience watching you perform, I created this elaborate backstory for you."

"Was it anything like what I told you?"

"Not at all! What's funny is that you literally could have worked in my dental office."

Our conversation is interrupted by a dark-skinned, curly-haired, female server asking for our drink orders. Lucy answers, "I'll have a Martini—dry." I take a minute to look at the menu and order an Appletini. "Really?" Lucy smiles at me. "That's such a John Dorian drink."

"You know that show?"

"Yeah, I love *Scrubs*."

"Wow, that's one of my favorites."

"It's the best. Right now, I'm binge-watching *Boy Meets World* with my daughter. I've got custody of her this summer while my ex is on an extended business trip to China. We started watching *Girl Meets World,* and she wanted to know how it all started."

I suddenly feel a foot on top of mine. *Bang.* Startled, my legs hit the inside of the table as I move my foot away. "Ouch."

"Are you all right?" Lucy takes a bread stick from the basket at the center of the table. The phallic image of the pencil thin bread stick being placed between her red lips gives me the same tingling under my pants that I felt at the pool. I awkwardly look away to avoid eye contact and the outside chance that she can read my perverted and misogynistic mind. She interrupts the silence and asks, "Do you want to dance?"

Do I want to dance? Like Al Bundy, I'm *Married with Children,* but I'm happily married, and I don't want to screw it up. Still, I make a list in my head of how cool this woman is:

1. She is reading *The Tibetan Book of Culture.*

2. She has spiritual views similar to mine.

3. She loves television shows.

4. She looks exactly like the redhead (in her wig) from my childhood dreams.

I figure it can't hurt to get to know her tonight. As a person, not a sex partner. Nothing will happen. I'm having a drink and some friendly conversation. That's all.

Now her feet are on top of mine again, but this time I don't move my legs away.

I respond slowly, "Do I want to dance? Great question. The answer is..." I look down to make sure that Charlie is still sleeping. I smile sheepishly and stand up.

Suddenly, I see Errol, Ryan, and Klein come through the door of the bar. Ryan and Klein head to the bar to order drinks. Errol spots us right away and pulls up a chair to join us. I sit down and pull my seat towards the table again. Lucy's legs are nowhere to be found.

"Vegas?" asks Errol.

"You recognize me?" asks Lucy.

"Of course I do. It's your eyes. They're captivating. I'm Errol, Adam's good buddy from home. You were great last night by the way."

Lucy blushes and waves her hand like a Mississippi southern belle. "That's kind of you to say."

I look at Lucy and then over at Errol. Does Errol really want to go head-to-head to compete for her affections? Can I take him on? Do I want to take him on? "Have you been to the bioluminescence bay?" asks Errol.

"Yes, it's amazing. You really should go and see it if you have time," responds Lucy.

I begin to get boxed out of the conversation, and lose my attention span altogether, as Errol turns up the charm. He slowly brings his left hand over and puts it on her shoulder, his patented pickup move. I can't believe women fall for that. Lucy laughs a little louder than before. Her eyes are not on me anymore. She is fully engaged in a conversation with Errol. Who knows what the hell they're talking about, and when they ask me what I think, I blink four times and excuse myself.

I find Ryan and Klein at the bar and pull up a stool. "Look at Errol over there, that smug, confident SOB."

Klein shakes his finger at me. "Freeman, you should be thanking him for stepping in the way he did. Who knows what would've happened if we left you alone with her."

Ryan agrees with him. "You're not that type of guy, Adam."

I realize I was deluding myself with the innocence of our encounter. "I didn't know what was happening. It all was going so fast. I wasn't thinking."

Klein can see I am a wreck. "Remember, last week you were at the Buddhist monastery learning to control your mind and thoughts. You don't want that to go by the wayside! Listen, nothing happened. But it's natural for you to have wanted it to. You're a married guy and what married guy doesn't struggle when he sees a beautiful woman? We always wonder what it would be like to trade up."

"I love Minnie," I say. "I'm blessed to have a beautiful wife. But I did wonder if this one time it would be worth indulging the fantasy—"

Klein snaps at me, "*Definitely not*. Adam, you're not the affair type."

Buzz. I see there's a text on my phone. They say timing is everything. It's a message from Minnie and the kids. I click on it. "We miss you Daddy, can't wait to see you soon!😊"

I begin to cry. "You guys are right. I love my family so much."

"Let's get you back to the hotel." Klein says as he and Ryan stand up. "Errol can handle Vegas from here."

* * *

Jesus, Adam, you nearly blew up your life. That was a narrow escape. It looks like my congratulations may have been premature. It's ironic that the same goofball buddies who sometimes get you into trouble saved your ass this time. And it's a good thing they stepped in when they did. It's obvious you didn't finish your medicine at the monastery. You only took half of your antibiotic, and you still haven't eradicated the infection. I have to say, writing your journey is painful, but like rubbernecking on the highway, I can't stop myself. Sometimes I'm not sure if I'm writing your story or if you're telling it to me. Let's see what happens next.

The Adventures of Adam Freeman, DDS
July 13—*Sanford and Son*

My eyes open, and it is the ungodly hour of 5:46 a.m. I turn over and close my eyes, but Klein's rumbling snore prevents me from going back to sleep. At 6:02 a.m. I realize sleep isn't in the cards for me. I hop out of bed, put on my shorts, T-shirt, and sandals, and rush out toward the beach.

I pass the winding pool where I had my serendipitous meeting with Lucy. I think about lying down on a beach chair to meditate but that's too cliché this morning, so I keep walking. I go through a large silver gate towards the beach and slip off my sandals. The white morning sand feels cool under my feet. I break into a jog along the ocean. This is perfect. Looking into the hazy yellow and orange sun peeking up from the horizon, I am no longer thinking. I'm at one with the universe or, at the very least, the morning runners on the beach as we exchange waves. The smell of the ocean calms my soul, and I don't want this moment to end. I keep running. Having no watch or phone with me, I lose track of time.

Out of breath, I turn away from the crashing ocean waves, slow to a walk, and head towards the edge of the beach. I spot a palm tree and sit down under its cool shade to get out of the hot morning sun. I lie back against the bark of the tree and close my eyes. This time it feels right to meditate. My mind moves a thousand miles a minute, but I ignore the monkey chatter. Just when I've gotten into a groove with my breathing, I overhear a conversation.

"Look at this frog, son."

"That's cool."

I resist the urge to open my eyes and see who is talking. I try and block out the conversation, but they continue to talk.

"Don't touch. Let him be."

"Poppy, I want to catch it."

"Willis, you have to respect animals and the environment. The frog is a powerful animal in nature."

"What do you mean?"

"Well, the frog undergoes incredible transformations throughout its life to reach the destination of full adulthood, like we do. It represents rebirth, renewal, and opportunity. It's powerful."

"I don't understand, Poppy."

"You will someday. Animals are signs from the universe that can point us in the right direction."

I hear a female voice. "Sanford, we're ready for breakfast!"

Sanford shouts, "We'll be there in a minute, Jeannie."

That was quite the apropos conversation for me to overhear. Like the frog, I'm undergoing my transformation. I have a moment of clarity. *Don't be so hard on yourself, Adam.* I need to be patient as I continue to grow and appreciate my time on earth and use it to show love, humanity, and grace to others. Reaching enlightenment is not going to be easy. If it were, then everyone would be a Buddha or Jesus.

July 13—*Three's Company*

"Get up, you idiot!" Errol is screaming at me with Klein and Ryan by his side. The three of them look pissed.

"What?" I say in a raspy, morning voice. "Where am I?"

"Puerto Rico, you dipshit!" answers Errol. "You fell asleep on the beach."

"I can't believe you left your room without your phone," says Klein. "We had no idea where you went, and we've got a flight to catch."

Errol is holding my sandals in one hand and my phone in the other. "Well, we had *some* idea where you went. What the fuck, man? I didn't think that you were that type of guy."

"The type of guy who falls asleep on the beach?"

Klein nods. "I have to agree with Errol on this one. Very stupid, Adam. I can't believe you decided to do that."

"I needed it. It was my time to refresh and energize before I got back home to the family."

Ryan says, "Dude, I didn't think you had it in you, but your secret's safe with us."

Errol adds, "You dirty dog! And you gave me shit for what *I* did."

I look at my friends. "What the hell are you talking about? I went for a run and then fell asleep meditating."

"That's your alibi? Meditating? That's a weak cover-up. Take it from someone who's experienced with this sort of thing." Errol throws me my sandals. "You'd better start by destroying the evidence."

I grab my phone from him and see the image: 4 Best Hummer Ever call (555) 229-5014. I stand up. "No, no, no. I swear there was no blowjob."

Klein asks, "Then why would you have a picture of this in your gallery?"

"It was on the bathroom wall in the airport. I want to write a book about graffiti."

"Graffiti?" repeats Klein.

"We're supposed to believe that?" asks Ryan.

"Guys, I swear. Why would I get a BJ from another woman?"

Errol answers, "Because you're a guy."

"Klein, you're the voice of reason. Please tell them you believe me. I didn't do anything this morning except go for a run, meditate, and fall asleep. Call the freaking number if you want. It was on the stall in the bathroom at LaGuardia. Whoever it is, I doubt they're in Puerto Rico."

Klein studies me, then turns to the other guys. "I think he's serious." Then back to me. "Shit, that's a really bad sunburn."

"I forgot my sunblock. And really guys, this is a big misunderstanding. I'm talking *Three's Company* proportions. I wouldn't risk my marriage. I need you guys to believe me."

Errol speaks up. "Your story's so lame that I believe you."

Ryan adds, "But I bet you still checked out the number. Let's check your call history."

"You won't find anything there either."

Errol continues, "Here's some free advice, Adam. Delete that photo. You don't want Minnie seeing it. Let's call a cab and get back to the hotel. We're going to miss our flight if we keep up this bullshit."

CHAPTER TWENTY-ONE
7:59 a.m.

For Christ's sake, Adam, delete the photo. You and I both know it was harmless, but if Minnie sees it, you're screwed.

Cuckoo, cuckoo, cuckoo… I turn my head and check the time. The clock reads 8:00 a.m. I don't have much time left to finish Adam's journey. I need to plow through, but my mind is frozen and needs a break.

I get up and scamper to the kitchen for breakfast before the kids wake up and the morning mayhem begins. I get out a bowl and pour myself Multigrain Cheerios. Opening the refrigerator, I smell the milk and it's still good, so I pour it over my cereal. After I cut up a banana, I walk into the family room and eat my breakfast in peace.

I see the book *The Perks of Being a Wallflower* on the glass coffee table. Leah and I watched the movie last week. It was a miracle in and of itself that I was able to get Leah to watch a movie with me. My wife is not a big fan of films. They depress her. It's always a coup when I can get her to watch something with me. I could list a hundred movies I've watched alone. *Pulp Fiction, Happiness, Fight Club, Requiem for a Dream, Ghost World, Garden State, Little Miss Sunshine, Dan in Real Life, Juno, Away We Go, 500 Days of Summer, The Kids are All Right, The Descendants, Moonrise Kingdom.* I could go on, but you get the picture—pun intended! I usually don't mind watching movies solo, but Leah next to me, her hair smelling like strawberry shampoo, is the perfect ending to my day.

I was able to get her to watch *The Perks of Being a Wallflower* after winning a bet. If I could be home for dinner with the family five days in a row, she'd sit through the movie of my choice from start to finish without complaining.

I connected strongly with the film and am planning to start the book by Stephen Chobsky next week. Watching it validated my beliefs that we're all connected. I empathized with Charlie as an outcast, and my heart went out to that kid. I love it when the writer understands the reader, when the film director understands the audience. The characters in this film made mix tapes for each other, the way I did for Leah when we were in college. The books referenced in the movie: *To Kill a Mockingbird, Catcher in the Rye, Of Mice and Men, A Separate Peace,* are all lined up above me on my office book shelves. I could feel the story running through me.

Leah didn't share either my love of the story or the personal connection to it. My wife couldn't get over Charlie's childhood abuse.

I explained to her that I was trying to look at things from a Buddhist viewpoint. "Remember that life is suffering. If you come at it from this angle, the movie should not be disturbing."

She countered, "Life doesn't have to be suffering for people. I don't understand that belief."

Even though I hold a different belief system than my wife, I accept her viewpoint as being hers, and mine as working for what my truth is in this life.

After Leah left the room that night, I spent the rest of it IMDbing the movie. I was inspired when I discovered that it took Stephen

Chobsky five years to write the book. I felt better after learning this. Maybe it's not so unusual that Adam's story has not seen the light of day for the past six years now.

Perhaps I still have a story worthy of publication.

The Adventures of Adam Freeman, DDS
July 13—Girls

Waiting at the airport, we are all in our own worlds as we sit by the gate. Errol is following up on some calls from the hospital. Ryan is texting. Klein has his eyes closed and is murmuring mantras to himself. I take out my phone and begin deleting suspicious graffiti photos as the guys suggested. There goes my book idea.

A baby begins to cry, and it agitates me like nails on a chalkboard. I can empathize with the rookie parents, three chairs to my left, trying to stop the child's tears. The dad gets out a stuffed animal and dangles it playfully over the baby.

Klein elbows me hard in the ribs.

"Ouch, what the heck was that for?"

"Look at that stuffed animal."

Annoyed, I reply, "It's a unicorn, so what?" I finish deleting and put my phone away.

"Well, last night I dreamt of a unicorn and now I see this! Remember what I told you, there are no coincidences. I have to google what this represents."

As I watch the father use the unicorn to help temper his upset child, Klein reads, "Unicorn is the symbol of magic, miracles, purity, innocence, and enchantment. This magical and enchanting animal appears to only a rare few and has the ability to bestow magic, miracles, and wisdom to those who are pure of heart and virtuous in their deeds."

"Really, Klein? I respect your spiritual journey, but a unicorn? That's ridiculous."

Klein continues, "To have a unicorn appear is both a great honor and a divine gift. Only a very few people are pure and virtuous enough to cross paths with a unicorn and should feel very blessed."

"Listen to yourself with this new age stuff. You're losing it."

Klein leans in. "I was meditating on one of my big issues that I've had to sort through in life. And the unicorn theme is validating my progress."

"What are you talking about? A stuffed unicorn is validating your progress in life? You've gone off the deep end."

"Don't judge me. Didn't you learn anything at that monastery?"

"You're right. Sorry, Klein. This is a judgment-free zone. Go on."

"Well, I'm surrounded by females everywhere. I have four daughters, and I'm a sixth-grade teacher in an all-girls school. Then, I get put into drag onstage by Vegas a few days ago."

"And then we bury you to look like a mermaid! Ouch."

Klein continues, "Exactly. Don't get me wrong—I love all my girls, and I wouldn't change having them for absolutely anything. But there was a time when I was very insecure about myself and my masculinity because everywhere I turned there was female energy. I began wondering why I didn't have any strong connection to guys."

"Come on Klein, you have us, the Four Horsemen."

"I know, but it's different. I wasn't close with my dad growing up, and I felt that void. I thought it would be cool to have a son to bond with, but since we have all girls..." He pauses, and I can see the sadness in his eyes. "I did a lot of work to recognize that this is my responsibility in this life—to help raise four special girls who are the sunshine of my days and see them develop into amazing women. Don't misunderstand me, I'm happy, but it's bittersweet. I love my ladies, but it's also a challenge being the only man in a house raging with estrogen."

"I'll bet!"

"But Adam—I've learned to embrace it!"

"You're preaching to the choir here. I've got two girls, and I get it. Are you gonna go for the boy?"

My old friend is smiling. "You know how many people *still* ask me that? It used to bother me, but now I laugh it off. It's human nature to always want what you don't have, but I'm completely comfortable with my family harem! It's taken a lot of work to get so comfortable with it."

I notice that the baby looks peaceful and serene sleeping on its father's shoulder now. The dad puts the unicorn toy away. Since Klein's being honest with me, I open up to him, "I admit that I'm happy we had Spencer. Good to have some testosterone in the house. God bless you, my friend. I'm glad you are at peace with everything."

"Hey, before girls I had no idea what conditioner was used for! Then I learned that girls can burp and fart as loud as the guys in my fraternity house."

"You're funny, Klein. I'm not half the girl-dad you are. I still get embarrassed when Minnie starts talking about her 'time of the month.' And now she tells me that Paige may 'become a woman' soon. Oy vey."

Klein puts his arm around my shoulder. "Oh, you have no idea. Your life is about to become a hockey game before you know it: three periods and a whole lot of fighting!"

I laugh at Klein's line. He must have read that somewhere. He continues. "Adam, my Miriam is fourteen now, and I still can't get over that she has breasts and is dating boys. I remember the time Joy told me that I couldn't give Miriam a bath because she was 'developing.'"

"I can't believe she's the same girl you used to run around the house holding like a football."

"It's hard letting go. I wish I could say it gets easier, but it doesn't." Klein smiles. "It's all good though. These children, from my enlightened viewpoint, are not really ours anyway—they're on loan from the universe, and we're blessed to have the opportunity to touch their lives."

I pat Klein on the back. "I never thought of it that way. Thanks for sharing."

"I've come to peace with the femininity in my life. And, I've discovered bulk tampons at Costco."

"But, do you still want that male dog you were telling me about?"

"Shit yeah. One with a really big shlong and balls hanging down to the ground."

July 13—*Alias*

I am looking forward to an uneventful plane ride as I start making my Hella-Rockin' Travel Playlist v23. Thoughts start to seep into my head about starting work next week. I'm ready to go back!

As if reading my mind, Errol turns to me and asks, "Are you ready to return to the office?"

I pause my mix. "I was just thinking about that. It's been a surreal journey. I've been such a mess, but between the meditation and my new JuBu philosophy, I'm ready. Bring it on."

"Are you glad you went on the brodeo?"

I grin. "God yes. I had a blast." I try to stifle what I'm about to say next, but the old Adam gets the better of me. "But it would've been nice to have gotten to know Vegas more—"

Before I can complete my thoughts, Errol interrupts me. "Listen, I know you think I'm a dick for that move, but can I be completely honest with you?"

"Of course."

"The Horsemen all saw you needed an intervention. Plus, I needed to talk to Vegas to find out more about hypnosis."

"What? You didn't sleep with her?"

He smiles. "I have a reputation to uphold, so I'll neither confirm nor deny those allegations."

"Oh give me a break; tell me the truth for once."

"Does it really matter? But if you must know, we kept our clothes on. No more fucking around for me. I miss my family, man. This trip helped me realize that Kristy is a good person. I'm a better man because of her. I hope she'll take me back."

"Then what'd you do with Vegas?"

"I picked her brain about how hypnosis works because I had an amazing experience with it recently."

"You did?"

Errol whispers, "Don't discuss this with anyone."

"It's in the vault, key locked!" I close my mouth and twist my hand over it.

"Well, it's no secret that I've been going through a lot with my marriage. I started to drink again. I was pulled over last month driving home from a bar, totally shitfaced."

"How come I didn't hear about it from Minnie? She reads the police blotter religiously."

"The cop who stopped me is a friend of mine, and he didn't make me take the Breathalyzer. If he had, I would've been screwed. He saved my ass big-time. I gave him my word that I would get treatment. And I agreed to see his hypnotherapist."

"The cop has a hypnotherapist?"

"Yeah, I can't make this shit up. As part of our agreement he referred me to this woman who helped him overcome his drug addiction. At first, I was hesitant, but my buddy, the cop, he was serious. He ended up taking me to her himself. She's a licensed hypnotherapist, and I had six sessions that really helped me. Adam, I swear I've never felt like that before. I'm a different person. I understand what you and Klein are searching for."

"That's amazing, Errol. But you're so skeptical about spiritual stuff."

"Sometimes I feel like Klein goes too far, and I hate when he preaches because we all have to figure it out ourselves. I know chasing ass has been a distraction for me and prevented me from dealing with my real issues. I understand now that your nervous eye twitch is your body's reaction to the stress in your life just like my drinking and womanizing are ways for me to numb myself from my pain. I have to search deep down inside myself and confront my inner feelings if I'm ever going to be able to let that pain go."

I see a tear trickle down his cheek. "I can't believe that this is the same Errol Naismith who I have known all these years. I'm impressed."

"I realized through Corinna that I would continue to have my bad habits and attract unhealthy incidents in my life if I didn't address my inner demons. I think you'd like her."

I see vulnerability and a transformation in my friend that I hadn't noticed before. And I like what I see. "I want to meet this woman."

Errol puts his arm around my shoulder. "I would love for you to see her. I really think she can help you too. Because, dude, I see your twitch is back."

CHAPTER TWENTY-TWO
8:23 a.m.

Wow, it took guts for Errol to admit his faults and give Adam the name of his healer and guru.

I went through a period when I was in search of my own guru, but I had a lot of trouble choosing one. I was jumping from guru to guru like a monkey jumping from tree to tree. I tried to temper my obsessive-compulsive personality with my questioning, scientific Ivy League background which caused me to be skeptical of the doctrines these gurus preached. But that made my search harder. I would get locked into books I connected with, but after googling the authors I became disillusioned. I would invariably find out that these gurus all had problems of their own from a history of drug addiction to being sued by their manager.

Finally, I came across one guru I connected with. This spiritual man was different. He was no charlatan; he had an Ivy League medical degree. But his writing wasn't stiff or scientific. It was totally accessible. He had a great way of mixing the science of neurology with spirituality. I loved his writing and podcasts that talked about the history of mankind's spirituality. He wrote extensively about how we have to sift through the extemporaneous human noise of preaching to uncover how the core beliefs of religion overlap. This was the Venn Diagram of religions that I was searching for.

I couldn't believe my good fortune when my new guru was on a book tour near Matingly. I eagerly went to see him speak. The first thing I noticed was that he had an exceptional way with words, which captivated the audience. I still remember some of his speech by heart:

"Look beneath the veil and know that what's going on is all an intricate and woven mosaic of life unfiltered. Stop thinking of the past, and put your thoughts and energies into the here and now. Be present. When you hold on to things, it causes anger and poisons you and those around you. Be strong. Be free. Be joyful. Do what feels right in your heart and soul. Don't overthink things, and ask yourself, what do you love?"

I was thoroughly enjoying the talk, but suddenly something snapped inside me. I noticed that the college students were sitting together like a flock of geese, leaning in to worship his every word. Didn't these people read the passage in his book that said we shouldn't put anyone on a pedestal? Yet, that's exactly what they were doing to the Ivy League guru, and he seemed to love it.

The money flowed from the congregation to the preacher as people took out their cash and credit cards to buy his books. I noticed grown adults waiting in line for his signature, reminding me of a kid getting an autograph from their favorite baseball player. The commercialization of selling his books and signing autographs overshadowed the important messages he was disseminating. My faith in this guru was shattered.

Right then I realized that the only one who can free you from the messy mind and the distractions of life is *you*. It's fine to get help, but don't expect a religious preacher or self-help guru to spoon-feed you the answers. It's more meaningful if you do the hard work yourself.

I hope that Adam proceeds cautiously. He's already jumped from guru to guru looking for answers. I wonder if he will learn the lesson that the only way to heal himself is to find the answers from within. I've found that a CliffsNotes version to enlightenment doesn't exist.

The Adventures of Adam Freeman, DDS
July 14—*Grey's Anatomy*

Coming home is like downing a huge glass of cold water after spending a day alone in Death Valley. Entering the house isn't as dramatic as my return from the monastery, but seeing the joy in Minnie's and the kids' eyes combined with the love I feel in my heart for them is euphoric. We spend all of Saturday hanging out together. I listen to Paige play her newest piece on the piano. I play basketball and have a catch with Rose, and Spencer and I tackle and tickle each other until our bellies ache.

At the end of the shortest day in the history of the world, Minnie and I lie alone in bed, cuddling. Wow, has it been a long time. No holds barred at this point in my journal since we've gotten to know each other really well—cuddling leads to making love—hot, heavy, steamy sex. It. Is. Incredible.

I do have to admit that I am a little out of practice. "Why are you stopping?" Minnie pants at one point.

"I have to calm down," I tell her as I move Charlie away from her mouth. "Now it's my turn to help you out!"

As I move my face downward between Minnie's thighs, I think back to my awkward anatomy lectures in dental school. I know you're wondering why the heck a dentist needs to learn about the genitalia. I asked myself the same question when I found out we were required to take classes with the med students. My face was as red as a tomato during those lessons, but the anatomy classes were a blessing in disguise. There were things I didn't know, and other things I didn't know I didn't know. I now have a GPS—that stands for Gynecological Positioning System—that helps me lead women, well, one woman—to their nirvana by pinpointing both the clitoris and the G-spot.

Tonight, however, even armed with my knowledge from *Grey's Anatomy* (the book, not the television show), I need a bit of direction.

Minnie moans, "Lower, Adam!"

"Shhhh," I mumble, "you're going to wake the kids," which is usually her line to me. I move down a fraction of an inch.

"Mmm. Do the thing where you go in circles."

I oblige.

"Oh, that's the spot! Yes, sooooo good... *Yes*! Adam, get in me now."

I come up for air. I have Charlie under control, and he's ready to be reunited with Minnie.

The rest is magic as Minnie and I move our bodies in perfect harmony, then crescendo together to the point of no return. I fall asleep spooning her, taking in the scent of her hair, and slip easily into dreams.

* * *

Adam, I thought we weren't writing any kind of *Fifty Shades of Grey* here, but I have to admit that I enjoyed it and how aware you finally were of pleasing someone else besides yourself. Minnie deserved it.

The Adventures of Adam Freeman, DDS
July 15—*Family Guy*

When I wake next to Minnie, I am painfully aware that this is my last day to focus on my family before returning to work, so we agree to have a Family

Fun Day and take the kids to the local Children's Museum and Planetarium. The museum is almost empty, and we enjoy the leisurely pace afforded by not having lines to wait on. There are exciting activity-based exhibits for the kids: a room full of Rube Goldberg machines, a ropes course, a moonwalk, and a building room where Spencer can play with the blocks. He tires himself out by running around the room at warp speed throwing and catching them. Although I'm exhausted, a few minutes in the baseball room energizes Rose and me before lunch.

This is the kind of morning that reinforces my new zest for life. The unconditional love I feel is delightfully overwhelming. I am a long way from being paralyzed in my own home as the five of us scamper through the museum laughing and enjoying each other's company.

We decide to break for lunch and go to the museum cafeteria. We're standing in line, and Paige, our eleven-year-old picky eater, expresses her dismay at the limited menu.

"There's nothing to eat," she complains.

"Come on, Paige. There's a whole menu," I coax.

She squints, then turns to Minnie. "I guess I'll have the broiled salmon and scallops combo."

"You can't get that," Minnie admonishes. "It is the most expensive dish. Find something you like on the kids' menu."

"There is nothing to eat on that menu," Paige whines. "And," she adds, stamping her foot, "when will you realize that I am *not* a kid, dammit!"

There's nothing like your tween daughter's hormone-induced temper tantrum to snap you out of your zen moment and test your commitment to being more Bu than Ju. I react instinctively before I can calm myself down, shouting, "Paige Freeman! Watch your language, and don't talk that way to your mother!"

Paige throws her hands up. Here it comes.

I expect Minnie to back me up, but instead she says, "Adam, please, lower your voice. People are staring."

"Minnie, she can't talk to us like that. That's disrespectful. I *never* spoke that way to my parents when I was growing up." I turn to Paige. "Is this how you treated your mother while I was gone?"

Paige glares at me. "Stop it. I can eat what I want. You can't tell me what to put in my mouth."

I snap. "I can if I'm paying for it."

"I *hate* you," screams Paige as those in the room stare at us.

I zone out for a moment, thinking of Lester Burnham in *American Beauty*. Like him, I'm a broken, beaten-down man trying to resurrect his life. My sweet little Paige has become snarky Thora Birch, and I can't handle her anymore. I come out of my daze and growl, "You, young lady, are about to drive me—"

Minnie steps in. "*Enough*! Both of you. Adam, take a deep breath. Paige, pick a meal from the second page of the menu or order one of the specials. Daddy's back with us, and I want you to stop fighting with him."

My eye is twitching involuntarily again. I feel like Harry Potter when his scar burns uncontrollably. I know Minnie is right; I need to disassociate myself from these feelings of anger and frustration. But I'm having trouble getting a hold of myself.

Minnie looks at me intently and whispers, "Adam, you're the adult here. Start acting like one. Please use what you have learned these past few weeks to make things peaceful."

I turn away to compose myself, then turn back and address Paige. "Honey, your mom is right. I don't want to fight with you. I missed you so much. I'm sorry I raised my voice at you. Your mother and I love you very much."

I wrap Paige in a big hug. Slowly, her shoulders relax, and her head slides onto my chest as she stifles a sniffle and hugs me back.

"I love you too, Daddy."

Looks like my time in the monastery, although terminated early, was well spent. I'm changing for the better after all.

CHAPTER TWENTY-THREE
8:45 a.m.

Leah always says Hillary Clinton got it right. "It takes a village to raise a family." Now I want to modify her quote. In this story, it's taking a *continent* of people—and one intervention after another—to raise Adam Freeman to enlightenment or at least to the level of a grown-up man.

Minnie is Adam's saving grace, the voice of reason in his life. At times, she's the only thing standing between him and the abyss. And I don't know how she does it. She has a sister dying of cancer, three young kids to care for, and a husband who's having an early onset mid-life crisis and trying to find himself. That woman has the patience of a saint, and she must love Adam very, very much.

And Adam? Is he worthy of that love? His heart is filled with goodness, but it's frustrating as hell to watch him continue to stumble on his stutter-step journey, even after all the help he's received. When he seems to be getting it, he slides back. He's in a game of Candy Land progressing to the finish line, but then he picks up that special card that sends him back to Peppermint Forest.

Come on, Adam. You're not a kid playing board games anymore. It's time to grow up, get your act together, and stand on your own two feet.

The Adventures of Adam Freeman, DDS
July 16—*Cheers*

I enter the office. "Hello everybody." I'm greeted like Norm entering *Cheers*, as the staff responds in unison, "Dr. Freeman!" But this can't be my office. I don't recognize anything around me.

Veronica sees the shocked look on my face. "We fixed things up while you were gone, Dr. Freeman. Minnie picked everything out. Hope you like it!" I am overwhelmed with the amazing redecorating job and the work everyone did to make the office patient-ready.

Taking in my bright, freshly painted waiting room, I have optimism in my heart and a clear head telling me that I'm ready to go. I look down at the new, natty, blue-and-brown carpeting. The walls are now pale blue, the color of the Caribbean Sea. I had grown so accustomed to the old brown walls that this feels like moving into a brand-new space. I bend down to pick up a plastic protective wrapper left on the new crystal-clear waiting room table.

On the blood-free reception room desk is a beautiful bouquet of flowers, courtesy of the staff. It is a sweet gesture.

I join the team for the morning huddle. Before we review the schedule, I address the team with a lump in my throat. "Ladies, I'm glad to be back. I don't say this a lot, but I'm blessed to be here and thankful to have you all in my life."

Veronica and Danielle wipe tears from their eyes and give me big hugs. I swallow hard and regain my composure as Veronica runs through the day's schedule. She calls my attention to the assistant we're interviewing before lunch to replace Sam. Gosh, Cellgate seems like an eternity ago.

"Good idea having a half day today," I tell the team. "This'll help me get back into the swing of things."

Veronica speaks for the group. "Oh good, we were a little worried you'd be upset that we didn't have as many production slots filled as you like. I wanted you to have a smooth first day back."

I smile at her. "The old version of Adam Freeman would've been upset. But Adam 2.0 is grateful."

The morning runs smoothly. I have sealants on two patients, four hygiene checks, three class IV composite fillings, and a new patient exam. Everything is copacetic. I'm looking through the get-well cards stacked on my desk when Veronica enters my office. She begins, "Well the applicant's been given the tour and met the staff. I've spent thirty minutes in the interview."

"Is she worth having back for a working interview?"

"Well...there's quite a discussion going on in the lunch room now."

"About what?"

"Gender."

"Excuse me?"

Veronica continues, "Well, the candidate seems to be portraying, um, herself as a woman, but there are a number of characteristics that lead me to believe she's a man. I wanted you to be aware so you're not caught off-guard."

I nod. "What's the name again?"

"Carter."

"What's the first name?"

"That is the first name."

"Well, that doesn't help. Thanks for the heads up." Veronica turns to leave, but I stop her. "Um, Veronica? Maybe you can help me out here. I'm a defined gender kind of guy, and I've never met a transgendered person. What's the protocol? I don't want to do or say anything stupid or awkward."

Veronica smiles; she's enjoying having the upper hand and how uncomfortable this is making me. "It's no big deal, Dr. Freeman. Treat her like anyone else you'd interview. And it's transgender not transgendered."

"Okay." I take a deep breath, and although there is no rational reason, I know this is going to take me out of my comfort zone. "Let's do this." I follow Veronica into the room.

The applicant stands and shakes my hand firmly and is nearly as tall as I am. "Nice to meet you, Doc," she says in a deep but feminine voice. I try not to stare as I sit down across the table from Veronica and the candidate.

Like a game of Texas Hold'em, I try to decode all of the physical signs to help me determine the sex of my interviewee. The hairless black skin and the long cornrows seem feminine, but the facial five o'clock shadow tells another tale. I can't sneak a peek under the table to check if there's a bulge in the pants, so I turn my attention to the chest. I don't see any breasts. The attire is a blouse and pants along with high heels. I'm trying to detect if an Adam's apple is present, but I can't get a good look at the neck. Although I am still undecided on the gender, I find Carter pleasantly smiling at me as I break the awkward silence. "Tell me about yourself."

"I had a rotten childhood. My mother abandoned me and left me at an orphanage. I was in and out of foster families until sixteen. I'm not proud of my actions as a teenager, but I really set myself straight and ran away to San Francisco where I finally felt at home—like I belonged. I went to hairdressing school but grew bored with it. While working at a movie theatre, I finally decided that I needed to do more with my life. I felt alone and without a path. Have you ever felt misunderstood? Like no one could relate to you?"

I take a deep breath and wipe the sweat from my lip. Suddenly, out of nowhere, my eye starts to twitch. "Interesting question, but let's talk about you."

Carter continues, "Although it took me a long time to figure out what I wanted to do with my life, I always loved when people smiled at me, so I decided I should do something in the dental field." She stops and crinkles her eyes. "Doctor Freeman, are you...winking at me? I'm feeling uncomfortable."

I'm sweating profusely, and my eye is throbbing. I clear my throat. Veronica interjects, "Dr. Freeman has a nervous twitch, and the eye movements are involuntary. It's kind of like Tourette's Syndrome."

Carter responds, "Oh, I understand. Sometimes I get an itch in my butt that I can't control, and I have to reach around and scratch it."

I get up to end the interview. "Carter, do you have any questions for us?"

"One question. Did I do anything at the interview that would prohibit me from getting the job?"

Veronica responds for me, "Your interview was fine. Now I have to evaluate you with respect to the other candidates and come to the difficult choice of choosing the best person to add to our current team."

Veronica escorts Carter out of the office, and I stand to leave. Veronica comes back in. "She gave way too much information about herself. I'm not sure she will be a good fit. Do you agree?"

I nod my agreement. "Veronica, Tourette's Syndrome...really? You know I don't have that disorder, it's a nervous twitch."

Veronica shrugs. "I was trying to make her feel more comfortable and get you out of that awkward moment."

The recurrence of my twitch depresses me. I sit down at my desk and slouch in my chair. All that work, down the drain.

Then it dawns on me. The way to get rid of my twitch once and for all. I pick up my cell phone and text: "In dire need of help, send me hypnotherapist's #" knowing Errol has his cell phone cemented to his fingertips. As expected, he texts me back right away.

I dial and, luckily, Errol's hypnotherapist answers. She tells me that her next opening is in five weeks. I feel a strong urge to bang my head against the desk again, because I can't wait that long to get my twitch under control. She must hear something in my voice, because she asks me to hold for a minute then comes back to the phone and says, "A moment ago I got a cancellation, and can fit you in today for a sixty-minute appointment. I take no insurance but all major credit cards. Can you be at my office at 2:00 p.m.?"

"I certainly can." I grab my keys and sprint to my car. I'm out on the road following Google Maps to her office. I speed through a yellow light. I don't want to be late. She may be my last hope.

July 16—*60 Minutes*

The first thing I notice when I enter the hypnotherapist's office is how open the waiting room appears. There's no reception desk, and no one is there to greet me except a clipboard with a pen and a blank medical history form, next to a brightly colored floral arrangement on a modern, white-and-red table. I grab the form and start writing, hesitating over the "nervous conditions" check box but finally checking yes.

A new butterfly emerges from its cocoon in my stomach every minute I wait. But the picturesque photos of waterfalls and majestic animals that line the walls calm me. Finally, she comes out.

"I'm Corinna Frasier, very nice to meet you."

We shake hands. Hers is ice cold and I wince. "Sorry, poor circulation," she says.

She's an older woman, probably in her late sixties—short, petite, maybe five foot two (to be generous), and wearing funky green-rimmed glasses.

She wears a white button-down shirt with a flower-patterned red skirt, and her greying hair is neatly held back in a bun.

Her warm smile facilitates my immediate trust in her. I want to believe more than anything that she is going to help me gain control over my body after all these years of being a marionette.

I follow Corinna into her office and sit down in her plush brown La-Z-Boy recliner. Before she reviews the forms, I burst into a twenty-minute Christian confessional about how I developed my nervous eye twitch. I elaborate that, despite my efforts, it's as bad as ever, and I need help getting rid of it. Corinna isn't the least bit judgmental as I pour my guts out. She sits in silence looking over my medical history. Finally, she asks, "Do you take any medications?"

"No," I respond.

"That's very unusual. Most of my patients come in with a laundry list of prescriptions. I'm surprised that you're not on anything."

"Funny you should mention that. My wife keeps pushing me to take antidepressants, but I want to cure myself naturally. I don't want to mask my symptoms."

She puts her hand on my knee. "You're a hoot! I like you. We're going to get along well. I agree with you—medicine can mask the underlying cause of the issue, but some people do need meds to stabilize themselves. It's always my goal to reduce my patient's medication and get at those internal weeds that cause the problems in their gardens. Have you ever had hypnosis, dear?"

"I recently went to a hypnosis show, but I've never done anything like this. How does it work?"

Corinna replies, "Hypnosis shows are nothing like what we'll do here. My work is to clean up your mind. I uncover the myths and false beliefs that the subconscious mind has imprinted on the brain. These fallacies and misguided thoughts block us from seeing love, feeling positive emotions, and being the best person we can be. Hypnotherapy gets to the core of what's bothering you. Being in my chair is like having therapy on steroids. I can help good clients address their issues in five to six sessions, while traditional psychotherapy can take five to six years."

"Are there bad clients?"

"You're funny. I don't have bad clients, only people who are resistant. It's extremely hard work to clear your mind and allow yourself to heal. If you can do the work with me, then we'll be successful."

"You think there's hope for me to be cured of this twitch?"

She chews on her pencil's eraser. "There are no guarantees in life, but there's always hope, and I'll be your healing coach. The cure may not be 100 percent permanent, and you might sometimes need a tune up every now and then. The subconscious mind is a powerful and persistent force. But I'll give you techniques to counteract it and reassert control over your life."

"Sold. I'm willing to give this everything I have."

"Right then, dear. Are you ready to begin?"

"Now?" I ask in surprise. I start to sweat and cover my eye to block the twitching.

"Of course. Take off your shoes and lie back in the recliner." I stretch out my legs on the footpad. She gives me a pillow to hold.

I look around and say, "Where's the moving watch to follow, so I can fall asleep?"

Corinna laughs. "You've been watching way too much TV. We're going to do simple exercises to expand your mind." She pulls out a notepad. Then, in a hushed voice, she begins to talk to me slowly. "Close your eyes. Relax your body and take deep breaths. Clear your mind. I'm going to ask your subconscious mind some questions. Answer fast, without thinking. Are you male or female?"

"Male."

"What is your favorite color?"

"Blue."

"What is your favorite movie?"

"*Fletch, American Beauty, Fight Club.*"

"I asked for one, but that's fine." She continues, "Take an assessment of your whole body from the inside. You need to relax. Keep breathing deeply. Inhale. Exhale. Good, that's great. Feel your body, dear. Be in tune with what your body is telling you. See what bubbles up."

I try to tame my nagging skepticism, and my burning desire to heal myself helps me let go of my mind's monkey chatter. I feel a lump in my throat. I'm overcome by a dense sadness. In the distance I hear Corinna again. "Search your mind, dear. A picture should start to emerge. Tell me what you see."

She's right. I begin to visualize a scene. I'm on a hospital gurney with my parents by my side. I'm six years old. I am seeing the scene from the outside, as if I'm watching a television show. The nurse is wheeling me down a long hallway to an operating room. I remember this is when I had my tonsils taken out. I see a frightened child wondering why his parents are letting the doctors take him away. I feel deep emotional pain. I'm afraid of the hospital and the operation. I begin to cry uncontrollably in Corinna's chair. "That's good, Adam. Tell me what you're feeling."

"Anger."

"Who are you angry at?"

"My parents, the doctors."

"Why?"

"I don't want to get my tonsils out. Why do they have to cut me open? Why are they doing this to me? Don't they care about me?" A waterfall of tears streams down my cheeks.

"It's okay, get it out. This is good. Get out your emotions." I clench the pillow that is on my lap. "Repeat after me, Adam. I am angry."

"I am angry."

"And I deeply and completely accept myself."

I repeat, "And I deeply and completely accept myself."

"I am mad at you, Mom, Dad, and doctors, for taking my tonsils out without my permission."

"I am mad at you, Mom, Dad, and doctors, for taking my tonsils out without my permission." I continue to cry.

"You're safe and secure here, Adam."

With my eyes still shut, I feel like I'm choking and start to cough uncontrollably. "What is wrong with me?" I ask Corinna.

"Absolutely nothing, my dear, this is normal. The coughing is a good thing. You're releasing the pent-up emotions that have been stored within you for decades."

I look at her out of my blurry, watery eyes. "Those feelings were so strong. This is really tiring." I pause to take a sip of the cup of water that Corinna hands me. She takes the cup back.

"You were upset with your parents because they put you through something you didn't understand. Your subconscious mind internalized this situation as not having a voice or control over your life. But you can think more clearly now, right?"

"I think."

"Don't think. Tell me what comes from your heart."

"My parents wanted the best for me."

Corinna smiles. "Exactly. They never meant to harm you. I can tell your parents are good people who had pure intentions."

With complete candor, I respond, "Yes, I know that my parents love me and meant well. They didn't want to hurt me. I even remember all the ice cream I had afterwards and the Colorforms they bought me."

"You need to grow from this and forgive them. You need to let it go."

"They meant no ill will towards me and only had my best interest at heart. I forgive them."

Corinna has a big grin. "You were a kid when you underwent that scary surgery. The experience was traumatic. And your subconscious mind became stuck on the trauma. Your rational mind understands that the operation was necessary for your health, but you had to clear out the weeds that had grown so high they were obscuring your vision. This is great progress for you to gain back control of your body."

Ding.

"I'm afraid that's the end of our session. How would you like to pay?"

I take out my AmEx gold card and hand it to her. She waves it away. "I forgot to tell you, I don't take American Express." I pay cash.

On the drive home, I feel more free and uninhibited by my emotions. Like a Morley Safer segment on *60 Minutes*, Corinna has finished her investigative reporting of my mind. She has exposed that my parents had good intentions by helping get my tonsils out, but I misinterpreted the surgery, allowing a flawed belief to grow and occupy my subconscious mind. My body is lighter, and my mood is joyful. Best of all, my eye feels great— no twitching. I look at myself in the rearview mirror and begin to smile. I'm feeling less anger than usual, and it cumulates in a feeling of euphoria.

This woman, Corinna Frasier, is a miracle worker.

CHAPTER TWENTY-FOUR
9:06 a.m.

I have a confession. I've done hypnotherapy too. It's helped me decipher why my body acts like it does and, most importantly, cured my nervous ear wiggle. Through the power of examining my mind, releasing my feelings, and doing meditation, I realized that my tension and built-up anxiety manifested themselves in the involuntary movement of my ear. Once I addressed the source of the angst and released it from my body, my ear wiggle went away.

Okay, I know what you are thinking—I lied to Leah when I said I'm not Adam Freeman. But I didn't lie. I'm *like* him, but I'm not him. Adam is my best friend. Well, my fictional best friend since Leah is my real one. Adam is the guy who holds up the mirror and helps me see my true self. And yes, we've been through a lot together, including hypnotherapy.

My hypnotherapist was Nadine—a lady in her mid-fifties. She had short, pixie-cut hair dyed dark red. She always wore slacks and a colored blazer with a large pearl necklace dangling over her blouse. And no funky glasses like Corinna. Her office featured an autographed picture of Kelsey Grammer. When I first saw Kelsey's picture, I was excited that she was a hypnotherapist to the stars, but then she divulged that a client with connections in the entertainment business had given her the picture as a gift. *That borders on false advertising,* I thought.

I vividly remember my first session with Nadine.

"Do you believe in God?" Nadine asked.

"Yes, I do," I told Nadine. "I pray, but I don't advertise my faith. When I was little, I would lay my head on the pillow at night and start talking to 'the big guy upstairs.' I thanked God for all that he had bestowed upon me and then I would make requests."

"Do you realize you're separating yourself from God by asking for things?"

"But I felt a connection with God. I remember closing my eyes and picturing a tunnel. It was a long black tunnel with a light at the end. I used to dream that I was moving down this tunnel, but I never reached the light. I fell asleep long before I got there."

"Visualizing the tunnel is good; it's like you were picturing yourself getting closer to The Source. In essence, we are all connected to God."

"I understand that, but does that mean we shouldn't ask God for things?"

"Great question. We can have aspirations and ask God for guidance, but the key is not to get attached to your desires. Your mind will want to reach for things to keep you in the future or relive things that are in the past—but always remember to stay present."

"I try to clear my mind and open up to what is out there when I meditate, but I also pray to God. What's the difference between praying and meditating, anyway?"

"Meditation is a way to connect to our Source. When you meditate, you clear your mind and free your true inner self to listen to the Source. Once you have eliminated the outside noises and distractions, you can unmask your truth."

"And what about praying?"

"Praying is a way to communicate to our Creator. It's great to be thankful and acknowledge the Source. It helps a lot of people to pray. But, I believe prayer perpetuates the idea that we're separate from our Creator. We all have God inside of us. It's our mission to try to uncover God in ourselves, to surrender to the universe and have faith."

I'm mesmerized by our conversation as I understand and absorb Nadine's perspective. "When I ask God for guidance," I say, "no one speaks back to me. No miraculous event happens; lightning doesn't figuratively strike. Do I have to beg, plead, and steal for divine intervention? I'm asking for help but I'm not getting anywhere."

To this, Nadine answered with something so simple but deep. "You're trying too hard, Jacob. Relax and let things come to you."

I closed my eyes and let all the tension flow out of my body. "I want inner peace."

I told Nadine I had tremendous feelings of anxiety and what was most disconcerting was my nervous ear wiggle.

"Wiggle? No euphemisms allowed in my office. Let's call a twitch a twitch." She shot me a stern look. "Sit back and close your eyes. Let's start with what you are feeling…"

As I lay back in her comfortable chair with my legs up on the ottoman and closed my eyes to relax, Dr. Rick Barker suddenly popped into my mind. I told her that I was surprised to be looking at my old professor.

"Tell me who he is. Why do you think your mind is stuck on him?"

I filled her in on the backstory. Dr. Rick Barker was one of my favorite faculty members during dental school. I admired his wit and wisdom. He would make patients feel comfortable in the dental chair. It was poetry in motion to see him interact with families and a privilege to learn from him.

"Why are you seeing him in your mind's eye. Only you know the real answer."

"I have a lot of John Dorian in me. You know—the lead character from *Scrubs*."

"I don't know that show."

I continued, "It's one of my top five favorite comedies of all time. Up there with *Seinfeld, The Big Bang Theory, Cheers, Modern Family.* You also have to put *Frasier* and *Curb Your Enthusiasm* up there."

"Focus, Jacob, you're getting distracted."

"Sorry. Like JD from *Scrubs*, I yearn for acceptance and love from people. I admired Rick Barker so much I guess I put him on a pedestal. I listened intently to his lectures, read his published articles, and spent countless hours chatting with him after clinic. He was quite generous with his time."

"It sounds like you found a mentor."

"And a friend. Leah and I even double dated with him and his wife. During my orthodontic residency, I started working for him as his hygienist on the weekends. I'm not sure what happened, but over time Dr. Barker became angry and standoffish with me. I was a good employee, but he treated me like crap. He turned from the affable Dr. Hawkeye Pierce in *M*A*S*H* to the contentious Dr. Perry Cox in *Scrubs*. This sixty-year-old man would rail off insults at me, like how my cleanings were second rate and how could they let me graduate from dental school."

Nadine listened intently. I continued, "He had another hygienist, Helen, whom he clearly favored and always compared me to."

"Go on."

"I was relegated to being the ugly stepson, whom he treated like shit. I sent him an email asking him to lay off, because his rudeness had become insufferable. He was acting like a bully."

"Yes, he was."

"He got really mad at me when I called him out on it one day at the office. He shouted back to me, 'How dare you call me a bully. I'm your boss.'"

"I told him that I deserved to be treated like a colleague. I was studying orthodontics and doing dental cleanings for some cash to cover my expenses, not to be treated like an intern."

"It's good that you stuck up for yourself."

"He fired me on the spot."

Nadine gathered her thoughts. "Good. You didn't need him. He's the type of person with no self-awareness of how his words and actions affect others. You will never be able to change that."

"But why did he turn on me?"

"It's a cycle he goes through. No doubt he eventually soured on Helen too. The hate he outwardly displays represents the way he feels about himself deep down. He doesn't love himself, and this deficit defines the way he treats other people. He probably became jealous of you and put you down as a way to deal with his own insecurity. Put simply, bullying you made him feel better about himself."

"I never thought of it that way."

Nadine pressed on. "We need to dig down deeper, to examine your feelings about how he treated you. What's familiar about those feelings? Your subconscious mind has made a connection to them and something from the past." She handed me a pillow.

"The words he said were like a scalpel that cut inside at my heart."

"Nice metaphor, Jacob, but how did that make you *feel*?"

"Hurt. Angry. Unloved."

"Yes. Now what's familiar about these feelings? Search, and let your mind relax. The thoughts will come to you."

My vision was as clear as a light-blue sky. "I'm at the dinner table with my family. My mom's telling my dad about the new bathroom curtains. My dad describes his day at the store. My sister Jessica tells the family the exciting boy news of eighth grade. There's a lull in that conversation and all eyes focus on me. I start to talk about my day, but now I'm talking to the empty chair in front of me. My mother and sister have started to clear the table as my dad washes the dishes at the kitchen sink."

"How did this make you feel?"

"Like a second-class citizen. No one's listening to me."

"Feelings, Jacob. Your core emotions."

"Angry...unloved." My ear started to burn.

"Good. Now what do you want to tell your family? Speak to them. They can hear you."

"Why did you exclude me? Why didn't anyone listen to me?" Suddenly, I could no longer control the emotions flooding out. I started to cry.

"Repeat after me. I feel unloved. No one listens to me."

I was finally able to release the feelings of not being loved. Nadine put things in perspective for me. "We all want that feeling of belonging. To be connected with our family and friends. You know that Dr. Barker cares about you but is incapable of showing it. And you know your family truly and deeply loves you, right?"

"I know."

"Feel the love your family has for you."

I unexpectedly started to laugh. "I *know* they love me. But, they have a hard time showing it. Truth be told, I also didn't engage them in a lot of conversations. They had a different way of looking at things than I did." I paused and took a deep breath.

"Keep going."

"When I was away from home in college, I felt free and unbridled with no constraints from my family. I truly was an uninhibited person. It's sad, but it was the first time I felt free to be myself, although my freshman roommates gave me a real hard time. On the whole though, people paid attention to me and noticed me for who I was, and that was a wonderful feeling."

"Great, Jacob, you empowered yourself. *Always remember, you are loved.* Take some more deep breaths, and open your eyes when you're ready."

I soaked in the new and refreshing state of total relaxation. After two minutes I opened my eyes and looked at Nadine.

"I'm so proud of you. Those were some serious feelings that you acknowledged and released today. Very good for our first session." She patted me on the back.

I gave her a warm smile. "Nadine, you're a miracle worker. This is the first time I've felt peaceful and content in a long time. You're magical. I feel exhilarated."

My favorite part was when Nadine summarized the session. "Jacob, you need to search within and not externally. Don't seek love from your mother, father, sister, even this Dr. Barker. You'll never get the answers you seek from other people. There are great guides out there, and everyone has a reason for entering your life, but no one can paint your picture for you; they can only hand you the paintbrush and the paints. Accept the tools that people give you, but never, ever expect them to do your work. When you create your picture from your inner self, the meaning of life will be clear and amazing to you."

That was my first experience with my hypnotherapist, and like Adam's, it was life changing.

The Adventures of Adam Freeman, DDS
August 1—*Good Times*

Two weeks after Corinna's session, I'm still seeing things more clearly and, like a great athlete in a critical moment of the game, life has slowed down for me. I'm having a good time at home with Minnie and the kids. Work is not only tolerable but enjoyable. I'm finally letting go of my pent-up emotions and negative thoughts. I'm responding to things now with more love in my heart than I ever have. But life still tries to test me.

I begin getting eight-year-old Ella numb for a cavity when Michelle comes in. "Um, Dr. Freeman, I need to talk to you for a second out here."

After the injection, I excuse myself and she leads me into my office. "Dr. Freeman, I can't find the round burs in the drawer that you'll need."

I say serenely, "There are no round #8 burs? How about #6 or #4?"

"No. I think they may have been misplaced or thrown out during the renovation."

Even though not having my equipment is a *huge* pet peeve of mine, I say, "Michelle, there must be some burs around here. Keep looking. I'm sure they'll pop up."

"Well, I looked all around, and I can't find them. I've no idea where they could be."

I feel my frustration surging, then morphing to anger as the words spring from my mouth. "I need these burs to do my work. This is completely unaccept—" and then something strange happens. My eyes engage hers. I feel the stinging hurt she feels, and I know in this instant I have to let my negative thoughts pass and bring positive love and good energy to her, my employee who is doing her best to help me. Without thinking, I visualize a bucket of hearts being poured over Michelle's head. Although that image is strange, it helps me dispel the negative thoughts that are germinating in my mind. I speak calmly, "Okay, mistakes happen, and I understand. Let's learn from this and make sure going forward that I always have the inventory I need. I'll use the pear-shaped 332 instead of the round #8."

With that, I go back into the room, and I start making Ella a balloon animal as Michelle finishes getting my setup ready.

* * *

I'm running out of time, unless I play hooky from work—which is tempting. Maggie's deadline to kill Adam—or save him—is looming. When I left that meeting, I was dead set against working with Maggie or even meeting her again, but having spent the past twenty hours with Adam, I can see the source of her frustration. I've got the new and improved Adam Freeman, DDS. He's still the snarky, oddball, Larry David-esque character I love, but I think that now the gold in his heart shines through. I'm fairly confident Maggie would be fascinated with his trip to the monastery and his antics in Puerto Rico. But even with all the work I've done, I'm not sure it's enough. Do I pitch Adam or ditch him? I'll have to finish the rest of the manuscript before I decide.

The Adventures of Adam Freeman, DDS
August 3—*The Wire*

I wake up on this lazy Sunday and take an assessment of my body. I feel no tension or anxiety. With a pep in my step, I enter the kitchen and announce to the kids, who are already locked into the television, "Good morning, Freeman family! Daddy's making his world-famous pancakes!" They cheer, then turn their attention back to the TV.

My pancakes turn out perfectly—customized for each child—as my Rockin' '80s playlist echoes throughout the kitchen. One by one the kids grab their flapjacks. Paige likes hers with blueberries and chocolate chips. Rose is all in with banana, strawberry, and sprinkles, and Spencer—being the pickiest eater and a hater of healthy foods—eats only a small bowl of chocolate chips for breakfast.

I am seated at our kitchen island slathering my own banana and chocolate chip pancakes with whipped cream and maple syrup when Minnie ambles in sleepy-eyed and groggy. I greet her, "Top of the morning to you, Schmoopy. Oh, I changed that lightbulb in the bathroom that you were asking me to do."

She grunts and proceeds to grab a chocolate chip pancake. "Children, go downstairs to the Kids Cave," she tells them. Minnie then turns to me with a dark look on her face and asks, "Why did you wire ten thousand dollars from our savings to your practice?"

Like Jeff Probst says on *Survivor*, "You've been blindsided." With a mouth full of pancakes, I answer her question with a question, "Why do you ask?"

"Don't answer a question with a question."

"I needed the money to meet payroll. My being out for so long created a cash flow problem."

"I thought you had practice savings set aside for emergencies."

"I did, but I ran through it. There were other expenses."

"You didn't pay off a complaining client, did you?"

"You mean the Cains? No way, I wouldn't give those people a cent."

"What then?"

Unlike Dexter Morgan, I'm not good at keeping secrets. I admit the truth. "My sister and I agreed to put in ten thousand dollars each to send my parents on a cruise to Australia for their forty-fifth wedding anniversary."

Silence. I know this is not good. Then Minnie speaks very quietly.

"Adam...you decided to fund your parents' trip—without consulting me."

"I was going to tell you," I whine. Suddenly my eye twitch returns—the first time since my session with Corinna.

"But you didn't tell me. Adam, you can't spend that kind of money without checking with me. It would be like me blowing ten thousand dollars on new furniture and not clearing it with you first."

"I was going to use my practice money, but I didn't have enough. I didn't want to ask you because I knew what your answer would be."

"Well that says a lot. You know I hate sneakiness. It's not fair for us to support their habits at this point in our lives."

"Come on, Minnie! Support their habits is kind of harsh, don't you think? We're talking about an anniversary gift." I turn away so that she can't see my twitching eye.

"Adam, are you forgetting how they got into their situation?"

Minnie does have a point. Unbeknownst to us, we discovered that my parents' bank account had been drained five years ago due to my father's gambling habit on football games. Although it wasn't easy to convince him, he agreed to seek help. After three years of Gamblers Anonymous meetings, he finally gained control of his demons. As a result of my father's bad decisions, though, they're both still working, even in their mid-70s. I feel bad. They're tired, and my sister and I wanted to give them a stress-free, debt-free vacation for their big anniversary.

I turn back to face Minnie and use my trump card. "You're forgetting they helped pay for my college tuition."

Minnie has her response ready. "Apples and oranges. That's part of their parental obligation. Don't let your father guilt you into feeling that you owe them for their help when you were a student. We're not responsible for your dad's financial recklessness."

Calmly, I plead my case. "I don't see the big deal here. Giving a gift to my parents shouldn't cause a fight."

"It is a big deal. You didn't work for three weeks, and we need to take care of our household *first* before we give money away. And, the fact that you took cash out of our account without asking me is the most disturbing."

I begin to raise my voice and exclaim, "Do you hear how selfish you're being by not wanting to contribute to my parents' forty-fifth wedding anniversary gift?" I pause, getting ready for the zinger. "Plus, it's *my*..." Before I put my foot in my mouth, I channel my inner Bu and remember that it's *our* money and avoid Armageddon.

"Minnie, I'm sorry. I know you care about my parents. It was rotten of me to say that."

Minnie is silent. Astonished.

Smiling, I say to her, "I will call my sister and let her know we have to change the trip."

"I already spoke with her."

"What? You did?"

"She's still doing research on the trip and hasn't decided on a cruise yet. And she agrees that it's a lot of money. We're talking about going on a more economical family vacation, with all the grandchildren and your parents, to a fun resort."

"Really? You're game for that?"

"Listen, Adam, don't make me out to be some kind of bitch. I'm not. That's a long time to be married, that's for sure, and I agree your parents deserve something special, but—"

"You knew all along, and you still had me undergo a confessional."

"I wanted to see if your Buddhist transformation is for real."

"You hate sneaky. And I hate being tested. But I passed, right?"

"With flying colors!" She gives me a big hug.

CHAPTER TWENTY-FIVE
9:26 a.m.

It's taken more than 90,000 words and over three hundred pages, and still my fingers resist the urge to type out my own final confession. The truth is, this book is about more than Adam Freeman's transformation. Even after all this time, exorcising my inner demons by writing about Adam's escapades, I've skillfully avoided one area of my life that forms an essential piece of the puzzle. I still haven't built up the nerve to talk about it. I would love to tweet it out there, share it on Facebook, blog about it, even wear a sandwich board in Times Square, but I'm not that brave. I've hidden behind the veil of my characters, because I'm afraid of the repercussions. I don't want to be labeled by my peers, colleagues, and friends. Sharing my secret goes against everything I've been taught growing up and in my years of education. Like ripping off a Band-Aid, I can't think about it and screw up my courage. I need to tell the world that—

"Jacob, are you still reading?" I turn around as Leah walks into my office. "I can't believe you stayed up all night. My God, you mean business with this book. You're usually showered and shaved by now. You need to get a move on, or you'll be late for work."

I clear my throat and take another drink of water. "Maybe I'll take the morning off and finish my rewrite so that I can show the book to Maggie again."

"You can't be serious. We've talked about this—the practice has to be your priority. What's going on with you? Are you okay?" Leah puts her hand on my back.

"What are you talking about?"

"You're sweating and your leg's shaking. You haven't had the shimmy legs since college."

"I'm fine, Leah. You caught me in the middle of something. Please, I need to finish this."

Leah leaves my office, and I shut the door behind her, trying to stave off a panic attack.

Once I'm sure she's out of earshot, I whisper the words to myself, needing to hear them out loud myself before I can share them with actual readers: *this Harvard-trained orthodontist believes in past lives. Reincarnation. The ongoing journey of the soul.* Suddenly, I feel a huge sense of relief. The purpose of my book comes into focus, and my connection to my soulmate Adam is now crystal clear. I can barely contain my excitement. I couldn't tell Leah, but that's why my leg was shaking and I'd broken out in a sweat. Confronting the truth is frightening but also exhilarating as hell.

I would normally need to see double-blind case control studies to prove to me that past lives existed, since research and evidenced-based medicine and dentistry were pounded into my head at Harvard. But the reason I can now articulate my belief is because of the powerful experience I had in a hypnotherapy session. I struggled with what happened at my session for a long time. However, my scientific world and spiritual world collided one afternoon when I was in Nadine's office. The session was so vivid, so real, that it caused a seismic shift in my thinking—a 9.7 on the Richter scale. I now know how my rewrite will end.

The Adventures of Adam Freeman, DDS
August 11—*The X-Files/Stranger Things*

The kids are in bed, and Minnie and I are washing the dishes together. "You've been really quiet ever since you arrived home, how did your session go today?"

I really want to tell my wife about the events that transpired earlier today, but I'm hesitant. They were surreal.

Rose shuffles into the kitchen with a smirk on her face. "Get back into bed," Minnie tells her.

"I can't sleep. Can you tuck me in?"

"I'll be right up." Minnie hands me the dishtowel, and I go from washing to drying. As Minnie leaves the room, I wonder if I should recap what happened with Corinna. I'm not sure Minnie would be able to relate or grasp the magnitude of it. And I wouldn't blame her if she didn't buy into my story. I'd be skeptical too if I hadn't gone through the experience. While I continue to clean up, I review what happened earlier today in my mind.

10 Hours Ago:

I sit down in Corinna's chair feeling more anxious than ever. She wants to know how the last week went and if anything is "bubbling up"—her code term for anything upsetting me. I tell her I am doing well at my office, but my eye twitch acted up during my argument with Minnie over my parents' anniversary.

"I regressed. My eye acted up again. I don't know why I can't control it in stressful situations."

Corinna smiles warmly. "Don't worry. We'll solve it. Close your eyes. Relax and do your breathing. Let your subconscious mind take you where it needs to go."

Without warning, I'm instantly transported to another time. I describe the scene to Corinna. I see a little boy in a dank, white room, walls barren. The boy couldn't have been more than six years old with bowl-cut hair, dressed in a surgical gown. He is lying on a dull brown, sterile surgical table with a bright yellow light shining in his eyes. The boy looks anguished and frightened. I open my eyes.

"I can't do this."

"You can, Adam. Go with it. You are safe and secure here. Tell me what you see."

"There's too much pain. I can feel the boy's torment. I can't."

Corinna demands, "Let go of the pain. Go back to the event and tell me what you see. What you are feeling. Trust me, Adam, you have to release this." I take some deep breaths with her guidance, and I begin to relax and let go. I go deeper and deeper.

Through the boy's eyes, I see a young couple in the corner of the room. They look nervous. The young man wears a blue button-down shirt and long green socks stretched up to his knees. His brown knickerbocker pants are tucked into his socks. My mind focuses on his unusual shoes. They look like Crocs, but they are made of wood. The woman wears a simple blouse and a long skirt that covers her legs right down to her feet. A white bonnet sits atop her head. They look transported here from the past.

An older man with a gray beard enters the room. He dons a white coat with an ID badge on his lapel. The language they speak is not English. Their native tongue sounds Germanic, or possibly Dutch. Even though they are not speaking English, I can understand what they are saying.

Dr. Gray Beard sternly tells the couple, "Like we agreed, you'll be compensated handsomely."

The woman wails hysterically, and the man by her side comforts her by saying, "This is for the best. You know he's very sick and dying anyway."

"You don't know that. I can't do it. We shouldn't do this. It's a mistake," cries the woman.

"We're done here. Ursula has your money." Dr. Gray Beard pushes them out of the door.

The boy starts screaming, "Don't leave me. Mommy, I need you."

The door opens again, but instead of the woman coming back in to rescue the boy, a handful of people dressed in scrubs march in. Suddenly, I become the boy. Like an eclipse, one doctor starts to block out the bright light shining on me as his face comes into focus. He is tall and graying at the temples, has a salt and pepper mustache and round villain-like glasses. He is saying, "What took so long?" as he puts a mask over my nose and mouth. Dr. Gray Beard responds, "The typical second thoughts."

My eyes become heavy. I notice Dr. Gray Beard taking a Sharpie and drawing marks around my eyes. Then a nurse hands Dr. Gray Beard a scalpel, and he makes an incision around my left eye. I give a piercing cry and try to shout to the people looking over me that it feels like I am not completely under. The pain in my eye sears through my body. My whole body is twitching in agony. Words cannot even come close to describing how excruciating the pain feels. I want to let go, to die right then.

I scream at Corinna, "*Stop this now*! I don't want to go back there and relive these memories."

In a calm and loving voice, she tells me, "You have to visualize and acknowledge these memories to release them."

"It hurts too much."

"Adam, you can do this."

"*Stop yelling at me!*"

"I'm not yelling."

My eye feels on fire as the blade pierces my orbital rim. The white sterile room suddenly disappears, and my mind goes blank. I see nothing. I'm numb and empty.

"Adam, stay in the moment. What do you see?"

"Nothing. What's happening to me?"

"You've let go. There was too much emotional and physical pain. You've passed."

The floodgates open. The emotion is like a steamroller speeding unimpeded down a hill, and I go full speed ahead. The sobbing pours out of me, and I can't stop it. Even though I want to open my eyes and walk away, deep inside my core I know this is good for me. I continue to let the tears drain down my cheeks. My nose is runny. I'm exposed and vulnerable, but I don't care. It is not me, but it is me. I don't understand what is going on. Deep down, I know that this is a healing moment. The most important part is to release everything. "Let it go," Corinna tells me. I keep crying and crying. Corinna pushes me to concentrate on my breathing.

The vision is back, and the little boy is standing next to me holding my hand.

"How old is he?" Corinna asks, realizing that my vision has started again.

"Six," I reply without thinking. "Corinna, I'm scared."

"Explore the moment you are experiencing," she says, as I feel pain in my left eye and a surge of emotion so strong that I begin to cough uncontrollably.

"Good, Adam, good. Let it out. Scan your body and tell me what you feel."

I feel tension in my head and pain from the burning in my left eye. My whole forehead twitches.

"Go with it. What do you see? Follow the emotions."

I'm rubbing the boy's head. I burst out, "I don't want to be given away. They will harm me. I'll never be the same. I need to escape. These people hurt me. I can't bear it any longer. I don't want to suffer through life with the experiment."

"Good, Adam. This is a necessary step for your healing. Your body has cells that remember from life to life. You are clearing out a past life."

"Am I the boy?" *Cough, cough, cough.* "Is the boy me? What the hell is happening?"

"*Stop thinking* and let go. Don't worry, I judge no one. Go with it. This work has taught me that there are no coincidences; the subconscious mind goes where it needs to take you to heal."

"Am I going crazy that I envision myself given away as a six-year-old child to a doctor who did experiments on me? Did my parents really sell me?"

"You need to stop thinking with your mind and trust your subconscious. It seems this child was given away to these Dr. Mengele-like doctors who did vicious and evil things to kids. Apparently, they experimented on your eyes."

I open my eyes; the boy vanishes, and I yell, "This is *crazy*!"

"Listen, Adam, this little boy needs to heal. What I want you to do is close your eyes again and envision your parents from that life. You need to talk to them and tell them what you're feeling."

I turn to my side and begin to cough again. Corinna grabs a bucket in time, and I vomit into the trashcan, missing the carpet by inches. I can't stop the sobbing and coughing that continues as the chunks drip from my chin. This morning's half-digested egg white omelet and turkey bacon are staring up at me from the bucket. Corinna senses I am about to snap out of the vision, so she forces me to stay in the moment. She tells me, "Don't worry, this happens all the time. Remember, talk to your parents."

I envision the young couple in a room, and I question them: "How could you give me away like this? What kinds of parents do that to their child? Your actions were reprehensible!" They don't respond but their faces burn with hurt and remorse.

"Adam, look them in the eyes. Feel what they were feeling. Can you forgive?"

Their pain sears through my body. Without thinking, the words pour out of my mouth, "Yes, I forgive them."

"Why?"

"They were children themselves when they had me, unable to cope with raising a sick child."

"Very good. I want you to speak to the doctor in the room."

I have words for Dr. Grey Beard. "You're a disgrace. The horror of your actions has loomed over my heart for ages. I cannot fathom that you experimented on innocent children for what you termed the benefit of science. Don't you see how wrong that was? You've scarred me for life. For *lives*."

"That's your rational mind. Tell him how you *feel*."

"Angry. Outraged."

"Where do you feel the anger?"

"In my heart."

"Good. Where else?"

"In my eye."

"Bravo. Now tell him that you are not going to hold onto him or your anger anymore. And while you do that, hit the pillow that's on your lap. Get your anger out."

"Hit the pillow?"

"Trust me, it'll help."

"I'm not going to hold onto the anger anymore." With that, I do my best Muhammad Ali imitation and hit the pillow hard over and over again. More tears.

"Take a deep breath. How do you feel?"

I inhale, hold it, and exhale slowly. "Better. I'm visualizing a white light now in the blank space of my mind."

"Excellent. You were trapped inside this boy for too long, which explains the childlike behavior you exhibit."

At that, I sit up in the chair and look at Corinna. "So I'm all grown up now?"

"You're getting there. Your subconscious mind is healing from this trauma and will help your inner child let go. How do you feel towards the doctor? What do you want to tell him?"

I'm silent for a long moment.

Finally, I say, "I *forgive* you."

Corinna looks at me, smiling. "Wow. Adam, I'm proud of you. Your healing has finally begun." On that note, she has me scan my body for anything feeling different, out of the ordinary, still lingering. I feel great. She asks me to open my eyes when I am ready.

I open them. "Did you turn on more lights? It's brighter in here."

"No, you're seeing things more clearly now."

"I'm drained. I can barely move."

"Make sure you drink a lot of water. Listen, this was a groundbreaking session for you. You've made great progress in your healing. Your eye will be cured."

"My body feels light, free, uninhibited. I feel more at peace."

"Adam, I've completed my work with you. You need time to sort the rest out on your own. That's the point, right? We can always go to people who will tell us what to do and how to act, but the secret, the key to life"—I lean in closer—"is for us to figure things out for ourselves. I have given you the directions to take on your journey. But you can guide yourself now; don't use me as a crutch. You must continue to do the work to help your subconscious mind be at peace and disassociate from your thinking mind and ego. Let go of the past."

"Thank you," I tell Corinna. I stand up, feeling light and completely unburdened. The whole thing was like an episode from *The X-Files* or *Stranger Things*.

My thoughts are interrupted. "Adam, do me a favor. Don't think too much. Continue to meditate, live in the moment, and call me if you need a tune-up. Remember these words. *By letting go of the past, you open up the future. When you hold onto the past, you are strangling the present. By looking into the future, you are letting the present pass you by and losing sight of your life.*"

With that, she gets up and I follow her out to the door. She gives me a big hug, and I wonder if anyone will really believe what transpired. I'm still unsure what happened to me. As I drive home, I feel an unbridled enthusiasm for life.

Now the big dilemma: how much do I really want to share with Minnie? I know she will think I'm crazy, but she's my wife, and I do want her to know my truth. More than that, I need her to accept it.

CHAPTER TWENTY-SIX
10:26 a.m.

I lift my head up from the computer. It doesn't escape me that I just wrote nearly the same scene of what happened to me with my hypnotherapist, Nadine, but I substituted the eye surgery for the ear surgery. They say, "Write what you know," and it's cathartic writing out my experience through Adam. More astonishing, my experience with Nadine validated my feelings that I came into this world with a weight pressing down on my shoulders which manifested in my nervous ear wiggle.

For years, I was at a loss with my two sides, the scientist vs. the spiritualist, unable to resolve this conflict. So I sat down and tried to sort it out the best way I knew how—I tried to be academic about it. I didn't know of any scientific, evidence-based, case-controlled, randomized, double-blinded study I could cite. To me, I was the only case report of having experienced a past life—not very scientific to a Harvard-trained brain. I needed evidence—documented research in a peer review journal. If there were no indisputable facts, then I would know my imagination conjured up these images in my mind.

But I couldn't let my experience go. I knew there were truths to what I experienced, so I began to delve into the research. My moment of epiphany came when I read *Many Lives, Many Masters*, written by

Yale-trained (I'll try not to hold that against him) psychiatrist Brian Weiss, MD. His book was about a patient who experienced past life regression during hypnotherapy sessions that made his cynical mind a believer. He was credible. I didn't feel like I was being sold a can of snake oil reading his book. This gave me the courage to explore my experiences with past lives too. Still, I kept this experience to myself—

"Jacob! You're really late for work now."

I rub my weary eyes. Leah stands in the doorway holding the copy of Irving Sharf's book that I bought yesterday.

"I decided I'm going to skip my eleven o'clock clinic session."

"You're what?"

"Don't worry, I'll text Dr. Smith now to have him cover for me. I need to have this finished for when I meet with Maggie." I take out my phone and type a message to Dr. Smith and Janet letting them know that I will be out until later that afternoon.

Before I can hit send Leah stops me. "Jacob, my dear, you know I support you in whatever you decide to do, but this book, your meeting with Maggie...I don't want to see you disappointed again. How about you focus on what's paying the bills?"

"Leah"—I roll my office chair over and grab *The Swan Song of the Dragon Menace* from her arms—"You lived through my heartbreak of missing out on the writing competition, and not a day goes by that I don't think 'what if.' I know it's not very Buddhist of me. But now I have a chance at redemption. This is *my swan song*."

Leah grabs Sharf's book from me, leans over, and gives me a kiss. "It wasn't that good anyway; he uses the same old plot every damn book. You do this!" She hits send on my cell phone and walks out of the office.

The Adventures of Adam Freeman, DDS
August 11, evening—*Home Improvement*

I arrived home from Corinna's still trying to wrap my head around what had happened. For a moment, I forget about my breakthrough session and enjoy having dinner with Minnie and the kids. Being in the moment makes everything more real and intense. I even feel a strange sense of serenity when my daughters fight over whose turn it is to set the table. Usually during their screaming match, I storm into the room and shout, "Calm down and stop yelling!" But tonight, I speak in a soft, yet stern voice and remind them it's Paige's turn tonight and Rose's turn tomorrow. Miracle of miracles, they listen. Minnie is blown away. "You must have had a big breakthrough today."

Minnie has put Rose back to bed and comes downstairs to dry the dishes while I finish washing them.

And then it happens. My story bursts out over the running water as I continue to wash the pots. I recount every detail of the day to my wife. After I'm finished, she stands there, mouth agape, dish towel frozen in her hand. I turn off the water, put the gloves away, and start making the kids' lunches. Minnie's silence is killing me.

"I'm different now, Minnie," I say, watching her face closely. "My eye feels like a cord has been cut from it. I'm regaining control of my body."

I let out a deep breath as I see Minnie smile. "Adam, that's great. I'm happy for you—and for us."

"God," I say, "I'm relieved. I thought you'd think I was crazy. I thought you might want to send me back..."

Minnie laughs, "If this works for you...go for it. I'm grateful for anything that makes life better for us."

"Okay, but it's important for me to know that you understand where I'm coming from."

"Adam, I'm not sure even *you* know where you're coming from. You said yourself you can't explain what happened. Don't try to understand it. Some things we just need to accept."

"True. But I think I uncovered a past life of mine. It helps explain a lot."

"It may, but be careful. Don't blame the past for how you're acting now. It's a cop out. Deal with what's going on in your life at this moment instead of going backwards."

"I can't be here and live in the moment if I don't let go of my past, and this session helped me do that."

"Look, if you want me to believe in reincarnation, that's not going to happen. I also don't believe your childhood—or any past life you may think you've lived—is responsible for all your present issues. But again, if hypnotherapy helps you be a better husband and father, so be it."

I look at Minnie as we finish putting the girls' lunch bags in the fridge. I know I can't convince her, so I decide to appreciate her for who she is. I walk up and give her a big hug and kiss. "Let's agree to disagree."

She smiles, then kisses me back. "Done."

I begin walking upstairs and remind myself that I can't control how Minnie—or anyone—views the world. I can only hope that one day she gains the same perspective and insight that I have been given. If Minnie can feel peace and tranquility in her way, which is different from mine, who am I to judge which way is correct? I know the path that I am following is the right one for me.

"Adam?"

I pause on the fourth step and turn.

"Thanks for sharing your journey with me. I do appreciate it, and I love you."

* * *

Adam, you are really kicking some spiritual ass now! A lot of people doubted you, but I think the world could learn to love the newest version of you, Adam 3.0. Maggie, Leah, and even Dr. Dennis Smith had issues with your immaturity, but that was before my all-night rewrite. Did I do enough to make you redeemable? Did I save you from the great slush pile of the unpublished, from the infinitely long list of characters who only lived in their creators' imaginations and were never realized on the printed page? Maybe after all this, Maggie will still want to discard you. Maybe I'll persevere anyway and self-publish. Maybe—I'm so tired that this is my last thought before my eyes close and my head falls forward and my mind goes completely blank.

Suddenly, I'm wide awake, and an unrecognizable stranger is looking down on me. My first thought is that Leah finally called the cable guy to fix the remote that's been on the fritz. But I rule that out because no cable guy I know wears a white robe and sandals. The morning light through the window makes his long, wavy, light-brown hair glow. I gaze into his eyes and instantly recognize who's in front of me. "Jesus?"

His smile radiates through the room. "Yes, my child."

Quick on my feet, I say, "I think you took a wrong turn. I'm Jewish."

"No, my GPS works fine. I know your doubts and fears. I'm here to tell you to embrace this journey that you're on. Write all about it. Tell your story to the world."

"But I'm only an orthodontist and not a prolific writer. What about Maggie's opinion of Adam?"

"Jacob, don't limit yourself to being 'only an orthodontist.' No one is labeled in the eyes of God. Keep putting your feelings into words.

Keep writing about your journey, and fear not people's judgment. Go forth to spread the word that we all need to seek our inner truth. Speaketh to mankind that there is more out there in this world if people open their eyes and become *aware*."

His words reverberate through the house. "Listen," I say, "your message couldn't be timelier, but would you mind whispering? I think Eva's still sleeping, she had a rough night."

Jesus smiles at me again and whispers, "I see you are deep in thought."

"Yes, I have a question. I'm a Jew and technically don't believe that you're the messiah and son of God. Am I in trouble? Will I go to hell or not be allowed in heaven?"

Jesus laughs. "Many of my teachings have been misinterpreted. We're all the children of God. There's no such thing as hell. That's a man-made place. Yes, there are always consequences for your actions, but there are no judgments. As long as you perpetuate love, forgiveness, balance, and truthfulness, you will leave the world a better place, and that's all that the universe hopes for from humans."

"Then why do people proclaim that if you don't believe in Jesus then you won't be saved? That totally screws a lot of people in this world who aren't Christians."

I'm suddenly worried that I said "screws" in front of Jesus, but he seems to be cool with it. He responds, "Putting me on a pedestal and worshipping me is what humans decided to do, not something I asked for. No one person is higher than another on earth. In the universe, we are all connected. Religion has complicated things tremendously on earth. Go forth and spread the word that we can break the barriers of religion and division. There's still hope, but we need to give love. Strive for inner peace, look inside and seek your truth."

"People are not going to believe I saw you."

"People don't believe in my miracles either, but that doesn't mean they didn't happen. I can speak to all: Jews, Muslims, Hindus, and Buddhists to name a few. But most people are not open to listening. Religion separates us, and the reality is that even though we speak different languages, the message is the same. We're all united by love in the universe. I'm no different from Abraham, Mohammed, Moses, Buddha, Rumi, Ghandi, the Dalai Lama, Mother Theresa, Tim Tebow, the list goes on."

"Tim Tebow?"

"I'm messing with you on that one! Seriously, be open to the light, and communication will commence with the Creator. But, here is the most important message: *We all have this potential to be Godly during our time on Earth if we open up our hearts and minds and listen for the signs.*"

"Jesus, this is surreal. I don't think anyone is going to believe—"

"And one more thing, Adam."

"Yes, Jesus."

"I want you to end the book with the Four Horsemen, they crack me up."

He's gone. I open my eyes and look down at the manuscript. I'm left with one final thought: during my long and arduous journey to discover myself, memories started surfacing that weren't even mine. They wanted to come out and be heard. I had an underlying sense that what I wrote could resonate with the masses and that this story should be told. It appears now that I wasn't telling the story, but the story told itself. Adam is more than a character, he's an author in his own right. I would buy his book on Amazon and write a 5-star review.

Maggie the Agent be damned!

The Adventures of Adam Freeman, DDS
August 18—*The Walking Dead*

During the afternoon, I get a message from Klein on my voicemail, "Adam,"—there's a pause—"I hate to leave this message on your cell, but my mom stopped eating, and they made the call to give her a morphine drip to make her last days peaceful. I'm in St. Louis on the way to say goodbye to her. I have a feeling I'll be back on Monday to sit Shiva."

Shit. I knew Klein's mother was battling breast cancer and, although she was in remission, last year they found it had metastasized to the lungs. Still, you're never really prepared for when a loved one passes. My heart goes out to my best friend. I know from being with Minnie when her mom passed away that it's a tough and traumatic time for the family. Even though I now have a unique perspective on death and dying because of my new belief in reincarnation, I still feel the unbearable sadness of being separated permanently on earth from a loved one.

I immediately call my parents to check on them. They don't pick up, so I leave a message for them to call me and send my love.

I text my condolences to Klein. He messages me back before bedtime that his mother's condition has stabilized, creating an awkward situation. His family assumed she would pass away late this afternoon, since she's been on morphine for over two days—but, bless her heart, she's still hanging in there. Now Klein's relatives are getting antsy, because they wanted to hold the funeral tomorrow—Friday—because the out of town relatives need to leave by late Saturday. You never want your loved ones to die, and suddenly they can't die soon enough so everyone can fly home.

Minnie is next to me on the couch while I read Klein's texts. "Why can't they hold the funeral on Saturday?" I ask her.

"Sometimes I wonder if you're really Jewish."

I smile. "Sort of. Remember, I'm a born-again JuBu."

"You should know that we have to bury someone within twenty-four hours in the Jewish religion. And we don't do funerals on the Sabbath."

"That's Saturday, right?"

"Oh Lord."

I get another text from Klein late Friday night: "We have a lot of relatives coming in from out of town, and they keep asking if she's passed. It's surreal."

"It's like *Seinfeld* meets *Six Feet Under*," I reply. That must have made him laugh, because he texts me a smiley face.

August 24—*The Leftovers*

Klein's mother finally passes Saturday evening. He lets me know he'll be back in town on Monday, and they'll sit Shiva on the twenty-fourth. I am debating what to put in my reply text to him and ask Minnie for help.

"Adam, sometimes you're quite clueless. You don't text a friend back after he tells you his mother died. For God's sake pick up the phone."

I call him and get his voicemail. I leave a heartfelt message. By the time I am done, I'm almost crying.

My parents arrive to watch the kids so that Minnie and I can sit Shiva with Klein and his family. As we walk in, Klein is holding court, telling a group of people a funny story. I sidle up and listen to him spin the tale. "...then Joy and I gave our kids the option to go out to St. Louis and be at Nana's funeral to say goodbye. They all wanted to go. We trek out to the Midwest. But typical of my mom, she had to do things her way and wouldn't pass no matter how much morphine they were giving her. After two days of her hanging on, my kids think they're on vacation—going to the hotel pool everyday—as I spend time by my mom's side. When we finally get the news that mom is gone and there's going to be a funeral, I inform the kids, and my eight-year-old daughter turns to me and says, 'Well, at least it was worth the trip!'"

Everyone laughs. Only Klein can make people laugh at such a morbid moment and turn the sick dynamics of his family into a story that provides healing.

I watch patiently as people wait on the long concession-stand-like line to offer their condolences. At last, the line dwindles, and Klein makes a beeline for the cold cuts table. I approach, express my sympathy, and ask how he's holding up.

As he fills his plate with potato chips, a sour pickle, and pastrami on rye, Klein tells me, "I'm hanging in there. Doing as well as can be expected. She led a good life, but it was her time. I believe funerals are a healthy way for us to say goodbye to our loved ones."

I make myself a turkey sandwich with lettuce, tomato, and swiss on whole wheat and place a side of veggies with blue cheese dip on my plate. "I'm glad you got to see her," I tell him.

"Yes, that was a blessing. It's funny; the one thing I'm sad about is that my mom won't go on the ten-day National Mahjong Tournament Cruise she signed up for." Klein starts to cry. He takes out a handkerchief from his suit jacket and dabs his eyes.

I give him a hug, then try to lighten up the moment. "Nice handkerchief. Are those coming back?"

Klein smiles. "She led a tough life these past few years after the divorce from my dad and him remarrying a woman half his age."

"Is your dad here?"

"No. He's flying in tomorrow. Don't get me started on him." Klein's voice is choking up. He takes a bite of his pickle. "Enough about me—how are you? What's going on with Adam 2.0?"

"It's 3.0 now. Two point zero was after my panic attack and the monastery. Three point zero is post hypnotherapy. Klein, I feel bad talking about myself during your tough time."

"Don't. I need the distraction." Before I start to talk, Klein points to a group that has entered the room. He grabs my arm and drags me into his study. Carrots and celery drop from my plate to the floor as he whisks me away.

We are alone in Klein's cramped study. There is a mahogany desk in the corner of the room that Klein uses and a white built-in table where his girls do their homework. "Sorry about that, but let's talk in here. That's my Aunt Narissa and her family. They're certifiably nuts. One of my sisters can entertain the loony bin contingency from Florida. I'll deal with them later."

Klein sits down at his desk and begins spinning the globe anchored on its gold stand. I sit across from him and pour out the details of my visits with Corinna. Klein is mesmerized. After I get done telling him what transpired, Klein is on his feet pacing. "You better put pen to paper. *Now*, Freeman. You need to write a book."

"I haven't told anyone this...but I've been journaling."

"Forget a journal. This stuff needs to be published."

"You mean share this stuff with the world? Who would believe it?"

"I believe you. And who cares if no one in the world reads your words except me. All that matters is you writing out your inner truth. Let the chips fall where they may."

"Really? I'm no prophet or sage. If I write a memoir everyone will think I'm cuckoo."

"Who the hell cares? You could be one of those protagonists we love to hate." I scowl at him. "I'm teasing, Adam. Get it out there and see what happens."

"You're serious, aren't you?"

"*Yes*. I can see the jacket cover now. Pediatric dentist Adam Freeman breaks free of his neurotic Jewish upbringing and goes on a mission to cure his nervous eye twitch. Along the way, he witnesses a violent act that shatters his faith in the world, then does time in a Buddhist monastery where he learns how to let go and live in the moment. By the end, Freeman has become a Jewish Buddhist—a JuBu!"

"I don't know, Klein, not sure the world's ready—" Ryan and Errol come barging into the office and give Klein a big bro hug.

The Four Horsemen are together again. Ryan breaks the silence. "Sorry for your loss, buddy."

Klein sits back down, and we all pull up chairs around his desk. "Yeah, it sucks, but when you put things in perspective, we know that energy is neither created nor destroyed, it just changes form. Death is an illusion."

Ryan is shaking his head. "You guys are preaching that wild shit again."

Not taking Ryan's bait, I ask Klein, "How do you reconcile everyone's extreme sadness with us knowing the truth that your mom didn't go anyplace but to another life form and that there's not an end to the universe?"

Errol has his hands over his head. "Guys, this is not the time."

I look at Errol and Ryan. "If Klein wants to be philosophical, let him. What's the big deal?"

Klein responds, "What better time to philosophize than at a Shiva, chomping down corned beef and pastrami sandwiches? You know, there's a part of me that feels this is a joyous occasion. My mom has now escaped her human body and can go through her life review. Isn't that cool? I've been reading up on it. I'm looking forward to my life review—when it comes. I mean, it's the ultimate answer key to your life. Letting you know if you made the right decisions along the way."

Ryan jumps in. "Klein, that's gobbledygook."

"Hey Ryan," I say, "lay off. What makes you the authority on all things religious?"

Klein looks at Errol and Ryan. "Guys, let's table this." Then he turns to me. "Adam, we're never going to enlighten these guys. They're not ready."

Errol and Ryan leave Klein's office. He continues, "Most people aren't ready to put in the work to find out their truth. What I've learned is that you must devote yourself completely to having pure thoughts and actions. Remember that everything you do can affect things beyond even your wildest imagination."

I add, "Sometimes I want to shake those who don't understand this and try to get them to see the truth. I want to remove the veil in front of their eyes. To clear the haze and have them see through the fog so that they know there's meaning behind everything. That death is an illusion. Disease and destruction are human creations caused by our separation from the life force of the universe."

"Wow, you've really been reading the books I gave you. Nice." Klein stands up and lets a knocking Minnie into the room. Minnie walks up to me phone in hand. "Your mom texted me, Spencer's having a meltdown. They want us home."

"All right, I'll see you later." I give Klein a bro hug, and he holds on longer than usual.

Before we leave, Klein says to me, "I need to get out of here. I can't be cooped up sitting Shiva without a break. Let's all meet for brunch tomorrow morning, Horsemen and women at the local diner." I look at Minnie and she nods her approval. "Oh, have Joy give you a plate of food to take home. We're going to have a ton of leftovers."

August 25—*Big Bang Theory*

As usual, we are the last to arrive at brunch with the other Horsemen and their spouses. The meal begins with a startling revelation. After we order drinks—Minnie a Mimosa and me a Bloody Mary—I whisper to Minnie, "What is she doing here?"

"You mean Kristy?"

"Yeah."

"Didn't you know, Adam?"

"Know what?"

"She and Errol are back together," she whispers. "They're trying to make it work."

"Errol never said anything. No matter, I'm glad for them."

It feels comforting to be around good friends. Minnie always tells me I regress to my college days when I'm with my boys, but I like feeling young and occasionally acting immature. Since all the wives are here, and because Klein's a little more subdued this morning, the guys are all on their best behavior.

I'm sitting next to Ryan's wife, Sally, and I lean over and ask how she's doing. Sally is a petite woman with pin-straight blonde hair who looks like Kaley Cuoco from the *Big Bang Theory*. I always got a kick out of seeing her and Ryan together when he was at his girth stage. They were as well matched as Penny and Leonard. But now that Ryan is thinner, they appear to be more physically compatible. Sally laments, "My stomach's been really hurting lately. I've had diarrhea for weeks, if not months, now."

"You poor dear," responds Minnie.

I was going to say, "A little too much information for my liking," but I nod in agreement with my extremely empathetic wife.

"It's been horrible. I can't digest most foods. They go right through me."

"What have you been doing?" asks Kristy.

"I've had to live on vegetables and Imodium. I've lost a ton of weight."

Minnie adds, "I can see that. You look very thin. What do the doctors say?"

Sally responds, "I've seen my physician, an osteopath, and a gastroenterologist. They've changed my diet to gluten-free and told me to avoid dairy. I had a ton of blood work done and even had a colonoscopy."

"My friend went on a gluten-free diet, and her skin is radiant lately," Kristy tells the table.

"What did they find?" Minnie asks.

"Nothing. They can't find anything wrong with me," answers Sally.

I'm feeling uninhibited and chime in, "You know, if they can't find anything medically wrong with you, maybe it's"—I hesitate then go for it—"something beyond what we can physically understand."

Suddenly I'm getting the strangest looks from everyone. Minnie kicks me under the table; she doesn't like where this is headed. "I'm a big believer that the body follows the mind. I'll give you the name of my hypnotherapist. She works miracles. I'm telling you, she can really help get to the root of your issues." I look at Errol as I feel the pain of his shoe digging into my shin. I grimace. Guess he's not ready to go public with his history of seeing a hypnotherapist.

"*You* see a hypnotherapist?" Ryan asks.

At that moment, I look around at the prying eyes of the table. What was I thinking? My journey will fall on deaf ears here. I answer back quickly, "I'm joking! I was thinking how stressful it must be to live with Ryan. That's enough to give anyone diarrhea all of the time!"

Everyone laughs. Errol and Klein smile at me. We all know this group doesn't want to hear advice about going to see a hypnotherapist. Guess you can't change everyone.

October 26—*Happy Days*

It's been months now since I've taken pen to paper. I'm living in the moment, meditating every night, and nothing journal-worthy has happened lately. My eye twitch? Cured. Even when there's a situation that starts to stress me out and my E.T. wants to rear its ugly head, I take deep breaths and let it pass. Everything is impermanent and knowing this means I don't have to worry. It's my choice if I want to be upset and let it affect my body. Instead I choose not to obsess about anything. It all melts away.

The truth—my new truth—is that we're in soul school. We need to learn love, patience, faith, honesty, healing, coping, and peace of mind. Every tragedy that enters our life is a lesson from the universe.

On my long, arduous journey, I've learned that God is within us, and we need to unlock that Divine love and presence with our thoughts and actions. Those monks at the Buddhist temple knew this. Rabbi Shekl taught me the same message during my Kabbalah sessions.

How can I synthesize everything I learned from Sufism to Buddhism to Kabbalah to Catholicism to Spiritualism? If I'm supposed to let go of the past, is it bad form to keep a diary and try to condense this mass of information into one big Venn Diagram and define it as "Freemanism?"

Here I am, on my fortieth birthday, at Klein's urging, preparing my diary, *The Adventures of Adam Freeman, DDS,* for publication. If you are like me, you'll want this story wrapped up neatly with a big red bow around it. You invest days, weeks, or months of your life seeing a movie, reading a book, or binge-watching a television series, and you want to be rewarded—

completely satisfied and fulfilled. But endings don't always happen like in the movies, TV shows, or books we love.

Do you want me to end the book with a switcheroo similar to the one in *The Sixth Sense*? I don't want to leave you unfulfilled, like the series finale of *The Sopranos,* or deeply disappointed, like the last episode of *Dexter*. I'd love to wrap things up, nail the ending, and answer all your questions, a la *Breaking Bad*. I wish I were creative or smart enough to think of a great ending for my life, as they did in *Six Feet Under*, but I'm just Adam Freeman, and I don't know what the future has in store for me. As much as I wish I could move my family to Hawaii for infinite relaxation, stress reduction, and life in paradise—that wouldn't be realistic. Was this all a dream, like the series finale of *Newhart*? Sorry, I'm still awake, but more *awakened* than I was at the beginning of the journal.

Maybe I will end up publishing this book and perpetuate a new spiritual movement for the masses. Maybe there are millions of people with nervous twitches or severe anxiety who will feel connected to my story. Maybe those for whom Western medicine is failing will find hope and solace in my journey. Maybe, after reading this book, some will decide that meditation and hypnotherapy are viable options along with traditional medicine. Maybe folks will take up meditation, and a new movement of Love, Inner Peace, Joy, and Gratitude will spread throughout the world. And maybe, just maybe, this random Jewish pediatric dentist who decided to go on a spiritual quest and became a JuBu will shine some needed light into the darkness.

CHAPTER TWENTY-SEVEN
12:58 p.m.

I walk into the High-Priced Café clutching my new manuscript. My patient Abby the Waitress greets me. "Morning, Dr. Silverstein. Can I, like, get you a seat? Will you be joining the woman from yesterday and her friend?"

"What friend?" I look over and notice Maggie sitting next to a gentleman in a tan blazer, eating a piece of bread and taking a sip of red wine. I'd recognize that silver hair anywhere. What the hell is Sharf doing here? I planned to meet Maggie and present my new and improved manuscript to her alone. Sharf's always impeding my progress. Forget about it. Who cares what Maggie Christiansen thinks about my novel anyway? "I'll take a Cobb salad to go."

"Got it. Can I, like, get you something to drink while you wait?"

"I'm good." I pull out my credit card to pay, and it falls on the floor. I bend down to pick it up and suddenly Maggie is standing over me.

"Jacob! I'm so glad you came. Quite honestly, I didn't think you'd show after our meeting yesterday. But here you are, which tells me something. You look tired."

I put the credit card back in my wallet. Before I can think, I blurt "It's all your fault!" She gives me a quizzical look. "After we met, and you expressed your, um, reservations about Adam, I let you get in my head. You challenged me to break my inner artist out of his cocoon and made me aware that I was playing it safe as an orthodontist straightening teeth for a living. Beyond that, you made me wonder if I should take a risk and give birth to Adam, or simply spit out my own memories, or kill the whole thing. I hit the pause button and reevaluated Adam's story. The reason I look tired is that last night I did a *massive* rewrite, and it made me realize that I've created characters who tap into our universal consciousness. I've developed an emotional connection with my characters, and...and Adam is my soul brother."

People around the restaurant are staring. I hadn't realized I was speaking so loudly. Abby the Waitress is practically beaming, and I think I detect the hint of a smile on Sharf's weathered face as he puts down his wine glass. Maggie looks nonplussed.

I hand her the manuscript. "It was painful—and scary—putting my alter ego out there, knowing he might be rejected and judged. After all, I'm human and yearn to be accepted and validated with my story."

"Jacob..."—Maggie puts a bony arm around my shoulder— "come over and join us to discuss."

"I'm holding true to my vision, Maggie. I'm *not* doing a memoir. You're not changing my book. While I was rewriting, I didn't know how the story would end. But all along, I was rooting for Adam to become enlightened and discover his peace."

Maggie corrals me back to her table, and I whisper to Abby, "Bring the Cobb Salad. And a bacon, mushroom and Swiss burger. And a big glass of red wine. Bring it to the table...and add it to their bill."

I sit, and to my utter surprise, Maggie smiles at me warmly. The ice in her face has melted, and I can even see a twinkle in her eye.

"Irving," she says, turning to Sharf. "I want to introduce you to Dr. Jacob Silverstein, my newest author. He's going to be the next big thing."

"Maggie," I say, doing my best Humphrey Bogart imitation, "I think this is the beginning of a beautiful friendship."

Author's Note:

I began writing *Journey of a Jubu* at a time when I was suffering from persistent anxiety and a nervous facial tic. Chronicling my experience through fictional characters helped me organize my thoughts about meditation, religion, spirituality, and hypnotherapy. While it began as a personal endeavor, I soon discovered that my journey was relatable to a larger audience while sharing chapters with my writing group at the Westport Writers' Workshop. Their responses were extremely encouraging and kept me motivated to complete the book.

Perhaps it's obvious that the narrator, Jacob, is my alter ego—an orthodontist who writes a meta-fiction, coming-of-*middle*-age novel about his conversion from Judaism to Buddhism. Like me, Jacob, is reluctant to face the intense personal scrutiny that accompanies publishing a memoir, so he, in turn, hides behind the veil of *his* alter ego, Adam Freeman, a Yale-trained pediatric dentist. This is where our journeys depart. While Adam manages to find a measure of spiritual enlightenment over a single summer, his transition in the book is accelerated for dramatic effect. The path to finding inner peace is an ongoing, often lifelong endeavor. Don't be discouraged if your own path is longer and more challenging—the journey is just as important, if not more so, than the destination.

I want to thank you for taking time out of your busy life to read my modern-day parable of finding spirituality in the twenty-first century. It is my hope that you were entertained by Jacob and Adam's quest. If you enjoyed *Journey of a Jubu*, I'd be grateful if you'd leave a review on Amazon and/or Goodreads and share the book with friends and family.

A portion of the proceeds of the book will go to the Silver Platter Foundation, which donates money to the families of those suffering from blood cancers.

Acknowledgements:

I foremost want to thank my wife, Rachel. One could not ask for a better partner or mother to our three amazing daughters, all of whom bring tremendous joy to my life. I also want to thank my parents, Phyllis and David Langberg, and my sister, Rebecca Weinstein, for providing a supportive, loving, and nurturing environment for me to grow up in.

I am eternally grateful to my editors, Randie Creamer, Thomas Fiffer, and D.J. Schuette, who helped move this book along and took it to levels beyond my imagination. They all played an integral role in the development of *Journey of a JuBu* and put their hearts and souls into the story to make it better. The novel would never have been published without their collaboration. Daniela Kinsbourne did a magnificent job creating cover art that reflects the spirit and theme of the book. Valerie Leff, Chris Belden, Adele Annesi, and Joanne Hardy all gave generously of their time and provided thoughtful advice.

Thanks to Fran Palumbo for showing me the effectiveness of hypnotherapy. I want to recognize my past writing partners: Hugh Jenkins, Vish Thanik, Keith Margolus, Christopher Griffin, Alex Lugones, and Todd Walkow for their collaboration and friendship.

I'm very appreciative to my advance readers, who were generous with their time and feedback. They encouraged me and gave me confidence that people would connect to the story. Many thanks to Brian Glassman, Craig Sherter, Bill Wolff, Andy Langberg, Scott Brown, Debbie Frishman, Andy Frishman, Adam Rubinfeld, Jane Zeitz, Eric Allen, Barbara Hoover, Andrew Weinstein, Ryan Alexander, Diane Brown, Anthony Tammaro, Katherine Greene, Frank Kirby, Toni Raissis, Bhante Sujatha, Dr. Henry Grayson, and Julia Bobkoff.

Made in the USA
Columbia, SC
24 March 2020